The First, Wild Clamor
of Desire . . .

Even now, Ileana could feel her treacherous body awakening beneath him, and silently, she cursed him for the things he was doing to her, things that made her flesh meld itself against her will to his, her bones melt inside her, like molten ore, as Cain's free hand explored her, touching her in ways and places that no man had ever touched her.

Her heart pounded too quickly in her breast; the tiny pulse at the hollow of her throat fluttered when he kissed it, teased it with his tongue. His lips slid hotly down the side of her neck, and his teeth nipped her skin there, causing a shower of electric shocks to tingle through her veins . . .

He raised her face to his, compelled her mouth to open; his tongue shot deep inside her lips to pillage the softness within until at last she was kissing him back, madly, as though she had no will of her own, but were a wild thing he might tame as he pleased . . .

Passion Moon Rising

Rebecca Brandewyne

POCKET BOOKS

New York   London   Toronto   Sydney   Tokyo

This novel is a work of historical fiction. Names, characters, places and incidents relating to non-historical figures are either the product of the author's imagination or are used fictitiously. Any resemblance of such non-historical incidents, places or figures to actual events or locales or persons, living or dead, is entirely coincidental.

Another *Original* publication of POCKET BOOKS

POCKET BOOKS, a division of Simon & Schuster, Inc.
1230 Avenue of the Americas, New York, N.Y. 10020

ISBN: 0-671-61774-5

First Pocket Books printing February 1988

10 9 8 7 6 5 4 3 2 1

POCKET and colophon are trademarks of
Simon & Schuster, Inc.

Printed in the U.S.A.

For Carl and Charlene,
the dearest parents-in-law ever.
With love.

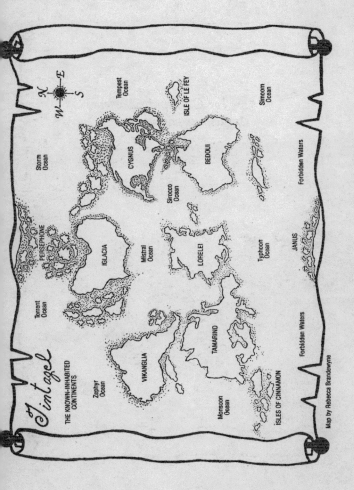

Tintagel

THE KNOWN-INHABITED CONTINENTS

Map by Rebecca Brandewyne

Zephyr Ocean

Torrent Ocean

PERSEPHONE

Storm Ocean

Monsoon Ocean

VIKANGLIA

IGLACIA

Mistral Ocean

CYGNUS

Sirocco Ocean

Tempest Ocean

ISLE OF LE FEY

BEDOUI

Simoom Ocean

ISLES OF CINNAMON

TAMARINO

LORELEI

Typhoon Ocean

Forbidden Waters

Forbidden Waters

JANUS

Forbidden Waters

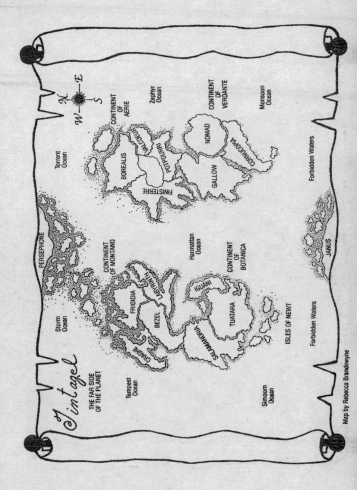

Map by Rebecca Brandewyne

The Players

THE ROYAL HOUSE OF ARIEL
The Lord Balthasar sin Ariel sul Ariel, the High King of Tintagel
The Lady Lucia sin Ariel sul Ariel, the High Queen of Tintagel; wife to the Lord Balthasar

Their children:
(Four sons)
The Lady Ileana sin Ariel sul Khali, the High Princess of Tintagel; wife to the Lord Cain
(Twin daughters)

THE ROYAL HOUSE OF KHALI
The Lord Yhudhah sin Khali, the High Prince of Tintagel (deceased)
The Lord Cain sin Khali sul Ariel, the High Prince of Tintagel; kinsman to the Lord Yhudhah

THE NUNNERY OF MONT SAINT MIKHAELA
The Ancient One, Gitana san Kovichi, the former High Priestess of Mont Saint Mikhaela (deceased)
The Reverend Mother Sharai san Jyotis, the High Priestess of Mont Saint Mikhaela
Sister Amineh san Pázia, a twelfth-ranked priestess; mentor to the Lady Ileana

THE MONASTERY OF MONT SAINT CHRISTOPHER
The Ancient One, Takis san Baruch, the former High Priest of Mont Saint Christopher (deceased)
The Reverend Father Kokudza san Dyami, the High Priest of Mont Saint Christopher

Brother Ottah san Huatsu, a twelfth-ranked priest; mentor to the Lord Cain

Brother Edu san Nahele, a third-ranked priest

THE RULERS OF
THE KNOWN-INHABITED CONTINENTS

The Lord Faolan sin Lothian sul Lothian, the King of Vikanglia

The Lady Pualani sin Gingiber sul Gingiber, the Queen of Tamarind

The Lord Tobolsk sin Tovaritch sol Kharkov, the King of Iglacia

The Lord Lionel sin Morgant sol Draca, the King of Lorelei

The Lord Xenos sin Ariel sul Ariel, the King of Cygnus

The Lady Nenet sin Khali sul Khali, the Queen of Bedoui

THE RULERS FROM THE COMMON HOUSES

Master Radomil san Pavel sol Antoni, the High Minister of Tintagel

Mistress Elysabeth san Villette sol Franchot, the High Electress of Tintagel

THE QUESTERS

Charis, handmaiden to the Lady Ileana

Mehtar, manservant to the Lord Cain

Sir Husein, chief protector of the Lady Ileana

Sir Ahmed, chief protector of the Lord Cain

Mistress Halcyone set Astra, a shipbuilder of Cygnus

Doctor York, a physician of Lorelei

Bergren Birchbark, a dwarf of Cornucopia

Jiro Juniper, a dwarf of Cornucopia

Syeira, a gypsy of Nomad

Garrote the Dispossessed, an Outcast of Gallow

Ulthor, a giant of Borealis

The Prince Lord Tarragon, an elf of Potpourri

The Princess Lady Rosemary, an elf of Potpourri

Mace, an elf of Potpourri

Dill, an elf of Potpourri

Contents

Passion Moon Rising

The heavens were unfurling to release the night,
The twelve signs opening all their pearly gates
To let the stars out slowly,
Like some prophecy of long ago,
Foretold but not yet seen.
Deep within the black and hushed Melantha Forest,
From bristly pines, the snowy owls,
With plaintive cries, were calling
And counting every flicker
Of the skies' illumination;
And the Weeping Wraiths fluttered
Like forlorn sighs
Upon the wings of the whispering wind.
The Eternal Bell chimed midnight,
As though it struck a galaxy away—so distant—
And two Mont-Sect cloisters answered it the same.
The luminaries glowed
Soft like the mist along the narrow wynds;
And Ariel Heights floated among gossamer clouds.
Past the desert bluffs, Khali Keep,
In which the mysterious obelisks stand,
Triangular, pyramidal,
Each based upon its proud faesthorses,
Guarded that fair mosque, Cain's bride,
Sorceress, daughter of the Light.

The Passion Moon was rising,
And shadows of the First and Blue
Had filled up all the planet to the brim,
Burning yonder castle
In some enchanted incandescence,
Compelling her who gazed with passionate desire
To smolder and ignite
And find a Flame Prince
Who hungered for her soul.
To kiss him was to bring away
His fire upon her lips.
Her body trembled at the thought.
Her aura blazed; still, he engulfed her with his own.
The Sword of Ishtar glittered bright;
And somewhere the Darkness drew near. . . . *

*Poem adapted from *Aurora Leigh,* Eighth Book, by Elizabeth Barrett Browning

NEW MOON

To Let the Stars Out Slowly

Place and Time Unknown

In the Beginning, there was only the Being.

Alone in the vast, cold, empty darkness that was nothingness, It floated, a massive, pulsating, efficacious, ethereal essence that stretched out endlessly to encompass all, for all that ever was or ever would be was within it. Yet It did not even know if It was real, for there was naught else to confirm Its existence.

I must know, *the Being thought*, whether I am.

And so thinking, slowly, It summoned Its boundless power, Its cogent energy, from every breadth of Its never-ending reach. Like an aura, the Being began to glow, darkly at first, then brighter and brighter, shimmering colors streaming from Its center until at last It was a white-hot light exploding into the black void, scattering Its tremendous force across the nothingness to illuminate the darkness, to fill up the emptiness, and to warm the coldness.

The Being was pleased by what It had created, for It saw that some of Its ethereal essence had been transformed by Its ebullition into gaseous and vaporous energy and solid particles that had coalesced to form dense bodies of matter. It saw, too, that the countless brilliant, fiery spheres It had wrought burned so intensely and radiantly, even those few that were cold and dark were heated and enlightened by the others. The Being called these fiery spheres stars and the dark spheres planets.

Presently, the Being realized that so potent was the power It had unleashed, all was now chaos, the stars colliding with each other and with the planets. Pieces of each had begun to break away and to spiral through the blackness, which the Being called the heavens. So again It gathered Its strength and brought order to what It had created, sending Its great force throughout the heavens so each of the stars might have its own place therein. Around some of these stars, It fixed the planets and set them into motion so they would circle these stars, which It called suns.

Soon the Being observed that the suns shone only upon one side of the planets, and so It once more called forth Its puissance and made the planets turn upon their axes so every part of the planets would once every revolution be bathed in light; and this, the Being called day.

Then It fixed even smaller, darker orbs, which It called moons, around the planets so even when the planets were not turned toward their suns, they would receive light, for the suns would shine upon the moons and this light would be reflected upon the planets; and this, the Being called night.

After that, It noted that upon some of the planets, Its energy had altered, had become liquideous instead of vaporous, engulfing the solid matter. So again It summoned Its power and caused upheaval upon these planets so the liquid, which the Being called the seas, was divided and some of the solid matter was once more revealed. Upon these exposed masses, which the Being called the land, It sowed the seeds of Its awesome force, and these, too, were eventually changed and grew to cover the land with earth and flora.

Again the Being released Its effluence, and the seas began to teem with swimming creatures. With the passing of time, some of the swimming creatures were transformed, and they left the seas to walk upon the land. Then some of these creatures left the land to fly in the heavens.

The Being saw that this was good, and It blessed all the creatures, for they were a part of It.

Still, this was not enough. So presently, as It had made the others, the Being created two more creatures, and these It fashioned from the ashes of Its indomitable, incandescent might and the land and the seas as well. Then, with the final remnants of Its power, the Being soughed gently, and the ethereal essence of Itself entered into these last two creatures. Thus, formed from fire, earth, water, air, and ether, they became Its image.

These two creatures, which the Being called the Kind, It placed upon the land beneath the Tree of Life and Knowledge born from the seed of Its force. Then, lightly, the Being touched the tree, and upon its branches the Fruit of Free Will burst into bloom.

The Being wished to know the truth of Its existence, and It knew that in order to discover this, It must give the Kind the freedom to choose between the Light that was Itself and the Darkness that was the nothingness. If the Kind chose the Light, then the Being's existence would be confirmed. If the Kind chose the Darkness, then there would be only nothingness.

After that, drained of Its strength, the Being rested and waited.

In time, the Kind ate of the fruit from the tree, and so the Seeds of Free Will were planted within them and took root; and the Kind learned that unlike the other creatures of the seas, the land, and the heavens, they had been given the freedom to choose their own LifePaths and Destinies.

As time passed, the Kind mated and begat children, and these children were nurtured so they flourished and grew to beget more children until the planets were peopled with the Kind; and these became the Tribes, for the Kind were many and, over the ages, grew to be different from one another.

Some of the Tribes worshiped the Being who was the Light, though they called It by many names. But there were others who chose the Darkness, the nothingness, and so the Being sent messengers to the planets to tell of It; and these became the Keepers and the Prophets.

But still, some of the Tribes did not believe in the Being, and they disrupted the harmony of all It had created; and the Darkness began to attain power.

The ethereal essence within those of the Tribes who

chose the Darkness began to metamorphose until it was no longer as the Being who was the Light had fashioned it. These creatures so changed became the Demons Fear, Ignorance, Prejudice, Hate, Greed, and Apathy.

Because the ethereal essence of these Demons had altered, they were no longer a part of the Being who had made them, and the Way to return to It, to become One with It, as they had been in the Beginning, was lost to them forever; and what had once been good within them was corrupted and turned to evil.

And so the Darkness spread and began to dim the Light.

Soon, the other Tribes became infected by the wickedness of those who served the Darkness, and mistakenly, they began to believe their name for the Being who was the Light they worshiped was the only name by which It could be called or known. They forgot what they had learned from the Tree of Life and Knowledge and from the Keepers and the Prophets, too, setting one's teachings above the other, male above female, and the Kind above Beast and Plant. Disorder grew rampant and at last prevailed.

In the Name of the Light, the Tribes began to war among themselves, shedding the Blood of Life and destroying those who did not believe as they believed. Many great civilizations passed into the Darkness, the nothingness, nevermore to be. This was the Time of the Tribal Wars.

Through Its messengers, the Being admonished the Tribes, telling them this was not the Way or the Truth of the Light; but they did not listen. At last, disheartened, the Being again summoned Its boundless power, and the heavens were filled with chaos, as they had been in the Beginning. This was the Time of the Cataclysms.

But still, the Tribes did not heed the Being's warnings, and over the ages, they turned from Its ancient teachings to a new learning in which they sought to discover the key to the cogent energy of the Being and to make it their own. They did not understand that *only fragments of Its tremendous force had been revealed to them. They thought themselves possessed of the Being's great secret.*

With their newfound pieces of knowledge, which they called Technology, the Tribes of each planet began once more to war among themselves, forgetting all that had gone before and not realizing that in the Name of the Light, they had again allowed the Darkness to seize them in Its terrible grasp. Great explosions shook the land, and the planets were devastated by the destruction wrought, as the Keepers and the Prophets had foretold. This was the Time of the World Wars.

Once more, through Its messengers, the Being admonished the Tribes; but still, they refused to listen, and they continued their pursuit of what could only be fully known and understood by those who had become One with the Being in the End, as had been promised to those who believed.

With their Technology, the Tribes on each planet discovered the existence of those on the other planets, and because they were different from one another, each viewed the rest as alien creatures, though they had all been One with the Being in the Beginning.

The Darkness was stronger now than It had ever been before, for over the ages, the Demons Fear and Ignorance had gained many followers. Now these Demons and their followers caused the Tribes on each planet to be afraid of those on the other planets, as they had once been afraid of those on their own planets, for all that is not understood is frightening.

Secure in the knowledge that their Technology was greater than that of the rest, some of the Tribes allowed the Demons Prejudice and Hate to enter their hearts and minds, and thus their ethereal essence was changed and given over to the Darkness. Others, those whose knowledge of Technology was less than that of the rest, hungered for what they did not have and let the Demon Greed inside themselves. Still others who saw what was happening cared only for the well-being of their own planets, and they withdrew from the rest, loosing the Demon Apathy among themselves;

and the Darkness spread throughout the universe.

In the Name of the Light, the Tribes of the planets set out to destroy one another. The worlds collided. Fire and ice such as had never been seen before swept across the planets, consuming them, and all were devastated by the destruction wrought, as the Keepers and the Prophets had foretold. This was the Time of the Wars of the Kind and the Apocalypse.

All things come full circle.

After the Apocalypse, all was as it had been in the Beginning, the Tribes scattered and unable to move physically through Time and Space as they had before. Many were so changed, they were unrecognizable as the Kind, and indeed, they no longer were, for they had regressed to creatures such as they had been before the Being had gifted them with Its ethereal essence and the Fruit of Free Will from the Tree of Life and Knowledge. Others were lost forever, their worlds having passed into the Darkness, the nothingness, and having ceased to exist.

Those who survived were few. These were the Tribes whose belief in the Being had never faltered, who had wielded the Swords of Truth, Righteousness, and Honor against the Darkness so the Light would not be extinguished, but would continue to burn, no matter how faintly, shedding its rays of hope and promise throughout the universe.

These were the Tribes who experienced the Time of the Rebirth and the Enlightenment, when Faith, the Keeper of the Flame, appeared and spake again of the Way to the Being, the Immortal Guardian of all things that ever were and ever shall be, the Light Eternal that forever holds the Darkness at bay so long as even one of the Kind believes the Being is.

And this time, on one small planet called Tintagel, the Tribes heard the Word—and they listened.

—Thus it is Written—
in
The Word and The Way
The Book of Eden

THE WAXING

*Foretold
But Not Yet Seen*

Map by Rebecca Brandewyne

Chapter 1

When one who has been Chosen sees Signs of the Things to Come, that one must take great heed to weigh the Portents most carefully upon the Delicate Balance of the Soul. This must be done in order to determine the Meanings of the Omens, for the Power is like a two-edged sword. It must be wielded wisely and with extreme caution, lest its blade be turned to the Hand of the Darkness, instead of the Light, and the Power be forever corrupted. . . .

—Thus it is Written—
in
The Gift of the Power
by the Sorceress Saint Sidi
san Bel-Abbes set Mosheh

Ariel Heights, Cygnus, 7250.5.14

THE FIRST MOON WAS JUST RISING WHEN THE TWO WOMEN MADE their way stealthily down a shadowed, seldom-used corridor of the castle and let themselves out through the portal gate into the darkness. Though it was summer, the moist night air was thin and cool, as it was always in the clouds that surrounded the fortress perched like an aerie among the Gloriana Mountains, and both women wore black djellabas as protection against the chilly mist. Still, the hoods drawn up close around their faces seemed to ward off more than just the damp; and once or twice, one of the women glanced back uneasily over her shoulder, peering intently into the quiet that swallowed all in their wake.

That their furtive flight had gone unnoticed did little to set her mind at rest, however. Timidly, she reached out and tugged at the other's cloak.

"Lady," she whispered, her eyes wide with apprehension. "I am afraid."

The Lady gazed at her faithful companion reassuringly for a moment but made no reply before continuing on, her booted feet echoing softly upon the empty, gold-cobbled streets as she disappeared into the swirling fog.

The handmaiden scurried after her, deeply fearful of what lay before them, but just as frightened of being left behind. Should anything go wrong this eve, the consequences of having deserted her mistress would be even more terrible than what they were about to face.

The city of Ariel slept on peacefully, oblivious of the silent, hurried passing of the two women. Once, a cat mewed plaintively from a narrow alley, but only the crystal luminaries that lighted the main streets spied the women's clandestine journey.

Though the handmaiden did not know it, the Lady, too, was troubled. Despite her determined attempt to quell it, a sense of guilt ate at her fiercely as she slipped through the darkness like a wraith.

In all the years she had been married, she had never once deceived her husband, and the thought of her betrayal of him this night preyed heavily on her. She wished desperately that she might have told him of the letter she had received less than a fortnight ago, the summons she had dared not disobey. But the missive had been explicit: She was to reveal its contents to no one. And so, fearing the consequences, the Lady had held her tongue and done as she was bidden.

Now she wished fervently that she had not kept still, that she had told her husband all and begged his guidance. He would have known how to advise her, she was sure. Then she would not now be filled with such uncertainty, such trepidation about her decision.

Why, the Lady asked herself for the hundredth time, had she been the one selected? She did not want the burden that had been thrust upon her and would, in fact, have rejected it had she been given a choice. But there had been no such option open to her.

The Lady sighed. There was naught to be done now in any event. It was too late to reconsider, to turn back, despite her misgivings. She had cast her fate to the four winds, and now she must go where they took her.

After a time, the two women reached the city's far wall.

They followed it to the place where they were to be met. Then, hesitantly, the handmaiden spoke again.

"Lady, is he come?" she asked.

"Yea."

The word was faint, as though the Lady, too, the handmaiden thought, had begun to fear what lay ahead.

Slowly, the women approached the man who waited for them in the shadows, his hands wrapped about the gleaming bridles of two nervously dancing alaecorns, one massive, heavily muscled, and bay, the other smaller, more delicate, and flaxen gold. The single polished horns of the beasts shone like burnished wood in the moonlight, matching the luster of their dark, solid hooves. Their diaphanous wings were folded, tucked close against their bodies, and their luminous eyes were wary.

"Ye were told to come alone."

The man's deep, harsh voice broke the stillness suddenly, startling the women and causing the handmaiden to clutch anxiously at her mistress's djellaba once more.

"The woman is my handmaiden, Ophelia," the Lady announced with a calmness she did not feel. "She has been my faithful companion since childhood. I do not go without her."

The man shuffled forward into the half-light, making the women gasp, for they could see now that he was one of the Misshapen, those who were a legacy of the Time Before, when the worlds had collided and the Wars of the Kind and the Apocalypse had almost destroyed them all. He stood over seven feet tall and towered over the women menacingly, making Ophelia cringe and the Lady cower slightly, though, bravely, she stood her ground. His features were grossly distorted and seemed even more hideous when seen by the wavering flames of the luminaries. He had only one eye; where the other should have been was a sunken piece of flesh, evidence that the socket and its orb had never formed properly. His broad nose was flat and lopsided; his thick lips were gruesomely twisted. His face itself was tightened with severe disapproval, further accentuating its malformation. His back was slightly humped, giving him, for all his height, an odd, stooped appearance, as though he were leaning over the women, intent on scooping them up and crushing them between his large, beefy fists.

For one terrifying instant, the Lady was afraid he would do her some injury for not following exactly the detailed instructions she had received, and she took a cautious step back from his hunched, looming figure.

At last, however, the giant nodded to her curtly, indicating his acceptance of Ophelia's presence. Then, loosing his hold on the reins, he bent and cupped his hands to assist the Lady onto the flaxen-gold alaecorn. When she was firmly entrenched in the saddle, he tossed her mute handmaiden up behind her. After that, without another word, he mounted his own prancing beast.

Lightly, he touched his spurs to the animal's sides, and after a short run, the alaecorn started to flap its translucent wings, then rose majestically into the night sky. The Lady was an adept WindRider and had no difficulty following the man as her own beast spread its wings wide and soared from the ground to bear her away upon the uplifting current. Ophelia hung on to her tightly as the lights of the city fell away beneath them.

Swiftly, they pursued the stars across the heavens, leaving the continent of Cygnus behind as they headed toward the Sea of Ice, which was home to the Forsaken Islands of the north.

Far away, on the isle that was their destination, an old hermit stood watchfully. Her eyes were upturned to the black-velvet firmament, searching for a glimmer of the alaecorns; her head was cocked a trifle as she listened intently for the steady beat of their powerful wings.

Soon! They must come soon!

Already the First Moon shone nebulously, a frosted silver crescent against the endless expanse of ebony, and the Blue Moon had begun its slow ascent above the horizon. What had to be done must be accomplished before the third moon —the Passion Moon—had joined its sisters in the sky.

The Ancient One shivered slightly, drawing the folds of her tattered cape more closely about her as the icy wind swept in from the sea, cutting her like a sharp knife. Summer came seldom to the tundra, and she longed for the warmth of her fire. Then she remembered what she had seen in its flames—what had brought this eve to pass—and she shuddered. If only she were wrong . . . But, nay, she thought grimly. The Darkness had been too strong; she had beheld its malevolent forces too clearly to have been mistaken.

O Immortal Guardian! she beseeched silently. *Hast thou deserted us? Or is what is to come so vile, only we can defeat its horrible evil? We, who have stood constant in our hearts since first ye cast the Light upon us? I have weighed the portents most carefully on the delicate balance of my soul. I know the answers to my questions, and still, I cannot believe; I do not want to believe. O Immortal Guardian! Tell me my aged eyes have grown dim with the years; tell me I have misread the omens I have seen. . . .*

She flung her hands up imploringly. Her jet-black eyes closed tightly, and she began to chant old magic words, feeling the Power, which had been sleeping, leap at her command, surging through her veins. Slowly, an aura started to emanate from her being. At first, it was only a swirl of purple mist. But gradually, as the Power grew in intensity, the halo changed until it was a glow of lucent blue, then a flash of yellow radiance, and finally a blaze of streaming, white-hot coruscation. A dazzling streak of sparkles shot up from the staff she held outstretched in one hand and was answered by a crackling bolt of lightning from the heavens.

The solitary cried out in anguish at the reply, slumping upon the snow-covered ground in defeat as, without warning, her aura darkened abruptly. Despair, sharp and bitter, pierced her being; and suddenly, she felt the full weight of her many years keenly. Once, there had been a time when the Power had scarcely tired her, when its strength had been her own and a meal, some wine, and an hour's rest had been all she'd needed to renew her vigor after calling it to her command. Now she felt drained and weary, oh, so weary. She was too old to undertake the task that had been given unto her this eve. But there was no one else to perform it. The High Priestess Sharai san Jyotis, who now served in the place that had once been the wisewoman's, had said as much.

"The Power is strong within me, yea," the High Priestess had conceded, "but even I do not have your knowledge of it, Reverend Mother. Ye are the Ancient One; ye alone must guide the Sisterhood in this matter. There is no other."

"Amen," she who was now called the Ancient One muttered to herself. "So be it."

She would do what she must, though she knew that it would be the last ceremony she would ever perform in this LifePath, that after it was done, she would leave the physical shell that kept her earthbound and Strom would scatter her ashes to the elements so her body would return whence it had come. In a way she was glad it would be so, glad she would not live to see what this night's work wrought.

Her eyes glittered as she raised her head at the sound of the alaecorns' wings above her. Once, in the Time Before, it would have been the purr of a motor she heard, the shine of melded substance as light as air and as hard as diamonds she would have seen skimming, wingless, through the clouds. But such machines had died with the Wars of the Kind and the Apocalypse centuries before her birth, when the Way had been lost and the Tribes had looked to the Terrorists and the Fanatics for leadership and had got propaganda and violence instead, for those the Old Ones had thought would guide them had served only the Demons, the Minions of the Foul Enslaver. In the Name of the Light, the Tribes had turned their hearts and hands to the Darkness, destroying the worlds. Only those few planets that had fought on the side of the Light had endured, though not unscathed. Tintagel was one of these.

Now the Darkness, which had been sleeping, only sleeping, threatened once more to awaken and to cast its black shroud over the slowly rebirthing land. Yea, the Ancient One must do what she could to prevent it. It would be her legacy to the Sisterhood she had served so faithfully all these years. She only hoped they would use it wisely and well.

For a moment, she glanced anxiously at the night sky, but the deep lilac Passion Moon had yet to make its appearance. With a sigh of relief, she struggled to her feet, leaning heavily on her staff as she made her way toward the two beasts descending from the clouds.

The proud animals skipped across the tundra, slowly folding their wings as they came to a halt some distance away. The two mounted women pressed against their alaecorn's sleek, silky coat, huddling close together for comfort as they watched the beldam's stooped trudge across the snow.

As she drew near, they saw by the light of the moons that, between her thick white eyebrows, her forehead had been tattooed with the Tyrian-purple crescent moon that marked her as a Druswid, a member of the Sisterhood. Set beneath her slanted brows were dark, penetrating eyes heavily outlined with black kohl, which made the orbs seem like empty sockets in her sunken, wrinkled face. Her nose was large and hooked, jutting out over dry, cracked lips. She was thin and hunched in body, with sharp, protruding bones. The wind tore at her snow-white hair, making her look like a madwoman, and her ragged djellaba flapped about her wildly, so she appeared like some ominous bird of prey swooping toward them.

The women shivered, wishing themselves safe at home in their soft, warm beds instead of here, where things beyond their comprehension waited. But no one, not even those of the Royal Blood, dared to ignore a summons from a sorceress as powerful as Gitana san Kovichi.

"Strom, is she come?" the seer asked quickly as the giant dismounted and stepped forward, touching one fist to his heart as, respectfully, he knelt before her.

At her signal to rise, he stood and nodded wordlessly before moving to assist first the Lady, and then Ophelia, from the saddle.

"'Tis good," Gitana murmured. Then, frowning with displeasure, she observed, "There are two. Ye were to bring only one."

Strom grunted.

"The Lady would not come without the other," he explained tersely, his face stony.

Gitana shook her head, mumbling to herself. Then she spoke again.

"There was no help for it, then. Ye did right to bring them both." Dismissing him, she turned abruptly, without greeting, to the Lady. "Come, Lady," she said curtly. "We have much to do—and little time in which to do it."

After that, without a backward glance, she strode as rapidly as her age would allow over the frozen earth toward her home—and her hearth.

Chapter 2

And so the Lady did a potion seek,
Tempting Fate
And the stars of night.
What cruel havoc did they wreak!
Oh, too late,
One who sought but the Light
Found its price so glorious dear,
Ne'er to still
With the wings of Time.
A soft refrain in chasm clear,
With silver rill,
Its echoes haunt the silent rime.

—Thus it is Written—
in
Tempt Not the Stars
by the Poet Ibadan set Samara

THE HOME OF THE SORCERESS, GITANA SAN KOVICHI, WAS NOTH-
ing more than a cave. Its entrance gaped, small and dark,
from the side of the mountain wherein it nestled snugly.
The promontory itself loomed forbiddingly overhead, and
the two women who followed the hermit shuddered at the
sight, clasping hands for solace.

Inside, the large, yawning cavern was filled with phospho-
rescent stalactites and stalagmites. Their multicolored glimmer seemed unworldly, and the shadows cast by the

flickering flames of the fire danced eerily upon the grotto walls.

The cheerless sight did little to alleviate the women's fear, and Ophelia clung tightly to her mistress's side, like a child to its mother's skirts.

Gitana did not seem to notice their fright—or to care that they shrank from her. The Lady was but the Ancient One's instrument this eve; Ophelia was less than nothing. Gitana did not welcome them, and only as an afterthought did she motion for them to be seated on the flat rocks that served as chairs. Then she turned away, taking off her cloak to reveal the silken folds of her tattered violet chasuble with its pattern of silver crescent moons and five-pointed stars. Talking to herself under her breath, she hung her cape upon a peg, then shuffled off to finish the preparations she'd started earlier.

The women watched quietly. Once or twice, the Lady gave Ophelia a slight, reassuring smile, but neither dared to speak. It was as though even a whisper would cause the sorceress's black, piercing eyes to fall upon them reprovingly.

At last, Gitana was ready. Ignoring the women, she knelt, closing her eyes and breathing deeply as, silently, she began to meditate to gather her strength for what must be done. For a moment, she did not know if she would be able to perform the ceremony for which she had taken such care to prepare. But she must. If she failed . . .

Ah, Takis, she thought, remembering her old companion, he who had once served the Brotherhood as she had served the Sisterhood. *In truth, I am too old and weak for this onerous task I face. I fear that my heart cannot endure the strain, that 'twill give way before the rite is finished. I fear, too, that my power will abandon me, that my magic will not be strong enough. . . . Oh, Takis! How I thank the Immortal Guardian that somehow ye withstood the forces of that night long past, that the spell ye wove succeeded, that there is another. They say he has much power, all that was yours—and more. Still, if ever he turns to the Darkness . . . Takis, I must not fail. I dare not! There must be a daughter of the Light to balance that son of Darkness ye conjured, he who carries the fire of death in his soul!*

The realization strengthened the wisewoman's resolve. Without warning, she felt the Power burst forth within her, pulsing through her veins like a forceful electric current. Before the sensation could slip away, she opened her eyes and waved her staff in command, and the iridescent stalactites and stalagmites of the cave darkened until only the dim light of the dancing fire remained.

The resulting effect was weird, ghostly. Once more, the two women, waiting tensely in silence, glanced at each other uneasily. Ophelia half rose upon trembling legs, intending to run from the cavern and whatever was about to take place. But the Lady shook her head warningly, staying her faithful companion. Obediently, the handmaiden settled back nervously on the edge of her seat, but her body remained rigid and poised for flight.

They should not have come! It was madness to tamper with forces even the Chosen could not always understand or control. If anything went wrong, Ophelia must escape—and the Lady with her. Despite her fear, the handmaiden's lips set with determination. Even if it cost Ophelia's life, no harm must come to the Lady. Surreptitiously, the handmaiden stared at the solitary.

Taking a lighted fagot from the fire, Gitana moved toward the curved stone dais that sat at the head of a great circle she had dug with her ceremonial knife, a crescent-shaped arthame, into the hard clay floor. There was a smaller ring within the larger one, and inside the border were evenly spaced a number of strange names and old magic symbols. Within the smaller circle was yet an even smaller one, which contained a triangle; inside the triangle was a pentacle. At the center of the pentacle, the fire burned.

Ophelia shivered at the sight of the diagram and, with difficulty, suppressed the strong urge she had to star herself for protection.

Upon the altar itself stood two tall gold sconces, each holding a single candle. One was white, representing the Light; the other was black, representing the Darkness. Gitana lit them both. When they were burning steadily, she planted her oak staff firmly between them in a hole that had been made in the dais for this purpose. Like an obelisk, the shaft thrust up defiantly, towering over the candles. The old, gnarled wood of which it was fashioned shone with a soft, burnished glow; the silver star that topped it gleamed in the half-light.

Then, once more taking up her fagot, Gitana stooped to ignite the ornate gold incense burners that sat upon the altar's base. Soon the pungent, heady aroma of sweet flowers and tangy spices saturated the air.

This done, the beldam lifted her tall, peaked hat, which sat to one side, and placed it upon her head. After that, she opened one of the oblong wooden caskets that lay upon the dais, unwrapped the purple silk within, and carefully removed a silver wand. This, she held in her right hand.

Sighing with satisfaction, she turned and looked appraisingly at the Lady. Then she motioned for her to remove her djellaba and step forward. Silently, the Lady did so, laying aside her cloak and reverently sinking to her knees outside the diagram.

"Do ye know and understand what is to be done?" Gitana inquired.

"Yea," the Lady responded, her voice quivering slightly with awe and more than a little fear.

"And do ye give your consent freely and willingly?"

"Yea."

"And do ye solemnly swear the Power that is to be revealed to ye and given unto ye this eve will be used only for the Light, to whom it rightfully belongs, else your soul be mortally damned for all eternity?"

"Yea," the Lady answered a third time.

"Then we will begin." Gitana gave Ophelia a sharp look. "Ye may observe, if ye desire, since ye have seen fit to join us this night. But be still, lest ye taint the ritual and the Darkness forever silence your tongue."

The handmaiden bobbed her head in assent, her eyes wide with alarm.

Gitana turned back to the altar and, lifting her palms, started to chant hypnotically words from an ancient language. Gradually, an aura began to radiate from the seer's being, blinding the women who watched, spellbound. They knew there were those with the Power, but until this very eve, they had never witnessed its use. It was a gift bestowed only on the Chosen, those who had been blessed —or cursed, some said—with more than the five senses.

Gitana turned to gaze upon the Lady, who knelt before her.

"Ye are the Lady Lucia sin Ariel sul Ariel, the High Princess of all Tintagel and named for the Light, which ye have sworn to honor, serve, and defend freely and willingly with all your body, mind, and soul?"

"Yea, I am the High Princess Lady Lucia, Defender of the Light."

"Then come, Lady, for the Immortal Guardian has need of your services."

Slowly, the Lady rose and stepped inside the diagram, where she again knelt. Gitana took her wand and passed it around the border formed by the outer two circles. Lightning flared jaggedly inside the grotto. When the cave was once more dim, the Lady saw that the boundary of the diagram now shimmered incandescently.

"Do not attempt to step outside the circle now," the hermit warned, "for it must remain unbroken if we are to be protected from the violent forces I will summon here this very night."

"Nay, I shall not," the Lady promised. Then she cringed as the Ancient One suddenly cried out thunderously.

"Hear me!" Gitana wailed. "The Passion Moon begins its ascent into the heavens! A fortnight ago, I looked into the fire and, in its flames, saw signs of the things to come. They were dreadful portents, Lady, omens like none my aged eyes have ever before beheld. The Light wavers, and the Darkness grows stronger." The Lady gasped. "Yea," Gitana intoned forebodingly. "Even as I speak, the Darkness lies deep within Its wet, murky depths, waiting, waiting. . . . And fools are they who will unleash It to prey upon us! I cannot prevent Its onslaught, for my weary bones are old and brittle. Their chill has warned me my Time of Passing draws near, and many of those who will unwittingly loose the Darkness upon us have yet to be born. Still, I must do what I can.

"Four times this eve, I will invoke the Spirits. Speak not unto them, Lady, for they come from the Far Beyond, that place of gloaming that lies forever between the Light and the Darkness; and only the Chosen may command them. Do ye understand?"

"Yea."

"Be certain, Lady." Gitana's eyes seemed to stab the Lady's very soul. "For there are those without the Power who have sought mastery over the Spirits—and failed. Their fate is a terrible price to pay, Lady. Do ye wish to know it?"

"Nay! Nay, Reverend Mother! I seek not the dreadful knowledge to which ye are privy!"

"Then I shall call up the first spirit."

With this dire pronouncement, Gitana turned back to her dais. She opened the ancient book that rested there, riffled its gold-leafed pages, and at last found the one she sought. She closed her eyes, took a deep breath, and started to chant once more.

"In the Name of the Light, O Spirit Aldinach, I, Gitana, do invoke and conjure thee. In response to my summons, do thou come peaceably and without tarrying from the Far Beyond. Do thou presently appear and show thyself visibly before this circle, in fair and comely shape, without guile, deformity, or horror. Do thou make true and faithful answers unto all my demands, and speak with a clear and intelligible voice, that I may understand thee. Do thou perform all my desires as are proper and that thine office permits, according to my will and intentions.

"Be thou disobedient, and lo! Behold! I shall curse thee with that by which the Elements are overthrown. The Sea will madden; the Earth will quake; the Wind will roar; the Fire will rage, and all Things Celestial, all Things Terrestrial, and all Things Infernal will tremble and be confounded together.

"Come, therefore, in the Name of the Light, O Spirit Aldinach. So I, Gitana, command thee."

The solitary waved her wand. Lightning flashed, illuminating the cavern. Then all was shadowed again.

For a moment, nothing happened. Then, slowly, softly at first, there came a gentle laughter, a gurgling, like that of a babbling brook. It was not at all terrifying, but rather spritelike and playful.

Surprised and puzzled, the Lady glanced toward the ceiling of the grotto. There, from a crooked crack, water had begun to trickle. Presently, the rivulet grew stronger until at last it burst forth in a silver stream, spilling down into the center of the diagram.

Reverently, Gitana selected a stoppered bottle from those arrayed upon the altar, uncorked the vial, and tossed some sparkling crystal salts upon the diamond ripples.

"I honor thee, O Spirit Aldinach. Thou hast responded to my summons as commanded. Doest thou hear and know my demands and desires?"

There was no reply save for the bell-like tinkling of the waves. This, however, Gitana appeared to understand and to approve.

"'Tis good," she said. Then, "This is the Element Water, mutable, ever changing, Giver of Life and Rebirth. Enter, Lady, as ye did during your Ritual of Beginning, that ye may be cleansed and purified anew."

Almost eagerly, for she was not afraid of this spirit, the Lady slipped from her boots, abayeh, and undergarments until she stood naked, covered only by her knee-length silver hair. Her pale, round breasts thrust up proudly. Her long, graceful legs seemed to glide as she stepped beneath the rushing water of the cascade and let the spirit envelop her.

Three times, she performed this ritual: once for her body, once for her mind, and once for her soul. The waves lapped over her soothingly, bringing peace and tranquility to her being, washing away the past and all its pain.

When she withdrew, she felt clean and refreshed, new, like a child untouched by the years. Joyously, she once more robed herself in the pale blue silk folds of her abayeh.

Gitana took a heavy silver chalice from the dais, blessed it, then held it out to capture a few drops of the precious water.

"O Spirit Aldinach," she uttered, "because thou hast truly and faithfully answered my demands and performed my desires according to my will and intentions, I do hereby give thee license to depart. Do thou go peaceably and without tarrying to the Far Beyond, whence thou camest. Do thou go without injury to Kind or Beast or Plant.

Depart, I say, but do thou be ready and willing to come again whensoever thou art duly invoked and conjured by the Sacred Rites of Magic. In the Name of the Light, so I, Gitana, command thee."

The stream spewing from the ceiling of the cave lessened to a mere trickle. Then it disappeared.

The beldam turned the pages in her book. The Lady tensed, her fright returning as she awaited the coming of the second spirit.

"In the Name of the Light, O Spirit Hecate, I, Gitana, do invoke and conjure thee. . . ."

The Ancient One waved her wand a second time. A ragged-edged bolt of coruscation again lighted the cavern. With a low rumble, the floor of the grotto suddenly cracked, slinging up earth from the chasm. After choosing another flacon from the dais, Gitana bent, scooped up the rich, wet red clay, and sprinkled her minerals upon it.

"I honor thee, O Spirit Hecate. . . . Doest thou hear and know my demands and desires?"

Once more, the ground shook softly.

"'Tis good," the seer declared. Then, "This is the Element Earth, fixed, constant, Sustainer of Life and Death. Embrace it, Lady, that your roots may grow deep and strong in its fertile soil and its dust receive your scattered ashes in the winter of your years."

The Lady closed her eyes tightly and held out her hands; her fingers wrapped around the ball of clay, molding themselves to its shape. It was only dirt; but still, she felt small and insignificant when she touched it, for it represented something much greater than her own humble self. She was but a tiny piece of its larger whole. Inexorably, she felt her blood start to pound with the earth's energy, bold and fierce, as it had been in the Beginning and would be until the End. Yea, the earth was strength. Someday, it would embrace her as she now embraced it. Her fear receded in its wake. She threw up her chin defiantly and opened her eyes.

Gitana gave a cackle of satisfaction. Then she sifted the earth so bits of it fell into the intricately worked chalice, mingling with the drops of water.

"O Spirit Hecate," she purred, "because thou hast truly and faithfully answered my demands and performed my desires according to my will and intentions, I do hereby give thee license to depart. . . ."

Deliberately, the crack in the floor of the cave sealed itself as though it had never been. Again, Gitana turned pages in her book. She was silent for a minute, as though the third spirit were not as easily commanded or controlled as the other two had been and required more of her strength and concentration to be summoned. The Lady shuddered at the thought.

"In the Name of the Light, O Spirit Bechard, I, Gitana, do invoke and conjure thee. . . ."

The Ancient One waved her wand a third time. Another blaze of scintillation shot through the cavern. Gently at first, then more forcefully, a cold, sighing whisper sounded through the grotto, sending shivers up Ophelia's spine, for it was as though a legion of ghosts had drawn near, bringing with them the chill solitude of the grave. Gitana picked up another bottle from the altar, opened it, and cast its crystals to the wind.

"I honor thee, O Spirit Bechard. . . . Doest thou hear and know my demands and desires?"

The soughing breath rejoined with a murmur.

The hermit nodded.

"'Tis good," she asserted. Then, "This is the Element Air, mutable, ever changing, Ferrier of the Soul. Fly upon its wings, Lady, that your spirit may know the joys of unworldly freedom as it seeks passage to the Far Beyond."

For the first time, the Lady hesitated.

"Do not be afraid, Lady. Touch my robe."

Timidly, the Lady stretched out one hand to touch Gitana's chasuble. Almost instantly, the Lady heard a low thrumming begin in her ears. It grew louder and louder until it echoed with a piercing ring. She longed to put her hands over her ears, to shut out the sound, but she dared not release her hold on the Ancient One's robe. The Lady's heart beat faster and faster until she thought it would surely burst within her breast. Then the horrible wrenching started. It felt as though an invisible fist had reached inside her body, grabbed her soul, and were now trying to yank it from her very being. She fought the terrible force with all her might, certain she would die if she yielded to it. But her struggles were in vain. Moments later, she had become a disembodied spirit floating in the cave.

Horrified screams clawed their way up Ophelia's throat as she watched her mistress's astral body leave its physical shell, only a slender, silver, ethereal cord binding the two. But the handmaiden was even more terrified of the sorceress, Gitana, and so she choked down her cries until they were only muffled sobs.

The Lady did not hear them. She was flying upon the wings of the wind down the black passage leading to the Far Beyond. Time and space as she knew them had ceased to exist. There was naught but the cold, dark tunnel that was nothingness as she rushed through it. Ahead, she could see the first lambent beams of the Light, dazzling in their effulgence. A glorious joy permeated her being. She did not want to go back . . .

But she was back, and the Lady saw it was as though she had never left her body. All was as it had been, as though it had been frozen, suspended in time for that fleeting eternity. She glanced about disbelievingly, and Gitana gave another small crow of laughter, holding forth the ornate chalice. The wind blew, stirring the contents of the silver cup.

"O Spirit Bechard," the wisewoman chortled, "because thou hast truly and faithfully answered my demands and performed my desires according to my will and intentions, I do hereby give thee license to depart. . . ."

The grotto was eerie in its sudden silence.

Gitana turned the culminating pages in her book. The Lady trembled violently, certain the last—and worst—was now to come.

"In the Name of the Light," the solitary crooned, "O Spirit Eblis, I, Gitana, do invoke and conjure thee. . . ."

She waved her wand again. A crowning streak of resplendent glitter erupted in the cave. Then all was still.

Slowly, a bitter cold started to invade the cavern. It was even more horrifying than the unworldly chill of the Element Air, for this cold brought with it the putrid stench of decay, the foul, rotten odor of things dead but uncremated. . . .

The Lady cowered on the ground, shielding her eyes, as

though by not seeing the final spirit, she could ward off its evil. For it *was* evil. Even Gitana seemed to sense that this spirit brought the Darkness with it, for she switched her wand to her left hand and laid her other warily upon the arthame at her waist.

Her voice rang out authoritatively again.

"In the Name of the Light, O Spirit Eblis, I, Gitana, do invoke and conjure thee. . . ."

Once more, she waved her wand, and the lightning sparked. And still, all was hushed and cold and rancid. Ophelia gasped as, with a wild shriek of fury, the beldam drew her dagger from its scabbard.

"In the Name of the Light," she howled ominously, her aura blazing like a spangled mass of shooting stars, "who rulest over all Spirits, Superior and Inferior, but especially over thee, O Spirit Eblis, I, Gitana, do invoke and conjure thee. . . . Behold! I shall curse thee. . . ."

Again she waved her wand, and the lightning crackled in reply.

For a time, all was silent. Then, suddenly, the fire flared with a roar, its tongues singeing the hem of Gitana's chasuble. With another shrill cry of anger, she struck out with her steel at the flames, forcing them back. Once more, they leaped high, scorching her robe; and the battle was joined.

Tears ran down the Lady's face and Ophelia screamed soundlessly as the seer stabbed repeatedly at the blaze and parried the wicked thrusts of its licking flames. It was vicious in its disobedience, as though possessed by a hideous diabolism. Twice, it appeared the fire would envelop both Gitana and the Lady, but at last, the flames were the hermit's to command. Breathing hard, she turned, prudently keeping one eye on the blaze. She decided on a final vial from the dais, opened it, and flung its minerals upon the fire.

"I honor thee, O Spirit Eblis. . . . Doest thou hear and know my demands and desires?"

The flames raged in response, belching smoke, as though they would attack again; but presently, they quieted at Gitana's remonstration.

"'Tis good," the Ancient One stated. Then, "This is the

Element Fire, cardinal, most important, Bringer of the Light—and the Darkness. Draw near, Lady, but not too near, for only a soul that has reached its Phoenix may rise from the fire's ashes."

Terrified, the Lady approached the blaze and felt its heat sear her. Gitana handed her the chalice filled with the potion prepared earlier by the other three spirits.

"Place this upon the flames," the sorceress instructed.

The Lady knelt, setting the cup in the center of the fire, taking care not to spill its contents, though her flesh was burned by the malevolent blaze and acrid smoke filled her eyes and nostrils. Afterward, she stepped away quickly.

"Give me your left hand," Gitana ordered.

Ophelia clapped her fingers to her mouth to stifle her screams as, without warning, the wisewoman jabbed her knife down, cutting the Lady's palm open with the blade's sharp point. Blood spurted from the jagged, arc-shaped wound. Gitana then slashed her own hand in the same fashion and pressed her palm against the Lady's. Their blood mingled as it dripped slowly into the chalice. The liquid within started to hiss and bubble, foaming over the edges of the cup into the fire.

Seeing this, the solitary bent and took the chalice from the flames. The silver of which it was made glowed hotly, and the Lady marveled that it had not melted and that the metal did not burn the beldam's withered flesh.

Gitana poured the cup's contents into a clear purple glass flacon, then sealed it with a silver stopper.

"O Spirit Eblis, because thou hast truly and faithfully answered my demands and performed my desires according to my will and intentions, I do hereby give thee leave to depart. . . ."

At first, it seemed the spirit would disobey the seer's command; but she raised her arthame threateningly, and gradually, the fire burned down until naught save embers remained.

Gitana pressed the purple bottle into the Lady's hands.

"The Power of the Elements lies within this small vial," the Ancient One said. "On Lugnasad Eve, when the Passion Moon starts to rise, ye shall lace Balthasar's wine and yours with this bitter brew and drink it, Lady. His desire for ye will be as it has never been before, as yours will be for him, and his seed will take root and grow strong within ye. From your mating will come a child, a sorceress more powerful than any Tintagel has ever seen. She shall be called Ileana, Chosen by the Light; and though she will be born from your womb, Lady, she shall belong to the Druswids. Remember that, for when the Darkness first casts Its shadow upon the land, she must be given unto the Sisters at Mont Saint Mikhaela."

"Nay, Reverend Mother!" the Lady protested, though fearfully. Still, the thought of parting from her unborn daughter fueled her sudden defiance. "Ye cannot ask that of me! Ye cannot!"

"I can, and I do," the sorceress insisted grimly, her obsidian eyes holding the Lady's ice-blue ones mesmerizingly. "All must be done as I have spoken, or we are lost. Do ye understand me?"

"Yea, Reverend Mother, I do." The Lady capitulated at last, defeated.

"Pray ye do indeed, Lady, for if all I have wrought this eve does not come to pass, I will know ye have failed me, and the penalty for your failure shall be more terrible than even I can name. Therefore, heed my warning well, and speak to no one of this night! So I, Gitana, command ye. Go with the Light."

It was done. The Ritual of Choosing was over, finished. It seemed as though it had taken hours, and yet as she and Ophelia stumbled through the snow to where Strom waited with the skittish alaecorns, the Lady saw that the deep lilac Passion Moon was just reaching its zenith in the heavens.

She clutched the precious flacon tightly to her breast and, starring herself with one trembling hand, began fervently to pray.

CRESCENT MOON

Daughter of the Light

Chapter 3

It is known that the Light Eternal set the Kind apart from other worldly creatures, and it has been written that this Uniqueness comes from the Kind's Investiture by the Immortal Guardian of a Free Will enabling the Kind to choose their own LifePaths and Destinies.

I say unto ye that this is not always thus, that sometimes Fate chooses us instead, and we are helpless against it. . . .

—Thus it is Written—
in
The Chosen
by the High Princess Lady Ileana I

Khali Keep, Bedoui, 7345.8.21

SHE WAS OLDER NOW—AND WISER—AND IF SOMETIMES LATE AT night the shadows of regret darkened her thoughts, like clouds the moons, they were only fleeting and she had learned to live with them.

It had not always been thus. Once, she had been young and foolish, a child in her father's castle, Ariel Heights, where the world had been hers and she'd had only to lift her hand to command it. She'd known nothing of the Light and the Darkness then, and the Power had not yet come to her.

She remembered it all so well, as though it were only yesterday when she stole among the winter-ravaged gardens of her father's fortress and felt the sharp, bitter wind prick her face with thorns of sleet, leaving it flushed like the dusky-pink roses that would bloom again in spring. They were dead now, brown and lifeless. The vines clinging to the snow-laden trellises were stripped bare save for the rivulets of rain that had turned to icy little waterfalls. They glittered like a young maiden's tears when touched by the pale twilight sun that struggled to pierce the hazy shroud of mist that always enveloped her father's castle. Like the Weeping Wraiths that few but the Chosen ever saw, tiny wisps of white-grey clouds floated among the branches of the stark trees, and brittle, dead leaves rattled on the nearly naked limbs and rustled on the ground where she trod. Once or twice, an owl hooted, its plaintive cry like the moan of some sorrowful ghost. But other than this, there was only the hushed stillness of winter's sounds soaked up by the thick, powdery white snow.

Even then, she was a child of winter, pure and untouched. Yet like the season, death lurked within her soul, a harbinger of the Darkness that precedes all rebirth. She did not understand it then, for at first, its images came only in puzzling, distorted fragments, as though seen through a vignette; and when she finally comprehended their import, it was too late to draw back: She was already caught fast in the throes of the Power for which she had been conceived and born. But in the beginning, as she knelt beside the pond that lay in a sheltered corner of her father's gardens, she saw only a brief glimpse of what would someday be hers, and so it had little meaning for her then.

How clear and vivid was her memory of it even now, keen and bright-edged, like the sun upon an arthame. It seemed strange that it should be thus when nearly a lifetime had passed since then and the Power had long since faded, never to come again with its brilliant, white-hot flashes of color and its wild, glorious cry of the Keepers. But it was so.

Ah, the Power . . . her ecstasy, her agony.

Sometimes her remembrance of it was so real that she awakened with the auras once more blinding her eyes and the call of the harps and flutes still echoing in her ears. Then, for a moment, the exciting, exhilarating rush of those days long gone would fill her body and lift her restless spirit before she realized she was only dreaming.

She could still see. She could still call up the flames as she had of old or find the pictures in a silver pool, a polished mirror, or a crystal sphere. Like reading the ancient cards and tea leaves, these were the simplest of magics, the first to be discovered, the last to be lost. But the images were now blurred with the shadows of age, of too many things seen in the fires and mists of long ago. All had left their marks upon her, making her hesitant now to gaze too closely through the portals to the Far Beyond. There is joy in knowledge, but there is pain also; and sometimes she wondered if she would have been better off not knowing.

Such was not her LifePath, however, for she was one of the Chosen, those precious few upon whose shoulders the choice between the Light and the Darkness forever rests and whose decisions determine the fates of worlds.

How heavy a burden for one so young as she was that day long past when she looked into the frozen mirror that was the pond.

Had she been older, wiser, as she was now, she might have hesitated and never grasped the Power that was hers, for it was a frightening force, an awesome thing to behold, a fearsome influence to control. But she had known only five years then, and the weight of the world had not yet crushed her with its ponderous load. So she stared at her reflection in the icy looking glass, and she was not afraid.

Her long silver hair, the pale, frosted color of the First Moon, shimmered about her like a shroud, making a curtain around her face and her figure as she knelt there in the soft, deep snow and studied herself solemnly.

She was small for her age and delicate, with wide lavender eyes set in her perfect, oval countenance. They were the eyes of a changeling child—or so her mother often said and would star herself to ward off evil when she glanced at the girl, although she loved her well.

But the child's eyes were for her windows through which to see the mysteries denied mere mortal beings. Young though she was, this she felt instinctively as, through the mist that had begun to settle low and thick upon its polished surface, she peered into the pond and watched her reflection disappear as though it had never been.

She knew no fear even then. Only a strange curiosity

possessed her as she stretched out her hands and laid them upon the diamond-hard ice. Her reflection had indeed vanished and was nowhere to be found.

This is what she saw that winter's gloaming, when the Power that was to shape her LifePath first came to her.

It was winter, as it was then, and cold, so bitterly cold and dark. Yet by the light of the moons, even through the snow that fell steadily, silently, she recognized the place where she stood. She had been there once before during her childhood. It was Dorian's Watch, the jagged headland that lay upon the far west tip of Cygnus, her birthplace.

Though the bristly pines that dotted the mountains bent beneath the lash of the cruel wind, the girl stood there tall and proud upon the naked edge of the high cliff, her hair streaming back wildly from her face and her djellaba billowing violently about her figure. She watched not the southern shore across the Gulf of Mab, as Dorian had done, but the Sirocco Ocean, the tempestuous, shifting sea that roared along the coast, waves crashing upon the rocks on the beach.

She was older, much older than the child she was then. But still, she knew it was herself who stood there staring with mingled apprehension and anticipation, waiting, waiting. . . .

After a time, there came a strange lull in the brewing storm. Her breath caught in her throat, for she knew that what she awaited was about to come.

The whitecaps of the madding sea gathered like ghostly steeds at the far side of their grey-green arena, as though preparing to gallop headlong into battle. Then, suddenly, they thundered toward her, merging into a vast wall of fury a league or more in height. On and on, the great wave hurtled toward her until she thought she would be swept away before it, crushed beneath its tremendous tide.

But at the last moment, by some peculiar trick of fate, the glorious wail of the Keepers filled the night and the waters broke apart to rend themselves on the spiny crags that thrust up from the slush upon the beach.

From the site of their parting was flung a man mounted upon a massive black faesthors. In one hand, he held a brilliantly flaming sword, its length fashioned of molten ore fallen from the heavens, its jewel-encrusted hilt, of gold.

A prince the man was, a high prince. But it was his blade that caught and held her attention, for it was an unworldly weapon, the Sword of Ishtar, Keeper of the Stars. The child trembled at the knowledge, for though she had never seen the Holy Relic, somehow she recognized it for what it was.

Aeons ago, it had been brought from the Far Beyond to Tintagel by a great lord, his body now long since dead, who had vowed that Ishtar herself had given the blade unto him to wield against the Darkness. The weapon had been handed down from one generation to the next until, during the Wars of the Kind and the Apocalypse, it had mysteriously disappeared.

Now the stories told of it were legend. Some said that Ishtar, angered by the Kind's turning from the Way, had retrieved the weapon and returned it to the stars, whence it had come. Others claimed the sword had been stolen by Tintagel's enemies and destroyed when it was learned they could not bend it to their will. Still others swore that before the blade could fall into the evil hands of the Darkness that had seized the world in Its terrible grasp, it had been spirited away and hidden by True Defenders of the Light, who, even in the Time Before, had guarded the land against the Foul Enslaver and Its Demons. Since then, it was said, the weapon had lain always in the secret Holy Place, never to be wielded again until one who had been Chosen by the Light should take it from its resting place. When that happened, it was said, the Darkness would once more cast Its shadow upon the land, and only two who had once been one would stand between It and the end of the world.

Now, the child knew, the Time of the Prophecy was at hand.

The sword flashed with blinding red-gold luminescence as the man mounted upon the mighty faesthors soared higher and higher, his blade cutting an arc of glittering flame across the firmament. Like some erratic comet, he rose, piercing the night sky and, with a deadly, unnatural determination that frightened her, battling an unseen foe.

Then, suddenly, the man and animal swooped straight

toward her. She saw the High Prince's dark visage clearly
—the Tyrian-crimson sunburst tattooed between his fierce
black brows, his black-velvet eyes, his carnal mouth
—before, loosing his hold on the faesthors's reins, he
reached out and swept her up before him. She gasped as the
warmth of the man's body flooded her own; and then, as her
face was drawn irresistibly to his, she shivered uncontrollably at the bloodlust revealed in his midnight eyes—eyes
that burned dark with passion. He wanted her, this Defender of the Light. She was the price of his salvation.

The sword he wielded still glowed hotly, like an ember,
but she no longer saw it. There was naught for her but the
hungry, haunting eyes of the High Prince and his sensuous
lips parting to claim hers possessively as his aura ignited
and melded with her own, overpowering her, enveloping
her, forging a bond between them that would never be
broken as long as they lived.

Abruptly, the image faded, and after blinking a few times,
the child slowly became aware once more of her surroundings. She shook her head a little, as though to clear it, and
drew the folds of her white wool cape more closely about
her to ward off the chill that had seeped into her bones.

She shuddered as she pondered what she had seen. What
did it mean? she wondered. *Was* it a portent of the future, or
had she somehow fallen asleep without realizing it and
dreamed the entire episode? She did not know, and because
of this, she was afraid, for it was frightening to think she
might have the Sight. Had she known that the extent of her
power was to be far greater than this, she would have been
terrified.

As it was, a sense of foreboding began to tingle eerily
along her spine; and for one wild eternity, she yearned to
turn back the hands of time, to obliterate the moment when
she had first looked into the pond.

But she could not, for she was the Lady Ileana sin
Ariel—Chosen by the Light.

Chapter 4

A wise Prophet of another world once saith: "In my father's house, there are many rooms." I tell ye this Prophet spake truly, for the Dimensions of Existence are indeed many. In a house, when one door closes, another opens so the one who dwells therein may progress from room to room. Thus do the Portals between the Dimensions of Existence open and close also so the Spirit may progress from Plane to Plane. And so it is that for every LifePath there is a Time of Passing, and this is but the Way to the Light Eternal.

—Thus it is Written—
in
The Word and The Way
The Book of Rani, Chapter Eleven, Verse Nine

Ariel Heights, Cygnus, 7258.4.9

ILEANA HAD KNOWN ONLY SEVEN YEARS THAT SUMMER WHEN THE body of the old High King Lord Gwalchmei died and her father, the High Prince Lord Balthasar, was crowned the High King of all Tintagel. Still, she recalled it well, for it was then the Power she had first glimpsed in the pond that winter in her father's gardens began truly to come to her.

It was the month of Cancri, and she was sitting in the schoolroom of her father's castle, Ariel Heights, hearing but not really listening to Master Zelotes's voice as he tutored her and her siblings at their lessons. The sun, Sorcha, was just setting on the far horizon of the endless sky, its rays slanting through the diamond-shaped, lead-glass panes of the narrow fortress windows, making filmy rainbows of gold tinged with lilac and azure upon the hard oak floor. The evening was quiet and peaceful, the silence broken only just now by the resonant chiming of the chapel angelus sounding the call to prayer, echoing—or so it was said—the unheard tolling of the Eternal Bell of the Far Beyond.

As Ileana obediently rose and knelt, facing south, as befitted the Vespers Hour, she remembered thinking she liked this part of each day the best, for it was as though time had ceased at the castle and the world outside its high, massive walls did not exist. Yet she knew even then it did, for without warning, she felt a strange ripple of joy mingled with sorrow shudder through her being, momentarily stilling the prayers upon her lips; and without knowing why, she sensed that the High King's body was dead. She was gladdened by the thought that his soul was no longer burdened by its physical shell, but she was saddened, as well, by the knowledge that those the Lord Gwalchmei loved must now be parted from him until they, too, experienced their Time of Passing.

Thus, of all her siblings, Ileana alone was unsurprised when, following the evensong, her mother, the Lady Lucia, appeared in the doorway of the schoolroom.

After a muted conversation with Master Zelotes, Lucia turned to her now seated children and gently informed them of the death of the High King's body a fortnight ago. At the news, they once more stood, then sank to their knees, starring themselves as, softly, they began to chant the Prayer of Passing so the Lord Gwalchmei's journey to the Far Beyond would be a good one:

> May thy Spirit hasten
> To where the Light awaits
> Past the Far Beyond.
> May thine eyes remain blind
> To the Darkness
> That would rob thee of thy Soul
> For all time.
> May thy footsteps never falter

On the path to the Immortal Guardian,
Leading thee astray,
Leaving thee lost.
May thy lips respond sure and true
To the questions of the Keeper of the Gate,
That thee are not turned away as Unworthy
At the end of thy travails.
May thy heart stand fast
And Understanding crown thy Essence
With its Joyous Delights.
May the Swords of Truth, Righteousness, and Honor
Be always at thy side,
And may the Light Eternal shine upon thee
With its Everlasting Flame.

Their prayer ended, the youngsters rose and waited expectantly for their mother to speak again. When she did, it was to tell them there were to be no more lessons with Master Zelotes until the various ceremonies engendered by the High King's passing had taken place. Although pleased to escape from the schoolroom, the children were at first somewhat confused by this announcement, for the Lord Gwalchmei had ruled Tintagel for as long as any of them could remember and they had never seen the rites their mother briefly described to them. It was only after she had gone and they began to discuss the matter among themselves that they realized that their father was now the High King and that a new heir or heiress to the High Throne must be chosen. Their voices rose with anticipation at the thought, for the forthcoming ceremonies were sure to prove exciting, with the Tribes from all the known-inhabited continents gathering for the occasion.

Only Ileana did not join in the bright chatter and laughter that now filled the schoolroom. She was too caught up in the dark feeling of premonition that had slowly crept upon her, making her distinctly uneasy. There was no rational explanation for it, she knew, for there was nothing ominous about the upcoming ceremonies. Still, she could not help but feel something terrible was going to happen.

Unaware she did so, she closed her eyes tightly, inwardly pleading for a glimpse of the future like that which she had seen in the pond. But she saw naught save darkness, and at last, she gave up the attempt, opening her eyes and laughing a little to herself to allay her fears. She was being foolish, she supposed, letting her imagination run away with her again, just as it had that winter in her father's gardens. Still, though she had assured herself she'd simply fallen asleep that twilit eve and dreamed, even now the memory of it sent a shiver down her spine. She'd never mentioned it to anyone, sensing instinctively that to do so would irrevocably change her life. She was not sure why this was so—only that it was.

Resolutely, Ileana thrust the recollection aside, relieved that this time, she had seen nothing untoward. It was, she felt, further evidence that she was possessed of a fanciful nature but nothing more. She was glad, for the thought that she might be one of the Chosen scared her. She had seen the Druswids, as those belonging to the Brotherhood and the Sisterhood were called, and she knew that some of them were privy to dreadful knowledge and had powers far surpassing those of mere mortal beings. The Chosen walked where none other dared to tread, and the roads they traveled were often hard and lonely. Ileana had no desire to make their LifePath her own, and she had no real reason to assume it would be.

Determinedly shaking off her apprehension and forcing herself to smile, she joined her siblings, who were still conversing animatedly as they exited the schoolroom.

With the coming of dusk, the torches set into the iron sconces that lined the walls of the long, winding corridors of Ariel Heights had been lit. The bright, dancing flames dispelled some of Ileana's gloom as she hurried toward her chamber, for they were a comforting reminder that the Light was always with those who believed, no matter how dark the hour. There was naught to fear. She was safe within her father's castle, and the land had been at peace for many long years now, the Demons who had once trespassed upon it having been driven from its shores. The final remnants of her trepidation dissipated at the thought.

Having reached her room, she opened the door and went in. There, her nurse, Agathe, and her young handmaiden, Charis, were waiting.

"Ye are late, Lady," Agathe observed, glancing at the clock on the mantel above the fireplace. "But no matter. The supper hour has been set back because of the Lord Gwalchmei's passing, so there is time yet for ye to wash and to dress properly. Your bath is waiting, and Charis has laid out clean clothes for ye."

"Thank you, Agathe," Ileana said.

Under her nurse's watchful eyes, she stood quietly while the seven-year-old Charis undressed her and pinned up her long hair. Then Ileana stepped behind the ornate screen that shielded one corner of her chamber. There, she slipped into her hammered-brass bathtub filled with steaming water and began to lave herself thoroughly with hyacinth-scented soap. When she had finished rinsing, Charis handed her a thick, fluffy towel with which to dry herself. After that, Agathe took charge, assisting her into her garments. Then the nurse removed the pins from Ileana's silvery tresses, brushed them, and plaited them into a single intricate braid.

"There, Lady." Agathe nodded with approval as she eyed her handiwork critically. "Ye look as fine as a newly minted platina. Run along now, for if I'm not mistaken, that's the sound of the supper gong I hear."

With Charis at her side, Ileana made her way to the great hall of the fortress and took her place at her mother's left at the high table. Charis stood behind her, leaning forward to fill Ileana's pewter plate with food from the many dishes arrayed upon the table and her pewter cup with watered, sweet red wine. Ileana ate hungrily but scarcely paid any heed to the lavish meal, for her attention was focused on her father, now the High King Lord Balthasar.

How tired and solemn he looked, she thought, as though the weight of the world had settled upon his shoulders. But then, of course, it had; and though Ileana had no real concept of all that being the High King entailed, she knew it must be an awesome task indeed.

Having known more than forty years, the Lord Balthasar sin Ariel sul Ariel was an imposing figure—silver-haired and blue-eyed, tall, lithe, and powerfully built. He easily dominated the great hall, and even had he not occupied the most important place at the high table, none would have mistaken him for a man of lesser rank. His bearing was regal, and he wore his authority like a mantle. It was evident he was accustomed to giving orders and to having them obeyed.

For over twenty-five years, he had been the High Prince of Tintagel, heir to the High Throne and second in rank only to the High King. Now Balthasar need kneel to no one. Tintagel was his to command.

He grieved deeply over the passing of the Lord Gwalchmei, who had, with wisdom and caring, prepared him for the burden of responsibility that was now his. He would miss his friend and mentor sorely, he realized, for already the weight of his new position was beginning to make itself felt. Still, though filled with sadness at his loss, Balthasar would not shirk his duty. He would rule as the Lord Gwalchmei would have wished him to rule, and he would do his best to ensure his reign proved a happy and prosperous one for the people. He felt confident it would. If he had any concerns at all, they were for his wife, Lucia.

Unobtrusively, Balthasar gazed at her. A frown knitted his brow. Ever since the scroll-bearing messenger-hawk dispatched from Vikanglia had reached them and they had learned of the Lord Gwalchmei's passing, she had seemed different somehow, deeply troubled in some manner he could not discern. Outwardly, she appeared unchanged. But she had been his wife for over two decades, and they were very close. Balthasar sensed that despite her composed facade, Lucia was a mass of turmoil. Yet when he had mentioned the matter to her earlier, she had only laughed brightly and said it was nothing more than simple excitement coupled with anxiety at being the new High Queen. Still, he reflected, there had been a false note in her laughter, and her explanation, while plausible, had not rung true.

The thought disturbed him, for it was not like Lucia to shut him out. He wondered what it was she feared. Yea, that was it: She was afraid. But why? Balthasar did not know, nor did he guess that more than anything, his wife yearned to take him into her confidence. But she dared not, for even now, after all these years, she could still hear the words of the sorceress Gitana san Kovichi ringing in her ears.

Speak to no one of this night! Speak to no one of this night!
And so Lucia had kept quiet. And on that Lugnasad Eve

long past, she had drugged her wine and Balthasar's with the bitter potion, as instructed, and later had given birth to Ileana.

From the beginning, Lucia had watched the child closely, unable to believe she did not bear some visible sign of her unorthodox conception. But except for her lavender-colored eyes, rare but not unknown among the Cygninae, she was no different from the others of her tribe. And so as the years had passed and nothing untoward had occurred, Lucia had started to breathe a little easier, certain that somehow the Ancient One's magic had failed. Lucia had determined she could not be held accountable for that. She'd done all that had been required of her; it was not her fault if the sorceress's spell had not worked. Relieved, Lucia had finally thrust the entire affair from her mind. In later years, it had been only occasionally that she'd looked at Ileana and felt a tiny chill of dread. At such times, Lucia had starred herself for protection and silently begged forgiveness for having betrayed Balthasar's trust in her.

But now the thought of what she had done that night so long ago preyed heavily on her conscience. Inadvertently, one hand strayed to her breast, where the missive she had received earlier this evening nestled disconcertingly beneath the bodice of her abayeh. No doubt the letter had been kindly intended, for it need not have been sent at all. But still, it tore at Lucia's heart. The words that were written upon the parchment had been indelibly branded into her soul: *It begins,* the note read. *Prepare yourself to be parted from the child.*

It was signed by the High Priestess Sharai san Jyotis of Mont Saint Mikhaela and had been delivered by one of the silent, veiled Sisters from the nunnery.

Though she will be born from your womb, Lady, she shall belong to the Druswids. Remember that, for when the Darkness first casts Its shadow upon the land, she must be given unto the Sisters at Mont Saint Mikhaela.

The words of the sorceress haunted Lucia.

Nay! I cannot bear it! she thought wildly. *They will not take my child!*

But they could, and they would, for no one dared to defy the Druswids. Their knowledge and power were too great.

Even Balthasar, who now ruled all Tintagel, would not challenge their authority, for they served a law higher than his worldly one.

Lucia inhaled raggedly, stifling with difficulty the sobs that choked her throat as she studied her eldest daughter, sitting quietly by her side. Ileana was so young, so innocent. It was not fair that she should be wrenched from her home and shut away in an abbey, where she would become a novice subject to rigorous training and hardships. Yet such was to be her LifePath, and there was nothing Lucia could do to prevent it. Nothing!

She felt that somehow she had failed her child—and Balthasar, too. What would he say when he discovered what his wife had done? He would be hurt and angry that without his knowing, she had pledged their daughter to the Druswids. Still, he loved her, Lucia thought, taking comfort from the knowledge. He would understand how afraid she'd been, how she'd seemed to have no will of her own when she'd gazed into the Ancient One's black, piercing eyes that night long past. Yea, he would know there was nothing else she could have done, and in time, perhaps he would forgive her.

Time. How much did she have, Lucia wondered, before they came to take her child?

Covertly, she glanced again at her daughter. How strange it seemed that Ileana would be a sorceress more powerful than any Tintagel had ever known. What need could the world have of such?

When the Darkness first casts Its shadow upon the land . . . The Darkness . . . It begins. . . .

Suddenly, Lucia shivered uncontrollably. She had been so distraught at the idea of parting from her child that she had not considered at all the reason why she must do so. The Darkness was returning to Tintagel; It might be here even now. Lucia recoiled in horror from the realization. Like those with the Sight, she had been given a glimpse of the future, and for the first time, she pitied those who must carry the burden of such knowledge upon their souls. To know that the Darkness was coming and yet to be powerless to prevent it . . .

What form would Its evil take? Perhaps even the

Druswids did not know for certain, Lucia speculated, frightened. Perhaps even they had seen only shapes and shadows of the things to come. But if so, even these had so horrified them, the Ancient One had dared to perform the Ritual of Choosing. She had dared to summon the Power of the Elements and to bestow it upon Ileana, knowing that if ever the girl turned her hand to the Darkness, all that she was would be corrupted and used against the Light. What a risk the sorceress had taken!

Now Lucia saw the wisdom of the Ancient One's insisting Ileana be given unto the Sisters at Mont Saint Mikhaela. There, at least, she would be prepared to wield the Power that was hers; she would learn how to recognize and to withstand the lures of the Foul Enslaver and Its Demons, whispered in honeyed tones and wrapped in velvet raiment. Yea, when Ileana joined the Druswids, she would be in the hands best suited to mold her into what she must be.

Lucia could ask for nothing more. Instead, she must think of Balthasar and the rest of their children.

Balthasar. She shuddered to think his reign as the High King of Tintagel would be a time of the Darkness. He must be warned. When the Sisters came for Ileana, Lucia would no longer keep the secret she had harbored all these years. She would tell Balthasar what she knew. He must be able to take what steps he could against the coming evil, even as the Druswids had done, and as she herself must do.

Amen, she thought. *So be it.*

Forcing herself to smile, Lucia reached out and took one of her husband's hands in hers, holding it tightly and blinking back the tears that stung her ice-blue eyes. She was the High Queen, and she would do her duty as such. But, oh, how she wished she were only Balthasar's wife, that they were only common folk, who bore not the weight of the world upon their shoulders.

Oh, my love, her heart cried out to him silently, *would that we could turn back the hands of time, for our past has been a happy one, and I fear the future and what it may bring.*

As though he sensed her despair, Balthasar's face filled with love and solicitude for her; and for a moment he, too, longed for the old days, when they wore not the High Crown and High Coronet of Tintagel.

Chapter 5

There are five elements: Fire, Earth, Air, Water, and Ether. Four of these belong to the Kind. The last belongs only to the Immortal Guardian. All are vital. But of those known to the Kind, Water is the most precious, for it is the Giver of Life and Rebirth.

—Thus it is Written—
in
The Teachings of the Mont Sects
The Book of Elements, Chapter One

THOUGH ONCE BEFORE, FROM DORIAN'S WATCH, ILEANA HAD seen the Mistral Ocean to the west, she had never before traveled upon its waves; and now, standing at the rail of the ship that was carrying her westward to the continent of Vikanglia, she was filled with awe by the water's vastness, its primeval force, and her own sense of aloneness and insignificance as she gazed upon it.

This must be what it was like in the Beginning, she thought, *when the world was empty and there were only the land and the sea, always the sea, mutable, ever changing, and so great and powerful that all who look upon it must feel diminished.*

The ocean stretched out endlessly around her in all directions, seeming to touch the far horizon; and for a moment, Ileana could imagine that it had somehow swallowed the land, that now there was only the sea and nothing more.

She had heard the tales the bards sang about ancient lands that had either fallen into the ocean or been swept away by its fearsome tide: Mu, Pan, Lumania, Lemuria, Atlantis, Lyonnesse, and Ys. Once, it was said, these had been great civilizations whose knowledge had been so vast, it had enabled them to colonize many planets. But here on Tintagel, the sea had claimed what they had built. Now all that was left of them were the sunken castles the pearl and sponge divers of Lorelei swore they sometimes spied fathoms deep beneath the water. Others said such sightings were only stories, that such "fortresses" were naught but mountains, cliffs, and boulders that had crumbled into the ocean, which continuously eroded the land, changing and reshaping it. Still, Ileana believed there must be some truth to the legends, and she stared raptly at the sea, hoping to catch a glimpse of the age-old keeps.

The sky arched above her, a delicate shade of blue made warm and bright by the mellow sun and streaked with white where cloud wisps reached across the firmament like slender fingers. The waves below reflected the heavens, gleaming clear and azure beneath the sun. A cool, gentle wind, tasting of salt, blew across the water and sprayed Ileana's face. Overhead, the white sails of the galley billowed and flogged in the breeze, and below deck, the oars wielded by the rowers moved in unison to the rhythmic beat of the deep drum that set their pace, echoing the sigh of the ocean as it whispered in her ear.

It was as though the sea spoke to her, and briefly, Ileana wished she could understand what it was saying, for she felt somehow that it knew secrets she must learn. For an instant, she strained her ears against the soughing of the wind and the water, listening intently to the voices that seemed to call out to her softly. Perhaps they belonged to the long-gone civilizations of yesteryear, she mused. Then, abruptly, she shook her head, laughing at her whimsies.

Though it was true that those who died before their LifePaths were finished walked the land as ghosts, they usually spoke only to the Chosen, who were sentient enough to communicate with them. They had little use for mere mortals.

Ileana smiled with relief at the thought, glad she was not burdened by more than five senses, for she knew if ever she really did see or hear a fetch, she would be quite frightened.

Pushing the unpleasant notion from her mind, she turned her eyes to the blue waves in the distance, where a school of grey dolphins had appeared. This was a welcome sight, for the porpoises were said to bring good luck. They sliced through the water, heaving up magnificently into the air, then plunging beneath the ocean's surface. Some twisted and turned in midair before diving. After reappearing from beneath the sea, they reared and bobbed a kind of bow when Ileana laughed and applauded their playful antics. Their happy, high-pitched cries rang out over the waves, attracting other people aboard the ship; and presently, Ileana realized she was no longer alone at the rail. Her mother had joined her.

Lucia had been occupied with her two younger daughters, the twins, Daphne and Phoebe, who had fallen prey to seasickness. Now, having left them in the capable hands of their nurse, she was drawn to Ileana, intent on spending as much time as possible with her, for who knew how many precious days together they had remaining?

Ileana did not know they were soon to be parted, but she sensed her mother's distress all the same and wondered at its cause. Ever since becoming the High Queen, her mother had been different somehow. There was a sadness in her eyes that had not been there before, and an air of what seemed almost like apprehension clung to her, though only the most observant would have noticed it.

Wishing to cheer her, Ileana pointed out the dolphins, relieved to see they brought a smile to her mother's face.

"The Loreleish say the porpoises bring good fortune, Mother," Ileana remarked. "Do ye suppose 'tis true?"

"I hope so," Lucia replied fervently, as though speaking to herself.

But still, she could not shake off the feeling of trepidation that enveloped her; and there were tears in her eyes when she laid her hand upon Ileana's head and drew her close, wondering why this beloved child, of all others, must be one of the Chosen.

It begins.

—Thus it is Written—
in
A Letter to the High Queen Lady Lucia II
from the High Priestess Sharai IV

It was two days later when they saw the craft—or what was left of it, for floating on the waves were only a few rough planks from what had once been a dinghy.

When the drifting pieces of wood were pointed out to him, the captain of the PT *Mystic Rose* ordered the crew to furl the sails, cease rowing, and drop anchor. Then a small boat was lowered so two sailors might retrieve the splintered planks.

Once aboard the galley, the pieces were carefully examined by Captain Theron; the first mate, Master Faustis; and the High King Lord Balthasar. It was evident that whatever had happened to the craft had occurred some time ago, for the battered wood was covered with seaweed, algae, and barnacles, and it had been burrowed through in places by teredo worms as well.

"Some fisherman's dinghy caught in a storm and capsized, most like." Captain Theron voiced this opinion for the benefit of the women present, for there were several deep, bloodstained gouges in the planks, and the marks appeared as though they had been made by powerful teeth or claws. Privately, Captain Theron thought the boat had been set upon by some sea monster. "From the look of things, I'd say there isn't any use in searching for survivors, Lord." He addressed Balthasar respectfully, his tone underlaid with tacit meaning. "The oceans' currents are strong and swift. No telling when or where the craft went under."

"Nay, I should think not." The High King shook his head gravely, hoping the dinghy's crew had not suffered long, for he had not missed the strange furrows in the wood. "We will take a moment for the Prayer of Passing, Captain, then continue our journey."

"By your command, Lord." Captain Theron bowed.

He was just turning away to issue the necessary orders to the sailors when he was stopped by the first mate.

"Stay a moment, Cap'n," Master Faustis said. "Look here . . . beneath this seaweed."

The first mate pushed aside the tangled strands of kelp wrapped around a curved piece of wood. After scraping away the patches of algae and barnacles that clung to the plank, the captain could just distinguish the faint letters that had once been painted so boldly on the boat's bow: CV *Far Explorer*.

"Why, this was no fisherman's craft, Lord," he told Balthasar softly. "This was one of the lifeboats from the *Far Explorer*."

His tone was solemn; but even so, he could not disguise his excitement, for over the past several years, in the hope of finding other tribes that had survived the Wars of the Kind and the Apocalypse, both the planetary and the continental governments of Tintagel had dispatched various ships to the other half of the world. None of these vessels had ever returned, nor had any trace of them or their crews ever been discovered. This, then, was the first tangible evidence of their fate.

"It's been nearly two years since the *Far Explorer* left Vikanglia," Captain Theron went on. "What remains of this lifeboat must have been drifting for months—and for as many leagues," he added.

"Yea," Balthasar agreed soberly. "This matter must be brought before the High Council as soon as possible. Until then, mention it to no one." His voice was low, but his tone left neither the captain nor the first mate any doubt that the penalty for their disobedience would be severe. Balthasar then continued. "There is no point in alarming the people until we know what it may mean. Captain Theron, I charge ye with the responsibility of protecting the remains of this lifeboat until we reach Vikanglia. Now let us pray."

After the Prayer of Passing had been said, Captain Theron sharply ordered the crew back to their duties.

"And send someone to tell the BeastMaster to quiet those animals below," he demanded, for ever since the galley had weighed anchor, the beasts in the hold had been nervous and restless, their hooves pounding against the floor of the lower deck.

The sailors dispersed reluctantly, wanting, like the passengers, to crowd forward to get a better look at the pieces of wood that had been the cause of the *Mystic Rose*'s unscheduled delay. The planks had been bundled up in a length of unused sail and tied tightly with twine, however, so there was nothing much to see; and presently, most of those still watching drifted away.

Only Ileana was unable to tear her eyes from the canvaswrapped parcel Captain Theron and Master Faustis were now carrying to the captain's quarters. Ever since the dinghy's remains had been brought aboard, she had felt, like the animals below, a distinct sense of unease. Now, as the two men passed her, an almost tangible horror rose to crush her in its grip. Waves of evil streamed from the bundle, engulfing her in a tide of darkness that blinded her.

Without her even realizing it, a deep purple aura began to emanate from her diminutive figure, and an awesome, frightening force like nothing she had ever felt before uncoiled itself in the pit of her belly and leaped through her body with an intensity that terrified her.

Afraid, unable to see, Ileana staggered wildly, thrown off balance by the sudden lurch of the *Mystic Rose* as the ship's slowly unfurling sails were caught by the breeze and the vessel moved forward.

The girl was unaware her aura was starting to glow brighter, to shimmer incandescently with gradually changing colors. Without warning, the wind rose with a roar and the ocean began to roil and eddy. Beneath her feet, Ileana could feel the galley shudder and heave, as though it were caught in the grip of some horrendous storm. From the hold, the shrill, anxious cries of the beasts split the air, and the calls of the crew rang in her ears as, thinking a squall was about to descend, the sailors ran to secure lines and hatches.

Suddenly, the sounds started to fade until at last Ileana could hear them no more. Then, startlingly, a vague, shadowy image like none she had ever before beheld began to take shape in her mind. But she could not gain her footing on the now violently rolling deck; and before she could wholly discern the dark, gruesome form in the vignette, she fell, striking her head against one of the capstans. She was momentarily knocked unconscious, and when she came to, all was once more calm and the dreadful picture was gone. There was only her mother bending over her, her face filled with concern—and fear.

"Ileana, are ye all right?" Lucia inquired anxiously, her voice trembling.

O Immortal Guardian! she pleaded silently. *Please let me be the only one who saw what truly happened. Please let me be the only one who saw that terrible light in my daughter's eyes, the aura that surrounded her, the Power that burst forth from within her. . . .*

Now, more than ever, Lucia acknowledged that the Ancient One, Gitana san Kovichi, her body dead these many years past, had been both a great sorceress and a wisewoman indeed. Lucia had not only seen the Power that had radiated from Ileana's small figure; she had *felt* it! She had been standing so close to her daughter that Ileana's sudden trance had been like a physical blow, nearly knocking her to her knees. What had scared Lucia even more, however, was the fact that she'd realized her daughter could not control the tremendous force. It was Ileana who had caused the wind to blow so fiercely, the sea to swirl so savagely, and the galley to buck so wildly upon the waves. Had she not lost consciousness, the girl might well have destroyed everyone and everything around her!

Heaven's Light! Lucia thought frantically. *She must be given unto the Sisters as soon as possible! Only they can teach her what she must learn before 'tis too late!*

Lucia helped Ileana to her feet, scarcely even hearing her assurances that she was uninjured save for a nasty bump on her head.

"'Twas—'twas the sun," Ileana lied, panic-stricken by the way her mother was staring at her. "It blinded me for a moment so I could not see, and when the ship began to pitch, I—I tripped . . ." Her voice trailed away as she recognized that there was no use in trying to deceive her mother. Lucia had seen. Lucia *knew.* "Mother, what is it? What happened to me?" Ileana asked, her voice barely a whisper.

At first, Lucia did not reply. Instead, she drew her

daughter into her arms and hugged her tight. It was only after swallowing hard that she managed to speak again.

"Forgive me, Ileana," Lucia begged quietly. "Please, forgive me. I—I cannot tell ye. But ye will know the answers to your questions soon enough, I promise ye. Until then, speak not of what really occurred. Do ye understand? 'Twas the sun that blinded ye, the ship that unbalanced ye, just as ye said. 'Twas only the sun and the ship—nothing more.''

"Yea, Mother, I understand," Ileana agreed, bewildered and afraid.

To those who were now gathered around her, she repeated the false explanation hesitantly, cursing her tongue, which stumbled over the words. Ileana was certain all knew her for a liar. But to her vast relief, none save her mother had seen the terrifying incident. The others had been too intent on their duties; and so the story the girl told was readily believed.

"Master Faustis will escort ye to sickbay, Lady," Captain Theron declared firmly to Ileana, all too aware of his fate if one of the Royal Blood should be harmed while in his care. "Doctor Clement, the ship's leech, ought to take a look at that wound, for you've a bruise and a cut there—and some swelling as well."

"Thank ye, Captain. My head does ache something fierce," Ileana admitted, rubbing the injured spot.

She was certain Doctor Hilary, her family's physician, had already been summoned. But as she did not want to offend Captain Theron, she allowed Master Faustis to lead her away without protest. Once in sickbay, Doctor Clement treated her wound carefully, then advised her to lie down in her quarters until she was feeling better. Ileana was only too happy to do so, for she wished to be alone to think.

Even now, she could still see that hideous, blurred image taking shape in her mind, feel that strange, electrifying energy coursing through her body. What did it all mean? she wondered, for this time, she could not dismiss the episode as being born of her imagination. Was it possible, after all, that she was one of the Chosen? Was that what her mother had meant by her cryptic words?

At the thought, Ileana, now huddling on the bunk in her cabin, pulled the covers up over her head for comfort, as though they might somehow keep her safe and secure. She did not want to be burdened with more than the five senses; she did not want to see signs of the things to come.

Eventually, her heart aching, she cried herself to sleep; and it was only later, much later, that she remembered the sail-encased pieces of wood and knew they belonged to the Darkness.

Map by Rebecca Brandewyne

Chapter 6

So come with me to Vikanglia, fair maid,
Distant land of laughter and love,
And there, on the shores of Lake Tostig, we'll bide
For a time 'neath the blue sky above.

—Thus it is Written—
in
Songs of Vikanglia
collected by the Bard Alsandair set Windestun

THE CONTINENT OF VIKANGLIA WAS QUITE DIFFERENT FROM Ileana's own home, Cygnus; and for the first time since the incident aboard the *Mystic Rose*, she began to come out of the shell into which she'd withdrawn and, attracted by her surroundings, to take an interest once more in life. She had never left her homeland before, so she could not help but be excited by all around her.

Mounted upon her dapple-grey alaecorn, Ketti, who pranced along friskily, glad to be out of the galley's hold, Ileana gazed about eagerly as the large procession headed by her father traveled over the hard dirt road to Lothian Hold, the castle belonging to the rulers of Vikanglia.

Unlike the mountainous, thickly forested Cygnus, Vikanglia was a continent of rolling hillocks and flat plains filled with tall, sweeping green grass and golden grain. It was dotted with small woodlands and, here and there, an occasional lone tree. To the northeast was a vast marsh known as Cerdic Bog, and rivers tinged reddish brown from the rich coppery earth, as well as the muddy black peat of the swamp, wound through the countryside.

It was a peaceful, placid land, warm and welcoming, for the sun shone bright yellow overhead and the summer sky was a startlingly clear, deep blue. Because the countryside was so open, the firmament so endless, it made one feel as though one stood in the hollow of the Immortal Guardian's palm; and Ileana, who was used to the closeness of the mountains and forests, found her slight disquiet at being so exposed lessening as she rode along.

The Vikanglians who had met them at the northern shores of the continent to accompany them to Lothian Hold also fascinated her, for she had never before seen so many of them. They were all red-haired and bronzed by the sun, tall and muscular. Even Balthasar seemed dwarfed in their presence. Ileana, used to the serene hush of Ariel heights, was half enchanted, half mortified by the boisterous warriors. Their manner was rough and easygoing; their voices were booming and hearty, and their laughter was loud and ribald. They shouted and joked among themselves unrestrainedly, clapping one another exuberantly upon the back and grinning widely when they were cuffed playfully in return. They reminded Ileana of the roly-poly bear cubs she sometimes spied frolicking in the forests of Cygnus, and she could not suppress her smile of delight at their antics.

Both the men and the women wore short, colorful, coarsely woven cotton tunics and ornate steel breastplates. Horned helmets adorned their heads; wide leather bands with metal cleats encircled their wrists, and leather thongs that laced up to the knee were upon their feet. Some of the soldiers sported an array of weapons and shields, but these were mainly for show, for the land was at peace; and though there were bands of reivers who, having lost the Way, roamed the countryside, looting and—rarely—killing, they would not attack a cavalcade as large as Balthasar's.

Some of the warriors carried brightly colored banners and pennants that rippled gaily in the breeze. A few bore hawks upon their shoulders or wrists. All were mounted upon sleek-coated, antlered dēor and perytons.

At last, the procession neared the city of Lothian, which lay upon the northern shore of Lake Tostig and spanned the River Owein. A great noise arose as the crofters lining the

dirt road outside the city's walls crowded forth in an effort
to catch a glimpse of the new High King. As the sound of the
cheers and the trumpets announcing his arrival rang out,
Balthasar smiled, nodding and waving to his subjects.
Ileana's heart swelled to bursting with pride as she saw how
the common folk loved her father.

When the party reached the city gates, where the Lord
Gwalchmei's widow, now the Past High Queen Lady
Daogmar, stood waiting, Balthasar dismounted and stepped
forward to exchange the Kiss of Peace with her.

Though she had known over seventy years, Daogmar was
still a beautiful woman. Like all the Vikanglian women, she
was tall, her bearing proud and regal despite her age. She
was clothed in an emerald-green caftan with gold trim that
set off the honey tones of her finely lined skin and made her
gold-flecked green eyes stand out brilliantly in her face. Her
long auburn hair streaked with grey was plaited and wound
neatly about her head, upon which perched the High
Coronet she would soon bestow upon the new High Queen
Lady Lucia.

Daogmar's eyes were red-rimmed from weeping, evidence
of her sorrow. But now, her decades of duty sustaining her,
she held the tears at bay, and her lips lifted in a smile as she
stretched out her hands to Balthasar.

"Welcome, Lord," she said warmly, remaining upright, as
was her privilege.

"Lady, ye do me honor," he responded, bowing.

Once she had greeted Lucia as well, Daogmar mounted
her peryton to lead the cavalcade through Lothian.

As the procession wound along the stone-cobbled streets
teeming with people, Ileana glanced about raptly, drinking
in the unfamiliar sights.

The rectangular marketplace at the center of town reverberated with the loud cries of the merchants hawking their
wares, each trying to win business away from his competitors. Some of the hucksters offered roasted chestnuts and
hot cross buns, fresh fruits and vegetables; others advertised
little stuffed dolls, carved wooden toys, and other cheap
trinkets. The bolder tinkers accosted passersby, thrusting
goods on these reluctant customers, who either paid for

things they did not want or escaped by threatening to call the guard.

Ileana saw a bin filled with produce accidentally over-turned as a group of heedless young men mounted on stags galloped past. One grinning rogue paused to toss a handful of coins to the fat, irate vendor, who shouted and shook his fist at the youth before laboriously stooping to gather the isarns and peltros. They were already being snatched up by a hoard of dirty street urchins, who were also stuffing their pockets with the lettuce, tomatoes, and carrots that had fallen from the crate. Farther on, Ileana spied an impish lad sidle up to the edge of a dozing old crone's booth and attempt to steal a small tin soldier from a shelf. The hag roused herself immediately, shrieking and waving her cane at him angrily as, sputtering passages from *The Word and The Way*, she drove him off. Past that, narrow wynds buzzing with swarms of people began to branch off from the marketplace.

Cloth Row was a close huddle of fabric marts, before which peddlers had set up carts filled with bolts of material of every color and weave. There, Ileana observed two women arguing so fiercely over a piece of pale muslin each clutched determinedly that, finally, it split in half, much to its weaver's fury. He gave both customers the sharp side of his tongue before he adamantly demanded money from each, then chided them for their behavior.

On Armor Avenue were the stalls of the ironmongers and the blacksmiths, where the violent pounding of hammers on anvils assaulted Ileana's ears. In sharp contrast to this were the quieter, more elegant establishments of the goldsmiths, silversmiths, and jewelers to be found in Girandole Square. Near these, in Time Circle, were located the clockmakers and the watchmakers, and here, Ileana heard the soft ticking and chiming of intricate timepieces.

On Candlewick Street were the chandlers and the perfum-ers, from whose stores wafted the fragrant aromas of tallow, soap, and scent. Spicy sandalwood, pungent lemon verbena, and delicate heather mingled intoxicatingly with the sweet bouquets emanating from the shops of the vintners on Nectar Lane and the florists on Foliage Boulevard. Not far from this, the savory redolence of clove, cinnamon, and ginger issuing from Spice Path rose to blend aromatically with whiffs trailing from the open tins of cheroots and jars of snuff displayed by the vendors on Tobacco Road. From the bakeries along Mill Way drifted the rich, yeasty fragrance of hot breads and the delicious, enticing scent of chocolate pastries. Sprawled haphazardly along the banks of the River Owein were the shops of the butchers, where the gamy aroma of newly slaughtered venison, pork, and fowl pervaded Ileana's nostrils, as did the tangy smell of freshly caught trout, bass, and salmon exhibited by the fishmongers. The muddy river itself exuded a dank, peat-tinged smell.

A damp breeze stirred, rippling the water that lapped gently at the hulls of the many ships, boats, and barges anchored at the docks.

On the wings of the wind flew the harmonious twang of lutes and trill of flutes as the traveling minstrels attracted to the city by the forthcoming ceremonies moved among the crowd, passing their caps for small donations. There were mimes and mummers, jugglers and acrobats, too; and once, Ileana spied an old grinderman with a monkey on a leash. The little beast danced to the tune of the carillon played by the man and held out a battered tin cup for coins. The gay jingle-jangle of zins, magnesis, and alumes clattering in the cup was drowned by the raised voices and the raucous laughter of the throng.

Occasionally, here and there, as was to be expected in so large a gathering, Ileana saw fights break out, especially around the warehouses lining the wharves, where exotic goods from far-off places were half unloaded from the vessels that clogged the river, the dockhands having paused in their work to watch the passing procession.

Most exciting of all were the people pushing and elbowing their way through the now flower-strewn streets to reach the heart of the city. Here, brightly striped tents had been erected, and barkers promised for a zin the sight of wondrous things or prizes for winning various games.

"Three balls for a peltro," one man called to lure prospective customers. "Three balls for a peltro. Topple the dolls and win a trinket for your sweetheart."

Above all this were the periodic blasts of the trumpets and the loud cries of the heralds as they cleared a path for the cavalcade.

"Make way for the High King!" they shouted. "Make way for the High King!"

Finally, the party reached Lothian Hold. Set on a small knoll overlooking the city, the ancient castle rose above them, magnificent in its glory. It was not a beautiful fortress, for it had stood since the Time of the Rebirth and the Enlightenment and it had been built for defense. But its massive grey stone walls were compelling, and Ileana was filled with awe as she cantered over the drawbridge spanning the deep, wide moat.

Once in the courtyard, the procession was greeted by the King and Queen of Vikanglia, the Lord Faolan sin Lothian sul Lothian and his wife, the Lady Mathilde. After that, all were shown to their quarters.

Because the keep was filled to overflowing with guests, Ileana had to share a chamber with her younger sisters, Daphne and Phoebe; but she didn't mind. She listened with half an ear to their chatter as she ate the meal that had been brought to her on a tray. Then, after bathing, she climbed into the room's big, canopied featherbed and snuggled down beside the twins, exhausted. There, for the first time in weeks, she fell into a deep, dreamless slumber, untroubled by thoughts of the future.

> *Now thy Spirit has left its shell to journey past the*
> *   Far Beyond,*
> *And the Light in the distance is glorious to behold.*
> *It beckons sweetly with open heart, its every mystery*
> *   now revealed,*
> *And holds thee safe forevermore, as promised true of*
> *   old.*

—Thus it is Written—
in
The Hymnal of Requiems
collected by the Priest Yannis san Kastor
set Mont Saint Christopher

* * *

It was a beautiful day, Ileana thought as she walked across the courtyard with the others who had journeyed from far and wide for the ceremonies engendered by the passing of the old High King Lord Gwalchmei. Ileana knew many of her companions by sight, for they were persons of importance and had visited her father's court in the past. These were the kings and queens of the known-inhabited continents; their heirs and heiresses; the High Priest Kokudza san Dyami of Mont Saint Christopher and the High Priestess Sharai san Jyotis of Mont Saint Mikhaela; the High Minister Radomil san Pavel sol Antoni, the people's representative, and his wife, the High Ministress Jenica; and the High Electress Elysabeth san Villette sol Franchot, Radomil's successor, and her husband, the High Elect Tarn, both of whom, before the Lord Gwalchmei's passing, had been part of Balthasar's court and had traveled aboard the *Mystic Rose* to Vikanglia.

There were others whom Ileana did not recognize, but whom she deduced, from their clothing, were of the Royal Blood and belonged to the Royal Houses. The priests and priestesses, too, were easy to discern from their garments. The rest, she suspected, were various ministers and elects of the continental cabinets or masters from assorted guilds.

One young man in particular caught Ileana's eye, for he had a handsome profile and looked familiar besides, although she could not place him. It was only when he turned and she saw his entire face that, startled, she realized he resembled the High Prince she had seen in her vision that winter two years past in her father's gardens. After her initial shock had receded, she secretively studied the young man, relieved to find that upon closer scrutiny, he was not, after all, the High Prince of her foreboding dream.

What would she have done if he had been? Approached him, spoken to him, accused him? Of what? Ileana did not know. Troubled by the thought, her heart still beating too quickly in her breast, she turned away, forcing herself to concentrate on the courtyard instead.

Here, tall ancient trees with massive trunks and spreading

branches grew: gnarled oaks and twisted yews, towering elms and slender birches. The hot sun peeked through their deciduous, green-leaved limbs, dappling the stone paving blocks of the courtyard with gold. At the bases of the trees, a profusion of multicolored flowers bloomed, and verdant vines tangled along the ground.

Ahead lay the chapel of Lothian Hold, its weathered grey stone walls reflecting every nuance of light and shadow, its leaded stained-glass windows bending the sunlight, casting rainbows on the earth. For a moment, it seemed as though the chapel were aglow, its slender spires rising from the heart of some unworldly fire. Its heavy, carved oak doors stood open; but because the chapel was small, there was not room for everyone, and many of those who had come to witness the old High King's funeral were left standing outside.

Once Ileana had taken her place in the pew reserved for her family, she observed that the Lord Gwalchmei's body lay in state upon an ornate litter resting on a magnificent catafalque. His corpse had been preserved in the ancient way by the embalmers, so it looked as though he were merely sleeping. He was dressed in his finest accoutrements: a royal-blue velvet gallibiya trimmed with gold and an ermine burnous lined with cloth-of-gold. A horned helmet was upon his head; leather boots adorned his feet.

Ileana, along with the others in the chapel, knelt and bowed her head as everyone quieted and the ceremony started. The High Priest Kokudza, resplendent in his white mourning chasuble, turned to face the stone altar and, lifting his palms, began to chant melodically the prayers that constituted the Last Rites. He was joined by the High Priestess Sharai and the other priests and priestesses who had been selected to perform the ritual. Their harmonious voices rose and fell, floating up to the arched beams of the high gabled ceiling and echoing softly along the wooden pews. Later, the appropriate dirges were sung, and the deep sanctum bell sounded the death knell through the chapel.

The many tall white candles on the altar blazed brightly, and the sweet fragrance of frankincense and the pungent aroma of myrrh mingled to fill the air with smoke and a heady, almost overpowering scent. This, combined with the cloying smell of perfumed bodies pressed close in the summer heat, made Ileana, after a time, feel quite nauseated. She shut her eyes tightly and swayed a little upon her knees, fearing she was about to be sick. She tried to quell the spinning of her head and the roiling of her stomach by breathing deeply, but this only exacerbated her malady. The acrid smoke and the intoxicating incense permeating the chapel filled her lungs to bursting, and for an instant, as she struggled for air, she thought she might faint.

She gripped the back of the pew in front of her and slowly opened her eyes, seeking to regain her equilibrium. As though in a trance, she saw that the white-robed priests and priestesses were now lifting from the catafalque the litter that bore the old High King. Only it was no longer the Lord Gwalchmei who lay there. It was instead the handsome young man from the courtyard. His face was ashen and drawn; his lips were compressed and twisted, as though he had been in agony when death had claimed his body. His skin hung in folds from his emaciated frame, and the hands crossed over his breast were skeletal. Ileana scarcely recognized him.

Dazed and uncomprehending, she blinked her eyes. The vignette blurred, then faded; and seconds later, it was again the old High King that the priests and priestesses were carrying down the aisle. Still feeling slightly disoriented, wondering if she had imagined the misty moment out of time but fearing she had not, Ileana tardily stood to follow the others, who were now exiting the chapel in the wake of the corpse.

The procession wended its way through the crowded streets of the city, where the common folk had gathered to watch the funeral silently. Finally, the official party of mourners reached the northern shore of Lake Tostig, where the Lord Gwalchmei's ornate ceremonial karve, its bow and stern curving up in the slender shape of a peryton's head and tail, lay at anchor. The old High King's body was placed aboard. Then the longship was set afire; its gaily striped sail was unfurled, and its lines were cast off. As the wind rippling across the water caught the canvas, the burning karve moved forward gently, trailing wisps of smoke.

The golden sun shone upon the gleaming azure waves and was reflected into Ileana's eyes, and for a minute, blinded, she saw not the peryton-headed longship drifting slowly across the vast lake, but a gigantic sandstone dragon stretched upon desert dunes and enveloped by flames. On the back of the dragon lay the corpse of the handsome young man from the courtyard.

At the sight, the girl buried her head in her hands, knowing that like the hazy picture she had seen in the chapel, it was not real.

O Immortal Guardian, she begged silently, *tell me I am going mad. Tell me these are not signs of the things to come. I do not wish to know the future. I do not want to be one of the Chosen. Have mercy. Have mercy. . . .*

She wanted to run away, to hide, to think. But she dared not leave before the funeral had ended.

At last, when the Lord Gwalchmei's body and the karve were naught but ashes scattered upon the waves, Ileana turned away, her eyes bleak and her heart heavy at the remembrance of what she had seen.

The land had become a madhouse guarded by fools, for those who might have changed the course of history could not reason with those who were afraid, ignorant, and filled with hate and greed. To give the former credit, they did try. But by then, the political structure of the land was so needlessly massive and complex, and so riddled with corruption as well, that those who wished to alter it for the better found it impossible to do so. Frustrated and disheartened, they soon gave up the attempt, condemning the land to its terrible fate.

Because of this, after the Wars of the Kind and the Apocalypse, during the Time of the Rebirth and the Enlightenment, the Survivors determined that in order to prevent a reccurrence of the Time Before, only the best and the brightest must henceforth rule.

Thus were the Games established. It is only by winning these that those of the Royal Blood ascend their thrones and those of the common folk achieve their chairs.

—Thus it is Written—
in
Tintagel: After the Apocalypse
by the Historian Fala san Mocambique
set Kazatimiru

The following day, the coronation of the Lord Balthasar and the Lady Lucia took place. It was a grand affair followed by a long night of feasting and celebration. After that, bright and early the next morning, much to the dismay of those who had overindulged themselves with food and drink, the Games began.

These were a series of physical and mental tests that grew progressively harder. Because these were the Royal High Games, which would determine who would claim the Lesser Crown, Throne, and Scepter, they were the most strenuous and difficult of all.

Only those of the Royal Blood were permitted to enter this competition, so there were not as many contestants as there were when the Common High Games were held; but still, the field was crowded with hundreds of would-be victors.

Although Ileana might have placed her name on the lists had she so wished, she had realized she was too young and small to have any serious hope of prevailing over others many times her age and size. Now she was content to watch from her father's box.

Though the rows of stone tiers in the coliseum provided a good view of the arena, there would not be much to see initially, for the first event was a marathon and the runners would follow a twenty-five–mile dirt path that would take them out of the stadium. They would race along a winding, obstacle-ridden course until they returned to their starting point. Judges would be stationed at each barrier to ensure no one cheated. Though it was not expected anyone would, a chance to rule could entice even the best of men from the path of righteousness. Only those who successfully cleared each obstacle and were among the first hundred competitors to reach the coliseum would go on to participate in the next event. That way, the field was narrowed immediately to a manageable size.

The trumpets blared as the heralds announced the start of the marathon. At the sound, Balthasar stood, raised one hand, then lowered it sharply, the signal for the race to begin. The arena rang with the cheers of the spectators as the mass of contestants rushed toward the stadium's huge wooden doors, all of which stood wide open. Most of the runners headed for the southern exit, for it was closest to the actual race course. Correctly deducing that they could cover the extra distance around the outside of the coliseum in the time it would take those jamming the southern portal to get through it, the rest of the competitors jogged toward the remaining three exits.

Ileana surveyed the field speculatively, wondering which of the contestants would be lucky enough to be among the first hundred to finish. To her surprise, she spied the handsome young man from the courtyard. He wore a short red tunic emblazoned with a golden dragon, and because of this, she knew he belonged to the Royal House of Khali. As he disappeared through the eastern doors, a faint sense of perturbation assailed her. Remembering her visions of him, his body wasted, then dead, she fervently hoped he would not be one of those who successfully completed the race.

But he was. And day by day, as the Royal High Games wore on, he continued to emerge triumphant. A fortnight later, only he and two other participants remained.

A hush fell over the crowd gathered in the arena for the final event as the King Lord Faolan mounted the dais in the center of the stadium. Solemnly, he faced the three competitors who had managed to come so far.

"Lord Yhudhah sin Khali, Lord Valentin sin Lorelei, and Lady Hoshie sin Gingiber," he addressed them, "this is a momentous occasion in your lives. Ye are to be congratulated for attaining it, for the tests each of ye has passed have been the most strenuous and difficult ever devised. They have been so for one reason—and one reason only: The burden of responsibility that comes with the Lesser Crown, Throne, and Scepter is great. The one who would undertake such a task must be fitted to do so. Such a one must be strong and decisive, wise and just, and honest and compassionate. Above all, such a one must act always with honor and on the side of right." The King's voice reverberated through the coliseum.

"The events in which each of ye excelled have proved that ye have such traits and that ye are, in truth, Defenders of the Light. Any of ye would be capable of carrying out the duties entailed by the high rank ye seek, and I know I speak for all when I say Tintagel would be proud and honored to bestow the Lesser Crown, Throne, and Scepter upon any of ye.

"There can be only one winner, however, and so now we come to this, your final test—The Riddles. Please take your places."

After the three contestants were seated at the long table that stood at one end of the dais, Faolan slowly unrolled the scroll he held in one hand and began to read the first riddle. The participants then wrote down their answers, and all were revealed as correct. On the second riddle, the Lord Valentin, obviously downcast, was eliminated. The anticipation and excitement of the audience mounted as he strode from the arena, nodding and waving to acknowledge the appreciative applause that accompanied his exit. The Lord Yhudhah and the Lady Hoshie gazed at each other soberly, knowing that in moments, one of them would claim the Lesser Crown, Throne, and Scepter.

A terrible sense of impending doom rippled like icy water along Ileana's spine as the King raised his hand and a tense, expectant hush fell over the stadium. She did not need to hear the third riddle; she did not need to hear who gave the proper response. She already knew it would be the handsome young man from the courtyard, the Lord Yhudhah sin Khali.

O Immortal Guardian, please let me be wrong, she beseeched silently; but she knew her prayers were in vain.

Gruffly, Faolan cleared his throat. Then he read the third riddle:

Once, of molten ore, I was, born of heaven's light,
Part of something greater, and then a thing in flight.
Sisters small, cold, and dark, at last, I came to be,
Fragments of what was, with faces numbering three.

Now, like jewels, I shimmer, bright with stolen flame,
Seen and then unseen, ever changing yet the same.
A thousand centuries old am I, though sometimes I am new.
What's the answer to my riddle? Can ye tell me true?

The throng watched with bated breath as Faolan unrolled the small scroll upon which the Lady Hoshie had written her response.

"'What am I? I am the Swords of Truth, Righteousness, and Honor,'" he read aloud. "I'm sorry," he told her, shaking his head. "'Twas a good guess, but 'tis incorrect."

As she bowed her head in defeat, Faolan moved to the Lord Yhudhah. If he, too, were wrong, the two competitors would be given another riddle to solve. But Ileana knew this would not be necessary. Somehow she knew that despite all her hopes to the contrary, the handsome young man had got the right response.

Faolan read the Lord Yhudhah's answer.

"'What am I? I am the three moons of Tintagel.' That is correct, Lord," the King said.

The spectators went wild and leaped to their feet, cheering and applauding.

"Hail, High Prince Lord Yhudhah!" they shouted. "Hail, High Prince Lord Yhudhah!"

A flurry of activity quickly followed. Disappointed, the Lady Hoshie politely congratulated the Lord Yhudhah, then left the dais. The heralds blew their trumpets, and the Royal Lesser Guard marched into the coliseum to line up on the field in stately formation. The ornate Lesser Throne, which Balthasar had brought from Cygnus, was carried to the dais, along with a large red velvet pillow bearing the Lesser Crown and Scepter. Then Balthasar left his box to assist the High Priest Kokudza, the High Priestess Sharai, and the High Minister Radomil with the coronation. After that, following a solemn ceremony, the Lord Yhudhah was crowned the High Prince of all Tintagel.

"Long live the High Prince Lord Yhudhah!" the crowd roared. "Long Live the High Prince Lord Yhudhah!"

The cries in the arena dinned in Ileana's ears like the sound of drums or the thunder that presages a storm. It seemed to her that a cloud passed across the sun, casting a shadow over the field, and suddenly, she saw not the Lord Yhudhah seated upon the Lesser Throne, but the mysterious, dark High Prince of her dream. He was gazing at her triumphantly and holding out one hand to her. . . .

Nay! It is not real! It is not real! Ileana repeated over and over in her mind.

She felt strange, light-headed, as though she had drunk far too much of the sweet amber nectar that had been served to her earlier. She felt limp, too, as though all her bones had somehow melted.

The High Prince Lord Yhudhah held up one hand to quiet the spectators. At last, they resumed their seats, and silence fell. In the hush that followed, as though in a trance, Ileana felt herself stand. It was as though she had no will of her own and had been pulled to her feet by some invisible force. Then, to her everlasting horror, she saw herself point straight at the High Prince, and in a voice that was hers yet not hers, being older and deeper somehow, she heard herself utter quite distinctly, forebodingly: "He shall not live to wear the High Crown."

As her words echoed through the stadium, a dreadful stillness enveloped the coliseum and everyone stared at her, aghast. Then many of those present starred themselves to ward off evil.

The last thing Ileana remembered clearly was the startled look in the High Priestess Sharai's eyes, an expression of surprise that soon changed to one of speculation and then, oddly enough, satisfaction. But why? Ileana wondered. Why should the High Priestess find gratification in her unspeakable act?

Ileana had no answers to her questions, and before she could ponder the matter further, a veil of blackness swirled up like mist to engulf her.

Chapter 7

> *Now comes a priestess,*
> *Aged, wise,*
> *A maiden child to behold.*
> *Is she the promised one?*
> *Yea, it is so.*
> *Daughter of the Light,*
> *A journey lies ahead*
> *And your destiny.*
> *Many names shall ye know,*
> *But of these,*
> *Sorceress,*
> *Cain's bride,*
> *Shall be everlasting.*

—Thus it is Written—
in
Ode to a Fair Maid
by the Poet Ibadan set Samara

IT WAS PAST MIDNIGHT WHEN ILEANA'S MOTHER CAME TO WAKE her. The girl was wide-eyed in moments, for she had not rested well after the awful episode in the coliseum. Indeed, she had lain awake for hours, horrified by the afternoon's events and wondering how she would dare to face the world in the morning. Everyone would be talking about her, whispering behind her back, and pointing at her. Overnight, she would become a person of notoriety and scandal—she, the daughter of the High King! She didn't know how she

73

would bear it. The shame was even worse than the realization that retribution, too, would no doubt be forthcoming for her conduct.

When she finally had fallen asleep, Ileana had been haunted by strange, disjointed dreams that had frightened her with their diabolical images.

I must have cried out in my sleep, she decided. *That is why Mother has come to my chamber.*

Still, by the light of the flickering candle Lucia held in one hand, the girl could see that the others in the room slumbered on; and her mother seemed anxious and afraid—not comforting, as Ileana had at first thought.

She would have spoken, to tell her mother about the nightmares and to ask her why she was so upset, but Lucia held one finger to her lips, motioning for Ileana to rise and dress quietly. Puzzled and apprehensive now, too, the girl did as she was bidden. What was her mother doing at this late hour? And why had she come for her? Ileana could not guess, and it was obvious Lucia did not intend to enlighten her.

Silently, her mother opened the door of the chamber to lead her down the narrow corridors of Lothian Hold. Ileana followed wordlessly, her soft leather boots whispering over the stone floor, the folds of her abayeh rustling against her body. The torches lining the castle walls still burned, lighting their way, but Ileana found little solace in this. The shadows cast by the wavering flames appeared to loom over her menacingly, and the cool night air filtering through the passages made her shiver.

Eventually, they reached a part of the Vikanglian fortress with which she was not familiar. As they neared a door set into a small alcove, she could hear the sound of voices, one raised in anger, the others muted and calmer. After knocking upon the portal, her mother turned the knob and went in. The heated conversation broke off abruptly.

Once they were inside, Ileana saw to her surprise that the room contained her father and the High Priest Kokudza and the High Priestess Sharai. She thought her father looked wroth, but the two Druswids appeared unmoved by this, for their faces were stoic in the half-light.

"Ah, here is the child." As Sharai spoke, she turned

toward Lucia and Ileana. From the chair in which she was seated, she beckoned to the girl. "Step closer, child, that I may see ye better. My eyes are not what they used to be."

Ileana looked to her mother for guidance, but Lucia only shook her head warningly and gave her a little nudge forward. Hesitantly, recalling the strange expression in the High Priestess's eyes that afternoon in the arena, Ileana moved to stand before the Druswid, suddenly apprehensive.

Sharai's face reminded her of a hawk's, proud and fierce, determined and filled with purpose. The cowl of the High Priestess's habit was thrown back, revealing gleaming coal-black hair threaded with grey, and she had dispensed with her yashmak, the veil that priestesses often wore to conceal their identities. Like all Bedouins, she was dark-skinned; her face was etched with fine lines born of time; her clawlike hands were spotted with age. Her beaked nose was set above thin lips now pressed together grimly as she studied Ileana closely, probing, appraising.

She seeks to know what is in my heart and mind, the girl thought uneasily, for she could almost feel the Druswid reaching out to her mentally, attempting to delve into the darkest chasms of her soul.

Though Sharai had known over sixty years, she had never felt her age. Her knowledge and power were great, and she had used them to her benefit, for her rank and the attendant responsibilities were onerous, and only one of strength could bear them. But tonight, as she gazed at the child before her, she felt a weariness in her bones and a chill that warned her that soon she must think of giving her place to another. She would be called Wisewoman then and perhaps, if she lived that long, the Ancient One.

She shuddered a little at the thought, recalling, without warning, another who had borne that name, the sorceress Gitana san Kovichi, her ashes scattered these many years past.

O Reverend Mother—the High Priestess spoke to her dead mentor silently—*now I know how ye felt that winter's eve when I came to ye so long ago. What I would give for your words of wisdom at this moment! The Foul Enslaver has cast Its shadow upon the land; this, we know. But none can see what form Its evil will take, and there are only he whom Takis*

*conjured and this child born of your own magic to stand
between the Light and the Darkness. Has this one the
strength and the power to do so? I do not know.*

The Druswid continued to scrutinize Ileana, her coal-
black eyes seeming to pierce right through the girl, ferreting
out her innermost thoughts and secrets.

"How many years have ye known, child?" Sharai asked at
last.

"I have known seven years, Reverend Mother," Ileana
replied respectfully, wishing the High Priestess would stop
staring at her so intently.

So young, the Druswid mused pityingly. *I pray there is yet
time to see she is properly prepared, or she will surely be
lost—and all Tintagel with her.*

"Do ye know why ye are here, child?"

"Nay, Reverend Mother. But I—but I . . . that is—"
Ileana paused to lick her lips nervously. "Is it—is it
something to do with what happened in the stadium this
afternoon?" she asked timidly.

Vaguely, she remembered how, stricken, her mother had
snatched her up and carried her from the coliseum, determinedly pushing past those who had closed around them
like vultures, squawking a multitude of questions; how, her
head held high, her bearing regal, Lucia had eyed them
fiercely, silently daring them to try to prevent her from
leaving the arena. Though angry and frightened, no one had
attempted to stop her, for to lay hands upon the High Queen
was a crime punishable by death.

Upon reaching Lothian Hold, Lucia had deposited Ileana
in her chamber and instructed her to remain there until she
was sent for. Scared and confused, the girl had not dared to
do anything else. Miserably aware of the havoc she had
wreaked, she had spoken to no one, turning away from the
comfort her sisters, nurse, and handmaiden had offered.
Somehow Ileana had forced down a few bites of her supper.
Then she'd gone straight to bed, wondering unhappily what
dire consequences would result from her behavior. Surely,
she would have to do penance of some sort, she'd thought,
and hoped she was not to be an Outcast—for then she
would be shunned, forbidden contact with anyone else, and
left to make her own way in the world.

When no one had come for her, Ileana hadn't known whether to feel relieved or more anxious. Now, though she was glad her judgment had fallen swiftly, she wished her mother had waited until morning before seeking her out. Dull with sleep, she was not thinking clearly, and added to her confusion was the fear she felt at having been so mysteriously roused from her bed and brought here. It was not what she had expected.

"I—I do not know what made me—made me act as I did at the Lord Yhudhah's crowning," Ileana went on, faltering, "for 'twas as though some strange force looked through my eyes and spoke through me. But 'tis not true what I heard some say later—that I cursed the High Prince. I did not! By the Light, I swear I did not!" she insisted vehemently.

"I know, child," Sharai told her, not unkindly. "And I know, too, that ye must be very bewildered by all this. But do not be afraid. No one here means to punish ye for what ye did. Though I wish things had occurred differently, 'twas not your fault ye lacked the training necessary to have handled the affair otherwise. We should have taken steps earlier to prepare ye, but there had been no sign yet that ye were indeed the one. . . ." She shrugged. "Well, one cannot change the past, no matter how much one might yearn to do so. 'Tis the present and the future with which we must be concerned now. Have ye ever had such revelations before, child?"

Ileana, uncertain how to answer, glanced at her mother. But it was her father who responded to her silent plea for assistance.

"Speak, daughter," Balthasar demanded. "It is as the Reverend Mother has said: No one here means ye harm. But we must know the truth of the matter, Ileana."

"Yea, Father," the girl replied, her eyes downcast. "I—I have . . . seen things in the past and—and felt them, too. But not very often!" she added quickly, looking up to gauge the expressions on their faces, for she did not want them to think she was one of the Chosen, and she was afraid they did.

She shuddered. That would be terrible, for then perhaps the High Priestess would take her away to Mont Saint Mikhaela. Already the Druswid's talk of training had frightened her, for how could that be accomplished anywhere but at the nunnery? It was there, Ileana knew, that those in the Sisterhood studied. Sometimes they left the abbey afterward to take their assigned places in the world. But most of them remained secreted behind Mont Saint Mikhaela's walls for the rest of their lives and were never seen again —except by the Sisters themselves, of course.

"And what have ye seen and felt, child?" Sharai inquired, her countenance showing nothing of her suddenly churning emotions.

Hoping she was not somehow sealing her fate with her answer, Ileana softly told the High Priestess about her visions, beginning with that winter when she had first seen the High Prince of her dreams. The eyes of the High Priest Kokudza flickered briefly at her description of the unknown lord. But other than this, Ileana could discern no reaction whatsoever by the Druswids to her words, and she began to breathe a little easier, feeling that she must have been mistaken, that they did not believe she was one of the Chosen after all.

When she had finished her tale, she stood silently, waiting for Sharai to speak again. Instead, wordlessly, from the folds of her robe, the High Priestess drew forth a small silver casket, which she placed on her knees. She gazed at it steadily for a time, as though debating whether to open it. But in truth, she was wondering if she had the strength to do what must be done.

'Tis late, and I am tired, she thought. *Perhaps I should wait until tomorrow. . . .*

But, nay. She had never shirked her duties before; she must not do so now. Who knew what the dawn might bring? Oh, if only there were not so little time. . . .

"Do ye see this box, child?" she questioned Ileana. Then, at the girl's nod, she continued. "'Tis very old and extremely valuable, for it contains a crystal sphere within which glows a shaft of the Light. Yea." She nodded, noting Ileana's amazement. "There is only one other like it in the entire world, so 'tis Mont Saint Mikhaela's most precious possession, for no one, not even the Druswids, knows how 'twas fashioned, and thus 'tis irreplaceable. 'Tis used in our initiation rites, for it may be looked upon only by those who serve the Immortal Guardian. All others must perish before its ray." She paused, then went on slowly. "In a moment, I am going to open this box and release the Light so 'twill shine upon ye, child. Ye must not turn away from it, no matter how brightly it glows or how intensely it burns. Do ye understand?"

"Yea, Reverend Mother," Ileana said, starting to tremble.

Did this mean that she was indeed one of the Chosen, that she would be taken away to Mont Saint Mikhaela?

Covertly, she peeked at the silver chest, and as she examined it, she felt a finger of fear brush her nape. What would the Light do to her? she wondered anxiously. Would it blind her? Scorch her? She glanced once more at her mother for reassurance. But Lucia had closed her eyes and was moving her lips soundlessly in prayer. Alarmed, Ileana turned to her father. His expression, though filled with concern, was implacable, and she knew no aid would be forthcoming from him. This was a test; *that,* she understood. But now, terrifyingly, she grasped the fact that if she failed it, she would die!

"'Tis good," the Druswid asserted, startling the girl, for she realized that somehow Sharai had read her thoughts. "Ye have comprehended the import of the box and what it contains, and ye are afraid. Fear is a demon. It interferes with the processes of the mind so one cannot think clearly or rationally—if at all. Ye must face the Demon Fear and recognize it for what it is. Then ye must conquer it by driving it from your mind and willing yourself to concentrate on the Light. Breathe deeply, and think of the Light. Think only of the Light."

The High Priestess's eyes bored into Ileana's. Slowly, the Druswid took a heavy silver chain from around her neck and inserted the key that dangled from it into the casket's lock. After turning the key and removing the lock, she lifted the lid to reveal the crystal sphere within.

Initially, Ileana saw nothing. But gradually, as she continued to study the glass ball, it began to shimmer. A soft flicker grew inexorably stronger until at last it was a steady, lucent emission. Its ray swept the chamber, finally coming to rest upon Ileana. There, it remained.

She swallowed hard, suppressing her desire to cringe as

the beam probed her tentatively. Suddenly, the Light burst forth like a beacon from the heart of the crystal, dazzling her with its brilliance. Ileana longed to shut her eyes against the knifelike glare, but Sharai's warning rang in her ears, and she dared not disobey it. Instead, she continued to gaze at the sphere until the Light was all she could see and she thought she must be blinded.

Slowly, horribly, the pain started. At first, it felt as though tiny tongues of fire were licking her all over, singeing the fine hair upon her skin. But soon the flames started to grow hotter and hotter until Ileana was certain she was burning alive. She wanted to scream, to run away from the atavistic agony that enveloped her. But still, recalling the High Priestess's words, she stood rooted to the floor. She could feel her flesh sizzle like frying meat, and she thought that, surely, it must be blackening and peeling away to expose her bones, charred and crumbling into ashes.

Heaven's Light! She was going mad. The pain! *The pain!*

And then, just when Ileana knew she could bear no more, she felt a comforting essence touch her own.

Fear is a demon, the unfamiliar soul reminded her. *Think only of the Light. . . .*

From deep within herself, Ileana drew upon some resource of strength and courage she had not known she possessed. Fiercely, she concentrated on the Light, willing all thoughts of the Darkness to leave her. To her astonishment, the pain stopped and the white-hot ray of the Light vanished. Though she was glad of this, to her dismay, the consolatory essence was gone, too, and she felt bereft, as though she had lost something very important.

"By the moons," the startled Druswid muttered as, with a sharp click, she closed the casket. "'Tis enough. 'Tis more than enough. Only one other has ever withstood so much. . . ." Her voice trailed away as she drummed her fingers upon the lid of the chest.

Is she the one? Sharai wondered. *Is she truly the one? Yea, 'tis so. There can be no mistake. Even without training, she absorbed more of the Light than even I could have borne. O Reverend Mother, what a terrible risk ye took in conjuring this girl. She is only a child, and already the Power is strong within her. I shudder to think what will be hers when she is fully grown. She will be a formidable foe indeed if ever she turns her hand to the Darkness. Thank the heavens, there is another. . . .*

Abruptly, the High Priestess brought herself back to the present, realizing those in the room were awaiting her decision.

"Well, at least we now know ye do not presently serve the Darkness," she informed Ileana, causing Balthasar and Lucia to exhale with relief.

The girl herself, however, was unmoved by the Druswid's words. The sadness that had engulfed her with the solicitous soul's leaving remained; and though the Light had disappeared, a hazy vestige of Its luminescence still lingered, clouding her vision. Ileana was afraid she was now permanently blind, and burned beyond all recognition, too. She wished desperately that she could see, that she could look at herself, could touch herself to determine whether she was now truly the monstrosity she feared. But she was not brave enough to attempt to focus her eyes, to lift her hands. If she was now a thing of horror, she did not want to know it.

As though she had read Ileana's mind, Sharai spoke again.

"Lesson number one: Have the courage to try," she asserted firmly. "If ye do not, ye will allow the Demon Fear to take possession of ye, and ye will fail in all things—not because ye lack the ability to succeed, but because ye are afraid. Such are the wages of the Demon Fear. Do ye understand, child?"

"Yea, Reverend Mother."

Deliberately, Ileana forced herself to breathe deeply, to focus her eyes, to look at herself. She was stunned to discover that she could once more see and that there was no mark upon her. Marveling, she touched herself. The Light had been so bright. The pain had been so real. . . .

"'Twas all in your mind," the High Priestess said, correctly interpreting the girl's amazement. "'Twas all only in your mind."

"Does that—does that mean I passed the test?" Ileana ventured.

"Yea, of course. If ye had not, if ye had for even an instant turned from the crystal sphere, you would be dead now." The Druswid displayed the crescent-shaped dagger she held in her hand, which had previously been concealed beneath the folds of her habit. "I would have plunged my arthame into your heart," she said chillingly. Then, brusquely, she declared, "Fortunately, that was not necessary." She paused briefly, then continued.

"Though ye no doubt wish it were otherwise, ye are one of the Chosen. Ye have always been so. And though ye were born to the Royal House of Ariel, ye belong to the Druswids. Ye were given unto us before your conception, and 'tis time now that ye take your place among us." She paused, waiting for this to sink in. "Ye do not believe me? Well, 'tis true."

But Ileana remained unconvinced.

She is stubborn, Sharai reflected. *She will have a hard row to hoe because of that.*

Sighing, wishing she did not have to do so, knowing how shocked and betrayed the girl would feel, the High Priestess related the details of Ileana's birth.

"Go now and gather those few things most precious to ye," she ordered once she had finished her tale. "We leave for Mont Saint Mikhaela this night."

"Nay!" Ileana burst out, blanching. "I shan't go with ye, and ye can't make me! Father! Mother!" She turned frantically to her parents. "What she said isn't true, is it? Oh, tell her it's not! Tell her she can't take me away!"

But Balthasar cleared his throat gruffly and commanded Ileana to do as she was bidden. Lucia said nothing, for she was crying so hard, she could not speak.

It is true! the girl thought, stricken. *Everything the Druswid said is true! And in my heart, I have known it all along. I just didn't want to face it. Oh, Father, Mother, how could ye do this to me?*

Ileana stared at her parents accusingly for a long, painful minute. Then, her emotions overwhelming her at last, she turned and ran sobbing from the room, feeling as though her world had suddenly shattered into a million pieces.

QUARTER MOON

The Flame Prince

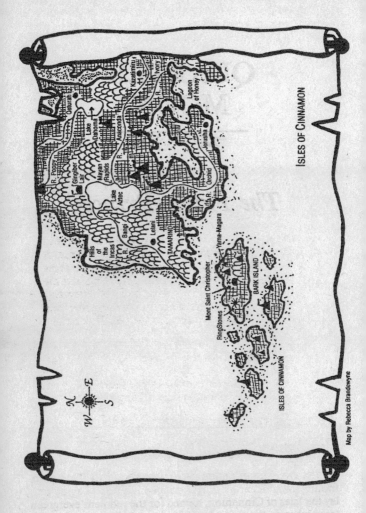

ISLES OF CINNAMON

Map by Rebecca Brandewyne

In the Isles of Cinnamon, native to the western verge was
trees whence the spice is at came and that grew in wild
abundance in the dense, steaming jungle that developed the

Chapter 8

It may seem strange that the Rebirth and the En-
lightenment occurred on Tintagel, for never once was
there a planet more truly besieged by the Darkness. But
the Immortal Guardian, in Its Infinite Wisdom, knew
the ember of hope that glows most hotly is the one that
rises like a Phoenix from the ashes of destruction. And
so, after the Wars of the Kind and the Apocalypse, It
bade Faith, the Keeper of the Flame, to appear to those
upon Tintagel and to speak again of It. Thus did the
Survivors, finally hearing the Word and understanding
the Way, establish the Mont Sects to honor, serve, and
defend the Light Eternal that sustains all True Believ-
ers in their Hour of Darkness.

—Thus it is Written—
in
The Teachings of the Mont Sects
The Book of Beginnings, Chapter Four

Mont Saint Christopher, Isles of Cinnamon, 7258.6.34

AT THE FAR WESTERN EDGE OF THE CONTINENT OF TAMARIND,
trailing away from the dragon-shaped land like a spiny tail,
lay the Isles of Cinnamon, named for the redolent evergreen
trees whence the spice itself came and that grew in wild
abundance in the dense, steaming jungle that enveloped the

large main island and smaller islets. A traveler who knew not of the isles' existence would have had difficulty locating them, for though they thrust up like massive boulders from the depths of the vast, dark blue Monsoon Ocean, they were often cloaked by the cool, thick, rolling white-grey fog carried northward on the wings of the bitterly cold winds that blew up from Janus, the southern polar cap.

Produced over the ages by massive volcanic eruptions, the terrain of the isles was mountainous, hard and craggy and black with lava that stretched like fingers to the coasts, where beaches of pale gold sand and, occasionally, coral reefs were kissed by whitecapped waves. But as though in recompense for its violent beginnings, the land itself was an emerald-green paradise shot through with bursts of brilliant color.

The giants of the tropical rain forests—the great silk-cotton trees, fruit-laden sapucaias, and blue-blossomed sucupiras—towered over the archipelago, cutting a jagged verdant line across the hazy, pale blue horizon and shading the myriad smaller trees that huddled beneath them, struggling to find a place in the sun. Hard, fragrant rosewoods and rubber trees sticky with sap fought for space alongside thorny acacias and leaf-crowned palms hanging with coconuts. Banana trees, bombacaceaes, and pink-blossomed cacao trees intertwined with tall stands of bamboo and clusters of cecropias, cedrelas, and figs. Climbing bignonias with branches laden with trumpet-shaped flowers, and coffee trees dripping with seeds, thrived among laurels, mauritias, and myrtles heavy with blackberries and white-rose blooms. Most prolific of all were the cinnamon trees, with their rough, spicy bark.

All the trees were wrapped in a thickly woven blanket of peperomia, moss, pineapples, liana vines, pipers, ferns, cacti, and a never-ending profusion of bright yellow daffodils, fragile, multicolored orchids, delicate water lilies, and other exotic tropical flowers. From the branches of the trees, tendrils of hanging moss flowed to the ground.

Above, aerial plants, whose roots never touched the plush tapestry of grass and moss, flourished, embedded in their larger, stronger brothers for nourishment and support. Beneath these, nut bushes and other shrubs crowded together to compose a tangled undergrowth, and exposed tree roots and trailing plants reached out like tentacles to feel their way through the mazelike jungle.

Here and there, huge, ropelike stranglers encased their hosts, gradually squeezing them to death in an effort to gain a precious bit of space, a vital ray of sun.

Because the latticelike canopy formed by the uppermost reaches of the vegetation was so tightly interlaced, the interiors of the rain forests were nearly impenetrable, swathed in constant darkness. Only one who knew how to follow the treacherous, often hidden path that twined through the jungle might make his way to the very heart of the main island, Bark Island, where, in a cleared glade at the base of the mighty snowcapped volcano Yama-Magara, the meticulously designed and stoutly constructed, high-walled abbey of Mont Saint Christopher stood.

Centuries old, the monastery had been built of solidified magma wrested from the earth, then hewn into square blocks and polished until it shone like the volcanic glass, obsidian, with which it was studded. At each corner of its four battlemented walls was a square, crenellated tower. The structure itself was quadrangular in shape, the church at its center surrounded by the wings. A square, gold-domed bell tower thrust up from the steep, pitched roof of the chancel. The gable-roofed wings were three stories tall and lined on all sides with mullioned casement windows of amber glass that appeared to stare like the gleaming eyes of panthers. In the mornings, when the rising sun was high enough in the sky to look down upon the edifice, the diamond-shaped panes caught and reflected the brilliant red-gold rays, making the abbey look like a powerful jaguar springing from a shimmering pool of liquid fire. It was a perfect black jewel for the splendorous jungle setting that held it.

There were few who ever trod the secret monastery's long, narrow, winding corridors as did Brother Edu san Nahele this eve, though he wished fervently that he were abed, as most of the other inhabitants were. He did not like to prowl about the halls at night, and he was tired besides. But neither fear nor weariness kept a priest from his assigned duties, and Brother Edu was no exception to the rule. So he continued toward the north wing of the abbey, the novitiate, where the novices were housed. It was there, he knew, that at this late hour, he would find the Lord Cain sin Khali, now known only as Sirrah Cain, since he was merely a novice and his rank beyond Mont Saint Christopher's walls had no meaning within them. It was he Brother Edu had been instructed to fetch.

The slight, bent priest shuddered at the thought of the dark Bedouin novice; and then, glancing about to be certain he was unobserved, he starred himself surreptitiously for protection and drew his brown cowl more closely about his face. There was something different about that one, he mused soberly, though he did not know what it was. He knew only that Sirrah Cain was not like the other novices, that his power was such that he had been singled out for special training and attention.

Brother Edu frowned at the thought. Though each novice's talents must, of course, be carefully nurtured, he did not hold with permitting any one of them to learn too many of the Mysteries before taking their Final Vows. He felt this encouraged them to entertain ideas above their present station. Then they sometimes foolishly attempted tasks for which they were not fully prepared—producing disastrous results. Why, just a few years ago, one young novice had nearly blown up the entire monastery when a spell he ought not to have been casting had got out of hand!

Brother Edu was only a third-ranked priest, still restricted to the Lesser Mysteries and not likely to progress any higher. When he thought that Sirrah Cain, still a novice, was to be admitted this eve to one of the abbey's most closely guarded and revered places . . .

Ah, well, the priest sighed, shaking his head.

It certainly was not for him to question the wisdom of Brother Ottah san Huatsu, a twelfth-ranked priest and the designated successor of the High Priest Kokudza himself. Still, Brother Edu was glad he did not stand in Brother Ottah's sandals tonight.

Seeing he had finally reached the small chamber he sought, Brother Edu carefully composed his face into an expressionless mask. Then he took several deep breaths in an attempt to calm his racing nerves. After that, only because he didn't want to disturb those novices who might already be asleep—or so he told himself—he knocked softly, very softly, upon the wooden door of Sirrah Cain's room.

It was only fitting that I first saw her in a dream, though I did not know that at the time. Nor did I know what an important role she was to play in my life, though this was told to me by Brother Ottah from the start.

Perhaps I did not want to believe it. I don't know.

When I had known only five years, I was taken away from my home, Khali Keep, by the High Priest Kokudza to the monastery of Mont Saint Christopher on the Isles of Cinnamon; and there, I was prepared for my fate, which, I was told, had been written in the stars before my time and could not be changed.

It was only natural, I suppose, that being proud and fiercely independent, I should rebel against this and seek to attain some measure of control over my destiny.

I did this in small ways at first. But later, I did it with the girl, fighting the feelings that drew me inexplicably to her, though in truth, I wanted her from the very beginning. . . .

—Thus it is Written—
in
The Private Journals
of the High Prince Lord Cain I

Since the hour was late, the Lord Cain sin Khali, now called Sirrah Cain, was very much surprised to hear the hesitant rap upon his door. Curious, he at once closed the book he had been reading and, after turning up the oil lamp, rose to make his way across the bare floor of the sparse cell that had served as his private domain these many years.

Its lack of comfort had ceased long ago to disturb him, though once, in his childhood, he had been accustomed to fine furnishings—and to having his every need met by one servant or another. Now, though he had progressed in his studies to the point where he had been given an acolyte, he mostly waited on himself.

After reaching the wooden door, he pulled open the shutter to peer through the mesh grill, thinking that if it were Jahil or Iskander, they could enjoy an hour or so of conversation and share a bottle of stout ale from the monastery's brewery before retiring.

Vaguely disappointed to see it was neither of his friends in the hallway, Cain did not at first recognize the stooped, hooded figure outside.

"Who is it?" he asked impatiently, now slightly annoyed at having his studies interrupted.

"'Tis I—Brother Edu—sirrah," came the low reply. "Your presence has been requested. Would you come with me, please."

Wondering why he had been summoned—and by whom —Cain abruptly closed the shutter, then opened the door and followed the priest down the corridor. Due to the lateness of the hour, only a few torches still burned to light their way, but Cain, unlike Brother Edu, was unperturbed by the shadows dancing on the walls. Without haste, he tagged after his thin, anxious superior, now scurrying like a mouse down the stairs to the novitiates' refectory. After crossing the dining hall, Brother Edu opened the doors that led to the cloister, passed beneath the colonnade, then descended the short flight of steps to the paved private courtyard. Here, skirting the ornate central stone fountain, he hastened his already rapid pace, and Cain altered his own measured stride accordingly, smiling.

Everyone knew that Brother Edu was as twitchy as a rabbit; it was only his considerable skill as a manuscript illuminator that had earned him a place in the Brotherhood.

Cain sighed. He wished his superior would tell him where they were going, but he knew from his many arduous years of training that unlike some of his more talkative fellows, Brother Edu never relayed any information he had not specifically been told to impart; and so Cain did not even bother speaking to him. The novice knew his questions would be answered soon enough. There was no point, he decided, in further agitating the nervous priest.

As they neared the church, the fragrant scent of cinnamon

wafting from the incense burners pervaded Cain's nostrils.
He breathed deeply of the spicy aroma. It was one of the
things he liked best about the abbey—the inevitable smell
of cinnamon. During the rainy season, the priests harvested
and processed the bark, and later, it was shipped to the
continents and sold to merchants.

Brother Edu entered the church, Cain following close on
his heels. There was a sense of peace and harmony here that
never failed to touch the novice, and briefly, he longed to
stay a while to meditate. But to his surprise, the priest did
not stop, but passed on through the nave and the chancel to
the small alcove behind the altar. There, he pushed aside
the thick, beautifully patterned carpet that covered the
floor, then unlocked a stout oak door set within the intricate
parquet. Once he had lifted the portal, he pulled up two
small, curved handrails attached to either side of a wrought-
iron ladder that was bolted into one wall of the yawning
chasm below. After he had firmly fastened the handrails
into place, he indicated Cain should go on alone.

Startled, the novice quirked one eyebrow questioningly,
but Brother Edu shook his head and refused to meet Cain's
eyes. Slowly, the novice began to descend the ladder into the
dark pit that gaped before him like the open maw of some
monster and that grew even blacker when, behind him, the
priest closed the door. Cain, alone now, heard the sound of
the key grating in the lock, and for a moment, he wondered
if he was to be shut away in here forever. Then he laughed at
the foolish notion, knowing a priest did not stoop to murder
without an extremely good reason.

He paused to accustom his eyes to the darkness. Then,
feeling carefully for the ladder's rungs, he continued on
wondering where the aperture led. The climb seemed endless, and the air was chilly and drafty, too, the metal ladder
cold to the touch, making Cain wish somewhat irritably that
Brother Edu had told him to wear his gloves.

At last, just as he was starting to wonder if the descent was
ever going to terminate, he discerned a dim, flickering light
below and felt a gust of warmer air brush his skin. Presently,
he dropped the short distance to the ground and exhaled
faintly with relief.

Once his feet were firmly planted on the solid rock floor,

Cain glanced up into the blackness whence he had come. The door was nowhere in sight, and he calculated he must be one to two hundred feet beneath the earth's surface. Thank the Immortal Guardian he had not slipped and fallen, for he would surely have been killed!

Slowly, the novice examined his surroundings. The light proved to be a flaming torch in an iron sconce set into a wall of a long, curving tunnel. At regular intervals along the passage, Cain could see additional torches; observing no other route to follow, he started down the corridor, wondering where it would take him.

After a time, hearing the faint hiss of steam and a low rumble, the novice recognized with a start that he was in an offshoot of Yama-Magara, the massive volcano that had given birth to Bark Island. Though the powerful giant had lain slumbering for many years now, there was still always the chance it would once more awaken and erupt; and Cain did not relish the thought of probing its interior.

Sweat beaded his brow as, realizing he could not turn back until he had fulfilled whatever duties awaited him this night, he continued forward. Eventually, he reached a large cavern, and there, he drew up short, stunned.

The grotto before him reminded him of the inside of a pyramid, the mysterious structure that, in the Time Before, had been used by the Old Ones as a burial place for their dead. Once, during his childhood, Cain had dared to explore one of the strange triangular buildings that, in solitary magnificence, towered over the windswept dunes of the Haghar Desert in Bedoui, his homeland. He remembered entering the edifice and following its steep decline until at last it had angled up sharply to open upon the great tomb itself. There had been a peculiar stillness within the chamber, and an awesome sense of power had seemed to emanate from the core of the stone crypt in the center of the vault.

Now, as he had then, Cain felt a chill of morbid fascination and dread tingle along his spine. The odd hush of the volcanic cavern seemed to envelop him like a shroud, and he could almost feel the power that throbbed within the room. It was as though its very walls were alive and closing in on him, pulsing with the ethereal essence of a thousand cloaked priests, long since scattered ashes, who had come and gone over the ages, leaving behind only the sound of their chanting voices, their rustling robes, and their whispering footsteps to mark their passing. Some would have said it was only the hissing of steam and the growl of the earth's bowels that echoed in the silence. But Cain, shivering a little, knew better.

Yea, it was a place as old as time, he thought, witness to a millennium of rites and passages.

Over the centuries, some of the magma that flowed through the subterranean fissures had cooled and hardened, and the chamber itself was composed of layer upon layer of dense black basalt—polished until it gleamed and subdivided by jagged, crystalline streaks of amethysts, topazes, rubies, aquamarines, sapphires, diamonds, and emeralds. Here and there, rivulets of molten lava trickled along the ground, casting an eerie glow upon the walls, and the entire grotto flickered as though it were ablaze, the glittering jewels melting and running into one another.

Set upon solid gold bases and positioned so they formed the five points of a star were white marble statues of the primary Keepers: Faith, who fed the Eternal Flame, kneeling, her hands uplifted and cupped to hold secure the fire that burned within them; Harmonia, who kept order in the universe, placing an object into the neatly arranged shadow box that sat upon a pedestal at her side; Epochē, who maintained the Circle of Time, bending to turn slowly the upright wheel, an hourglass at its center, that rose before him; Rocca, who guarded the gate leading to the Immortal Guardian, standing in front of the gate itself, a sword and shield held purposefully in his hands; and Judicium, who recorded the deeds of the Kind, sitting with an open book in his lap, his quill poised to write, a balance at his feet.

The figures appeared so lifelike, Cain half expected them to move. Uneasily, he turned away from the sightless statues to the strange pool, unlike any he had ever before seen, that lay at the heart of the vault.

It glimmered like quicksilver, reflecting the brilliant colors of the rough-cut gems in the walls so it looked as though a rainbow were held prisoner in its mercurial depths. Random droplets cast out by the gently rippling waves sparkled like prisms around its edge; from its center, white steam rose in swirling clouds.

Wondering why he, yet a novice, had been brought to this obviously secret and revered place, Cain peered into the darkest reaches of the chamber, searching for some sign of the priest who had summoned him here this night. Finally, he spied Brother Ottah san Huatsu, who was seated upon a flat-topped rock in the shadows, waiting mutely for the novice to become aware of him.

"Ah, so ye have arrived at last, sirrah," the priest remarked unnecessarily upon observing that Cain had seen him, for he had been watching the novice for some time. "I was beginning to think perhaps ye had got lost—or, worse yet, had fallen down the shaft, which would have been a very great pity indeed. But I see my faith in ye was not misplaced after all. Ye are here, safe and sound, as I assumed ye would be, and not so blinded by your surroundings that ye failed to notice your old mentor." Brother Ottah paused, glancing about proudly at the cavern that held Cain spellbound. "'Tis very impressive, is it not? We call it the Hallowed Hall." He seemed about to say something more, then obviously decided against further explanation. "Well"—he stood and rubbed his hands together briskly as he stepped forward into the half-light—"so much for the amenities.

"No doubt ye are wondering why I sent for ye, sirrah, so I will not keep ye waiting long for an answer. Come." He motioned with one hand to Cain, indicating the shimmering silver pool. "There is something I want to show ye. I believe ye will find it . . . most interesting."

Puzzled but expectant, Cain joined the priest, who now knelt at the edge of the pool. The novice, impatient to be enlightened as to why he had been brought here, had to fight down the urge to break the silence as he waited for his mentor to speak again. To do otherwise, he knew, would be a thoughtless breach of etiquette, displaying his chafing curiosity and his lack of control over his emotions —something for which he would be strictly chastened.

So, wordlessly, Cain studied his mentor. Though he guessed Brother Ottah had known over fifty years, the priest appeared ageless. He was bald and rotund, with smooth skin, which made him resemble a newborn babe. Because of this, others often assumed he was as innocent and guileless as a child. But there was a wealth of wisdom, insight, and knowledge in his eyes, and since he had been Cain's mentor for many years now, the novice did not make the mistake of thinking him a harmless old fellow. Brother Ottah, though he did not presently look in the least menacing, wielded a power that was almost as great as that of the High Priest Kokudza.

Steadily, Brother Ottah returned Cain's unblinking gaze, well aware of his restlessness, his longing to be told why his presence had been requested this eve. Yet the novice hid his turbulent emotions superbly, the priest thought with satisfaction, for Cain had made no movement, however imperceptible, since they had first knelt at the edge of the pool. Yea, the novice had learned well, Brother Ottah decided, remembering the sullen, rebellious child who, when he had known only five years, had been brought to Mont Saint Christopher for training.

There were those who had despaired of ever teaching him anything, above all discipline, then; and those who had known what he was to become had been afraid that Takis san Baruch, the Ancient One, his body dead these many years past, had, in performing the dangerous Ritual of Choosing, conjured a force that would easily be turned to the hand of the Darkness.

But Brother Ottah had sensed in the boy a hunger and an ambition that would be fed and nurtured by knowledge, and an innate sense of justice that would grow with time. So the priest had set for himself the task of imparting all he had learned to the novice.

At first, Cain had proved a rude and an unruly pupil. But Brother Ottah was nothing if not patient, and he had persisted in his endeavors. Gradually, the child had come to grasp the fact that the training he would receive at the abbey would be far more difficult and comprehensive than any he would have got at home and that he would be privy to many secrets besides. Recognizing an opportunity for advancement that might not otherwise have been accorded him,

Cain had buckled down to his studies with an intensity that, while startling to those who had not suspected the depths of his character, had not surprised his mentor at all.

Satisfied he had reached the boy at last, Brother Ottah had then embarked on a strenuous and daunting course of guidance and teaching. Now, he knew, there were areas in which Cain, though yet a novice, far surpassed him. Brother Ottah accepted this with equanimity, understanding that all were not created equal, but were gifted with whatever intellect and talents the Immortal Guardian chose to bestow upon them. The secret to success and happiness lay not in coveting the attributes of others, but in recognizing one's own abilities and developing them to the utmost.

Secure in the knowledge that he had done this, Brother Ottah felt no envy of others, especially Cain, whose LifePath was chilling to contemplate.

Mentally, the priest starred himself at the thought. Then, aware he would need a great portion of his strength and power this night, he closed his eyes and began to meditate, willing himself to forget the past and to concentrate on the present. Finally, he was ready. He opened his eyes and spoke.

"How many years have ye known, sirrah?" he asked, though he knew the answer well.

"I have known eighteen years, Dominus," Cain replied respectfully.

"Yea." Brother Ottah nodded. "And for thirteen of them, I have been your mentor, have I not?"

"Yea, Dominus."

"And during that time, I have always spoken to ye truthfully, have I not?"

"Yea, Dominus," Cain responded.

"Then ye know that this night, too, I shall speak the truth." The priest paused to allow this to penetrate. Then he continued slowly. "Ye are aware, sirrah, of the circumstances of your birth, that ye were conceived and born of the Ritual of Choosing and promised to the Druswids. That is why ye were given unto the Brotherhood. But ye do not yet know why. Nor do ye know there is another such as yourself."

"Another, Dominus?" Cain raised one eyebrow, astonished by this information, for he had thought he was alone, the only one. . . .

"Yea, a female. Even now, she undergoes the Trial of the Light, as ye yourself once did."

Brother Ottah turned to the pool. He waved one hand, and moments later, the steam rising from the waves thickened, darkened, and began to eddy like the blanketing mist that presages a snowstorm. A low rumble sounded deep in the earth, growing steadily louder and fiercer until it shook the ground beneath them. Then, suddenly, the pool started to bubble and churn violently. At last, it erupted with a roar, water spewing from its core to shatter the shroud of steam.

"Behold," the priest commanded softly.

As Cain looked into the geyser, the image of a beautiful young girl slowly started to take shape. She was small and delicate, a Cygninae, he knew, because of her long silver hair and wide lavender eyes. Her eyes were filled with fear as she stared at the Light issuing from the crystal sphere, which had once held him spellbound, blinding him, burning his very soul. It was a torturous test, for if one failed it, one was instantly stabbed through the heart by the arthame of the High Priest or the High Priestess who held the glass globe. Did the girl know that? Cain wondered. Or did she, as he had, sense only that she would die if she turned away from the Light? She seemed so tiny and vulnerable, too young to have her ashes scattered to the elements.

Instinctively, Cain felt a kinship with her, knowing what she was feeling at this moment, and inexplicably, he was drawn to her. Without his being consciously aware of it, his essence reached out to her across the miles that separated them.

Fear is a demon, he repeated the litany silently to himself —and to her. *It interferes with the processes of the mind so one cannot think clearly or rationally—if at all. Ye must face the Demon Fear and recognize it for what it is. Then ye must conquer it by driving it from your mind and willing yourself to concentrate on the Light. Breathe deeply, and think of the Light. Think only of the Light. . . .*

Whether his soul had touched hers, Cain did not know. Still, he saw that the girl was not shying away from the Light, but was continuing to face it, drawing on her inner reserve of strength and courage to stand fast before the lambent beam that pierced her eyes and penetrated her body, mind, and soul.

"As ye yourself were, she is very brave for one so young, is she not?" Brother Ottah queried, bringing Cain abruptly back to the present.

"Yea, Dominus," the novice answered soberly.

"Do not forget her face, sirrah, for she is to play a very important part in your life." The priest paused, then went on quietly. "She will someday be your mate."

"But . . . she's only a child!" Cain burst out, momentarily stunned into losing his composure.

Brother Ottah smiled, amused.

"Yea, now, of course," he agreed, "for she has known only seven years. But she will grow, sirrah, and 'twill be a while yet before ye shall be joined—a decade or more, if we are fortunate, though when one considers the whole of time, even a century is merely a fleeting moment in the scheme of things."

"A decade . . . yea . . . 'tis indeed little time, as ye say," Cain admitted. "And even then, she will still be very young." He frowned. "I mislike the idea of being bound to this child, Dominus," he asserted firmly, regaining control of himself. "Though she is beautiful and has much courage, too, who is to say what she may become in the future? I know her not; and besides, I seek no mate, and even if I did, I would prefer to choose my own."

"So I surmised," Brother Ottah said calmly, unperturbed. "But I'm afraid ye shall have no choice in the matter, sirrah. Ye are fated for each other. The Ritual of Choosing by which each of ye was conceived and born made certain of that. She is the other half of your soul—and is in your blood, as ye are hers. There shall be no escaping that, as ye will discover for yourself when the time is right. Then ye will understand why it must be so."

The priest knew that Cain was angered by the words, for the novice's black eyes narrowed and a muscle worked tensely in his jaw. Briefly, Brother Ottah felt a twinge of apprehension prick his spine. There was still a rebellious streak at the core of Cain's nature. He would not without a struggle accept his destiny—or the fact that it could not be changed. Instead, he would fight his feelings for the girl, and in doing so, he would more easily be turned to the Darkness that had been so hazardously bred into his soul by Takis san Baruch, the Ancient One. Still, that was the chance that must be taken if Tintagel were to be saved from the horror that threatened it. Brother Ottah could only pray that the girl, instilled with the Light, would prove strong enough to balance and, if necessary, combat the Power that would be Cain's.

It was indeed a pity she was so young. But even those who had risked performing the Ritual of Choosing had not dared to do so twice in one night. The forces unleashed by the ceremony were so powerful and the rite itself was so fraught with peril that to have carried it out two times in a single eve would have been mad. Since the ritual could only be performed when the heavenly signs were right—and the stars and planets assumed such favorable aspects rarely —the Druswids had despaired of bringing forth more than a single child of the Chosen, so they had selected a male, thinking he who faced the Darkness would have need of great physical strength.

Then, eleven years later, much to the Druswids' amazement, the heavenly signs had once more moved into position for the Ritual of Choosing, the stars and planets aligning themselves auspiciously, if differently from before. The Druswidic astrologers had considered this no less than a miracle and had interpreted it as a fortuitous omen.

Now a female child could be produced to counterpoise the male, thus ensuring that the symmetry found throughout the universe could be maintained.

Still, the girl *was* very young, Brother Ottah thought again sadly, and there was little enough time to prepare her. He did not envy her mentor's task. Sighing, he gazed once more at the image of the girl, still hovering incandescently in the fountain of water that sprayed from the pool.

"She has passed the Trial of the Light," he noted unnecessarily, for Cain could see this was so. "Now she will be taken to Mont Saint Mikhaela for training."

Abruptly, the priest waved his hand, and the geyser collapsed, taking the girl's image with it as it vanished into the pool. Then, once more, he turned his attention to Cain.

"Listen well, sirrah," he intoned. "In the time before your birth, those who possessed the Power looked into the fires and mists and saw signs of the things to come, dreadful omens like none their eyes had ever before beheld, shapes and shadows of a terrible evil that can belong only to the Darkness." Cain inhaled sharply in sudden, dawning comprehension, and Brother Ottah nodded. "Yea, our old enemy returns to the land; indeed, It is already here, though few yet know it. Now the Foul Enslaver is weak. But as It did in the Time Before, It will feed upon the land, and soon It will grow stronger—strong enough to unleash Its Demons and their deadly forces upon us all.

"Those who foresaw Its coming did not know what form Its wickedness would take or how powerful It would be, and so unto Takis, the Ancient One, was given the arduous task of performing the Ritual of Choosing so one of the Chosen might be brought forth to defend the land and the Light. That one so conceived and born of his magic is ye, sirrah."

The priest fell silent, waiting for the novice to grasp the import of this. Cain was wooden with shock; his mind was a mass of confusion. Though he had understood that the manner of his birth was significant, never in his wildest dreams had he imagined that its consequences would prove so treacherous and far-reaching. Now he knew why he was yet a novice, why his training had been and continued to be so much harder and more extensive than that of any of the other novices. The revelation stunned him, intrigued him, excited him, even while it sent a cold prickle of fear down his spine. Inwardly, he struggled to bring order to his chaotic thoughts and emotions.

"And the girl?" he inquired at last, wondering what part she was to play in all this. "What of her?"

"She is a part of ye, as ye are of her, as I have said. Ye are tied to each other by bonds more powerful than mere worldly ones," Brother Ottah reaffirmed. "This cannot be changed. When the time is right, ye will be mated with her. She was conceived and born for this purpose of the magic of Gitana, she who served as the Sisterhood's Ancient One in Time Past. Much as ye dislike the idea, sirrah, your joining is inevitable, as ye will come to understand."

There was more to it than this, Cain realized, much more.

But it was obvious his mentor meant to offer no further explanation, and the novice did not press for one, knowing that to do so was pointless. All things had their own time, and he would learn the answers to his questions soon enough.

At the priest's signal, recognizing that he was being dismissed, Cain stood. He was halfway across the chamber when, suddenly, he stopped and turned to glance back at Brother Ottah, still kneeling beside the pool.

"Yea, sirrah?" The priest raised one eyebrow expectantly —and somewhat censuringly as well, since the interview had ended.

Cain cleared his throat.

"The girl . . . she whose image I saw in the pool"—he spoke hesitantly, then swallowed hard. "I—I . . . that is . . . I would know her name, if it is permitted."

Brother Ottah smiled, his features softening with affection for the novice he had trained.

"It is," he said. "She is called Ileana. Do ye know its meaning, sirrah?"

"Yea," Cain replied, realizing he did indeed, though the answer had come to him from nowhere and he had not known it until this very instant. "It means 'Chosen by the Light.'"

"Think about that," the priest advised enigmatically, "and remember what ye have been taught. Go with the Light, sirrah."

For every force in the universe, there is an equal and opposite force.

—Thus it is Written—
in
The Teachings of The Mont Sects
The Book of Laws, Chapter Two

Think about that, and remember what ye have been taught.

The cryptic words rang in Cain's ears as he strode swiftly down the tunnel to the dark shaft at its end and began to ascend the wrought-iron ladder. Upon reaching the end of his long climb, he rapped peremptorily upon the closed door. In his haste to reach his cell, where he could consider more clearly all he had learned this eve, Cain nearly knocked Brother Edu into the aperture after the priest had unlocked and lifted the door to allow him to exit.

Not caring that it was said with ill grace, the novice muttered a curt apology, then bid Brother Edu good night, not bothering to wait to be dismissed. Deeply affronted, for he had longed to ask Cain what the Hallowed Hall, which he had never been privileged to view, was like, the priest stared with thin-lipped condemnation at the novice's retreating figure.

To Brother Edu's further vexation, instead of returning immediately to the novitiate, Cain entered the warming room just west of the chancel to make his way down the long hall known as the night passage.

Headed for the brewery—or the cellars—no doubt, the prim little priest decided sourly, *and without so much as a thank ye for all the time I spent here waiting for him!*

Instantly mortified by the censurious thought, Brother Edu hastily begged the Immortal Guardian's forgiveness and promised to repeat a litany of prayers as penance. Then, sighing, he stooped to pull the carpet back into place over the closed door. Moments later, the priest heard a whisper of wind sough through the night passage, and he knew his earlier conjecture had been accurate: Cain was crossing the public courtyard to the almonry, beneath which the cellars were housed.

Well, perhaps he is in need of a small glass of wine, Brother Edu reflected more charitably. *They say the Hallowed Hall is a powerful place. Who is to know what may have happened within its walls tonight?*

Shrugging, then giving a final glance around the chancel to be certain no trace of this eve's trespass remained, Brother Edu entered the night passage to make his way to the dormitory.

After taking a bottle of burgundy from the cellars, Cain retraced his steps to the novitiate and his small cell. There, he poured himself a glass of the dry red wine and settled back upon his bed to contemplate Brother Ottah's parting words.

Think about that, and remember what ye have been taught.

Tired, the novice shut his eyes. What had the priest intended to convey to him by that advice? It was something important, Cain knew, else Brother Ottah would not have mentioned it. It was something to do with the girl's name. Ileana. Chosen by the Light. Ileana . . . and Cain. Cain. The name was an old one, yet oddly enough, the novice had no idea what it meant. But . . . wait. Wasn't there a reference to it in one of the books his mentor had given him just this past week to study? Yea . . . now he remembered. He had just started to read it when Jahil and Iskander had come to drag him away for a game of Pharaoh.

Faintly excited, certain it was indeed so, Cain rose and began to examine the ancient tomes that lay upon his desk. At last, he found the volume he thought contained the entry. Quickly but carefully, he riffled the book's pages. Yea, here it was. Eagerly, he read the passage:

> CAIN/'kān/ n [Bd *Qayin*, fr. OBd *Qanah*]: "One who is given a choice: to possess or to be possessed." On the now extinct planet of Terra (noted for its warlike tribes and destroyed during the Time of the World Wars), Cain, a member of the Hebrew Tribe, was the brother and murderer of Abel. According to the Terran Holy Bible, for his crime, Cain was accursed and sentenced to wander the earth; and so none might strike him down, he bore the mark of Yahweh[1]. He settled at last in the land of Nod, east of Eden.
>
> [1]One of the numerous Terran names for the Immortal Guardian.

One who is given a choice: to possess or to be possessed.

As he closed the tome, Cain shuddered involuntarily, feeling a little sick as he grasped the implication of what he had read. Now he understood fully what Brother Ottah had not told him, what the priest had known Cain must discover for himself. The girl—Ileana—had been Chosen by the Light. He, Cain, had been given a choice. He could either

possess the girl—and the Light—or he could *be* possessed
. . . *by the Darkness!* Yea, it was so, for had he not learned
that the universe was symmetrical, that each force it contained had an equal and opposite force to balance it?

Now he understood why there were those at the monastery who feared him, who starred themselves when they
thought he was not looking. Though they might not know
what it was, somehow they sensed there was something
different about him—as he himself had sensed it in the
past.

Cain was accursed . . .

The words printed on the page he had read burned like a
brand in the novice's memory. Like that Cain of another
world, was he, too, accursed? He did not know; but though
he could not understand how or why, still he recognized
that somehow a part of the Darkness dwelled within him.
Determined to ferret It out, Cain searched every nook and
cranny of his body, mind, and soul, probing, dissecting. But
try as he might, he could find no trace of the Light's
antithesis. Yet he felt certain It was there somewhere,
lurking inside him.

Deeply troubled, he blew out his oil lamp and went to
bed. But sleep was a long time coming, and when he finally
did close his eyes, it was an uneasy slumber that claimed
him, one haunted by dreams of the girl Ileana, fully grown
and shining with the Light as she held him in her arms
—and destroyed him.

Map by Rebecca Brandewyne

Chapter 9

*And so it was that when I had known only seven
years, I was taken away by the High Priestess Sharai to
the nunnery of Mont Saint Mikhaela on the Isle of Le
Fey; and there, for the next ten years of my life, I
dwelled and learned the Art of Sorcery.*

—Thus it is Written—
in
The Private Journals
of the High Princess Lady Ileana I

THE SUN WAS JUST BEGINNING ITS SLOW ASCENT ABOVE THE
eastern horizon when they finally came to the vast River of
Separation, which poured into the Sea of Oriana, where, in
the distance, the Isle of Le Fey rose in majestic splendor
from the golden waves crested with white froth. The island,
though large, was difficult to see at first, for it was veiled by
pale greyish white wisps of drifting mist that intermittently
obscured it from view. Thus when it did appear, it was all
the more startling.

Ileana was never to forget her first glimpse of it, for she
thought it was the loveliest place she'd ever seen. Involuntarily, she gasped as the haze shifted to reveal the island: the
coral reefs, the cream-colored beach, the green plains, and
the verdant forest beyond. The clear waves washed gently
over the ivory sand and, here and there, nudged clumps of
weeds and stands of slender golden-green reeds that edged
the shore, swaying in the cool, tangy breeze. Farther on, the

tall green grass of the sweeping plains rippled with each sighing gust and the leaves of the trees in the thick woods rustled softly.

At Ileana's sharply indrawn breath, the High Priestess Sharai, mounted upon a greyish yellow alaecorn with a black mane and tail, turned to look back at the girl who sat so still upon her own beast, her tiny, pale face, drawn and expressionless for most of the trip, now filled with wonder and awe.

So I was when first I saw it, Sharai remembered, and smiled a little to herself as she thought of the many years that had come and gone since then. *Poor child. She must be tired and hungry, too; but still, she has made no complaint. In truth, she has been far too silent. I fear the winds of change have buffeted her hither too hurriedly and harshly.*

The journey had indeed been long and hard, for the Druswid had left behind the *Enchanted,* the galley that belonged to the Sisterhood. It was still anchored in the harbor at Ethelred, the southernmost city of Vikanglia, whence Sharai and the other priestesses had made their way overland to Lothian Hold for the ceremonies just past. The Sisters would need the ship to return to the abbey. The High Priestess, not wanting Ileana to be interrogated by the High Council over the incident in the coliseum, had determined the girl must be spirited away from Vikanglia as quickly and quietly as possible. Had the entire retinue from Mont Saint Mikhaela departed before the end of the rites, this would not have been possible. So only Sharai and Ileana had left, riding the alaecorns, which had borne them here on favorable air currents.

They had traveled rapidly, with only a few stops here and there to rest the weary animals, who could not remain aloft indefinitely.

'Twas indeed a trying pace for one so young, the Druswid reflected.

Then, resolutely, she thrust aside her pity. Ileana's LifePath would not be an easy one. She must learn to endure the many trials she would face, and she might as well begin at once. Still, when the High Priestess spoke, her voice was kind.

"'Tis not much farther now," she said, "and then we will be able to bathe and to break our fast, too."

Ileana made no reply, but sighing wearily, she gathered up her reins, so Sharai knew she had heard and understood the words.

"Nay." The Druswid shook her head as she observed the gesture. "The beasts are useless to us now. The mist makes it too dangerous to attempt to land from the sky. I will summon the barge."

So saying, she dismounted and moved to stand at the river's edge. She pressed her hands together at her breast and bowed her head so it touched her fingertips and her chin rested upon her thumbs. Then, after taking several deep breaths and closing her eyes and ears to shut out her surroundings, she willed herself to concentrate on the silent call she sent out across the water to the nunnery, which rose from the very heart of the island, its slender spires surmounting the treetops. When she was sure her message had been received, Sharai glanced up expectantly, spreading her palms wide before dropping her arms to her sides.

Presently, gliding noiselessly over the sea, there appeared a small, ancient boat with gracefully curved bow, sides, and stern fashioned to resemble a swan. A single square sail billowed from the mast; six veiled Sisters manned the oars.

When they reached the place where the river joined the sea, the priestesses guided the *Swan Song,* as the barge was called, to shore. Then, heedless of their long robes, they disembarked and waded through the water to haul the boat a little way up onto the beach.

In later years, Ileana herself was to learn how to summon the barge, a simple enough thing once one knew the secret. But now she could only gaze at the boat with amazement, wondering how it had come to be there. Her eyes flicked with curiosity to the High Priestess, but Sharai only smiled enigmatically, offering no explanation.

"'Tis but a taste of the feast of knowledge that awaits ye within the abbey walls," she averred. "Come."

She spoke no more, not even to greet the Sisters, but motioned for Ileana to dismount and to lead her alaecorn up the short ramp now positioned near the stern of the barge.

Once the passengers and the animals were aboard, the Sisters removed the ramp and pushed the boat back into the water. Then, deftly, they climbed over the sides to take up their positions at the oars. Slowly, the barge headed toward the open sea and the Isle of Le Fey.

Ileana knew it would be many years before she saw her homeland again, and she could not resist looking back for a last glimpse of Cygnus—at the vast Melantha Forest with its tall evergreen pines, the snowcapped peaks of the purple Gloriana Mountains that cascaded down from the north, and the continent's towering cities that seemed suspended in the soft white clouds. Silently, she pressed the sight like a flower into the pages of her memory, telling herself it was only the spindrift that caused her eyes to blur.

Then, determinedly, her head held high, she turned toward the island, firmly shutting the door to her past.

The wind was stronger upon the water, and cool. The salt-tinged spray cast up from the waves slapping against the slicing bow of the boat felt chilly against Ileana's skin, despite the summer heat. Overhead, the sail flogged in the breeze; beside her, the silent priestesses rowed in perfect harmony, guiding the skimming barge over the water. The Isle of Le Fey lay ahead, beckoning to them like a siren playing hide-and-seek in the mist, luring them deeper and deeper into the haze.

Soon, the fog closed around them, thick and enveloping, like a blanket, and it was as though the sun had not risen in the sky, so dark and grey was the day. Now Ileana, who could see only shapes and shadows of what moments past had been so clear, understood why the High Priestess had forborne to fly upon the alaecorns to the island. The thin appearance of the mist was deceptive; they would surely have become lost within it and ridden the beasts into the sea. Ileana's heart pounded with sudden fear at the thought; perhaps the boat, too, would wander aimlessly to be driven upon the coral reefs or the rocks scattered along the beach. Then she remembered how the High Priestess had called the barge and how swiftly and surely it had come, and she knew those at the nunnery possessed knowledge far beyond her wildest imaginings. They knew how to pass safely through the haze that guarded the island and the abbey. At the realization, Ileana's fright receded, but still, she shivered a little and tightened her grip upon the swan's wing that formed the side of the boat.

A few minutes later, they broke free of the mist and the island lay before them. As before, Ileana's breath caught in her throat when she saw the golden sea shimmering along the sloping borders of the creamy beach, the sun-dappled ridges of the coral reefs that protruded above the water's surface to catch the whitecapped breakers in midair so they were like a fleeting fermata, held for a breathless instant and then released.

Presently, the barge neared the shore, and the Sisters waded into the water to drag the boat up onto the sand. Then they led the animals away, Sharai and Ileana following close behind them along the narrow concealed path that wound its way through the tall grass and the dense woods to the nunnery.

Ileana, surreptitiously casting a glance back to reassure herself that she had indeed safely arrived, was startled to see that the shore had disappeared and that the grass had swallowed the path behind them so no trace of their passing remained. She shuddered a little, for such things were beyond her comprehension. Surely, there was more magic here than she had ever dreamed existed! For the first time, despite her apprehension, she felt a tiny thrill of anticipation and excitement at the thought that she was to be privy to such secrets. Almost eagerly, she increased her stride to keep pace with the rest as they entered the forest known as the Woods of Pallas.

Here, the oaks revered by the Druswids grew tall and strong, their branches green with strange, fingerlike leaves and heavy with dark acorns that shone smooth and glossy in the sunlight. There were aromatic cedars and straight, sturdy ashes, too, both highly prized for their wood. From the former could be fashioned sweet-smelling wardrobes and coffers; the latter yielded bows and arrows, as well as flutes, harps, and lutes. Ancient, twisted yews and feathery, green-needled pines thick with ornate brown cones stood alongside red hawthorns bright with fruit, and junipers lush with purple berries. Hazels with hanging clusters of reddish-brown nuts provided a pleasing contrast to crab-apple trees with pink blossoms. The trunks of spire-shaped poplars and slender birches gleamed like pieces of silver among the rich browns and greens of the forest.

Wisps of greyish green moss as fine and soft as hair trailed from the branches of the trees, and clinging ivy and fungi in shades of blue and green enveloped their trunks. Wildflowers of every color bloomed in gay profusion amid the tangled vines that stretched along the ground. Here and there, edible mushrooms and poisonous toadstools sprouted and patches of damp black peat covered the earth.

Ileana's nostrils twitched with pleasure as she inhaled deeply the fragrant scents, for they reminded her of the Melantha Forest of Cygnus, and for a moment, she could almost imagine she had come home. Tears pricked her eyes briefly for all she had known and left behind; and once more, silently, as she had so many times since learning the circumstances surrounding her birth, she cursed Gitana, the Ancient One, who had gifted her with the Power, and Lucia, her mother, who had pledged her to the Druswids.

Then, at last, they reached the foot of the hill from whose summit the abbey rose to pierce the mist and the sky, and in that instant, Ileana knew that all was forgiven and forgotten, that she belonged to this spellbinding place as surely as though she had been born here. She would always love Ariel Heights, yea; but somehow she knew with certainty that from this moment on, Mont Saint Mikhaela would take precedence in her heart.

It was a glorious sight to behold, surpassing even her father's castle in beauty. The wraithlike haze that wrapped its arms about the single high circular wall winding around the top of the knoll made it seem as though it were no earthbound place, but soared above the world to mind the clouds and all they surveyed. Centuries old, the nunnery had been built of pure white quartz hewn from the Snowflake Mountains on the continent of Iglacia. At various strategic points along the curving, scallop-edged wall, graceful flying turrets capped with conical silver roofs kept watch over the land. The edifice itself was cylindrical in shape, the church set in the middle of the circle formed by the surrounding wings. A round, silver-domed bell tower topped the rotunda roof of the chancel. The imperial-roofed wings were three stories tall and lined on all sides with elongated, oval muntined windows of lead glass that sparkled like diamonds when caught just so by the mellow rays of sun. The entire structure glittered like a fairy-tale ice palace, prismatic and unreal, the perfect opposite of its dark, fiery brother, Mont Saint Christopher.

Ileana half suspected that it was naught but a mirage and that, presently, it would disappear as the blurred images in her dreams did. Enraptured and expectant, she turned to the High Priestess, who had come to a halt to let the girl's eyes drink their fill of what lay before them. Wordlessly, some of them smiling behind their veils as they recalled their own initial reaction to the abbey, the priestesses went on ahead to allow Ileana and Sharai a brief interlude of privacy.

"'Tis lovely," Ileana breathed. "Oh, Reverend Mother, do my eyes deceive me, or is it truly there?"

Sharai smiled faintly, remembering how once she, too, had thought the nunnery was only a figment of her imagination.

"It is as real as ye or I," she stated. "'Tis unworldly in its appearance because of the great power wielded within its walls." At Ileana's puzzled glance, she elucidated further. "The magic of which I speak is so strong, it enables Mont Saint Mikhaela to exist not only here, on the physical plane known to mere mortals, but on higher planes as well. That is why it shimmers so, as though at any moment it might vanish. The abbey, if the Druswids so wish, can transcend this dimension to materialize in another. Then ye would indeed see no trace of it there upon the hill. Thus does the Light protect its own. But such a spell would never be cast lightly, for 'twould cause a warp in the Dimensions of Existence that might not be easily repaired—if at all. Come, now. The others will be waiting for us."

As they neared the nunnery, Ileana could see a few robed Sisters upon the walkway of the circular wall. From within its boundaries came the sounds of soft music and low laughter; and gradually, as she and the High Priestess passed through the arched portal of the gatehouse, Ileana became aware that the abbey hummed with quiet activity.

After crossing the public courtyard, they entered the cloister, where they were met by a beautiful, black-haired priestess with dark eyes and an impassive face.

"Ah, Amineh, there ye are," Sharai observed. She placed her hands upon Ileana's shoulders and gently guided the tired girl forward. "This is the Lady Ileana sin Ariel, who has come to us for training. Have a room in the novitiate prepared for her and a meal brought there on a tray; she can dine in the refectory this evening, once she has become a little accustomed to the nunnery and our ways here. But first, take her to the balneary, where she may soak the soreness from her limbs, for our journey was long and hard, and even I, who am used to traveling, ache with weariness." She turned to Ileana.

"Sister Amineh san Pázia is a twelfth-ranked priestess," she informed the girl. "That is the ultimate level a Druswid may achieve and the reason why I have selected her as your mentor. From this moment on, ye must remember ye are a priestess in training and do naught to disgrace yourself so ye become unworthy to take your Final Vows. Go with the Light, child."

She was gone before Ileana could speak, and it would be many years before she ever singled the girl out again for special attention. But Ileana did not know that then, and so, believing there would be time later to thank the High Priestess for her kindness and consideration, she turned to Sister Amineh, who had been studying her silently.

"Come, damsel," the priestess said, motioning for her to follow.

Ileana was startled by the common manner of address, for since she was of the Royal Blood, she had never before been called anything but Lady. Thinking perhaps Sister Amineh was one of the priestesses who never left the abbey and so knew little of the outside world, Ileana began politely to correct her, only to find herself abruptly quelled by the priestess's suddenly stern demeanor.

"There are no Ladies here, damsel," Sister Amineh said, deliberately repeating the title she had bestowed earlier upon the girl, "for those who are Chosen come from all walks of life, and it matters not whether their blood be

Royal or nay. Ye are no longer the Lady Ileana sin Ariel, but only Damsel Ileana, a mere acolyte and therefore the lowest of the low here at Mont Saint Mikhaela. Ye will have no special privileges here, damsel; none will kneel at your feet or wait on ye hand and foot as they did before. Indeed, 'tis ye who shall do the waiting!

"Ye are to call only your fellow acolytes by name. All others ye shall address as Domina, except for the High Priestess, who is Reverend Mother to us all. Only when ye have taken your Final Vows shall ye be known as Sister and know others as such. Then"—Sister Amineh's voice now held a subtle teasing note, and Ileana saw that the priestess's face had softened slightly and that her eyes were twinkling as well—"ye, too, may put those beneath ye in their proper place, as I have ye this morn."

"Yea, Do—Domina," Ileana stumbled over the unfamiliar title, duly chastened.

It was but the first of many lectures she was to receive at the nunnery over the passing years, for as the High Priestess had suspected, she was proud and stubborn, and her training was made difficult because of it.

As had been foreseen, Ileana's power was great; but to use it wisely was a sore trial. It is hard to respect what comes easily, and the small but important magics were simple for Ileana to learn. She had but to hold out her hands and concentrate and the mystical blue fire of the Druswids leaped from her fingertips. She had only to lift her palms and bring them down again and the mist fell like night about her. The Sight came naturally to her, too, and soon she could look into the fires and mists she had summoned and call the visions at her will. But to understand what she had seen, to correctly interpret the meanings of the omens —this was not so facile.

Time and again, she saw the dark High Prince of her dreams and felt somehow that he watched her covertly, was hungry for her yet drawn to her against his will. The ongoing struggle she sensed within him both disturbed and frightened her. There was a place deep inside him where she feared to look, and the few times she felt his essence touch hers, she shielded herself from him quickly and closed her eyes against the images.

She learned to see in other ways as well: to look into a silver pool, a polished mirror, or a crystal sphere, and to read the ancient cards and tea leaves. And she was taught other skills, too: how to gather the pith of the papyrus plant, cut it into thick strips, and press it into material that, in the workshops of the abbey, she numbered and illuminated so she had a deck of cards uniquely her own. Then, with wood garnered from a small cedar tree whose branch she herself chopped, she carved an ornate box to keep the cards in. Likewise, from rich red clay she herself scooped from deep beneath the earth's surface, did she find and melt the silver from which she fashioned her cup. She spent weeks on the beach, searching for smooth pebbles upon which she chiseled the runes; and from hides she had cured, she sewed the drawstring bag in which she carried the stones.

She studied the stars and discovered how their positions in the heavens at the time and place of one's birth determined one's LifePath, and she charted her own course and others'. She learned how to assign a number to each letter of a person's name and how to assess one's character from the sum.

In the nunnery's herbarium, she was steeped in herbal lore: how to heal, and how to poison—for the Darkness was ever present, and a priestess might be called upon to do battle with It in any manner of ways. There were drugs, too, derived from certain mushrooms, plants, and cacti, with which Ileana looked deep inside herself and, though sick and dazed and sometimes vomiting, set her spirit free to ascend from the physical plane to the astral one, where there was written the Akashic Record of all that had passed since time's beginning and all that would be until its end. If one possessed the knowledge to decipher the cryptic messages contained in the Akashic Record, one could read the whole of the future; but the key that unlocked this door was given unto very few.

Unlike these lessons, there were others that were sheer delight. Ileana would take up the harp or the lute she had made from the sacred oak tree and strung with gut from a beast slain when the moons were full, and she would play and sing, her voice sweet and clear as she told of ages past. At other times, she danced like the Weeping Wraiths that few but the Chosen ever saw; her body was graceful and supple as she performed the intricate steps, whether choreographed or impromptu.

She saw no one beyond the abbey walls and so knew nothing of the outside world, for such news was kept from the novices so their minds could remain focused solely on their studies. Thus Ileana was ignorant of her father's meeting with the High Council, where the broken planks of the lifeboat found by the *Mystic Rose* were displayed and discussed. Neither did she learn of the other bits and pieces of similar craft that, with the passing years, continued to be discovered. Nor was she told of the single strange but surely Kind skeleton that washed up on the western shore of Tamarind one dark eve, twisted and battered, as though it had been subjected to some tremendous force.

Though its bones were examined closely by the Druswids and the physicians, the former sensed only that it belonged to the Darkness; the latter could not even discern the manner of its death.

Lacking further information, it was the consensus of the High Council that a vast sea monster prowled the ocean depths, and it was agreed that until such time as new knowledge could be gained, no more ships would set sail for the other half of the world.

But Ileana knew nothing of these events, which were inexorably shaping her LifePath, even as those at the nunnery were molding her to their will.

Then, at last, nine years after she had entered the abbey, there came the day when she cast out. Carried by the *Swan Song* to the shores of Cygnus, she was left to make her own way back to Mont Saint Mikhaela, knowing that if she could not, she would be deemed unworthy to take her Final Vows and the gates of the nunnery would be closed to her forever.

For a long while, Ileana was afraid and she wandered aimlessly along the beach, knowing she had but to walk northward and, in time, she would come to Ariel Heights, her father's castle. But though she yearned to see it once more, it was no longer her home; she belonged body, mind, and soul to the Druswids, and she could not turn back the hands of time. Mont Saint Mikhaela was where her heart lay.

Tentatively, she pressed her palms together, then just as quickly pulled them apart, her breathing shallow, her heart pounding with fear. Then she remembered what the High Priestess Sharai had told her so long ago and what she had read later, too, in *The Book of Lessons: Have the courage to try.* Deliberately, she slowed her breathing and stilled the furious beating of her heart.

Once she had gathered her strength, she summoned the Power as she had been taught; and when she felt it surging like a tide through her veins, she clasped her hands and bowed her head, closing her physical senses to the world around her. Like a note struck clear and true upon a harp, she heard her silent call ripple across the golden waves, and when she opened her eyes and lowered her now uplifted arms to her sides, the boat came.

As surely as though she had done it a thousand times before, Ileana guided it through the mist to the Isle of Le Fey, and there, she knelt upon the shore and wept unashamedly with joy, knowing she was worthy of all she had learned.

This time, unafraid, Ileana faced the crystal sphere that contained the Light; and when she was found to be its true and faithful servant, Sharai herself, with the Tyrian-purple dye that came from the mollusks the Sisters harvested from the sea, tattooed the dark crescent moon, which was the mark of a priestess, between Ileana's silver brows and presented her with the sickle-shaped arthame she would carry at her waist from now on.

Then Ileana was permitted to fashion from precious metals and wood the seven wands of a sorceress and to sew the silken garments—cap, robe, and belt—she would wear as befitted her status. Last but not least, she was instructed to begin her grimoire, the book in which she would record her magical spells, studies, and experiences.

The abbey's edificium, which housed the library and the scriptorium, were opened to her so the Lesser Mysteries might be revealed to her eyes, and she saw that all she had been taught thus far was but a drop in the great ocean of knowledge that awaited her.

It was shortly after she had known seventeen years that she was again sent from the nunnery, this time to perform the Ritual of Beginning that would mark her passage from childhood to womanhood; and it was then she saw for the first time in the flesh the dark High Prince of her dreams, he who carried the fire of death in his soul.

Chapter 10

To be one with the Light Eternal is the ultimate
ambition of all those of the Kind who would seek
Perpetual Harmony, Grace, and Enlightenment of the
Spirit. To fail in this Ordained Destiny is to condemn
the Soul to an Everlasting Fate of LifePaths in the
Primal Dimension of Existence—the Physical Plane
—from which the Essence, thus trapped, will be unable
to escape; and so the Way to the Immortal Guardian
will be lost forever.

If this is the road ye would choose to follow, read no
further. If, however, it is your desire to achieve a
never-ending State of Blessedness, then ye must start at
once to prepare yourself for the challenge of the Arduous Pilgrimage ye have decided to undertake. For the
path to the Light Eternal is a long and difficult one,
fraught with temptations and pitfalls for the weak, the
vain, the ignorant, and the foolish. To complete this
journey successfully is a Privilege to be earned only by
those Worthy of its Sacred Heritage.

There are many trials ye will need to endure to prove
yourself deserving of this Hallowed Trust and many
lessons ye will need to learn and to remember if ye are
to answer the questions that will be put to ye by Rocca,
the Keeper of the Gate to the Immortal Guardian. For
even there, ye may be turned away, deemed as yet
Unfitting to enter the Most Precious Realm of the Light
Eternal.

*Ye thus stand warned of the adversities of your task.
If ye are now still ready to attempt your search for
the Imperishable Truth and Final Understanding and
to embark upon your travels to the Immortal Guardian
of all things Ceaseless and Universal, then ye have
already learned Lesson I: Have the courage to try.*

—Thus it is Written—
in
The Teachings of the Mont Sects
The Book of Lessons, Chapter Three

The Melantha Forest, Cygnus, 7268.12.24

IT WAS THE DARKEST HOUR WHEN ILEANA EMBARKED UPON HER
journey to the top of the mountain called Dorian's Watch,
where she would cleanse and purify herself for the Ritual of
Beginning. But the luminescence of the waxing moons—the
frosted silver First Moon; the pale, shadowed Blue Moon;
and the deep lilac Passion Moon—and the stars that
glittered like diamonds against the black-velvet facade of
the mute night sky lighted her path, and she, who was of the
gloaming, was not afraid.

The powdery snow lay in thick silence upon the fallow
ground, swirling up here and there in flurries when the
chilly winter wind breathed. Crystalline icicles and prickly
cones hung from the boughs of the soft, bristly pines that
huddled amid the dense and ebon stealth of the otherwise
lifeless forest. Brittle brown leaves, strewn in sorrowful
abandon upon the earth, rustled beneath the hooves of
Ileana's alaecorn. The weeping branches of the ice-laden
trees parted to kiss her shoulders when she rode beneath
them. Then they closed behind her so it seemed as though
their intricate embrace, even in death, had never been
disturbed by her passing.

The mountain that loomed far ahead was the place where
she had elected to perform the ceremony for which she had
returned to her homeland this eve. Of all the peaks she
might have had on Cygnus, she had asked for this one,

despite the fact that it had been named for a lowly hermit not of the Royal Blood. The Royal House of Ariel had been shocked and dismayed by her preference. True, the humble solitary, with his cry of warning, had saved Cygnus from being destroyed by the Bedouins during the Time of the Tribal Wars and had been especially honored for the deed of salvation. But as the oldest sister, Ileana, according to custom, ought to have taken Estoile Point for her own, it being considered by far the grandest of all the crags on Cygnus and traditionally selected for the rite by the highest-ranked Lady of each generation of the Royal House of Ariel. But inexplicably drawn to the lesser Dorian's Watch, Ileana had requested it instead and felt herself the richer for it. There, as at Mont Saint Mikhaela, she sensed deeply the presence of the Light Eternal.

Ketti, her dapple-grey silvery-winged alaecorn, nickered quietly as they traversed the wooded path; but only this and the beast's muffled hoofbeats broke the hush of the forest this night. It was as though even the trees sensed Ileana's need to remain undisturbed so she might mentally prepare herself for the fearsome ritual she was soon to undergo. It was a ceremony fraught with peril, for if she miscalculated and surpassed the seventeen years she had known, she would disrupt the Circle of Time and forever alter her LifePath—if she survived.

At last, after many long days of travel, the girl reached her destination and dismounted, loosing Ketti to wander freely, knowing the mare would not stray too far from the range of her voice. Then she walked to a place just below the summit of Dorian's Watch, where a small stream twined its way through the woods that covered the sweeping slope. The rivulet gleamed like a silver ribbon in the moonlight and sparkled with shards of ice. Though Ileana shivered at the sight, she was not swayed from her intent, for it was too late now to choose another spot.

Forcing herself to ignore the cold and setting her teeth so they would cease to chatter, she began to make her preparations for the rite, secure in the knowledge that the forest was still and empty, that she was alone in the darkness, as was meet and proper.

The Bedouins are a proud, fiercely independent, and highly sexual tribe, possessed of great physical power, insatiable ambition, and unwavering strength of purpose. Seldom do they fail to attain their most sought-after desires.

—Thus it is Written—
in
Desert Dwellers: A Study of the Bedouin Tribe
by the Anthropologist Sharif
san Al-Jabar set Zeheb

The Lord Cain sin Khali could not sleep. At first, he had thought it was the bed, so much softer than his own at the monastery, and the excitement of being back, after so many years, at Khali Keep, the castle of his kinswoman the Queen Lady Nenet, that kept slumber at bay. But now he knew it was not so. Despite the coolness of the night air, his sheets were damp with perspiration and warm from his body, and his blood smoldered with a heat that owed nothing to the change of climate, for unlike the humid Isles of Cinnamon, the continent of Bedoui was arid.

Finally, after tossing and turning endlessly, he rose, naked, to pace, like a smilodon stalking its prey, upon the multicolored mosaic floor of the chamber he had been assigned upon his arrival at the fortress. The marble was chilly against his bare feet, but his brain scarcely registered that fact as, restlessly, he moved to stand before the long, narrow, ogee open windows that lined the north side of the room.

Though the evening was cool, as it was always in the desert, it was nevertheless pleasant, for it was summer in the southern hemisphere. A gentle breeze stirred, rippling the moonlit hazel water of the Bay of Isis and bringing to Cain's nostrils the fragrant scent of the sultry white flowers that bloomed thick and sweet along the Jasmine Coast. The aroma did nothing to quell the fire in his blood, and his eyes swept the far horizon across the Sirocco Ocean, coming to rest on the place where he knew Dorian's Watch rose in the distance.

Inexplicably, he felt drawn to the crag. It was as though

soon something of import was going to happen there, something that would forever change the course of his LifePath; and try as he might, he could not deny the insistency that compelled him toward the mountain. Something—or someone—was calling him to it. He could feel in his bones that this was so. He must find out what—or who—it was, for he knew he would have no peace of mind until he did.

At last, snarling an oath at his probable foolishness, he gathered a few of his possessions, dressed, and left the chamber to make his way to the castle's stables. There, he saddled Ramessah, his massive black faesthors, then flung himself upon the back of the beast, whose hooves clattered over the sandstone blocks of the courtyard as they approached the portal gate at the rear of the fortress. Cain did not bother rousing the guards, but set his spurs to the animal's sides, urging it forward. With a single forceful leap, they cleared the ten-foot gate, sailing cleanly between its brass spikes and the gracefully curved stone arch above.

As they hit the ground on the other side, Cain laughed with delight, his teeth flashing white against his bronze skin. Then, still grinning, he turned to wave impudently at the sentries, who, wakened by the sound of his passing, were now shouting at him from the high walls of the keep, both angered and astonished by his daring feat.

"Ye damned fool Druswid!" one of them called. "Ye might have broken your Royal neck! And then where would we have been? Carrion for the vultures, that's what! By the Light! I'll wager ye did not pull such stunts at Mont Saint Christopher, Lord, for tricks like that belong in the arena, as well ye know. When ye decide to return, see that you're properly admitted!"

Cain only laughed again and bent to pat Ramessah's neck fondly.

"They will have quite a story to tell in the morning, won't they, my beauty? No doubt their fellows will think it the result of an ale-induced stupor. But no matter. We know otherwise, don't we?"

At the faesthors's soft whicker of agreement, Cain once more gathered up the reins and nudged the stallion forward. Quietly, so they wouldn't disturb the sleeping city, they trotted along the narrow sandstone streets, the flickering luminaries lighting their way. From a distant quarter of town, Cain heard a deep-tolling bell chime the hour and the nightwatchman's answering cry: "All is well; the land is at peace."

Yea, he reflected soberly, remembering the discussion he had been privy to earlier this day, the conference that had taken place behind the closed doors of the Lesser Court. *But for how long?*

Another skeleton had been found; this time, it had washed up on the western shore of Bedoui. Like those discovered in Tamarind, these bones were broken and distorted, as though they had been shattered by some great power. Cain shuddered at the recollection. Like the other Druswids who had examined the skeleton, he had sensed it belonged to the Darkness. Yet the bones had been Kind; he felt certain of it. They'd been different from those of the known Tribes on Tintagel, but Kind all the same, surely.

The theory put forth at the Lesser Court was that at least one tribe on the opposite half of the world had survived the Wars of the Kind and the Apocalypse and was attempting to make contact with the planet's other side. But something —a sea monster, some claimed—was preventing emissaries from reaching their destination. The young advisers with whom the High Prince Lord Yhudhah had surrounded himself at the Lesser Court were eager for recognition and adventure; and subtly guided by the High Priest Kokudza, they had suggested that at the next meeting of the High Council, the Lord Yhudhah recount their conclusions and propose that two new ships, mightier than any ever before built, be constructed to attempt another journey to Tintagel's far side. This, the Lord Yhudhah had agreed to do.

Remembering, Cain shook his head, thinking his kinsman would do well to remain at home and conserve his strength. There was a sickness in the High Prince's blood, small but growing; Cain had sensed it when he had greeted Yhudhah and exchanged the Kiss of Peace with him. As yet, Cain thought, none except a few Druswids suspected the presence of the disease; even the High Prince was unaware of it, although he had complained of being tired—the result of his many duties, he had said. But Cain, who was now a twelfth-ranked priest, had studied the symptoms of the illness and the drugs that might be used to ease its pain, and he knew, if others did not, that Yhudhah did not have long to live, for there was no cure for the wasting sickness.

"Why?" Cain had asked his mentor, Brother Ottah, whose equal he now was. "Why must Yhudhah die so young?"

"I do not know," the priest had replied gravely. "Perhaps he has already learned the lessons given unto him in this LifePath, or mayhap his Karma is heavy with debts that must be paid. I do not know," he'd repeated. "'Tis enough for us to understand that this is the destiny the Light Eternal has ordained for him. It is not for us to judge the rightness or the wrongness of the reasons why it is so. That is why the ways of the Immortal Guardian are so mysterious—and often incomprehensible."

"But even so, may one not still question those ways?" Cain had inquired, causing the priest to smile faintly at the brave, bright spirit of youth not yet tempered by the trials and tribulations of age.

"One may always question, yea." Brother Ottah had nodded. "'Tis accepting the answers one receives that is often so difficult."

Abruptly, Cain shook himself from his reverie. There was no point in dwelling on his kinsman's unfortunate lot; it could not be changed and must therefore be accepted, as Brother Ottah had said, no matter how hard it might be to do so. Still, Cain reflected, it was a shame. He had always liked Yhudhah; it was too bad that he must die so young, that another heir or heiress would claim his place upon the Lesser Throne. Cain flushed guiltily, for the thought brought to mind something else his mentor had told him.

"After Yhudhah's Time of Passing, when the Royal High Games will be held again, ye must place your name upon the lists, Cain," Brother Ottah had insisted.

"But why?" the younger priest had asked, startled. "I mean . . . I will, of course, if that is your wish; but I do not see why I should bother. After all, I am a priest—not a prince."

At that, Brother Ottah had smiled enigmatically, his eyes wide with feigned innocence and his palms uplifted as though to say that the idea of Cain's entering the Games had been just the foolish whim of an old man.

"Yea, ye are right, of course," he had agreed. Then, most provokingly, he had added slyly, "But still, theoretically speaking, that is—since it has yet to be done—one could be both, could one not?"

Now, at the thought that he might be the next High Prince of Tintagel, that Yhudhah's death might pave the way for him to ascend the Lesser Throne, Cain felt a sudden surge of excitement, a hitherto unrecognized desire to wield more than just a Druswid's power. Hard on the heels of this startling discovery came the realization that if he were honest with himself, he must admit he no longer felt so downcast by the fact that Yhudhah's Time of Passing was so close at hand. Then, stricken with shame by the dreadful thought, Cain roweled the sides of his faesthors almost fiercely with his spurs, as though this would exorcise his conscience.

Sensing his master's abrupt ill mood, Ramessah broke quickly into a wicked canter, sweeping past the delicate domes, spires, and minarets of the city, which cut a jagged edge against the star-streaked sky. Soon they had left Khali behind and were galloping savagely across the high mesas of the Raokhshna Bluffs, which glittered in shades of rust, pink, and gold beneath the moons.

Cain tossed his head back and laughed aloud as the wind rushed through his silky black hair, which brushed his nape.

"Go, Ramessah! Go!" he cried, leaning low over the beast and giving it its head.

The stallion needed no further urging. Its powerful muscles bunched and quivered as, the bit in its teeth, it lunged forward, its incredible speed thrilling, dizzying. Cain did not try to stop it, knowing it could outrun the wind for hours at a time without slowing or tiring. It was the fastest animal in the world. Its hooves pounded against the hard-baked clay of the tablelands, ringing harshly in Cain's ears, like discordant notes struck upon a lute. But still, he made no move to rein the faesthors in. He must be mad, he thought as the terrain flashed by him in a long blur; but he did not care. Tears from the cold night air stung his eyes; he could feel the cool wind against his flesh and deep within his lungs as, breathless with exhilaration, he gasped for air.

Ramessah's hooves left the solid mesas to plunge into the vast, shifting dunes of the peril-ridden Haghar Desert, rippling like an eerie, endless sea in the half-light. Suddenly sober, Cain cursed himself for a fool, for now, in the darkness, one could not see the Swallowing Sands, which might suck one down into the center of the earth; and horrible, venomous helodermas and fire-breathing dragons roamed the desert here at night, in search of prey.

Still, the faesthors was not only swift, but surefooted. It did not stumble in the blackness, but made its way instinctively, unerringly, over the moon-raked dunes. It did not falter as it skirted the treacherous places where they might have floundered in the quicksilver sand; and once, when they spied in the distance the horrendous silhouette of a heloderma, Ramessah came abruptly to a halt and stood motionless, every nerve and fiber of his being alert and quivering until the giant, orange-and-black-striped monster, its long tail slashing from side to side, had slithered on, unaware of man and beast.

Toward dawn, they reached the River of Separation, which was bisected by Tintagel's equator and divided Bedoui, Cygnus, and the Isle of Le Fey. The far shore of the channel was several miles distant, but the stallion was strong and unfatigued and could use the Stepping-Stone Islands to cross. At Cain's signal, without hesitation, the animal splashed into the cold brown water and began to swim. When it had gained the other side of the river, it waded up onto the beach. Then, after snorting and shaking itself dry, it clambered up the slope.

"Tread carefully here, Ramessah," Cain cautioned the faesthors, "and leave no signs of our passing. Otherwise, the Cygninae will wonder about our lonely sojourn to their land and perhaps be uneasy, for old memories die hard. The Bedouins nearly annihilated the Cygninae during the Time of the Tribal Wars and the Time of the World Wars as well; and they do yet fear us, I think, though they will not admit it."

Ramessah's dark eyes gleamed, and though the beast

made no sound, it picked its way carefully through the Melantha Forest.

Cain, wet from crossing the channel, shivered a little in the frost-tinged morning air, wishing he had thought to wear his burnous. In his impulsive departure from Khali Keep, he had forgotten it would be winter here in the northern hemisphere. The ground beneath Ramessah's hooves was blanketed with snow, and Cain glanced back at the trail of hoofprints behind them. So much for his attempt at secrecy. If it did not snow again soon, the deep, wide tracks of the animal would be clear and unmistakable. The Cyginae preferred the smaller, cloven-hooved alaecorns and unicorns as mounts. The great power and speed of a faesthors were of little use in the dense woods and the giant promontories that covered Cygnus. An alaecorn could soar above the forests and the high, craggy peaks. A unicorn could step lightly and swiftly beneath the branches of the trees and cling like a nimble goat to steep, rocky mountain paths.

Ah, well, Cain sighed to himself and shrugged.

There was no help for it now; he had already trespassed where he had no business being, and there was no practical means of erasing Ramessah's hoofprints. Cain would just have to hope for more snow.

Thoughtfully, he guided the beast through the forest, listening intently to the sounds that broke the stillness: the dead leaves that crunched beneath the stallion's hooves, the soughing of the pines swaying in the breeze, the distant hoot of an owl, the mournful baying of a lone wolf. His eyes searched his surroundings ceaselessly. Cain was not a twelfth-ranked priest for naught, and there was little that escaped his notice.

Presently, he observed the dainty, cloven-hooved tracks of an alaecorn, and instinctively, he knew that if he followed them, they would lead him to Dorian's Watch. Briefly, he gazed through trees to where the mountain towered far above the land in the distance. Then, feeling its strange, urgent cry more strongly than ever, he spurred Ramessah forward along the trail of hoofprints that wound enticingly through the forest.

Finally, after many tiring days of riding at an unaccustomed slow pace due to the denseness of the woods, Cain attained his goal. He drew Ramessah to a halt. By the light of the moons, he studied Dorian's Watch, which now soared above him in the darkness. Why had it drawn him here? he wondered. It was only a mountain, like any other. Why, then, had it haunted him so, enticed him from his bed, and driven him to embark upon this ill-considered journey? Why, then, did he have the peculiar feeling that his fate would be waiting here for him? Cain didn't know. But he was a Druswid, and he would answer the silent, sentient call he had heard.

Filled with curiosity, expectation, and a twinge of foreboding, he urged Ramessah up the side of the crag.

At the summit, at last, Cain saw her. He inhaled sharply at the sight, for she was naked and breathtaking in her beauty. Before the babbling, snow-fed brook that flowed down from the snowcapped peak, she knelt, the Cygninae woman of his dreams, she whom he had seen so long ago in the mercurial pool of the Hallowed Hall at Mont Saint Christopher. No more than a child then, now she was a woman fully grown, a woman with a face and figure to enslave any man.

Her long silver tresses cascaded down her back in soft, shining waves that whispered against her narrow hips and curving buttocks. Her lustrous, pearl-white skin gleamed like evening dew in the moonlight; her high cheekbones, with their delicate hollows, glowed like dusky roses where the cold winter wind had wooed her with icy caresses. Her exquisitely drawn silver brows arched gently above wide, lucent eyes that glittered like precious amethysts and were starred with thick, pale lashes. Beneath her finely chiseled nose, her tender, tremulous mouth, parted sweetly and moist from the frosty kiss of winter, glistened, pink and inviting. Her classic jaw sloped down to a swanlike neck that met her small, sweeping shoulders in dainty planes and angles at her throat. Her full, round breasts were like twins, perfectly formed above the slender waist and hips that tapered into long, lithe legs and feet that were as elegant and artistically fashioned as her graceful hands.

She seemed as fragile as a fairy, as ethereal as a wraith.

But for all her elusiveness, she had a quiet, inner strength, a mystical power that radiated from the very heart of her being in iridescent streams of dazzling violet and shimmering silver light.

For a moment, Cain could not quite believe she was real.

"Ileana," he breathed, her name like music upon his lips. "Ileana."

She did not hear him, did not sense his presence, or she would have veiled her mood-revealing aura against his prying eyes. But Cain was not ashamed of himself for spying on her; he was glad her deep meditative state had made her oblivious of him.

With difficulty, he fought down the sudden wild, primitive urge he had to possess her, to leap from Ramessah's bare back and force her down upon the cold snow, to impale her with the heat of desire that throbbed in his loins. By the Passion Moon, how he wanted her!—wanted her more than he had ever wanted a woman in his life! But rape was a crime punishable by death, and so he dared not lay hands upon her.

He cursed the law that kept him from her and the fact that he could not even ride away to find another upon whom to slake his lust. On all the known-inhabited continents, prostitution and promiscuity were forbidden. In the Time Before, they had spread killing diseases that had decimated the Tribes, as the Keepers and the Prophets had foretold. And though concubines and consorts were still permitted, each was allowed to take only one lover at a time and, after severing a relationship, must be pronounced clean by a physician before entering into another union. Cain had a concubine, Takuhi; but she lived in the city of Jerusha on Tamarind, far from his reach this eve—and besides, suddenly, she did not seem that appealing.

Cain's heart filled with guilt at the thought of Takuhi, for deep down inside he knew, after seeing Ileana tonight, that he would never touch the concubine again. Ileana was in his blood, as Brother Ottah had told him so many years past.

Cain watched her hungrily, torn between his yearning for her and the memory of how she had come to him in his dreams, when, with the Power that was hers, she had held him in her arms—and destroyed him.

Naked, we are born from the Water of Life that gives us sustenance and provides us with passage into the world.

How many times do we float upon those serene waves, guarded by the Maternal Host who nurtures us with her body? Those who would distort the words of the Prophets would have us believe it is but a single time that we are born and die, and that in that brief moment, we have only to accept the Light, and we will be joined with It instead of condemned to the Darkness at the End.

I say unto ye that this is not so, that the path to the Immortal Guardian is not so quick, so simple, or so certain, but fraught with many trials to ensure we are True Defenders of the Light. Such a road cannot be traveled in a single LifePath. One has only to gaze up at the heavens, as I have gazed up at them, to know this is so.

And thus I say unto ye we journey through the Water of Life not once, but once for each of the Twelve Signs that are set among the stars to mark the Way to the Light Eternal. And if the lessons each such guidepost teaches us are not learned in the LifePath in which they are set forth, then we must return to the Sign that held captive the sun during our failure and try again to grasp the things the Immortal Guardian would have us know.

And so it is that the Twelfth Sign, Piscis, is called the Old Soul and has no traits of its own, but represents the sum of the rest. Its symbol, The Fish, is appropriate, for the two fish, each holding in its mouth the other's tail, swim both upstream and downstream so they come full circle, as all things must do. Thus did the Immortal Guardian, in Its wisdom, create first the swimming creatures; and so, too, will they be the last to perish. And thus is it that one who is born under the sign of Piscis and successfully completes that LifePath is given a choice: to be reborn on the Physical Plane, as before, or to enter another—higher—Dimension of Existence, for which all LifePaths are preparatory.

Consciously, with the exception of those that, each in

its own time, are present instead of past, we have no memory of these LifePaths. But they can be recalled in a moment if one but knows how to seek them, how to plunge once more into the Water of Life to wash clean the Darkness that precedes all rebirth and lingers to obscure the Light. Then may one see clearly—and remember; and all that has gone before will be freed from the Chasms of the Soul and made known.

Such is the Ritual of Beginning.

—Thus it is Written—
in
The Word and The Way
The Book of Baptiste, Chapter Seven

It was time. It was the darkest hour, as all had been dark before the Immortal Guardian had brought forth the Light, put the celestial bodies into the cosmos, and fashioned order out of chaos.

Slowly, Ileana, who had been kneeling, meditating to gather her strength and her power, rose. Naked and unaware of the man who now watched her from the shadows, she stepped into the clear silver stream that lay before her.

It was cold, but she had expected that, and though she gasped with shock as the freezing water closed around her, she forced herself to continue wading forward until she stood submerged to her waist. Her teeth chattered, and gooseflesh prickled her arms, but still, she did not hurry, keeping to the deliberate pace of the ceremony, as was meet and proper.

Lifting her palms unto the heavens, she began to sing softly the Sacred Chant that would enable her to perform the rite:

O Hallowed Water of Life born of the Light Eternal
Who watcheth over all things Ceaseless and Universal,
Naked, as the Immortal Guardian shaped me,
So do I come unto thee to pray
And to ask for thy Blessing of Rebirth.
Receive my body into thy womb;
Take my mind into thy matter,

And accept my spirit into thy heart
That I might not suffer condemnation
To a fate of LifePaths of Darkness Everlasting,
But be found Worthy to enter
The Most Precious Realm of the Light Eternal
When I stand at last before the Keeper of the Gate.
This, I do most humbly beseech of thee, O Water of Life,
Who bringeth new beginning to the earth each spring,
Who washeth clean the wintry scent of death,
And who sustaineth all life in all seasons.

When she had finished chanting, Ileana took a deep breath, then started to lower herself into the rivulet. Finally, she was completely immersed. She could feel the current eddying past her, through her, cleansing her body, opening her mind, and purifying her spirit.

At last, a great swirling darkness fell upon her, sucking her down like a whirlpool into its emptiness. This was the passage that linked the Dimensions of Existence to the Far Beyond, that place of gloaming wedged between the Light and Darkness, where all souls came in the End to join with the Immortal Guardian or to be cast out to Its antithesis, the Foul Enslaver.

LifePaths of the past flitted before her eyes. Ileana saw herself being born, growing old, and dying. Sometimes the images were fleeting; sometimes they seemed to endure for aeons. So many LifePaths there were. But the kaleidoscopic pictures flashed by her so swiftly, she could not count them, could only remember and weep for what had been and was no more. A deep sadness filled her being as she watched the vignettes, the faces and places she had once known and loved. Once, she was as dark as night and dancing upon the cool marble steps of some ancient mosque; once, she was fair and running across the sweeping moors of a strange and long-forgotten land; and once, she was like flame, a sword in one hand, a shield in the other. And always the man was at her side. No matter how he changed, she recognized him still, the dark High Prince of her dreams, his eyes boring into hers before he pressed his mouth hotly to her throat. . . .

Suddenly, the images blurred, then cleared, and Ileana

saw herself as she looked now. This was the most crucial, dangerous part of the ritual. If she failed— But she must not! Quickly, she struggled to the water's surface, gasping for air, shivering in the wind, and fearing she was not in time. Desperately, she peered at her reflection in the brook. It was not changed! She had not gone too far; she had not disrupted the Circle of Time and altered her LifePath. She had survived! Joyously, she threw back her head and laughed. It was over, and she had survived.

Humbly, she thanked the stream for its kindness to her, for the Blessing of Rebirth it had bestowed upon her. Then she returned to the bank, dressed herself, and tossed an offering of a single shining golden into the rivulet. The coin glittered brightly for a moment upon the diamondlike waves before they parted to swallow it up.

Ileana turned away. She was to spend what remained of the night in silent contemplation of what she had learned. She moved to sit, cross-legged, before the fire she had prepared earlier. Closing her eyes, she called up the Power and felt it awaken and unwind itself within her. She stretched out her hands. Presently, heat began to radiate through her body to her fingertips, where hot blue sparks ignited to become currents of crackling electricity that set the tinder ablaze. Hearing the sounds of the fire, Ileana opened her eyes to stare into the flickering flames that danced hypnotically before her. Soon she would be tranced and the dreams would come.

She breathed deeply, willing her mind to empty itself, to open itself; and then, slowly, surely, the vision for which she had waited began to appear in the fire. At first, the shapes and shadows were amorphous. But gradually, as they became clearer, she saw that what she had initially thought were figures were instead giant rough stones set into a circle with other megaliths laid on top so they formed a ring.

This was a place sacred to the Druswids, a place where the Light Eternal was worshiped above all other places, for here, the movements of the stars that marked the path to the Immortal Guardian could be charted, and thus the Way to It could be clearly seen. Here, too, the times of the Darkness could be forecast so the land would not be unprepared when the umbrages fell upon it.

At the center of the RingStones lay a single slab of rock upon which a fire burned, and so Ileana knew it was the month of Tauri, the time of Beltane, when Ceridwen, the Keeper of the Earth, was honored. Around the flames stood the simply robed priests and priestesses who had gathered for the celebration. Ululating, they laid their offerings of fruit, vegetables, and grain upon the blazing altar, for these were the blessings Ceridwen bestowed upon them and must be returned in kind.

Then, from somewhere in the darkness, there came the high, sweet trill of a flute, the harmonious intertwining of a harp and lute, and the resonant pounding of a drum. Feasting, followed by singing and dancing that lasted late into the evening, ensued. Ileana saw herself among the revelers, laughing and whirling in wild abandon, made dizzy by the wine and drugs she had consumed. The cowl of her habit was thrown back to reveal her flushed face, and the garment billowed out about her as she turned, displaying her naked legs and bare feet.

One by one, the others slipped away into the shadows, some standing at the edge of the RingStones, where they clapped in time to the music and urged her on, the rest drifting into the blackness, where they coupled in frenzy upon the earth, their cries of ecstasy piercing the night. At last, only Ileana remained. Alone, she danced, spinning faster and faster until, finally, she was caught up by strong arms and carried from the circle.

The man who had laid claim to her crushed her cheek against his broad chest, so she could not see his face, hidden beneath the hood of his robe. But she could smell the masculine scent of him, the wine that clung to his lips, the salt-tinged sweat that covered his body. She could hear his heart beating rapidly in her ear and feel against her thighs the quick pulsing of his loins, taut and aching with desire. Before she realized what he intended, he tossed her down upon the ground and divested himself of his habit.

Then, suddenly, his callused palms were pressing her down into the sweet summer grass; his dark eyes were ravaging her body and soul; his impatient hands were tearing at her robe and roaming over her bare flesh, arousing her in ways she had never dreamed possible. Ileana cried out, for still, she could not see his face, concealed by the shadows, and she did not know him. But he cut her off sharply, covering her lips with his fingers to silence her protests.

"I am for ye," he told her harshly. "I have always been for ye—then, now, and forever. . . ."

Roughly, he caught the shimmering cascade of her hair and twisted her face up to his, then brought his carnal mouth down upon hers, hard and possessive, causing her senses to reel, as though the earth had suddenly dropped from beneath her feet. His teeth grazed her tender skin, and she tasted blood, warm and salty, upon her bottom lip, and she realized dimly that some atavistic part of him had been loosed by the festival and was bent on conquering her—not gently, but savagely, as though she might not otherwise be taken. He compelled her mouth to open; his tongue shot deep inside her lips to pillage the softness within until at last she was kissing him back, madly, as though she had no will of her own, but were a wild thing he might tame as he pleased.

As though she had voiced the thought aloud, he laughed mockingly against her mouth; his lips slashed like a whip across her face to her temples as he ruthlessly entangled her hair with his fingers so she could not turn away from him. His breath was hot in her ear, his voice low as he muttered unspeakable words of passion, then bit her lobe, sending pain and pleasure coursing through her body.

"Sweet," he whispered. "Sweet . . ."

Ileana gasped with outrage at his violent assault and began to struggle against him. But she was no match for his brute physical strength, and he subdued her easily, pinioning her wrists above her head before his mouth covered hers again and his tongue plunged between her trembling lips. Over and over, feverishly, his mouth claimed hers until it seemed he meant to go on kissing her forever, draining every last ounce of resistance from her being so she would be weak and helpless against him.

Even now, she could feel her treacherous body awakening beneath him, and silently, she cursed him for the things he was doing to her, things that made her flesh meld itself against her will to his, her bones melt inside her as his free hand explored her, touching her in ways and places that no man had ever touched her.

Her heart pounded too quickly in her breast; the tiny pulse at the hollow of her throat fluttered when he kissed it, teased it with his tongue. His lips slid hotly down the side of her neck to the place where her nape joined her shoulders, and his teeth nipped her skin there, causing a shower of electric shocks to tingle through her veins.

"Damn you!" she sobbed, writhing beneath him in a futile attempt to escape. "Damn you!"

But he only laughed again and laid his hand upon her throat, tightening his fingers about it.

"Ye are mine," he said hoarsely, "forever mine. Why do ye fight me, *kari?*"

Kari. The lilting Bedouin word echoed in her mind. Woman, lover, mate—it meant all that and more, for the literal translation in Cygninae was "passion's slave."

"Nay," she breathed. "Nay, please don't."

But it was no use. He heard nothing but the blood singing in his ears, and Ileana knew that there was no reasoning with him, that he would not be swayed from his purpose by her pleas for mercy. Indeed, her soft cries seemed only to amuse him, to inflame him, to spur him on.

His hands swept down to fondle her breasts, his palms cupping the spheres swollen with desire, his thumbs flicking over her nipples, making them stiffen and flush in response to his caresses. Like spinning wheels, waves of fire radiated from the twin peaks as his hands glided over them sensuously, tormentingly. For an instant, Ileana felt a strange, warm throbbing in her belly. Then the feeling passed to be replaced by an even more primitive yearning as his mouth closed over one rigid bud.

Time passed; she did not know how much as she lay drunk and drugged beneath him, floating in a dark and ancient place where there was naught but hot, clinging flesh—and wanting. She did not even realize that the man no longer held her captive, that now, somehow, her arms were wrapped around him, clutching him to her. She could feel the powerful muscles in his back coiling and uncoiling beneath her palms as her nails dug into his skin, urging him on. Low moans of surrender emanated from her throat, insistent whimpers that told him without words of the desperate, aching need burning deep within her.

Tantalizingly, he stroked rhythmically the moist, secret heart of her that opened to him of its own accord as he nudged her thighs apart. Then, without warning, he was driving down into the very core of her, making her quiver and cry out sharply. She had not known what to expect, had not even in the most sentient depths of her soul understood until now this giving and molding of oneself to fit the other.

He took her fiercely; but she did not care. She was spiraling down into a black void with him, pulsing, primeval. Presently, they passed through its egress to soar among the stars, and she wept at the beauty of all that engulfed her.

When it was done, they plummeted to the earth; and Ileana, slowly emerging from her trance, discovered her cheeks were wet with tears. It had been so real. She gazed across the fire to where the man, his face still hidden by the shadows, was standing. She blinked once, twice, to clear her vision, startled that his image yet lingered, though her dream had ended.

Then, finally, to her horror, she realized that his form did not shimmer at its edges, that it had shape and substance; and she knew, stunned, that he was truly there.

Heaven's Light! What was he doing here, on Cygnus, upon her mountain; and how long had he been spying on her? Had he watched her Ritual of Beginning, which was forbidden? By the Passion Moon, if he had, he had tainted something very private and special!

Angry and frightened, she leaped to her feet. It was then that the man stepped forward into the half-light and she saw his face. It was the dark High Prince of her dreams! A Bedouin, she realized now, and shivered, for though the land was at peace, the Cygninae had feared the Bedouins, their enemies, in the Time Before.

Ileana gasped, stricken by his presence yet inexplicably drawn to him, for he was more handsome than she had ever envisioned. Beneath his black silk kurta, with its onyx studs set in gold, his shoulders and chest were broad, tapering to a firm, flat belly accented by a wide black silk hizaam wrapped tightly about his waist. Around the sash itself was a black leather belt; a gold scabbard bearing a steel sword hung at his right side, so Ileana knew he was the deadliest of foes: a left-handed warrior. His black silk chalwar trimmed with black braid were pleated and elegantly draped about his thick, corded thighs; the pantaloons narrowed at the knees to fit tightly around his calves and ankles, which were encased in high black leather boots, the left one bearing a ceremonial arthame, its straight blade like a sharp ray of the sun.

He wore a heavy, solid gold torque about his neck, and Ileana's eyes narrowed as she discerned the dodecagram, the emblem of a twelfth-ranked priest, engraved upon its sunburst medallion. Unthinkingly, her hand went to the similar collar at her own throat, a silver crescent moon with the heptagram that marked her as a seventh-ranked priestess. His knowledge was greater, then, than hers. Perhaps his power, too, was stronger.

His long, shaggy hair was ebon, the color of a night without moons or stars. Between his thick black brows was the Tyrian-crimson sunburst tattoo of the Brotherhood. His skin was swarthy and gleamed like bronze. Dark hollows punctuated his high cheekbones, his lean, hawklike face. His nose was aquiline, bespeaking the gypsy blood that had mingled with that of his Bedouin ancestors; and Ileana felt a small, smug sense of pride and satisfaction that her own blood was undiluted, the product of centuries of pure Cygninae mates. As though he had somehow guessed her thought, the man's full, sensual mouth curved into a mocking smile, and his jaw thrust forward arrogantly, determinedly, as though he meant to punish her for scorning him.

But it was his eyes that caught and held Ileana's attention, for they were deep-set and compelling. Beneath his fierce, swooping brows, they glittered like obsidian, heavily fringed with black lashes and dark with longing; and she knew he, too, had stared into the flames she had summoned and seen the RingStones on that Beltane night yet to come, when he would press her down into the sweet summer grass and . . .

With a little cry of fear, Ileana turned and fled, calling frantically for her alaecorn. If only she could reach the mare, the Bedouin would not be able to follow her through the woods. The black faesthors he'd led behind him when he'd padded like a stealthy cat into the moonlight could not put to use its speed and strength in the forest.

"Ketti!" the girl shrieked as she ran, her voice piercing the night. "Ketti!"

Behind her, she could hear the sound of boots thudding into the sodden earth, and she knew the man had given chase. Faster and faster, she raced on, blindly, for it had started to snow again. She could see the wet flakes upon the tips of her lashes and feel them in her hair, where the hood of her cloak had fallen back, exposing her to the elements. She screamed hoarsely for her mount, and the cold winter wind was sucked into her lungs. She tripped and fell, then staggered to her feet and rushed on, panicked by the delay, sensing she was but a heartbeat from capture.

Then, at last, he was upon her, knocking her to the ground and momentarily stunning her. She inhaled sharply as she felt the full weight of the Bedouin's body cover her own, pressing her into the snow. Dazed, Ileana struggled against him—but to no avail. She was caught and held fast in his steely embrace.

Why had he pursued her? Cain did not know. He thought he must be crazed, maddened by her vision, which he, too, had seen in the fire, or perhaps by the Passion Moon, which did strange things to men. He knew only that he wanted her, wanted to kiss her, to caress her, to take her. . . . Was she not his, after all, bound to him by the Ritual of Choosing and promised to him by the Druswids? Yea. Surely, she, too, knew it was so.

"Stop fighting me, witch!" he snarled in her ear. "I do but want a taste of the feast we both know is mine."

So saying, he grasped her jaw with his fingers and tilted her face up to his. His breath caught in his throat as his black eyes raked her countenance: her wide, scared eyes, like lavender pools in the moonlight; the finely drawn planes and angles of her face; her tender, trembling lips. With a fierce growl, he brought his mouth down on hers, hard, as though he meant to devour her.

Ileana moaned and writhed helplessly beneath him, shocked and dismayed by the violent, unexpected, overwhelming sensations that swept through her as his tongue forced her lips to part and licked the honey it found therein.

An ember of desire she had never known flickered within her, then suddenly leaped into flame, matching the fire she sensed raged within the Bedouin. For a moment, it seemed as though they would be consumed by it.

But then, finally, breathing raggedly, reason overriding passion, Cain released her.

"Go, witch!" he grated. "Go now, before I change my mind and take ye here in the snow, as though ye were a whore from the Time Before."

Ileana needed no further urging. Shaking, scarcely daring to believe he did not intend to ravish her, she scrambled away to stumble toward her alaecorn, which now pranced skittishly nearby, sensing its mistress's distress. Sobbing, the girl flung herself onto the saddle and gathered up the reins. Then, heedless of the trees, she set her heels to Ketti's sides, giving the beast the command to take flight. The animal nickered nervously but did as it had been instructed, spreading its silver wings wide. They scraped against the overhanging branches that canopied the woods, and belatedly, Ileana realized her mistake. It was too late to rescind her order, however. With a shrill whinny of pain, the mare broke free of the trees to bear her aloft.

"Oh, Ketti, I'm sorry, so sorry." The girl wept against the alaecorn's mane. "Your wings! Heaven's Light! Your wings!"

The fragile, diaphanous membranes that covered the skeletal frames of the beast's wings were torn and bloody in places. The animal attempted to compensate for the damage; but still, she barely skimmed over the treetops and was listing badly. Ileana's already heightened, chaotic emotions soared to a sharply honed edge at the realization. Pain and fury filled her being. Of its own volition, the Power sprang to life within her; her aura burst into a dazzling halo around her. She must reach the southern shore of Cygnus and call the boat! But it would be days before she could do so, perhaps even weeks, with Ketti injured.

Though it was not easy, the girl suppressed the Power raging inside her and forced herself to breathe deeply, to drive the Demon Fear from her mind. She must think!

By the light of the moons, she spied a gleaming glade beneath her, and recognizing that Ketti was on the point of collapse, she guided the alaecorn downward. Slowly, unsteadily, the beast came to rest upon the frozen earth, its trembling evidence of its fright and agony.

Her eyes blinded by tears, Ileana hurriedly dismounted, then began to search frantically through the leather bags looped over the pommel of her saddle. At last, she found the clay jar of healing balm she always carried with her. She yanked the cork free; then, scooping out some of the fragrant salve, she started to rub it on the animal's wounded wings. She crooned to the mare as she worked; and presently, as the ointment's soothing ingredients penetrated the alaecorn's flesh, its breathing grew less labored and its eyes closed tiredly. At that, after carefully resealing the jar and putting it away, Ileana turned to take stock of her surroundings.

Through the trees, she could see the glimmering water of the Gulf of Mab to the north, and to her dismay, she realized Ketti had landed on one of the Guardian Islands. The girl knew she would not be safe here, for if the Bedouin were still following her, once he reached the shoreline, his powerful faesthors would be able to swim rapidly across the narrow channel that separated the islands from the far west tip of Cygnus. Because the forest here was not as thick as it was on the continent, the stallion's speed would then prove an advantage. Ileana knew she had no choice but to move on.

Wearily, she climbed into the saddle and, explaining to Ketti why they could not stay, signaled to the beast to rise. Valiantly, the animal began to flap its wings, and soon they were once more gliding over the treetops.

Once they had gained the eastern shore of the Gulf of Mab, Ileana brought Ketti to rest upon the beach. Then quickly glancing back over her shoulder toward the islands, she led the mare into the shelter of the woods. The girl did not know if she was still being pursued, but she dared not take any chances.

They spent the remainder of the night trekking through the forest, and only when the sky began to lighten with the approaching dawn did Ileana draw Ketti to a halt. After dismounting, she stripped off the beast's saddle and blanket and rubbed her down hard. Then she slipped the animal's feed bag over its nose and spread more of the healing balm upon its wings. After that, she ate a few strips of dried meat and drank some watered wine from her flask. Then, wrapped in the folds of her fur-lined djellaba, she huddled against a tree trunk and tried to sleep. But Ileana did not rest easy, and after a few hours of inadequate slumber, she stood and indicated to the mare that they must go on.

At last, after several days of slow travel, they reached the southern shore of Cygnus. There, dazed from lack of sleep and inadequate food, the girl stumbled from the saddle, her breath coming in tortured rasps as she staggered toward the edge of the River of Separation.

She was now certain the Bedouin had followed her. She had seen him just yesterday, his black faesthors weaving in and out of the trees upon a small hill in the distance, rapidly closing the gap between them as the woods started to thin with the nearing of the coast; and now she feared he was almost upon her.

Nervously, Ileana licked her lips, trying to gather her strength and praying her power would not fail her. Then, beneath the light of the moons that had risen in the night sky, she pressed her palms together tightly and cried out silently, desperately, for the *Swan Song*. Her heartfelt, anguished call rang out wildly across the river and the sea to Mont Saint Mikhaela, on the far Isle of Le Fey. Presently, to the girl's vast relief, borne on the wings of magic, the barge came. Like a ghost detaching itself from the mist, quickly, noiselessly, it skimmed over the water, its single sail billowing in the wind.

Dimly, Ileana realized only two priestesses manned the boat's oars when there ought to have been six. But her mind had been dulled by her travails, and now, glancing uneasily over her shoulder at the outskirts of the dark forest behind her, she did not think to ponder this curious fact.

Finally, the bottom of the barge scraped upon the beach, and hurriedly, Ileana led Ketti up the short ramp. It was not until the Druswids joined her on the shore to help her push the boat back into the water that she recognized the High Priestess and Sister Amineh.

"Reverend Mother!" Ileana whispered, shocked, and at once sank respectfully to her knees.

"Rise, child," Sharai commanded softly, laying one hand upon the girl's shoulder, "and tell me what has happened, for we expected ye two days ago and never in all my years at the abbey have I heard the barge summoned as it was this night."

She helped Ileana to her feet, her eyes searching the girl's face, noting her fear and confusion, the faint purplish blue marks that shadowed her jaw and throat. Her cloak was wet and dirty from the snow, and beneath its folds, the Druswid could see that Ileana's abayeh was torn, as though strong hands had ripped it. Still, the older woman said nothing, waiting instead for the younger to speak.

"I—I will tell ye what ye wish to know, of course. But please, Reverend Mother!" Ileana begged. "Let us first put to sea. I—I am afraid." She did not have to say more, for as she cast another look toward the woods, she saw clearly silhouetted against the moonlit horizon the shadowy figure of a man astride a black faesthors, watching them silently, speculatively. "Oh, please, Reverend Mother!" the girl insisted, pushing frantically at the boat. "We must get under way at once!"

The High Priestess caught her breath sharply as she spied the Bedouin in the distance. Slowly, she exhaled, her piercing black eyes narrowed in sudden recognition and understanding.

"Have no fear, child," she stated calmly. "He will not harm ye." *Indeed,* she thought grimly, *he shall pay for it with his life, the Darkness or nay, if he has taken her maidenhead before 'tis time, before she is strong enough to withstand the Power that is his.* She turned to Ileana. "Did he lay hands upon ye, child?"

"Y-yea." The girl nodded, flushing with shame. "But in truth, I was not . . . hurt."

Sharai sighed with relief, comprehending the fact that Ileana was still a virgin.

"Get into the barge," the Druswid directed. Then, tersely, she addressed Sister Amineh, who was standing silently at her side. "Wait here for me. I shan't be long." Then, her robe flapping in the wind, Sharai pivoted to make her way up the beach.

Cain watched her laborious progress across the sand, and for an instant, he was tempted to ride on before she reached him. He was well enough acquainted with the High Priestess to see she was furious with him. He had no doubt that he was in for a wicked tongue-lashing that, deserved or nay, he had no desire to hear. Still, he remained where he was, for no priest defied his superior without severe penalty.

At last, Sharai came to a halt some yards away, and Cain saw it was as he had surmised: Her cold eyes flicked over him disdainfully, as though he were some insignificant, odious creature. Then, haughtily, she made a small movement with one hand so he would know she had found him lacking. When, finally, she spoke, her voice shook with rage.

"How did ye dare, sirrah?" she asked through clenched teeth, the demeaning title by which he had not been called for ten years cutting him like a whip. "Get down off that beast!" she snapped. "At once! And abase yourself before me! Ye are not so high and mighty that ye cannot be brought down!"

Duly chastened, Cain dismounted slowly and knelt before her. He saw that some of her wrath had been mitigated by the gesture, though not much.

"Well?" the High Priestess questioned. "I'm waiting, sirrah, and will have your explanation. What did ye mean by coming here to Cygnus and laying brutal hands upon that child? And do not try to tell me ye did not, for I saw the marks ye left upon her."

"Child, Reverend Mother?" Cain lifted one eyebrow and laughed shortly. "She was scarcely that when she lay in my arms and yielded to my kisses."

Her indrawn breath audible, Sharai took a few steps forward, and Cain briefly thought she would strike him.

"Ye are insolent, sirrah, and your crudity disgusts me!" she spat.

"I am no cruder than ye, who would give that 'child,' as ye call her, unto me to do with as I will!" he sneered, his voice low and mocking.

His words stung, as they had been intended to do, and the High Priestess drew herself up proudly so she seemed to tower above him, although he knew it was but a trick to fool the eyes, a small magic he himself had employed in the past. Still, he marveled at the Power that was hers, which enabled her to deceive even him, a twelfth-ranked priest.

"I do what I must to defend the Light," she replied stiffly, looking down at him reprovingly.

"Yea, as do we all," Cain rejoined bitterly. "But somehow that does not make it any more palatable."

Instantly, Sharai ceased her illusion of height, returning to her normal size.

"Then tell me truthfully ye do not want the girl, and I will inform Kokudza he must choose another to take your place," she uttered harshly, knowing what a risk she was taking. If he responded . . . She paused, allowing the silence between them to grow pregnant with tension. Then, when Cain did not answer, she snorted with satisfaction, relieved and smug that her reckless gamble had paid off. "So I thought! Very well, sirrah. When the time is right, ye shall have her. But until then, leave her be. She is not yet yours for the taking!"

Then, frostily, she turned her back on him, leaving him kneeling there upon the snow-covered sand, cursing himself and her and, most of all, the girl who had bewitched him.

Chapter 11

I do not know how we came to be so fortunate, but it is so; and my heart goes out to Gitana, the Ancient One, when I think of what it cost her to bring forth the child Ileana. My old mentor, she who was once called Reverend Mother, even as now I am so called, wielded a power greater—much greater—than ever I realized; and I know now that she used every ounce of it to perform the Ritual of Choosing that was her legacy to the Sisterhood.

With her body's last breath, she told me Ileana would be the other half of Cain's soul. But the thought of the Darkness once more casting Its shadow over Tintagel weighed heavily upon me, and as I held the Reverend Mother's dying body in my arms and felt her growing colder and colder, I was afraid. I did not know how I should go on without her, for even when her place in the Sisterhood was given unto me and she became the Ancient One, I looked to her for guidance. And so, frightened and feeling more alone than I had ever felt before, I failed to sift her final words carefully with my mind's sieve.

Instead, I assumed she spoke metaphorically, meaning Ileana would be the daughter of the Light who would balance Cain, the son of the Darkness whom Takis, the Ancient One of the Brotherhood, had conjured and so hazardously imbued with wicked umbrages, that he who was so fashioned might know intimately the Foul Enslaver.

147

This was indeed so, but it was not what the Reverend Mother meant, as I now know. For Ileana has told me of her Ritual of Beginning and, too, of the vision she saw in the flames when she was tranced upon Dorian's Watch; and now there is no doubt in my mind that Cain is her SoulMate, bound to her through the ages since the beginning of time. To think my mentor journeyed to the Higher Planes of the Dimensions of Existence and, out of all the Spirits her magic might have summoned to serve the Light, chose Ileana fills me with awe. Such was no accident, surely, but the feat of a truly magnificent sorceress.

If Tintagel survives the coming Darkness, I will see that she who was born Gitana san Kovichi set Rostòv is remembered not just as the Reverend Mother who became the Ancient One, but as a saint and a savior who flinched not in the face of adversity, but stood fast, a True Defender of the Light.

Now unto me falls the task of seeing that her legacy is used wisely, and my burden is heavy indeed, for I know without a doubt that the Time of the Prophecy is upon us. Slowly but surely, Tintagel begins to spiral down into that black void that is the Darkness, where the Foul Enslaver reigns supreme and Its Minion Chaos sits at Its left hand. These pieces of lifeboats that have been found, these strange skeletons . . . all are signs of the things to come, the things that will seek to destroy us.

The High King Lord Balthasar and the High Minister Radomil will do what they can to protect the people and the land, but it will not be enough; and the High Prince Lord Yhudhah, whose foolish young advisers are so easily swayed by Kokudza, is dying. It has been decided that once Yhudhah's body has been scattered to the elements, Cain shall take his place, for the Druswids must rule the planet if we are to save it. With Ileana at his side, Cain will be able to bend Balthasar, and thus Radomil also, to our will. . . .

Ileana. She has loved Cain since first the Immortal Guardian released Its essence and divided it so they who were once one became two. When fitted together, *they are a perfect whole. But she is afraid of him in this LifePath; she senses the fire of death in his soul. And he—he, too, is uneasy; he knows she may prove capable of destroying him. If they can put aside their fears and let their love for each other once more fill their beings, the Darkness will never defeat them, for united in the Name of the Light, they will be a power glorious to behold. But if only one of them loves and the other does not . . . ah, therein, I fear, lies Tintagel's doom.*

Ileana has seen their joining on Beltane eve, which is two months distant. There is so little time left, then, to prepare her, to see she is not crushed and defeated by Cain before she is needed at his side. His power is great, greater than I ever dreamed possible, for never have I felt such strength within a Druswid as I did that night when he knelt before me. For that reason alone, to say nothing of my own feelings for the girl, I weep at the thought of how I must betray her to him. Even now, she believes I will protect her from him, as I did upon the beach at Cygnus; but I cannot. I can but make her willing in his arms so she does not pit her strength and power against his when, yet, 'tis too soon.

So though 'twill not be an easy task, I must do what I must do. If I fail— Nay, I shall not even consider that, for to doubt is to let the Demon Fear take possession of one's soul, and that, I, who am a True Defender of the Light, will never do. I shall persist in my duties, no matter how unpleasant, and I shall succeed. I must, for otherwise, I am afraid all Tintagel will be condemned to the Darkness.

—**Thus it is Written**—
in
The Private Journals
of the High Priestess Sharai IV

DAWN WAS JUST BREAKING OVER THE EASTERN HORIZON WHEN Cain stormed through the halls of Khali Keep to enter rudely the chamber that had been assigned to Brother Ottah upon their arrival at the castle. Without bothering to knock, Cain flung open the door and strode angrily into the room.

"May the Blue Moon fill ye with a thousand sorrows, Ottah," he cursed the elder priest, "for ye tricked me! 'Twas not just to examine a set of strange bones that ye brought me here to Khali, but to see *her*, Ileana! Ye knew that she would be upon Dorian's Watch that night and that I would be drawn by her presence; and so I was. But mark me: Though she would tempt any man, I have not changed my feelings in the matter! I would have her if I could, yea; I would join with her and get her out of my blood—the witch! But by the Passion Moon, I have no wish for a mate—as I've told ye often enough in the past—and especially one who would seek to destroy me!"

Brother Ottah, who had been breaking his fast, now calmly dabbed his lips with a napkin, then tossed the muslin square upon his plate and raised one eyebrow.

"Indeed?" he inquired coolly. "I thought 'twas ye who had laid savage hands upon Ileana, but perhaps I misunderstood the TelePath I received from the High Priestess."

Cain had the grace to flush. Silently, he swore at himself for his stupidity. He should have known that Sharai would waste no time in informing on him, and obviously, she had not.

"Sit down, Cain," Brother Ottah said quietly but firmly, indicating a large satin cushion to one side of the low table at which he sat. "The sweet rolls are excellent, and the honey is the finest I have tasted in a long while."

Cain's jaw tightened perceptibly, and for a moment, the elder priest thought the younger would refuse to do as he had been commanded. Finally, however, resignedly, Cain lowered himself to sit cross-legged upon the pillow, glaring at his mentor. For a time, there was no sound but the trickle of the coffee Brother Ottah poured and, afterward, the clatter of the cup and saucer he wordlessly handed to Cain.

Slowly, the younger priest sipped the rich, syrupy espresso, feeling its warmth spread through his body. He had not realized until now how cold he was; the wintry chill of Cygnus the past fortnight and the cool night air of the desert upon his return to Bedoui had seeped into his bones. But he had been too torn by his conflicting emotions to notice or to care. He was hungry and exhausted as well, for he had had little food or sleep during his pursuit of Ileana. But the hot coffee revived him, and the two honey-dipped rolls he ate with relish filled his empty belly. After a while, feeling better, he recognized how boorish he had been, and he apologized to his mentor.

"I am sorry, Ottah," Cain said more gently, "if my behavior earlier offended ye. I—I was angry and over-wrought. I meant no disrespect."

"I know." With a wave of his hand, the elder priest dismissed the younger's breach of etiquette as unimportant, understandable under the circumstances and now forgiven and forgotten. Brother Ottah considered his next words carefully, wondering how much to reveal, how much to conceal. "I am, of course, guilty of that of which ye accused me, Cain," he admitted at last. "But I did not undertake such a deception lightly; this, ye must believe. There was —and still is—a purpose to my . . . callousness, if ye will, my disregarding of your emotions and your wishes.

"The Darkness is upon us, Cain. Ye, who were born of the Ritual of Choosing and given unto the Brotherhood, know what that means. Ye are a Druswid, a twelfth-ranked priest, as I am. Ye have sworn to honor, serve, and defend the Light—freely and willingly, with all your body, mind, and soul. Do ye say now that this, ye will not do?"

"Nay, Ottah," Cain replied. "But I would know why I must do it in this fashion. Is there no other way?"

Brother Ottah sighed.

"I do not know," he confessed. "We have naught but legend and the Prophecy to guide us, and the words of this last are shaped in riddles, many of whose answers we can but guess. Further, those who have seen the Darkness have not yet been able to discern Its form, only Its growing strength and power. For these reasons, the manner in which It must be fought is not clear, only that It must be battled by one with like strength and power. Thus were ye conceived and born—and Ileana also." The priest shrugged. "Those who performed the Ritual of Choosing did what they believed they must do in order to protect Tintagel and the Light. We of the Brotherhood and the Sisterhood did not question those Ancient Ones who brought ye forth into this world. We did, and still do, seek but to preserve that for which they gave their lives in this LifePath." He paused to study Cain thoughtfully for a minute.

"We believe that your destiny and Ileana's are inextricably bound," Brother Ottah continued, "that your joining is necessary if we are not to be doomed to the Darkness, for together, your power will be such, we feel, that ye cannot be defeated. But if ye are divided, so is your strength halved; and there is the chance then, we suspect, that one of ye may be corrupted by that which we would see ye destroy." Cain inhaled sharply, and Brother Ottah nodded. "Yea, there is always that possibility to consider when one is dealing with the Foul Enslaver and Its Demons," he said.

"However—and this, I say so ye may understand more clearly our dilemma—we do not know for certain this of which I have spoken, for the signs we have seen have been inexplicably clouded; even the High Priest and the High Priestess have not been able to determine clearly the meanings of the omens. Thus we have been and remain like blind men groping our way. It may be that we are mistaken in our speculations, that we have misunderstood the Prophecy and misread the portents that have come to us in the fires and mists. But"—Brother Ottah's voice was sober now—"we dare not make such an assumption, Cain, not when so much hangs on the balance of our thoughts and actions.

"What are two LifePaths, then, when one considers how many others are at stake? Did I not love the Light and the Kind who are Its image, I would say unto ye: 'Go, Cain. Forget all I have told ye and seek your destiny where ye may find it.' But as much as ye, who have been like a son to me, would have me tell ye this, I cannot. *I dare not,"* the priest asserted fiercely.

"The Way to the Immortal Guardian is never easy, Cain, and some who would follow it are tested more strenuously than others. Such ones are ye and I. But in the end, no man can decide for another the path he will take. One can but point out to the other the forks in the road, as I have done for ye, and say where they may lead. And I use the word *may* deliberately, for even if one has journeyed down the forks before, what lies at their end may have altered in the meanwhile or no longer be there at all. Such is the way of things, that only change is constant.

"The time is coming when ye will stand at a parting of the road, Cain. Whether ye go right or left or straight ahead is up to ye. I only hope ye choose your fork wisely, and well, for if ye do not, the whole of Tintagel may be consumed by the Foul Enslaver. Already It begins to feed upon us and Its Demons snatch crumbs from our souls. If we would save ourselves and our planet, we must strike now, before the Darkness has grown too strong and powerful for us to defeat It.

"Balthasar and Radomil, while good men, lack the knowledge necessary to combat the Foul Enslaver and Its Minions and, paralyzed by the Demons Chaos and Fear, may wait until 'tis too late to act. And soon Yhudhah, who would have pressed for battle, will be dead and the time will come when we will be plunged into confusion and terror. Then we will need someone both strong and powerful at the head of our army, a high prince who will not hesitate to lead us against the Darkness, a Druswid who knows how to fight the Foul Enslaver and Its Minions. I believe ye to be that man, Cain. But the decision must be yours—and yours alone.

"Go with the Light, ye who have been as a son to me, and choose carefully the path ye would follow."

Brother Ottah said no more. Indeed, he did not even seem to notice when Cain stood and slowly made his way to the chamber's exit. There, the younger priest glanced back at his mentor expectantly, half hoping further advice would be forthcoming. But Brother Ottah's eyes were closed and his lips were moving soundlessly in prayer; Cain knew there were be nothing else.

Quietly, so as not to disturb the elder priest, he closed the door behind him, tired and troubled and yet knowing that once he reached his own room, he would not sleep.

Chapter 12

"MOST WORTHY LORDS AND LADIES, GOOD MINISTERS AND Ministresses, I tell ye a ship of that size cannot be powered by sails and oars alone," Master Stiggur insisted adamantly to the members of the High Council, trembling a little at the thought of the idea he intended to put forth. "The vessel will be too slow and too unwieldy. If what we are up against is indeed a sea monster whose like none has ever before seen, such a craft would be at its mercy!"

"Then what would ye suggest?" the High King Lord Balthasar asked wearily, for the lords, ministers, and advisers who composed the High Council had been arguing for days over the High Prince Lord Yhudhah's proposition that two new ships be constructed and dispatched to the other half of the world.

"Lord"—Master Stiggur paused and took a deep breath, then hesitantly began to unroll the scroll he held in one hand—"I fear to venture my notion, certain, as I am, that it shall not find favor with the High Council. Indeed, my soul should take flight unto the heavens, my mind crumble to dust and ashes, my heart cease to beat forever before I utter the words against which my lips should remain sealed. But I fear some madness has come upon me, for only that can explain why I am thus emboldened to speak, to make known to ye the plan I have been considering ever since I was summoned to this meeting."

"Pray, good sir, get to the point," Balthasar ordered a trifle curtly, made impatient by the master shipbuilder's lengthy rhetoric. "The hour grows late, and we have yet to reach an agreement. If ye know of a method for improving the ships, by all means, let us hear it."

"Very well, Lord." Master Stiggur bowed. "In the Time Before, vessels such as we are discussing did not need sails and oars. They were powered instead by mechanical devices—"

At his words, the High Council, which had previously been listening in quiet respect, erupted with a roar, for those present were shocked and horrified, appalled that the master shipbuilder had dared even to mention that of which it was forbidden to speak. Several of the councillors starred themselves visibly to ward off evil.

"Blasphemer!" the High Priest Kokudza shouted above the sudden cacophony and confusion, abruptly silencing the entire room as he leaped to his feet to point accusingly at Master Stiggur. "How do ye dare, sir," he inquired, his voice shaking with anger, "to profane this assembly hall with such hideous heresy?"

"Yea! How does he dare?" several of the councillors cried, then began once more to mutter to one another, frightened and enraged.

"Silence!" Kokudza thundered, glaring about the chamber. When all were again still, he went on fiercely, once more addressing the master shipbuilder. "Do ye not believe, sir, in the Light Eternal, the Immortal Guardian of all things ceaseless and universal?"

"Yea, of course. But—"

"Silence, blasphemer!" the Druswid bellowed again, causing Master Stiggur to quake in his boots, wishing he had never worked up the courage to submit his proposal to the High Council. Relentlessly, Kokudza continued his interrogation. "Surely, ye have read, sir, *The Word and The Way?*"

"Yea, of course. But—" Once more, Master Stiggur was quelled by the High Priest's reproving words and severe demeanor.

"Do not interrupt me again, blasphemer," Kokudza warned. "If ye have read *The Word and The Way,* then ye have read within its pages that which we call *The Book of Dämmerung,* wherein the Time Before is described in great detail: the vast, sprawling cities of the land, with their tall skyscrapers set side by side—so close, they obscured the sun and obliterated the horizon, so close, not one single tree, not one single flower, *not one single blade of grass* born of the Light Eternal and guarded by Ceridwen, the Keeper of the Earth, might grow from the ground covered by these concrete monstrosities, these steel affronts to all of nature!

"Ye have read, then, of the diabolical factories wherein the materials for these unnatural structures were made, of the evil computers that replaced skilled journeyworkers, whose arts and crafts were thus lost over the ages. Ye have read of the littered asphalt highways, great, six-lane, many-tiered roads over which gasoline-fueled automobiles traveled, and of the grimy railroad tracks, along which steam-driven trains journeyed, that criss-crossed the countryside, boring through mountains, uprooting forests, and besmirching plains to join these cities; and ye have read, too, of the huge iron tankers that sailed the seas between these cities, leaving behind them large pools of oil that floated on the water to kill fish and fowl alike, and of the winged metal crafts, the jumbo-jet airplanes, that flew like birds through the sky to these cities, spewing fire and smoke into the firmament. Ye have read of the satellites, the rockets, and, finally, the spaceships that pierced the heavens above these cities, strewing the stars, the planets, and the moons with nuclear waste and debris.

"And so we know, Master Stiggur," the High Priest intoned forbiddingly, "that ye are aware of these dangerous machines the Old Ones created, these gruesome instruments of the Darkness that emitted filth and poison into the air so that in the end, the Old Ones were forced to wear filter masks over their faces so they would not breathe these unclean substances, these pollutive gases and foul inert compounds that corrupted and destroyed the earth's atmosphere so treated-glass domes had to be erected to protect all from the radiation that streamed to the planet's surface, bringing sickness and death, as the Keepers and the Prophets had foretold.

"And yet, in spite of all this, ye dare to suggest to this High Council, Master Stiggur, that a *mechanical device* be constructed to power our ships! Fie on ye, sir, I say! May the Blue Moon cause ye to shed a thousand tears!

"Lord"—Kokudza turned to the High King Lord Balthasar—"I urge ye to have this man . . . this—this *blasphemer!* taken into custody at once! He is in dire need of counseling if his immortal soul is not to be imperiled."

"Yea. So it would seem," Balthasar agreed gravely. "Guards! Arrest Master Stiggur at once and see he is confined in solitary until such time as he can receive the instruction necessary to redirect his misguided spirit."

"Yea, Lord," the four warriors who had stepped forth from the ranks of the Royal High Guard chorused as one.

Stiffly, they marched the master shipbuilder, now audibly bemoaning his foolishness, from the chamber.

For a moment, all were silent, stunned by what had occurred.

Already the Darkness spreads, Balthasar thought, dismayed, *else Master Stiggur, a fine man, would never have put forth such a proposition. 'Twas as he said: Some madness has come upon him, as 'twill beset all of us if we do not put an end to it. But how?*

"Lord"—GuildMaster Demothi stepped forward, breaking the now subdued atmosphere that had enveloped the assembly hall following the Druswid's outburst and the master shipbuilder's arrest—"I must apologize for Master Stiggur; he has worked very hard lately, and perhaps the stress to which he has, as a result, been subjected has indeed affected his mind. But I assure ye, Lord, as head of the Shipbuilders Guild, that no such scheme was ever discussed at any of our halls. Indeed, I was as startled as anyone else to hear of it. Be that as it may, however, I am afraid poor Master Stiggur was correct in his assessment of the proposed ships—though he was, of course, grossly mistaken in his notion for powering them," GuildMaster Demothi added hastily.

"However, I believe I may have the solution to our difficulties. If I may, Lord, I would like to introduce to the High Council a young journeywoman from Spindrift Hall." He turned to a slender girl, who stood respectfully behind him, and motioned her forward. "This is Halcyone set Astra, Lord. She has drawn up a set of designs for an entirely new vessel, one I think may meet with your approval and satisfy any objections to the project, for such crafts, if built, would be powered by sails alone. If ye wish, I shall have her elucidate to the councillors her highly unusual concepts."

"Very well," Balthasar said. "We will hear Damsel Halcyone."

After the young journeywoman had displayed and explained her designs, demonstrating, with the aid of a strange-looking model ship she had made, the manner in which the new vessels would operate, it was seen her suggestions had been well thought out and held promise.

The High Council decided to construct the two ships, one of which would be dispatched immediately upon completion to the far side of the planet, the other to be kept in readiness, to follow its sister in the event she did not return.

Chapter 13

There are many ways to induce a tranced state in one who has difficulty achieving such or in one ye wish to remain ignorant of what is intended. One such method is to seek out the flower known as papaver somniferum *and to gather its immature fruits.*

The fruits should be lightly pricked with an arthame to release their white juice, which should be collected in a flat container, then placed in the sun to dry. After the juice has turned brown or black and hardened, it should then be fashioned into small lumps, which, when needed, should subsequently be ground into powder, mixed with some drink, such as wine, which will heighten the drug's effect, and ingested.

One who has imbibed such a potion will gradually reach the desired tranced state, providing that not too much of the drug has been taken, in which case a deep sleep or even death will result.

—Thus it is Written—
in
The Grimoire
of the High Princess Lady Ileana I

THEY HAD DRUGGED HER. ILEANA KNEW THAT NOW—NOW, when it was too late. What had they used? It did not matter. Several drugs perhaps, or she would not have danced with such wild abandon around the altar that lay at the center of the RingStones, where the fire of Beltane burned, for she

159

had not drunk enough to addle her wits, and in sharp contrast to her previous energy, she would not now be filled with such lethargy, as though her limbs were too heavy for her body and she could not move them.

Or perhaps it had been *his* doing. Mayhap he had been waiting, hiding in the shadows and watching her, for she had not seen him earlier, though, carefully, surreptitiously, she had scrutinized the faces beneath the dark cowls of the robed figures who had cast into the flames their offerings to Ceridwen, the Keeper of the Earth. He had not been one of them, she was sure. Nay, he who was the son of the Darkness had stood concealed by the megaliths, biding his time. Then he had slipped through the blackness to drug her wine. Yea, that last cup had been sweet, so sweet. . . .

Was that how it had happened? Ileana did not know or care. She had felt herself borne up in strong arms, as though she had been carried aloft by her alaecorn, then tossed upon the earth roughly. She had struggled against the unrelenting weight that had fallen upon her, crushing her, she had thought at first; and from some deep, dark corner of her mind, unbidden, there had come a picture she had seen once in a beautifully illuminated manuscript in the library at Mont Saint Mikhaela, a picture of a woman, a witch, her flesh naked and gleaming beneath the door that had been laid over her prone figure. All around her had danced strange, gleeful forms, their macabre faces twisted with unholy joy in the moonlight as they'd cast stone after stone onto the door, crushing the woman—the witch—beneath.

My body is dying, Ileana had thought dazedly. *They are crushing it.*

But then she had felt powerful hands, hard as an alaecorn's horn, tearing at her habit, touching her bare skin; and she had realized it was *him,* the Bedouin, the dark High Prince of her dreams, who lay atop her, not a stone-laden door at all. Now she tried again to escape from him. But she could not, for he held her too tightly. She could feel his fingers digging into her flesh, and dimly, she thought that she would have bruises there tomorrow. She could feel the grassy earth pressing against her back, as though it were swallowing her up; and in her mind's eye, she saw herself taken deep into Ceridwen's womb like an unborn child. She cried out—in ecstasy or agony, she did not know which —and the man stilled her lips with his fingers.

"I am for ye," she heard him mutter. "I have always been for ye—then, now, and forever. . . ."

Ileana did not answer. It was only a dream, just a dream, for had she not seen it before, in the flames of the fire?

The music of the earth pulsated in her veins, like the primeval beat of the taut drums to which she had danced earlier. She could hear her blood pounding in her ears, taste it upon her lips where the Bedouin had kissed her savagely.

His laughter mocked her. She was helpless beneath him, dizzy from the wine and drugs she had consumed. His lips seared like a brand across her cheek, whispered unspeakable words in her ear, words whose meanings were plain to her, though she had never heard them before.

"Sweet," he breathed. "Sweet. . . ."

'Tis the wine, she thought. *I drank it from a gold-chased cup set with amethysts dark as the Passion Moon.*

She was a flower, silver and fragile, and the Bedouin was stripping the petals from her, breaking her stem to hold what was left of her, weak and quivering, in his cupped hands. Inexorably, he opened them, blew upon them with his breath, scattering the seeds of her senses to the winds. She spoke to him, but he only laughed again and bent his head once more to kiss her. Time drifted by; the seasons changed. Gently, she came to rest upon the ground, a single seed of what she had once been. Burrowed now into earth, she struggled to break free of it; and he—he was Regan, the Keeper of the Rain, pouring down on her, wakening her with his stormy kisses and caresses. She grew as he fashioned her, shaped her to his will, a tender bud that ached with yearning.

Slowly, exquisitely, unlike before, he unfurled her petals until she was a flower come full circle, bursting into bloom, opening to him, wanting him. Like a hummingbird, he pierced the dark, moist core of her, plunged deeply into the warm, sweet nectar of her, causing her to tremble and cry out. On the wings of the wind, he carried her through the blackness, her petals showering about them like tiny stars to illuminate their path. And then their flight was ended, and she was once more a part of the earth, reborn. . . .

With a start, Ileana came to her senses. She sat bolt upright and clutched her torn habit to her breast. Her head throbbed horribly, and there was a dry, bitter taste in her mouth. Her heart was thumping much too quickly in her breast, and she was sweating yet chilled, as though, crying out, she had wakened herself from a nightmare. She shivered uncontrollably as the cool predawn air touched her skin, and for a moment, she did not know where she was.

Dazed and bewildered, she gazed at her surroundings. This was not her cell at the nunnery. Was she still tranced and dreaming? Nay. In the misty grey half-light, she could see she was huddled just beyond the RingStones on the Isle of Le Fey. It had not been a dream at all, but real, she realized finally, sick and mortified as she spied the traces of her virgin's blood still visible upon her inner thighs, exposed by a tear in her robe. Never again would she be pure and untouched like the First Moon. The dark High Prince of her dreams had taken her innocence, and willingly had she given it to him, she remembered as the night past came flooding back to her, its every detail clearer than when she had lived it. She blushed crimson with shame as she recalled now how wantonly she had clutched the Bedouin to her, had reveled in his kisses, his caresses.

Ah, Heaven's Light. What had she done? What had she done?

Without warning, the full aftereffects of the wine and drugs she had ingested hit her, and she retched violently onto the ground. When it was done, she wiped her mouth with her trembling hand. Then, still shaking, she stood unsteadily, her head reeling, her stomach yet roiling. She staggered across the dewy grass to a small pool, undressed, and washed herself and rinsed her mouth, bruised and swollen from the Bedouin's fierce kisses. Then, slowly, she garbed herself, trying to restore some semblance of order to her muddled mind. She could not think, and finally, she sank once more to the ground, distraught.

What was she to do? Her reflection in the pool told her that her habit was ripped and dirty, her hair disheveled. Except for the Tyrian-purple crescent moon tattooed between her brows, the silver torque still hanging around her neck, and the narrow leather belt with her ceremonial arthame and silver cup, which she had discovered lying in the grass and tied about her waist, none would believe her a priestess now. She looked worse than any peasant, like a—like a whore from the Time Before, defiled and unclean.

For the first time, Ileana thought of the others who had celebrated the festival, and she glanced about fearfully, wondering if they had spied her. But they had left her here alone. Was she to return to the abbey, then? Nay, she could not go there, *would* not go there to those who had drugged and betrayed her. The thought was like a dagger stabbing into her fresh wounds, hurting her anew, and at last, she began to weep uncontrollably, her shoulders heaving. She felt herself an Outcast, cut off from those who had loved her and been her friends. How could they have done this to her?

After a time, she felt a warm dampness brush her skin, and startled, she looked up to see her dapple-grey alaecorn, its dark sapphire-blue eyes puzzled and disturbed.

"Ketti. Oh, Ketti," Ileana whispered raggedly.

She did not know or care how the creature had come to be there. No doubt, sensing her pain, it had wandered from the field in which the animals of the nunnery grazed. She hugged the beast close, finding comfort in its nearness.

Presently, she drew the edges of her robe together and rose. She could not stay here. Doubtless, when she did not return to the abbey, the High Priestess and the rest would come searching for her, and they would find her. She must get away before that happened.

One hand wrapped in her alaecorn's long, silky mane, Ileana made her way furtively northward through the forest to the plain and the beach beyond. There, she knew, the barge, the *Swan Song,* would be resting upon the shore.

When she had reached it, she pushed the boat halfway into the water. The barge was so old, it was said to have survived since the Time of the Rebirth and the Enlightenment; but Ileana thought this was only a tale, for surely, the whitewashed teak would have long since rotted.

She fastened the small ramp into place near the stern and led her animal aboard. Then she pushed the boat free of the sand and waded out into the water to pull herself over the swan's wing that formed the side of the barge. As she had done a hundred times before over the years when answering a priestess' silent call, she raised the sail and bent her back to the oars, moving swiftly across the sea.

When finally she had gained the southern coast of Cygnus, she set the boat loose to drift upon the water, hoping the swift currents would carry it back to the Isle of Le Fey, though she did not care if they did not.

Then, tiredly, she mounted the barebacked beast that stood at her side.

"Home, Ketti," Ileana commanded softly. "Take me home to Ariel Heights."

The alaecorn, its wings long since restored by the healing balm its mistress had rubbed upon them, took to the sky, soaring above the treetops of the Melantha Forest and then, at last, the majestic, snowcapped peaks of the purple Gloriana Mountains, where Ariel Heights floated among the clouds, cool and serene, like a welcome sanctuary.

And so it was that I left Mont Saint Mikhaela, much as I had come to it, mounted upon my alaecorn and with little in my possession. I did not see the nunnery again for many years, and by then, I was a woman wed and heavy with my first child.

But I get ahead of myself. I must speak now of the present.

It was many days before I came to my father's castle, for I ached in every bone in my body and traveled slowly. But I needed time alone, time to think and to decide what I must do; and I did not lack for aught, for I had learned well at the abbey how to live off the land, and Cygnus, even in winter, was bountiful if one but knew where to look for roots buried beneath the snow, how, with a leather belt, to trap a small animal, and how to melt ice or snow over a fire.

So I did not hunger or thirst. But I knew anguish all the same; it engulfed my body, mind, and soul. I felt as though I bore the mark of Cain upon me, and I wondered if the Bedouin, he who was also called Cain, as I had learned when I lay with him, was accursed like he who had settled east of Eden on the planet Terra, which was no more, though I had read of it in the nunnery's library. I wondered if I would ever see the dark High Prince of my dreams again, and I sensed that I would, that somehow our fates were inextricably interwined, like the pieces of a puzzle, the passages of a maze.

I had loved him once, in all my LifePaths past; this, I knew. And our joining had wakened within me those tender feelings of old. I knew that if Cain but shared them, I could forget and forgive what he had done to me that Beltane eve, for perhaps it had not been of his choosing, but the only way to bring me to him. I did not know. But I felt somehow that he, too, had been guided by the Druswids, who were, I was now certain, using us both for some ominous purpose of their own.

I knew not for what, for I knew little of the Darkness then, only what had been told to me by the High Priestess Sharai, and she had not sought to enlighten me as, later, I would learn Brother Ottah had enlightened Cain, though, still, all was not made clear to him.

But this is the way of the Druswids, to enshroud all in mystery, for they guard terrible secrets, secrets kept locked away in their edificia, secrets to which even the higher-ranked priests and priestesses may not be admitted, for it is not meet or proper that this knowledge be revealed.

But once more, I digress.

Suffice to say that, eventually, I learned these things, and then I understood why they had been concealed from me. But that was long after I had reached my father's fortress and shut myself, like a hermit, behind its high walls.

—Thus it is Written—
in
The Private Journals
of the High Princess Lady Ileana I

"We have searched everywhere, Reverend Mother, but Sister Ileana is not to be found," Sister Amineh said, her voice quivering, her face troubled, for she had come to care deeply for the girl who had been like a daughter to her. "Her bed has not been slept in, though her possessions are still in her cell."

The High Priestess's countenance whitened at the news, and for a moment, she was afraid. Had she misjudged Ileana's strength after all? Had the girl awakened, alone, and been unable to bear the knowledge of what had been done to her? Sharai remembered how once, in ages past, a young novice who had lost the Way had thrown herself into the sea and drowned; and she wondered if Ileana had committed this mortal sin, damning her soul for all eternity, for to destroy that which the Light had given was an unforgivable crime indeed.

Feeling old beyond her years, the Druswid rose and made her way blindly from her chamber, leaving the priestesses gathered there staring after her with concern. They started to follow her; but with a sharp movement of her hand, she bade them stay behind, permitting only Sister Amineh to accompany her to the beach.

There, they saw in the sand the small, cloven hoofprints of Ileana's alaecorn and, a few minutes later, spied the swanlike barge of Mont Saint Mikhaela drifting, empty, through the mist. The High Priestess had not realized she was holding her breath until, slowly, she released it.

Ileana was strong enough, then, for the joining, she thought. *She survived. She was not crushed and conquered by Cain's power and his taking her, as at first I feared.*

Relieved, the Druswid raised her hands and, summoning her great power, called the boat to shore. Of its own accord, it came, filling Sister Amineh with awe, for to move an object with one's mind was strong magic indeed. Sharai turned to the priestess at her side.

"Tell the others they may discontinue the search for Sister Ileana," she said, gazing out over the golden Sea of Oriana to Cygnus in the distance. "She has gone home, like a hurt animal, to lick her wounds so her body and soul may be healed. Thus will she gather her strength and become more powerful for her scars. No doubt we shall not see her again at Mont Saint Mikhaela for many years, and so, deprived of her presence, we are punished for our betrayal of her. Oh,

Amineh!" the High Priestess suddenly cried in anguish. "The path to the Immortal Guardian is a hard one indeed."

Then, silently, she turned and walked slowly back to the nunnery, pausing only to brush away a solitary tear that glittered on her aged cheek.

Through the ages, many Houses, both Royal and Common, have fallen, never to rise again. This is especially true of several of those Ruling Houses in power during the Wars of the Kind and the Apocalypse.

The Royal House of Ariel, however, has always reigned supreme over the continent of Cygnus.

—Thus it is Written—
in
Royal Blood: A History of the Royal Houses of Tintagel
by the Historian Fala san
Mocambique set Kazatimiru

Ileana paused, gasping a little for breath, for the air was thin and cold here in the mountains, quite different from below. Then she blinked to adjust her vision, momentarily blinded by the splendor she beheld, ensorcelled by the spell her birthplace cast upon her. How could she have forgotten how lovely it was?

The tall crystalline towers, turrets, and spires of the city and her father's castle, all of which had been built of pure clear or pastel rock hewn from the Crystal Mountains of Iglacia and brought by sea to Ariel, rose in delicate filigree against the grey winter sky, shimmering like exquisite diamonds beneath the mellow sun. The crystal luminaries that lined the streets sparkled, catching the sun's rays and bending them to cast a thousand rainbows upon the earth. The streets themselves were paved with gold and gleamed as though they were molten, pouring through the narrow wynds of the city cloaked by a mantle of snow and ice. Here and there, feathery pines flourished, their snow-laden boughs dripping with icicles and sighing with each breath of the chilly winter wind that whispered through the city. Snowdrops, hyacinth, and other alpine flowers bloomed in bright splashes of color upon the ground. It was a place of beauty, of harmony, of grace. No trace of ugliness or discord marred it. Eagerly, Ileana embraced it.

Here, she would be safe for a time from the world, safe from the Druswids and from Cain, ah, most especially from Cain, who still haunted her dreams. Did he ever think of her? she wondered. Did he ever lie awake at night, as she did, remembering that Beltane eve when she had lain in his arms and opened herself to him? Or had it been for him only a moment in passing, a moment lived and forgotten, as so many in one's LifePath were?

Angered and saddened, too, by the thought, Ileana deliberately thrust the Bedouin from her mind and set her heels to Ketti's sides, urging the alaecorn forward toward the gates of the city—and home. There would be time later, when she had rested, to think of him, to mend the heart he had taken and broken, and to build around it a wall higher than that which encircled the abbey that had given her unto him for all time.

Until then, Ileana would not let him invade her thoughts. But she found, as she rode on, that this was easier said than done; and for a moment, blinded by tears, she could not see the road that lay before her, silent and twisted, like the strings of her heart.

HALF-MOON

Heavens Unfurling

Chapter 14

I am dying. I have known for some time that this is so, though I have tried to hide it, to spare my loved ones pain. But now I can no longer conceal the truth from them. Even in my drug-induced stupor, I see their dear faces bending over me, filled with anguish; and that is somehow harder to bear than this agony that racks my body, despite the sweet potions the physicians have given me to dull the pain. But only that, for there is no cure for this wasting sickness that saps my blood, this disease that is a legacy of the Time Before, when part of the atmosphere of Tintagel was ripped away by that which the Old Ones had created.

Oh, would that they had kept to the path of righteousness instead of disrupting the harmony of all with which the Light Eternal blessed the cosmos. For if only they had done so, they would not have loosed the Darkness among us and I might have lived to see my work brought to fruition.

Instead, this LifePath has been cut short, so short; and while I know the Immortal Guardian, in Its Infinite Wisdom, has ordained that it must be so and has good reason to call me now to the Light, still, I feel there is much I leave unaccomplished, much I longed fervently to finish before my Time of Passing.

Somewhere on Tintagel, the Darkness has awakened and stretched out Its hand to lay claim to us, we who were once so safe and secure and now are threatened. Those who have seen the evil shadows cast by the

171

twisted fingers of the Foul Enslaver are afraid, and even the common folk, who know nothing, sense there is a wrongness in the land.

I, too, have felt it and thought to go out and meet it, as the High Priest Kokudza and my advisers urged me to do. Now that will not be possible. Instead, I must take comfort in the fact that the ships I proposed the High Council construct and dispatch to the other half of the world are finished and that others will take up the sword and shield I would have wielded against the Darkness to defend the people and the land, as was my arduous task.

Soon another will sit upon the Lesser Throne where I have sat, wear the Lesser Crown I have worn, and hold the Lesser Scepter I have held. Eagerly, that one will embrace these symbols of rank, as once I embraced them. Oh, would that I knew who will take my place when I am gone, for I would say unto my successor: Have no envy of those who rule as ye would seek to rule, for despite its power and glory, a crown weighs heavily upon one's head, and the heart and soul are fragile vehicles upon which to carry the world's ponderous load.

—Thus it is Written—
in
The Private Journals
of the High Prince Lord Yhudhah II

The City of Astra, Cygnus, 7269.3.18

THE SHIP THAT HAD BEEN CHRISTENED THE PT *STORM CHASER* moved slowly out of the harbor of Astra into the Gulf of Mab. It was a beautiful vessel, unlike any ever before seen. Fully two hundred feet long, it was the largest craft the Shipbuilders Guild had ever produced. It had three masts, the main one towering nearly a hundred feet above the top deck. All carried more canvas than Ileana had ever before seen, and not just square sails, but strange, narrow triangular sails, some set between the masts, the rest fastened to the long bowsprit. The craft's hull was lean and sleek and constructed entirely of teak attached to a frame of iron —rather than wood—ribs, something previously unheard of. Also unusual was the fact that below its waterline, the ship was sheathed with sheets of copper held to the hull with bronze nails. Most startling of all was the complete absence of oars. The unorthodox design was not called a galley, but had been given the name "windjammer" by its creator, the former Damsel Halcyone set Astra, who had been raised to the rank of mistress for her masterpiece.

So its crew could familiarize themselves with the operation of the vessel, the *Storm Chaser* was to follow a circuitous route, leaving the Gulf of Mab to sail through the Guardian Islands, around the far west tip of Cygnus to the Mistral Ocean and the Mercia Islands. From there, it would travel past the Lost Islands of the Tempest Ocean, which, farther west, became the vast Zephyr Ocean. The ship would hug the coast and make several stops along the way so the High Council could remain apprised of its progress. Once it had reached the Zephyr Ocean, it would continue westward into The Unknown, the far side of the planet.

If within one year it did not return, the second craft, the *Moon Raker*, would follow the same route in search of its sister.

From the wharf, Ileana watched the great windjammer until it disappeared over the horizon and she could see it no more; and she, who had not set foot beyond the high walls of her father's castle since her arrival there a year ago, suddenly felt a reckless longing to be aboard the magnificent ship, journeying to the other half of the world.

What would they find, those brave, adventurous few who had dared to set sail upon that splendid vessel? No doubt their course would be ridden with peril, perhaps even death. Mayhap they, too, would never return, as so many others before them had not returned. Why? What was out there, lying in wait for the unsuspecting, the unwary? Was it a giant sea monster, as some had claimed? Ileana did not know. Like the other Druswids, she had seen only shapes and shadows of the things to come, hideous, blurred images that had filled her with fear. She shivered a little in the sunlight, remembering.

A fortnight ago, the visions had come to her again, and

she had awakened in a cold sweat, her heart pounding fiercely. Quietly, she had risen and gone to her father's gardens, where she knelt beside the small pond in which she had first seen Cain. As she had so long ago, she had looked into the clear water, willing the trance and the dreams to come. But there had been little to comfort her, for she had seen only the harbor of Astra and the tall ship and then . . . nothing. Had it been a sign that the vessel, like all its forerunners, was doomed, or had she lost her great power when she had run away from Mont Saint Mikhaela? She did not know. Still, she had felt compelled to come here to Astra.

Her years of relative isolation at the abbey had left Ileana with an aversion to crowds and courtly circumstance; and not wanting to be surrounded by people and pomp, she had traveled to the city alone, waiting until her father's large procession had left Ariel Heights before taking her alaecorn from the stables and setting out on her own.

Now, sighing and drawing her yashmak more closely about her face, she began to make her way down the docks, ignoring the curious glances of those who stared at her. Still, no one bothered her, for the common folk were in awe and always a little scared of the Druswids.

Thus Ileana was startled when, without warning, she felt strong fingers close tightly around her arm. Thinking a person in the throng had mistaken her for someone else, she tried to pull away, but the hand held her fast. Turning, she gasped with shock, suddenly riveted to the ground, as she looked up into the fathomless black eyes of the Lord Cain sin Khali, who, after the Lord Yhudhah's death, had won the Royal High Games to ascend the Lesser Throne, as Ileana had long ago foreseen.

Like a tide, the crowd ebbed and flowed around them, noisy, raucous, and jostling. Cain put his arm around her still figure to protect her from the others. Ileana did not hear them, did not see them, did not feel herself roughly bumped and shoved. Time and the world had ceased to exist for her. Now there was only Cain, the High Prince, he with the fire of death in his soul.

How could she have forgotten how tall he was, how lithe and muscular? Though he was clothed in the fashion of a priest, the deep scarlet habit he wore was trimmed with gold braid set with jewels, as befitted a high prince. On the robe's left shoulder was embroidered his shield, a rampant, regardant sable faesthors, properly inflamed, surmounted on a gold sunburst centered on a sable field. Around his neck hung the gold torque with the dodecagram that marked him as a twelfth-ranked priest. At his waist was a gold belt bearing his ceremonial dagger and gold cup.

Ileana marveled at how well he had combined the trappings of his two offices, how handsome he looked, his hawklike face set with determination, his body rippling with savage grace as he drew her close.

In that moment, she was back again among the RingStones, where the fire of Beltane—and she—had burned. As though it were happening even now, she could feel Cain's weight pressing her down into the sweet summer grass, his callused hands roaming over her flesh, touching her intimately, taking her to the heights of rapture—and beyond.

His dark, intense eyes told her he, too, had not forgotten what they had shared. Keenly, his gaze raked her.

Though she had been gone from Mont Saint Mikhaela for over a year, Cain saw that she still wore the habit of a priestess and her silver collar with its heptagram, and that wrapped around her waist was the narrow brown leather belt from which hung her sickle-shaped arthame and silver cup. She still considered herself a Druswid then, bound to the Sisterhood by the vows she had taken, though she no longer trod the long halls of the nunnery. The hood of her robe was drawn up over her head so he could not see her long silver hair. But he remembered the feel of the satiny tresses intertwined with his fingers, and suddenly, he had a wild urge to push back her cowl and rip the yashmak from her pale, delicate countenance, to tangle his hands in her hair and tilt her face up to his so he could kiss her mouth as he had that night when they had lain together in the moon-cast shadows of the megaliths. He observed the small pulse beating at the hollow of her throat, and he knew she was not indifferent to him. But then, her eyes had told him that.

Ah, Ileana's eyes. Like amethysts reflecting the sun and

moons, they were, first light and clear, sparkling like lavender ice, then dark and opaque, gleaming like violet velvet. He could drown in those eyes, he thought, those twin pools that entranced him like a crystal sphere.

Once, Cain had believed that taking her would extinguish the fire in his blood. But he had discovered it was not so. She had haunted him, though he had tried to drive her from his mind; and with the passing of time, his desire for her had but grown stronger. Now he no longer cared if she destroyed him, as he had seen her do in his dreams. He wanted her, and he intended to have her, whatever the cost.

He looks older, Ileana reflected, *harder, and tired, as though he has not slept well for many nights.*

For an instant, she wanted to reach up and caress his cheek, brush his glossy black hair from his eyes and smooth the furrows from his brow. But she did not.

"Lady," Cain said at last, his voice low and impassioned, shattering the silent moment that had held them spellbound. "I would speak with ye."

"I do not think, Lord, that we have anything to say to each other," Ileana murmured in reply, and would have left had it not been for increased pressure of his grip on her arm pulling her back.

"Lady . . . Ileana, I do not wish to make a scene, but I shall if I am forced to do so," he said grimly.

Realizing he meant what he said and noting that already they had begun to attract attention, that people could not help but stare at him, their Druswidic High Prince, and at her, a priestess veiled and mysterious, Ileana allowed him to lead her away without protest to a nearby portal.

Once they were free from prying eyes, she turned to him questioningly, trying not to tremble at his nearness.

"What is it ye would have of me, Lord?" she asked boldly, wanting to escape as quickly as possible.

Slowly, Cain lowered the hood of her robe and removed her yashmak. Then, gently but firmly, he cupped his hands beneath her chin to lift her face to his.

"Did ye feel nothing that night, *kari?*" he queried softly.

The Bedouin word was intended to remind her of all they had shared. Instantly, Ileana's eyelids swept down to hide her thoughts from him. But still, she could not conceal the blush that stained her cheeks; and ashamed of her revealing response, she bit her lip, attempting to concentrate on the pain her teeth caused so she would not think of how he had aroused her that Beltane eve.

"Ye make no reply, Lady," Cain pointed out, "but your silence is answer enough."

He kissed her then, lingeringly, with tender fury; and when it was done, he released her, his eyes holding hers mesmerizingly.

"When I spied ye in the crowd today, I could not believe ye were real," he told her, "for ye do not know how many times I have seen ye in my dreams. Ever since that night, I have thought of nothing but ye." He paused, then continued, his voice husky with desire, "I want ye, Ileana. Heaven's Light, how I want ye! And in your heart, ye know ye are already mine. Come away with me! Now!" he urged, his mouth raining hot kisses on her face and hair, then sliding down her throat to the valley between her breasts. "I will make ye happy, Ileana. By the Passion Moon, I swear I will! Do not deny me."

His feverish words washed over her, stark and unreal, stunning her. He did not speak of love; *that,* she would have welcomed and delighted in. Nay, he talked only of desire. Did he not remember the beginning of time, when from one, they had become two? Did he not recall all their LifePaths past, when they had come together out of love? Or had he not loved her even then, but only lusted for her, as he did now? Ileana felt sick unto death at the thought.

"Are ye mad?" she cried, attempting to wrench away from him. "I am no whore from the Time Before, nay, nor even a concubine of Time Present. I am the daughter of the High King, sirrah!"—the insulting word sprang, unbidden, to her lips. "What happened at the RingStones was born of the wine and drugs the priestesses and ye had given me so I would be willing in your arms—nothing more! *Nothing more!*" she uttered fiercely, as though by doing so she could make it true.

"May the Light damn ye for a liar!" Cain shot back, angered by her words. "For I gave ye no wine, nay, nor drugs either. I had no need of them, and never think ye otherwise! I am in your blood just as ye are in mine. Much as ye may wish it were not so, there is no escaping that, as I have learned. Ye are a priestess, Lady. Ye know that what is written in the stars cannot be changed. Ye are for me as surely as I am for ye."

"Nay, I don't believe it. I *won't* believe it!" Ileana insisted, though in her heart, she knew he spoke the truth. "Now let me pass. I have nothing more to say to ye."

To her surprise, Cain let her go.

"Very well, then," he said, his voice cold. "But mark ye this, Lady, and mark it well: This day, I came to ye as a priest so I might ask you in privacy to be mine. But if ye deny me, the day will dawn when I shall come to ye as the High Prince, your lord and master."

"On that day, ye shall rue the moment when first ye laid eyes on me, sirrah; this, I vow!" Ileana declared.

"So be it then," Cain rejoined, smiling mockingly. "I no longer care. Destroy me if ye can, witch! In the meanwhile, ye shall be mine—to do with as I please."

Chapter 15

There comes a time in each one's LifePath when a choice must be made. For most, it is the decision itself that is difficult. But for those few who have been Chosen, the way is clear, marked by the signs such a one sees in the fires and mists that are the portals to the Far Beyond. Though the guideposts may be clouded and obscure and therefore hard to read and interpret, they are there nevertheless and cannot be ignored. Thus, for the Chosen, it is not the decision itself that is often so painful, but the following of it that tries one's heart and soul.

—Thus it is Written—
in
The Chosen
by the High Princess Lady Ileana I

A MAN'S WORD WAS HIS BOND, AND THIS, THE LORD CAIN SIN KHALI did not give lightly. Thus, once he gave it, he honored it. And so it was that this day, astride his black faesthors, Ramessah, he was galloping along the road leading through the Gloriana Mountains to Ariel Heights, where he intended to lay claim to the Lady Ileana sin Ariel, she who had dared to reject him.

Cain's mouth tightened with anger at the thought; a muscle worked tensely in his jaw. He was a Bedouin, a twelfth-ranked priest, and now the High Prince of all Tintagel; his pride had not easily sustained such a blow.

179

Silently, he cursed the woman who had dealt it to him and those who had securely bound him to her with their powerful magic. Oh, would that he could undo what they had done, those Ancient Ones of Time Past! But he could not, for he did not know what secret spells they had woven into the Rituals of Choosing.

Had Cain been cognizant of these, he would have freed himself from the unworldly ties that held him fast to Ileana. Even without such knowledge, he had fought his feelings for her, hoping to disentangle himself from the gossamer cocoon of enchantment that had been spun around him, its silken threads drawing him inexorably to her, despite his struggles to escape.

Oh, if only he had not gone to the RingStones that Beltane eve! But the High Priest Kokudza himself had commanded Cain's presence there, and he had not dared to disobey. His years of training at the monastery had left their mark upon him after all, and his sense of duty had triumphed over his turbulent emotions.

Cain wondered if he, too, had been drugged that night. But he thought not. The dark, primitive instincts that had been unleashed within him as he'd watched Ileana dancing with such wild abandon had been enough to send his senses reeling, to cause his head to spin, his blood to pound, and his loins to throb with desire. It had been as though he had been transformed into one of his most ancient ancestors, brutal and warlike, seeking savagely to conquer and possess. This, Cain had done, and in doing so, he had sealed his fate.

His jaw set grimly at the thought; his swooping jet-black brows knitted together fiercely, and he laughed harshly. *Kari,* he had called her: passion's slave. But it was not so. It was she who had ensorcelled him—the witch! And when, finally, driven and obsessed by her to the point of near madness, he had sought to make her his, she had denied him!

It had not been easy, but Cain had reached a decision at last. Now he meant to carry it out: One way or another, he intended to have Ileana. She might scorn the thought of being the concubine of Brother Cain, the priest. But a proposal of marriage from the Lord Cain sin Khali, the High Prince of all Tintagel, she would not dare to refuse.

Heedless of the low branches of the trees and the loose shale that crunched beneath Ramessah's hooves, Cain set his spurs sharply to the stallion's sides. Instantly, he felt the muscles of the mighty beast bunch and ripple beneath him as it leaped forward, leaving those who accompanied him scrambling to keep up with him on the narrow, thickly wooded road that wound through the mountains around Lake Loon.

The advisers of the Lesser Court and the soldiers of the Royal Lesser Guard who had been selected to form Cain's escort party spurred their own mounts forward in silence, hesitant to attract his attention lest they provoke his foul temper. Surreptitiously, the counselors and warriors studied their lord, wondering what had caused his black mood. After all, was he not on his way to claim a bride—and a beautiful one at that? He ought to have been filled with joy at the prospect. Instead, one would have thought the hands of time had somehow turned back to the age when marriages were arranged and those who reigned wed in order to secure political alliances and to enrich their coffers. But such days belonged to Time Past; in Time Present, one who ruled married where he or she wished—or not at all, for ever since the Games had been established, there had been no need to produce an heir of one's blood.

"Do ye think perhaps the Lord cast some spell that failed?" one of the soldiers asked softly of his fellows, for they all stood in awe of their Druswidic High Prince. "Do ye suppose that is what has put him in such a bad humor?"

"If it is, it must have been a love spell," another warrior joked, his voice low, "for in truth, he looks as though he's on his way to a battle instead of a betrothal!"

The others laughed, but quietly, unaware that Cain's power was such that he might hear even their thoughts if he chose.

For a moment, it crossed his mind to chastise the two men who had spoken. Then, realizing their jesting was but a means of lessening the uneasiness they felt, he wisely held his tongue. All his advisers and soldiers were a little afraid of him because he was a priest, as well as a prince, and there was no point in feeding their fear and alienating them in the process.

Seeing the brilliant crystal turrets of Ariel Heights towering over the city just ahead in the distance, Cain abruptly drew Ramessah up short and, forcing himself to smile, turned to the others.

"I believe it will behoove us to proceed at a more . . . shall we say . . . dignified pace from here on out," he said wryly, the corners of his mouth twitching as he observed the expressions of relief on the faces of his escort party. "Indeed, I must apologize for the fact that we traveled so hard and fast to begin with," Cain went on. "There was no need for such haste. However, though I may be a priest and the High Prince of all Tintagel, I am also, at this moment, a prospective suitor, and like any other such man, I . . . ah . . . am afraid I'm just a trifle on edge."

At his confession, sudden understanding lightened the eyes of his counselors and warriors; amused and sympathetic laughter rippled through their ranks, dissolving the tension that had held them in its grip. Several of the men and women, who would not have dared to do so before, now called out various sly and witty remarks, making the others chuckle and cheer. In considerably higher spirits, they continued on toward the city; and Cain was glad he had sought to set their minds at rest.

In truth, he had not had an easy time of it since winning the Royal High Games to ascend the Lesser Throne. His intensive training as a priest, while proving advantageous in many respects, had in other ways been a severe handicap.

Cain had no liking for the pomp and circumstance that were expected of the High Prince. He enjoyed even less being constantly surrounded by people when he was deeply accustomed to solitude. He was naturally reticent, not outgoing, as his kinsman Yhudhah had been; and he found it difficult to be gay, charming, and gregarious.

Though his patience had stood him in good stead on more than one occasion, it had been sorely tried even then, for he was not used to being questioned. The lesser-ranked priests, novices, and acolytes at Mont Saint Christopher would not have dreamed of asking the motives behind his actions. But his advisers at the Lesser Court frequently demanded explanations, and even the soldiers of the Royal Lesser Guard were not above requesting that he elucidate the reasons for his orders. Such openness did not sit well with a priest who'd had secretiveness bred into his very bones at Mont Saint Christopher.

It was no wonder, Cain reflected wryly, that Druswids had little inclination to enter the Games.

Briefly, he wondered how well Ileana would adapt to life at the Lesser Court. Then he remembered that she had been a part of it during her childhood and that though she seldom put in an appearance at the High Court, she was now a member of it and was therefore aware of the rules and etiquette governing courtly behavior. Because she was a priestess as well, she would understand the difficult adjustments he himself had been forced to make—no doubt she had made them herself—and thus she would be a double asset to him.

At the thought, Cain abruptly roused himself from his reverie, the corners of his mouth turning down sardonically. What on earth was he thinking of? Ileana had no liking —much less love—for him. She would doubtless be more apt to stick a knife between his ribs the moment his back was turned than to help remove any obstacles with which his LifePath might be beset. Silently, he cursed himself for a fool. For a minute, he had almost deluded himself into believing a willing bride was waiting for him at Ariel Heights, a mate to whom he himself was looking forward to being joined. Highly irritated, he shook his head to clear it, wondering if the thin mountain air of Cygnus had somehow affected his senses.

He did not care for Ileana any more than she did him, Cain told himself sternly. He merely wanted her—and that only because the magic of the Ancient Ones had irrevocably bound them together. He must have her. Since she would not be his concubine, he had no other alternative but to take her to wife; and that was the sole reason he was determined to do so. Otherwise, he thought he would go mad from the spells that had been cast upon him before his birth, the incantations that had ignited this raging fire for her in his blood.

Without warning, the trumpets of his heralds sounded, bringing him back to the present.

"Make way for the High Prince!" the heralds cried as they

passed through the gates of the city. "Make way for the High Prince!"

With one uplifted hand, Cain acknowledged the cheers of the townspeople, who, hearing the commotion, were hurrying to welcome him, the shopkeepers even leaving their stores to join the crowds lining the gold-cobbled streets. But his mind was not on the throng. Instead, his jet-black eyes narrowed intently, he was gazing at the diamondlike fortress that lay to the north of the city.

The high walls that enclosed the keep rose before him, walls behind which Ileana had taken refuge after that night at the RingStones. There, Cain thought, she believed herself safe from him.

But ye are not, kari, his soul whispered to hers, *for I have come, as I said I would, not as a priest, but as the High Prince of all Tintagel; and I have come for ye. . . .*

I was in my father's gardens when I heard the blare of the trumpets and the heralds crying out; and even before I felt Cain's essence touch mine, I knew he had come for me.

My first thought was to run away. But even as I began to do so, I realized there was no place I could go where he would not find me; and I knew, then, that there was no longer any hope I would be spared the fate for which I was destined. And so, as calmly as I could, I walked to the north reception hall, where the High Court received visitors, to greet him.

I had thought to find him smug, triumphant. But to my surprise, his eyes were cold and calculating when they raked me; and though they flickered with desire, there was, too, the shadow of something else I could not name, though in another man, I would have called it fear.

Unbidden, Cain's words at our last meeting echoed in my ears, and for the first time, I thought to wonder what he had meant by them.

Destroy me if ye can, witch! he had said.

At the time, distraught, I had dismissed the dare, assuming Cain believed I would attempt to cast some spell against him to keep him from me. But seeing him in the reception hall, I knew that I had been mistaken, that it was not the thought of this that had driven him to issue such a challenge.

What, then, had prompted the provocative taunt? I did not know. He was a twelfth-ranked priest; his power and knowledge were greater than mine, surely, for I was only a seventh-ranked priestess. But perhaps, I speculated, since this was so, he had foreseen something I had not. Mayhap he had cause to be afraid of me. But . . . why?

I could think of no reason, and at last, I gave up the attempt, telling myself that all things had their own time and that I would discover the answer to my question soon enough.

The marriage proposal was read aloud to me and the rest of the High Court by one of the heralds; and all the while, Cain watched me, that strange, unfathomable look upon his face. I did not even think of refusing him, of course; he had known I would not. To have done so would have been to insult him unforgivably and thus to disgrace the Royal House of Ariel, which I could not bring myself to do.

And so I bowed my head, acknowledging my defeat, and said nothing while the arrangements that would shape the remainder of my LifePath were made. It was only later, in the privacy of my chamber, that angry and hurt, I cursed him, he who was now my betrothed, and wept bitterly because there had been no word of love inscribed upon the long scroll the herald had read.

—Thus it is Written—
in
The Private Journals
of the High Princess Lady Ileana I

They were alone now in the opulent room. Covertly, from where she sat upon a gracefully curved chair with cabriole legs, Ileana stared at the tall, dark man who, this day, had become her husband. Though for their lengthy wedding ceremony, Cain had worn the Lesser Crown, a gold satin cape, a red silk gallibiya, and soft gold satin boots with laces, now he was garbed simply in a deep purple silk aba trimmed with gold braid richly studded with jewels. Plain brown leather sandals were upon his feet. Had he donned his priest's cap and belt, he would have required only a wand to perform some ritual, Ileana thought, for the aba greatly resembled an ornate chasuble. She wished this were indeed his intent; but to her dismay, she knew it was not, and she wondered how much time she had before he claimed her as his.

If Cain were aware of her thoughts, he did not show it. He turned to a long table laden with food and drink.

"Will ye have wine, Lady?" he asked, breaking the stillness that lay heavily between them.

Fearing she would become drunk, Ileana had barely sipped the many liquors that had accompanied the wedding feast. Now she felt the need of something potent to bolster her courage, and she nodded, watching closely as Cain poured the sweet red wine into a crystal goblet, then deftly watered it.

The wide gold marriage bands that now encircled his wrists gleamed in the candlelight with each movement of his strong, sure hands, reminding Ileana that around his neck, beneath the loose folds of his aba, hung the slender gold chain and silver key that unlocked the silver bracelets he had clasped upon her wrists during their wedding ceremony.

Now she glanced down at the bands, noting their detailed engraving, the way in which Cain's shield intertwined with hers, the sinister rays of his sunburst overlaid with the dexter points of her crescent moon. His rampant, regardant faesthors, properly inflamed and surmounted on the sunburst, faced her own rampant alaecorn, which rose from a cloud-enshrouded mountain peak and was tucked into the concave curve of the moon.

No longer was her designation simply sin Ariel; now it was sin Ariel sul Khali. Since Cain's rank was higher than hers, their children, if she bore any, would be designated sin Khali rather than sin Ariel; and if she ever left him, she would not be able to take them with her. For that reason, to say nothing of the dishonor such an act would bring to her family, Ileana knew she would never offer to exchange her own silver chain with gold key for the one Cain wore.

"Your wine, Lady," he said, startling her, for lost in her reverie, she had not realized he stood so near.

Carefully, so she would not touch him, she took the glass he handed her. Then, unobtrusively, or so she thought, Ileana ran her right hand around the rim of the goblet. To her relief, the moonstone set into the intricate ring on her second finger retained its pearly luminescence.

Cain, who had not missed the subtle gesture, laughed, the sound harsh and mocking in her ears.

"By the First Moon!" he swore fiercely. "I told ye once before, did I not, that I had no need to drug ye. Did ye think me a liar?"

He towered over her, his eyes hard and cold; for a moment, Ileana was half afraid he would strike her or dash his wine in her face. Part of her hoped he would do one or the other, for then she would be able to declare charges against him before the High Court and get rid of him without bringing shame to herself or the Royal House of Ariel.

Cain's eyes narrowed as he heard her thoughts as clearly as though she had spoken them aloud.

"Do ye take me for a fool then, too?" he asked softly, his voice smooth as the hiss of a snake. When she didn't respond, he smiled grimly. "In time, ye will learn I am neither, Lady," he told her icily. "I suggest ye do so quickly, for I mislike being insulted, and there are other ways besides violence of driving such notions from your mind."

His gaze slid meaningfully to the canopy bed that sat upon a dais in the center of the room, and Ileana, stricken, blushed and screened her eyes with her lashes so he could no longer guess her thoughts.

Nervously, she raised her glass to her lips, relieved when Cain laughed devilishly again, then moved to sit down in the chair opposite hers.

As though she were not there, he closed his eyes, leaving her to wonder what he was thinking, for as she had shut him out moments earlier, now he effectively shielded his mind against hers. Foiled, she ceased her tentative, cautious probing, recognizing that to continue to press would be to force him into an open confrontation. Ileana wished to avoid that at all costs, for she did not know the limits of his strength and power, and she had no desire to pit her own against his without some inkling of the outcome.

Still, the past year had hardened her, Ileana knew, tempered her strength like steel and enhanced her power in a way that would not have been possible had she continued her training. With a sudden flash of insight, she realized wounds and scars were not always the breaking of one, but sometimes the making of one instead.

Without warning, the words the High Priestess Sharai had uttered to her before the wedding ceremony rang in her ears.

"I do not ask ye to forgive," the older woman had said, her keen, dark eyes moist, her hands holding Ileana's tightly. "I ask ye only to understand."

At the time, the girl had dismissed the plea, for the pain of Sharai's betrayal still bit deeply. Now, like a door opening and closing swiftly, a faint glimmer of comprehension flickered in Ileana's mind. It was gone before she could grasp it, leaving her angry and frustrated, for she felt that if she had been able to hold on to the thought, much would have been made clear to her.

Restless, she rose, passing through the open doors that led to the balcony. The night air was cool and damp, as it was always in the clouds that enveloped the castle. Wisps of white-grey mist floated like wraiths on the wind, intermittently occluding the black-velvet firmament, where the three moons of Tintagel glowed and the stars glittered like shards of a shattered mirror. Ileana could barely make out the sword of Ishtar, the Keeper of the Stars; the trident of Ōkeanos, the Keeper of the Seas; the sickle of Ceridwen, the Keeper of the Earth; and the horn of Vāti, the Keeper of the Winds, in the sky.

She laid one hand upon the elegantly wrought balustrade. Then, shivering a little, she withdrew it, for the crystal was cold to the touch. It gleamed like quicksilver where it was showered by sprays of moonbeams and seemed just as fluid, as though it were not solid at all. But this was only a trick of the moonlight, Ileana knew, made possible by the way the

crystal—of which all the edifices in Ariel were constructed
—had been cut.

Though the small triangular and quadrangular slabs used
for roofs and the larger, rectangular blocks employed for
walls were pure and clear—even those that were pastel in
color—they were so multifaceted that in reality, they were
impossible to see through, as was the translucent, gelatinous
substance with which they had been joined. Thus the clarity
of the buildings that formed the city and the fortress was
illusory. To those unaccustomed to their brilliance, the
crystalline keep, shops, and houses, when reflecting the
sun's rays, were blinding to behold. But the eyes of the
Cygninae, exposed to aeons of dazzling white snow and
glittering ice, had genetically evolved so they now compen-
sated for the glare.

From her vantage point on the balcony, Ileana could see
the whole of the city below. The luminaries that lined the
narrow streets flickered like the tiers upon tiers of votive
candles that burned always in the castle chapel, making the
city appear to be a cascade of spangled, multicolored fire
tumbling down the mountainside.

Unbeknown to Ileana, the dancing flames of the luminaries combined with the incandescent light of the moons and
stars to illuminate her face and figure, and Cain, watching
her silently from the room they would share this night, felt
his breath catch at the sight.

How beautiful she is, he thought. *Truly, only magic could
have brought her into being.*

Her long silver hair and abayeh of like color shimmered
in the half-light so she seemed as ethereal as a fairy and just
as unreal. Her skin shone like a lustrous pearl, casting into
prominence her high, delicate cheekbones and the hollows
beneath them. It was as though fragile dusky-pink roses
bloomed upon her cheeks and evening dew kissed her
parted pink lips. When she moved, it was with the grace of a
white winter swan, and Cain knew the Cygninae had been
aptly named, for the word itself meant 'Tribe of the Winter
Swan.' He wondered how she would fare among the Bedouins, the Tribe of the Fire Dragon, and briefly, Cain almost
regretted the fact that tomorrow, he would take her away
from the cool purple mountains, blue lakes, and green

forests of her homeland to the sunbaked rose mesas, brown rivers, and golden sands of his.

Unbidden, a hundred memories from Time Past filled his mind, images from LifePaths of long ago, when he and Ileana had laughed and loved and delighted in each other and known that, together, they could face anything.

Why must this time be different? he asked himself. *Why must this LifePath be touched by the Darkness? I could lose myself so easily within her; in her arms, I could forget what I have seen in my dreams. But I must not, for she was Chosen by the Light, and it is within her power to destroy me, though I think she does not yet know it. She is my equal in power; I feel it is so. If her strength, too, should match my own . . .*

Slowly, Cain stood and, one by one, blew out the lamps that lit the chamber. Then he strode to the balcony and laid one hand, light as a feather, upon Ileana's arm.

"Come," he said, drowning in her pale eyes even as she floundered and was lost in the dark depths of his. "'Tis time, *kari.*"

> *I know it is the bounden duty of each one of us to record our thoughts and actions in our private journals so that once our bodies have died and been scattered to the elements, our memories will remain, sealed in the Archives for all posterity to read and thus to know what has gone before.*
>
> *But even now, when this night has ended and dawn is tiptoeing across the far horizon, I cannot bring myself to write of what passed between my husband, Cain, and me. And so I will say nothing and hope those of Time Future will understand and forgive my silence.*

—Thus it is Written—
in
The Private Journals
of the High Princess Lady Ileana I

Cain was her husband, her SoulMate, and yet in this LifePath, she knew him not at all, Ileana thought. She had lain with him once before, in the moon-cast shadows of the RingStones. But even now, it was as though he were a stranger to her, an alien creature who had come to her on the wings of the night and mesmerized her with his eyes till she had no will of her own, but was his to command.

Naked, he stood before her, proud and arrogant, like one of the idols she had read about in the library at Mont Saint Mikhaela, the gods worshiped by the Tribes of far-off planets, who did not know of the Light and the Darkness. His skin was bronze, his tall, lithe form muscular and beautifully proportioned, without a single flaw; and she knew only magic could have made him so. But his hands, when they touched her, were real enough, hard and callused, in sharp contrast to the soft whisper of her silk abayeh that he loosed and sent rippling down her bare flesh to lie like gossamer at her feet.

Slowly, as though it were all happening in a dream, he laid his hands upon her shoulders and drew her to him, so near, she knew she could see the shallow rise and fall of her breasts, hear the pounding of her heart, and feel the trembling of her body against his.

Lingeringly, he slid his fingers up the sides of her throat to her temples, where he imprisoned her silver hair and lifted her face to his. For a fleeting eternity, he stared down at her, and in that moment, Ileana thought he would speak. Her heart stopped in anticipation, then started to beat again too quickly in her breast. If only he would murmur some word of love to her, she would give herself willingly unto him, without fear or reservation. When he did not, she swept her lashes down to hide her pain.

Ah, Cain, her heart cried out to him silently. *Do ye not remember what we shared before? Or is it that now, for some reason I cannot fathom, ye choose to forget?*

Ileana had no answer to her question, and before she could ponder it further, his mouth captured hers. In a swirl of kaleidoscopic color and sensation, memories of Time Past engulfed her, when he had been gentle and deliberate in his lovemaking, as he was now. For an instant, she was almost persuaded into thinking that naught had changed between them, that they were as they had been before entering this LifePath. But it was not so, for even now, she could sense his inward battle as he fought to distance his mind from his body.

Suddenly, Ileana felt as though Cain's strong embrace were a leather thong, wrapping about her tighter and tighter as though to crush her; and she began to struggle against him. But he held her fast and went on kissing her; and presently, realizing she could not escape from him, she stood quietly in his arms, letting his kisses and caresses wash over her like the waves of a sea upon which, helpless, she drifted, carried by the current.

Tantalizingly, Cain's tongue traced the perfect outline of her tremulous lips before compelling them to open so he could taste the wild honey within, sweet and warm and melting on his tongue, wakening in him the first stirrings of sensate pleasure. Like a man starving, he hungered for more; but still, he did not hurry, knowing a feast such as this was best savored. His teeth nibbled her mouth, sinking gently into her soft flesh, taking small bites of her, morsels that only whetted his appetite, leaving him greedy for the banquet to come. Slowly, he began to devour her, his lips feeding upon hers, his tongue dipping into hers and licking the dark, moist crevices of her mouth. He reveled in the taste of her, like mulled wine. The warmth of her filled his belly; but still, he was not sated.

His mouth slanted across her cheek. Ileana could feel his hot breath against her skin, could hear him whisper huskily in her ear. But the words eluded her, fell into and were enveloped by the whirlpool of emotion that eddied around her, dragging her down into its black depths. She could not think, her head was reeling so; and she knew now that it had not been the wine or drugs that had made her feel so dizzy and faint that Beltane eve, but the man himself and the things he had done to her.

Now, as then, Cain touched her unerringly in ways and places that ignited her desire for him and set her aflame. His hands smoothed her hair, lifted it, and let it fall to brush gently against her hips and buttocks. His fingers tensed and spread wide, he gripped her back tightly, making her aware of how small and fragile her bones were beneath her skin, how much stronger he was than she. Expertly, he kneaded her flesh, causing her taut muscles to relax. Little by little, his palms slipped down her back, following the curve of her spine to her round buttocks. He cupped them firmly and pulled her nearer.

Fleeting impressions of him invaded Ileana's mind: the sharp, masculine scent of his body mingled with the pungent sandalwood oil rubbed into his skin; the rough texture of his bronze flesh made sleek by the same rich emollient; the linenlike crispness of the dark, glossy hair that matted his chest, where her hands were pressed against his nipples so she could feel the hardness of the twin peaks and the unevenness of the brown areolae.

She remembered the feel of his chest against her own in LifePaths past and beneath the megaliths on the Isle of Le Fey, and a wave of intense longing suddenly coursed through her being. If only they could be now as they had been before! But this was not possible. Something in Cain had changed. Perhaps she, too, was not the same. Was that it? Was that the cause of this distance between them?

Ileana did not know, and as Cain swept her up into his arms and carried her to the bed, she no longer cared. Whatever was wrong between them could be put right, some way, somehow. She would not fight him, would not resist his taking her, his bending her to his will. Perhaps then they could recapture what they had lost. . . .

The satin sheets felt cool and smooth against Ileana's skin, but the realization was a subconscious one, barely recognized before it was lost amid the feel of Cain's mouth and hands upon her flesh. As skillfully as he did his harp, he played her until she was taut and thrumming with desire; her lips were bruised and swollen from his kisses, her breasts full and aching with passion. The melody was as old as time yet sweet and true, for he had not forgotten how to call it forth, nor she the harmony that accompanied it and made it all the richer.

Time passed and kept on turning, yet to Ileana it was as though it had ceased, no longer existed. There was only she—and the song of Cain, kissing her with notes that pealed strong and clear, stroking her with chords that rang deep and vibrant, leaving no part of her untouched, unsounded. She echoed what she heard and felt, every last pause and breathless trill, until he was as caught up in the music as she, and she knew that he, too, could hear his blood singing in his ears, could feel his heart and loins throbbing with a primitive beat.

Lightly, he trailed his fingers along the insides of her thighs in a caress that made her gasp and quiver; and then he was thrusting into her, faster and faster, in a crescendo that took her breath away. In dulcet tones, she cried out her surrender and was answered by his own low, euphonious moan as they reached the shattering climax of their rapturous rondo.

Silence fell, broken only by the rasp of their breathing and the pounding of their hearts. The night air, wafting in from the balcony, felt cool against their sweat-dampened skin. They did not speak. They did not know what to say, though once, in so many other LifePaths past, the words had come easily and eagerly to their lips.

But now they had only memories—and whatever they might make of their future, uncertain and shadowed by the Prophecy and the Darkness.

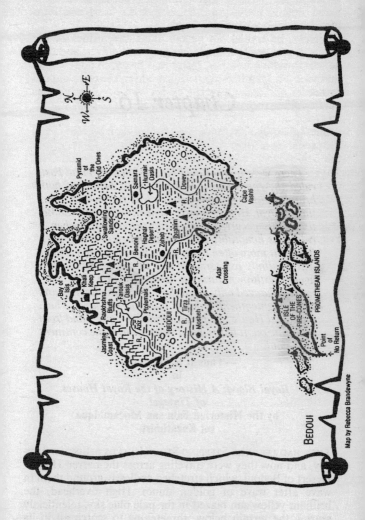

Map by Rebecca Brandewyne

Chapter 16

There were many Royal Houses that, in Time Past, ruled the continent of Bedoui, for its history is both brutal and bloody, and many of its rulers—and thus their Royal Houses—were violently deposed. Sometimes this occurred during intratribal wars, when a ruler was honorably confronted and slain on a battlefield. But more often than not, it happened that a ruler was stealthily assassinated and the Royal House savagely overthrown during a resulting coup.

This changed only when the Time of the Rebirth and the Enlightenment brought peace to the land. Then, the Royal House of Khali ascended to power, and from that time on, it has reigned supreme over the continent of Bedoui.

—Thus it is Written—
in
Royal Blood: A History of the Royal Houses
of Tintagel
by the Historian Fala san Mocambique
set Kazatimiru

THEY HAD LEFT THE STEPPING-STONE ISLANDS BEHIND AT MID-day, and now they were traveling across the barren Haghar Desert of Bedoui, which stretched endlessly around them in wave after wave of golden dunes. High overhead, the brilliant yellow sun blazed in the pale blue sky, relentlessly searing the terrain below, threatening to scorch all in its path.

Ileana, mounted upon her alaecorn, was thankful for the white cotton djellaba she wore. The loosely woven fabric shielded her fair skin while allowing it to breathe and soaked up the perspiration that trickled down her body. The oversized hood shaded her eyes against the glare of the sun. The desert sheen was different from the way in which the light reflected off the snowcapped Gloriana Mountains and the crystal cities of Cygnus, and Ileana was experiencing eyestrain during the initial adjustment.

For the hundredth time, it seemed, she drew forth the lacy handkerchief tucked in the sleeve of her etek and wiped away the sweat that beaded her brow and upper lip. Then, a trifle resentful, she glanced at the warrior, Sir Husein, whom Cain had appointed as her Chief Protector and who rode at her side. Did he not feel the heat? she wondered. It seemed he did not. His face was impassive, coated with only the faintest trace of perspiration. The material under the arms of his cream-colored kurta was barely even damp, while the sides of her etek felt wringing wet.

Sighing, Ileana turned to her young page, Leiandros, who, astride his small unicorn, was carrying a parasol to help protect her from the sun. Poor child. He looked nigh to swooning in the saddle. Still, the boy had pride and determination; he would be insulted if she were to suggest he abandon his post to ride in one of the wagons, so Ileana said naught.

There was really nothing she *could* say to make the trip any better. They were used to the cool air of the purple Gloriana Mountains, with their jagged peaks white with snow, and the pleasant shade of the verdant Melantha Forest, with its blue and green lichens and rich brown loam—not this dreadful hot sun that beat down upon the arid land ceaselessly, this stifling heat. Even Ileana's alaecorn was flagging, its head hanging listlessly, its wings and tail drooping. If this was Bedoui in the springtime, the girl shuddered to think what the continent was like in the summer.

Already she hated it—the flat, empty terrain that surrounded her in every direction as far as the eye could see, the pale gold of the sand made stark and colorless by the lack of contrast. There wasn't a mountain—or even something that might pass for a hill—in sight, not a gnarled tree or a scraggly shrub or a lone flower. Not even a single blade of grass grew in this vast, inhospitable wasteland. Even the blue of the sky appeared washed out, as though the fierce sun had burned away its intensity. Ileana didn't know how she would bear it. She yearned desperately for home, for Ariel Heights, where the white clouds trailed across the azure firmament like gossamer and the damp grey mist clung and filled the air with welcome moisture.

Once more, she dabbed at her face with her handkerchief. Then she licked her dry lips. Though Ileana knew it was only her imagination, they still felt cracked and parched. Never before had she known what it meant to suffer thirst. Now she wished fervently for a tall, frosted crystal glass packed with slivers of ice and overflowing with clear, cold water. But unlike on Cygnus, where the mountains and forests were rife with silver streams, the life-giving element was precious here in Bedoui. Only a few muddy brown rivers flowed sluggishly through the land; even rarer oases dotted the harsh, vacuous expanse. Water was not simply had for the asking, and thus it was carefully hoarded and guarded; not a drop was ever wasted, for it might mean the difference between life and death here in the desert.

Ileana had three full flasks hanging from the pommel of her saddle; Sir Husein had filled them from the River Pelagos before leaving Cygnus. She eyed them longingly. Then, made drowsy by the heat, she glanced at Cain, her husband, who rode at the head of the procession. Perhaps soon he would signal a halt, and then she could rest and wet her mouth with a cool drink of water from one of the leather containers.

That, by merely lifting her hand, she could bring the caravan to a stop herself, Ileana did not even consider. She was proud. She would rather die than let Cain and the warriors think she could not keep up with them. Squaring her slender shoulders, she pressed on determinedly.

Suddenly, a high, shrill scream pierced the air, startling Ileana from her reverie. She drew her alaecorn up short and turned in the saddle to look at the remainder of the procession, which wound like a phalanx of army ants across the terrain. Her face blanched at the terrible sight that met her eyes. Somehow one of the vehicles, loaded with tents, supplies, and possessions that were part of her dowry, had strayed from the path on to one of the treacherous patches of ground that were known as the Swallowing Sands.

The desert is alive! she thought wildly. *It is eating the cart!*

Slowly, like a stormy wave crashing against a shore, the caravan lurched to a halt amid the ensuing cacophony and confusion. Many in the procession barely avoided colliding with one another; others were not so fortunate, and the impact of two faesthorses added to the pandemonium as the beasts went down, their riders leaping hastily from their saddles in order to avoid being crushed by the massive, rolling animals.

Those soldiers who were not natives hauled sharply on the reins of their nervous, bewildered mounts, uncertain as to how to proceed; their hesitant, meaningless actions only further disconcerted the beasts, who pranced about skittishly, posing an additional hazard. The Bedouin warriors, however, well accustomed to the perils of their homeland, reacted quickly to the unexpected disaster, breaking away immediately from the rest and galloping toward the scene of the accident. Ileana spied Cain, his Chief Protector, Sir Ahmed, and Sir Husein racing along furiously with the others, their faces grim.

The hapless wagon, which had buckled at its center where the front axle joined the tongue, was now disappearing with frightening rapidity into the quicksand. The loud, panicky whinnies of the four unicorns harnessed to the vehicle split the air sickeningly, making Ileana cringe. The terrified animals were thrashing about convulsively, their hooves flailing, in a valiant effort to free themselves from the mire. But their frantic struggles only served to hasten their descent into the loose bowels of the earth.

Above the pitiful din of their unKind cries and the shouts of the soldiers rose another thin, wailing shriek of terror, and aghast, Ileana saw that atop the contents piled high on the cart, her Chief Handmaiden, Charis, knelt, scrambling for purchase as she tried desperately to save herself from a certain, grisly death. Tears streamed down her face as she clawed at the sand, attempting to pull herself to solid ground.

"Charis!" Ileana screamed. "Charis!"

Instinctively, she wheeled her mare about abruptly, intending to go to the handmaiden's aid. But before she could set her heels to the alaecorn's sides, one of the warriors milling about suddenly came to his senses and remembered his duty; quickly, he reached over from his saddle to grab Ileana's reins.

"Let go, ye fool!" she spat, and for a moment, the man feared she would strike him. "Let go!"

"Lady," he said, swallowing hard, "I dare not let ye endanger yourself. 'Twill mean my head if I do."

To the girl's fury and despair, despite all her threats, he stubbornly refused to release her, claiming that if he did, the Lord Cain would without a doubt order his immediate execution. There was naught for her to do but watch and wait helplessly while the wagon sank deeper and deeper into the quicksand, knowing that soon Charis, too, would be devoured.

Feeling quite ill but unable to tear her eyes away from the gruesome picture, Ileana stared at the unreal tableau being played out before her.

Earlier, the driver of the vehicle had rashly jumped from his seat to the back of the nearest unicorn in an attempt to avoid being swallowed alive by the mire. Now, at last, he was dislodged from his precarious perch by the violent, writhing movements of the beast. Thrown clear, he fell into the center of the deadly patch of ground. Within seconds, he had vanished, only his arms, swaying gently in a final, macabre plea for assistance, remaining above the earth's surface. Shortly thereafter, they, too, were sucked under.

Fearing she was about to vomit, Ileana closed her eyes tightly and choked down the bile that rose in her throat. One's Time of Passing should be a natural, peaceful transition, not an abrupt snapping of the slender, ethereal cord that tied the soul to the physical shell. She sorrowed for the brutal, untimely demise of the driver's body and hoped his next LifePath proved more propitious, for though she had not known him well, he had been a good man and had served the Royal House of Ariel faithfully for many years. Her lips began to move soundlessly in prayer so his journey to the Far Beyond would be a smooth one.

Suddenly, in the respectful silence that had fallen at the driver's death, Ileana heard a rapid succession of *whoosh*ing noises, sounding like the slithering of a heloderma's tail. Her eyes flew open wide. With the ropes they carried slung around the pommels of their saddles, Cain, Sir Ahmed, and Sir Husein had fashioned running nooses to form loose lariats, which they were now twirling expertly over their heads. They let the hemp fly, and the wide coils, cast with skill and accuracy, hit their marks. Two of the lassos closed neatly about the necks of the lead team of unicorns, still floundering wildly in the quicksand as, inch by inch, they slid toward the heart of the shallow, innocuous-looking depression that had already consumed the rear pair of beasts and the entire body of the cart as well. The third loop dropped over Charis's shoulders to gird her slim waist just as the last of the wagon's contents were engulfed, leaving her without support. Hurriedly, the men reined their mounts in short, drew the ropes taut, and wrapped the trailing ends several times about their pommels.

"Somebody cut the traces!" Sir Husein yelled as he struggled with his anxious faesthors. "Heaven's Light! Somebody cut the damned traces!"

In a flash, one of the soldiers hovering on the fringes set his spurs to the sides of his beast, whipped his dagger from his belt and, clenching the steel between his teeth, leaped from the saddle of his now swiftly cantering animal to the bare back of one of the unicorns staggering up the slight incline of the scarcely discernible pit. Moments later, the warrior sliced through the leather harness that held the team fast to the partially buried tongue of the vehicle.

Carefully, Sir Husein and Sir Ahmed began to back their faesthorses away from the mire; gradually, the men managed to haul the two unicorns up onto firm ground. As the ropes about their necks suddenly slackened, the animals stumbled a little. But they regained their footing quickly; still white-eyed and snorting with fear, they were led away by several of the journeyworkers who served the BeastMaster.

"Back, Ramessah, back . . . slowly . . . slowly, my beauty," Cain crooned as, deftly, he maneuvered the massive black stallion away from the indentation.

A few minutes later, Charis, too, was dragged from the quicksand. She lost her balance at the abrupt release of tension in the rope about her waist and hobbled forward, finally crumpling to her knees. Shaking uncontrollably, she reached for the left stirrup of Cain's saddle to steady herself. Tears poured down her cheeks; her breath came in rasps.

"Oh, thank . . . ye . . . Lord," she got out between gasps for air. "Ye—ye saved . . . my life! Ye . . . saved my life!"

"'Twas nothing," Cain replied kindly, bending awkwardly to pat one of the trembling hands that clutched his boot. "I'm just glad I was able to help. Are ye hurt, damsel?" he asked, concerned.

"Nay, just—just . . . scratched and bruised and—and . . . frightened, I think," Charis answered.

"Good." He paused, and when he continued, his voice was stern; his eyes were narrowed intently. "Damsel, how came your wagon to stray so far from the path? Where was your guard?"

"I—I don't know, Lord," the handmaiden confessed. "Some of—some of the ropes binding the Lady Ileana's possessions to the cart had come undone. I—I climbed up to retie them, and—and the next thing I knew, Theo . . . the driver . . . was flying through the air and the wagon was—was . . . sinking! Oh, Lord, if I had not been looking after the Lady Ileana's things, I—I—" Charis buried her face in her hands, sobbing so hard at the thought of her narrow escape that she was unable to go on.

"'Tis all right, damsel," Cain said softly. "I understand." He motioned to Ileana, who, having finally been released by the dutiful soldier, was now standing to one side. "See to her, Lady," he said curtly, but she knew his anger was not directed at her. "I will have a tent prepared for ye both."

Without waiting for her response, he spurred his faesthors forward sharply, shouting orders as he went and calling for Captain Westbroc, who was in charge of the escort party accompanying the caravan.

"Ye there, erect a tent for the High Princess Lady Ileana." Cain pointed to a nearby group of servants. "Fetch food and drink and whatever else she or her handmaiden may require. At once!" he barked when they continued to stare at him uncomprehendingly, still dazed and shocked by what had occurred.

At last, however, they began to carry out his commands, eyeing the quicksand warily and taking care to keep well away from it, though some of the Bedouin warriors had formed a ring around it to prevent further mishaps.

Once Captain Westbroc had arrived and saluted smartly, Cain addressed him tersely.

"Who is responsible for the safety of the High Princess Lady Ileana's personal attendants and possessions, sir?" he questioned, his black eyes blazing with fury, a muscle working in his rigidly set jaw.

"I am, Lord," Captain Westbroc rejoined promptly and unflinchingly in the face of his master's wrath. The soldier was well aware that, ultimately, it *was* his duty to be certain nothing untoward befell the Lord, the Lady, and those who served them; and he would not shirk it by attempting to blame another. "'Twas I who assigned Sir Masselin to his position. If there's any punishment to be meted out, Lord, I'm the one who deserves it."

"Your willingness to accept responsibility for the actions of your subordinate is admirable, Captain," Cain noted dryly. "Nevertheless, Sir Masselin shall not escape so lightly. Have him brought here immediately!"

"If that is your wish, Lord, then I shall certainly do so. But I beg ye not to be too hard on him," Captain Westbroc pleaded. Then, as one of Cain's eyebrows quirked devilishly at his temerity, he hastily explained the reasons for his presumption. "The lad is from Lorelei," he elucidated, "and he was only recently admitted to the Royal Lesser Guard. This is the first time he has ever been to Bedoui, so, naturally, he is unaccustomed to the heat. When ye cautioned us to conserve our water, Lord, the damned idiot rationed his own most strictly, even though he knew he needed more than the rest of us. He passed out, Lord. That's why he wasn't at his post. I found him unconscious a few miles back. He's lucky to be alive, and I've already reprimanded him severely for his foolishness," Captain Westbroc ended. Then he paused, waiting expectantly.

"The damned imbecile," Cain muttered, shaking his

head. He knew instantly what had happened, for the Loreleish were an amphibious tribe; they did indeed require a great deal more water than was usual. "The Light preserve us from overzealous soldiers." He sighed. "I meant only that water was not to be wasted, Captain, not doled out in spoonfuls! But perhaps my instructions were unclear. See they are clarified at once and thoroughly understood by all. I want no one else collapsing on this journey! As for ye and Sir Masselin . . . well, ye shall ride drag the rest of the trip! That is all."

"By your command, Lord." A wide grin split the captain's face at Cain's generosity. The two warriors would have to eat dust for several miles, but that was certainly better than being dishonorably discharged from the Royal Lesser Guard or executed for dereliction of duty, either of which Cain might have ordered had he chosen to do so. "Thank ye, Lord!" Captain Westbroc uttered enthusiastically. "Thank ye."

Cain smiled wryly.

"No doubt ye shall not be so grateful once ye have swallowed a crawful of sand," he remarked. "But no matter. We will rest here for an hour, during which time we will repeat the Prayer of Passing for the driver. Then we will continue on our way. Have everyone assembled and ready to go at that time."

"Yea, Lord. By your command."

Once he had acknowledged the captain's parting salute, Cain wheeled his stallion about and headed toward the large striped tent that had been hurriedly pitched at the impromptu campsite. There, he dismounted and tossed his reins to one of the guards standing stiffly at attention outside. Then, after stripping off his gloves, he lifted the flap and bent to pass beneath it. Upon entering the tent, Cain paused for a moment to allow his eyes to adjust to the relative darkness within. Then he gazed about sharply to be sure all had been prepared as befitted his wife, the High Princess Lady Ileana.

Plush wool carpets woven with elaborate patterns and fringed with knotted yarn at either end had been unrolled and laid upon the ground so their edges overlapped to cover the sand. Here and there, generous tasseled satin pillows had been scattered about to provide seating. In the center of the tent sat a low wooden table, its top inlaid with mosaic tile of ornate design. Artfully arranged upon this were several baskets of fresh fruit and two clay pitchers, one filled with cool water, the other with sweet red wine. Ileana, who had glanced up at his entrance, knelt nearby, a basin of fragrantly scented water in her lap. Charis was resting comfortably upon some of the pillows; her eyes were closed; a damp cloth was pressed to her forehead.

"How is she?" Cain asked his wife softly so as not to disturb the handmaiden.

"It is as she told ye: She was more frightened than hurt, though she is not without a few scrapes and bruises," Ileana reported. "She'll be fine once she's got over the initial shock of what occurred. Theo, the driver, was a friend of hers, I believe. Seeing him die in such a way was not pleasant. Even I, who knew him little, was aggrieved by the manner of his passing. I can't imagine how Charis must have felt."

"I'm sorry," Cain said. "I apologize for the loss of the driver and the wagon, Lady. Many of your possessions are forfeit, too, as a result. If, after we reach Khali Keep, ye will give me a list of what is missing, I shall make certain all is replaced."

"That is not necessary, Lord," Ileana replied. "I know that 'twas an accident, that what happened was no fault of your own. Ye need not feel responsible for it."

"Nevertheless, I do. Had my instructions regarding the water been made clearer, perhaps it would not have occurred. Sir Masselin, whose duty it is to ensure the safety of your personal attendants, is unused to the heat of our continent and passed out. I can only assume that without him to keep the wagons in line, the driver somehow strayed from the path, which often, as it did today, proves a fatal mistake here in Bedoui."

"'Tis indeed a harsh and hazardous land," Ileana murmured.

"Yea," Cain agreed. "'Tis not for the weak or the timid. But there is beauty to be found here, too, Lady, if only ye look for it. I hope the mishap will not blind ye to it, for this is to be your home now and I would have ye content," he declared, startling her. He paused, then continued. "We shall depart here within the hour. Be ready to go by then."

"As ye wish, Lord. And Cain—" she called as he strode to the exit, causing him to pause in the act of raising the tent flap. Sunlight streamed in, bright and golden, illuminating her fair countenance as he glanced back at her questioningly. "Thank ye for saving Charis's life. She has been with me since childhood, and her loss would have filled me with much sorrow."

"Then I am glad I was there to rescue her," he said quietly.

He was gone before Ileana could say anything further. For a long moment, she stared after him, contemplating the dark, brooding man she had wed. She had believed him hard, cold, and uncaring. But he had not hesitated to endanger himself to free Charis from the quicksand; and his words moments past had told Ileana he was not without some feelings for her, no matter that she had thought otherwise.

She plucked an orange from one of the baskets and peeled it deftly. When the last of the rough rind had dropped away, she pried the fruit into halves and bit into one section with relish, savoring the sweet, warm taste of the juice upon her tongue. The liquid ran down her chin and squirted over her hand as, hungrily, she took another bite. Peeking about to be certain no one was watching, Ileana wiped her face off with her sleeve, then licked her fingers, one by one. The orange was good. It had been a long time since she had eaten one, for they did not grow in Cygnus. But here in Bedoui, Cain had informed her earlier, the delicious fruit was harvested along the Jasmine Coast, where groves of orange and lemon trees flourished among stands of fig and olive trees.

There is beauty to be found here, too, Lady, if only ye look for it.

Soberly, Ileana pondered his words. How strange that he had spoken them and talked, too, of wishing her to be content here. Such a little thing it was, and yet perhaps it had been intended to offer much more—if only she could read his thoughts and learn what was in his heart. But Cain kept these aspects of himself hidden from her, revealing only what he chose to let her see.

She gazed down at the rich, pulpy orange halves in her hands, concealed until, little by little, she had peeled away the hard rind to expose the succulent inner fruit. It was only an orange, yet beneath its deceptive exterior lay a surprising sustenance native to Bedoui. To Ileana, it was evidence of the unexpected qualities that might be discovered in even the harshest of lands—or of men.

It was with a considerably lighter heart that sometime later, she mounted her alaecorn and took her place among the others, her face turned toward the towering bluffs in the distance, her eyes searching eagerly the far horizon.

Some days later, toward sundown, the caravan at last reached the city of Khali, where Ileana was stunned to see crowds of people thronging the narrow wynds to welcome her. As the heralds blew their trumpets and cried out to clear a path for the procession, a roaring cheer rose from those gathered to wish her well, and the fragrant scent of jasmine from the blossoms strewn before her filled the air. The girl had not anticipated such a reception, for the Royal Houses did not generally intermarry, and no doubt Cain had been expected to choose a Bedouin wife, preferably a distant kinswoman. Ileana was the first sin Ariel bride brought home to Khali Keep in decades, and she could not help but be moved by the warm, overwhelming display of approval that greeted her.

Finally, they arrived at the keep itself. There, before the stout, ornate brass gates that had been opened to allow them to pass, Cain raised his hand to bring the caravan to a halt so Ileana might view her new home. Her eyes widened with surprise and appreciation at the sight, for she had not realized until this moment how magnificent it would prove.

High atop the Raokhshna Bluffs, it stood, a capacious, sprawling castle, built, as all fortresses belonging to those of the Royal Blood had been, to house an extended family and four courts, if necessary. It was constructed entirely of huge sandstone blocks that had been backbreakingly hewn from the massive bluffs and transported by wagons to the site. There the blocks had been laboriously laid one atop another and joined. Here and there in various strategic spots, the high walls themselves, in variegated shades of rust, pink, and gold, were inlaid with mosaic tiles that formed elaborate pictures of Time Past. Intricate patterns painted in gold leaf and accented with the strange, pale whitish blue turquoise to be found in the land bordered the beautiful tableaux. Great stone pillars with tops chiseled to resemble the crowning leaves of palm trees lined the many wide, arched porticos that jutted from the imposing edifice, sources of welcome shade.

Flanking either side of the large portals were colossal statues sculpted to resemble both the Keepers and animals that held special significance for the Bedouins. Ishtar, the Keeper of the Stars, posed alongside Vāti, the Keeper of the Winds; crouching smilodons with sharp teeth and claws stalked slithering helodermas, spiny-tailed dragons, and humpbacked camels. At the four corners of the main portion of the building slender obelisks, each based upon proud stone faesthorses, rose to pierce the sky like needles threaded with trailing cloud wisps.

The doors themselves were gigantic, fashioned of heavy bronze overlaid with gold, silver, or copper, which was engraved, in turn, with labyrinthine designs and studded with precious jewels of every cut and color. On each story, long narrow ogee apertures, with gold-leafed wooden shutters that could be opened to permit cooling breezes to circulate or closed against violent sandstorms, were set in the walls at regular intervals. Smaller, inverted cordate windows dotted the castle like whimsical afterthoughts. Carved wooden lattices interwoven with lush green vines intermittently climbed the walls, helping to shield the mighty fortress against its two enemies: the relentless heat of day and the constant, merciless effects of erosion.

Graceful minarets that served as watchtowers and bell towers soared above the endless, flat roofs. These were ornamented with immense cupolas capped by onion-shaped domes sheathed in metals that matched the portals below and reflected the sun's brilliant rays.

Set apart in solitary splendor from the rest of the keep was the intriguing ziggurat. This was a tall, solid, conelike temple with a gradually rising path that spiraled up to the very peak of the structure, where the mosque was located.

But most impressive of all, as Ileana was to discover in the days that followed, were the gardens.

From the very heart of the castle grounds, a series of terraces, which grew progressively smaller the higher they got, ascended like steps up the rear wall of the fortress. The rectangular stone foundations had been filled with rich red earth brought by the cartload from the Farouk Oasis; in the resulting beds of dirt had been planted a vast array of vegetation. The spreading branches of orange and lemon trees intertwined with those of fig and olive trees. A gay profusion of exotic multicolored flowers bloomed amid squat shrubs laden with aromatic blossoms and bright berries; spongy blue and green lichens and moss carpeted the ground. Tangled tendrils of vines cascaded over the sides of the short foundation walls of the terraces, so the gardens seemed to hang.

On the roof directly above all this was an enormous copper tank that served to collect rainwater during the short, violent stormy season; this was carried by a system of copper irrigation pipes to the terraces below. During the long, hot dry season, when the tank was often empty, it was filled by pumping into it water from a small nearby river that snaked through the Raokhshna Bluffs.

Ileana, her eyes shining with emotion at the beauty of her new home, turned in the saddle to Cain, who was waiting silently, expectantly, at her side, his well-trained faesthors motionless beneath him.

"'Tis lovely," she breathed.

"Fuw-hatke imashín cholla khen jipor, kari," he repeated the traditional Bedouin words of welcome to a bride. "May ye find happiness within this house, Lady," he then translated the greeting into the common Tintagelese for Ileana's benefit.

"Y tam fuw-dizaba imashín a yah, cid," she replied fluently in his own language, surprising him. "And may I also bring happiness to it, Lord."

"I didn't know ye spoke Bedouin," Cain said.

"Ye forget: Sister Amineh san Pázia, my mentor at Mont

Saint Mikhaela, was from the Numair Oasis region," Ileana reminded him. "But, yea, there is much we have yet to learn about each other. May the Light grant us both the time and the wisdom to do so."

Cain studied her intently for a moment, his eyes suddenly so opaque and fathomless that she could not read his thoughts.

"Yea." He spoke at last. "Let us hope for that."

Wordlessly, they rode on toward the castle.

Chapter 17

And so it was that I came to Khali Keep, a young bride—but not beloved, though sometimes, in the most secret recesses of my heart, I did, in truth, yearn to hear Cain, my husband, speak such words to me. But he did not. Instead, there remained between us that inexplicable distance and doubt that had been present since the beginning of our relationship. It eluded my understanding—and perhaps Cain's as well—and mayhap because we never talked of it, the chasm that kept us each separate and alone seemed unbridgeable.

Yet in the days that passed, I came to know him well—not just as a priest and the High Prince, but the man himself; and I believed if our circumstances had been different, we might have been happy together, for we had much in common.

We were both very private people, accustomed to the hush and isolation of a cloister. In sharp contrast, the Lesser Court was a place of constant hustle and bustle from which it was not easy to slip away; and though a Druswid is nothing if not patient, there were times that tried us sorely. On occasion, I would glance over at Cain seated on the Lesser Throne by my side and see a muscle working tensely in his jaw, and I would know it was only with the greatest of difficulty that he held his temper in check. At such moments, he would suddenly rise and silently, without warning, stride from the reception hall or the assembly hall, his guards scrambling to keep pace with him.

Then it would fall unto me to deal as best I could with the many problems with which the Lesser Court was beset. Sometimes, though I knew in my heart I had done what was right for the good of all, the look of pain and disappointment upon the face of a petitioner I had decided against pierced me to the core; and so it was that in time, I came to grasp the meaning of the High Priestess Sharai's words to me the day of my wedding and, indeed, not only to forgive, but to understand her.

I saw now that she could not have loved me more if I had been her own daughter and that she would never have betrayed me had she not believed with every fiber of her being that it was necessary to do so. I realized that both the act Sharai had felt compelled to carry out and my subsequent coldness to her afterward must have hurt her deeply; and for the first time since leaving Mont Saint Mikhaela, I knew a deep sense of shame that I had been too upset, angry, and selfish to give her a chance to explain. Something of such import, that had so greatly affected my life, I, though a priestess bound to do as I was bidden, might have questioned and received an answer.

And so it was that late one eve, when all at Khali Keep slept, I made my way to the hanging gardens I had come to know and love; and there, I laid a fire and knelt before it, as I had not done for many a long night. I closed my eyes and breathed deeply, willing the Power to awaken within me, and after it had stirred to life, I let it flow through me unhindered. Blue sparks shot from my fingertips to ignite the kindling I had prepared; and when I heard the crackling of the dry wood, I opened my eyes to stare into the flames and wait for the trance to come upon me.

I did not look for dreams, for that was not my purpose that eve. Instead, I meditated at length, and at last, I heard the low thrumming I had sought sound in my ears. It grew louder and louder; my heart pounded in frantic harmony to its savage melody. But I was not afraid, for I knew this was but the battle between my mind and body for control of my spirit. I channeled my great energy to my mind, and at length, it prevailed, and I was free. Like a sigh, my essence floated from its physical shell to fly upon the wings of the wind, the slender, ethereal cord that joined it to my body trailing behind it like a spiral of silver ribbon across the sky.

Through the night, I soared; and when at last I stood before the High Priestess Sharai, I saw she was glad to see me. I knelt and asked for her forgiveness and her blessing. Silently, her dark eyes moist, she made the ancient sign above me, and I knew she loved me still.

When the TelePath was ended and my soul had returned to my body, I felt a sense of inner peace I had not known for a long while.

Dawn was just breaking over the far horizon when, finally, I left the gardens, determined—whatever the cost—to discover the answers to the questions that still plagued me, the reasons for the fear and mistrust that lay between Cain and me, who were SoulMates and had once loved so deeply in Time Past.

Why had our joining been so important in Time Present and yet so inexplicably tainted? Why had he come for me when he loved me not? And why did I feel that even now, we were heading toward some inescapable destiny irrevocably intertwined with the magic of the Druswids and the Light and the Darkness?

I did not know, nor did I have even a clue, then, of the terrible price I would have to pay for my insistence on learning that which was better left unknown.

—Thus it is Written—
in
The Private Journals
of the High Princess Lady Ileana I

NIGHT AFTER NIGHT, LONG AFTER THOSE AT KHALI KEEP HAD retired, Ileana slipped stealthily from the bed she and Cain shared to tiptoe into her sitting room, which lay to one side of their chamber. There, furtively—for she feared that if she were discovered, an attempt would be made to stop her—she lit a single candle and took her few precious, treasured books, her private journals, and her grimoire from the coffer in which they were stored.

These, she studied intently for hours on end, poring over the many pages filled with beautiful illuminations and elaborate handwriting—hers and others'—trying to make some sense of it all. She had been conceived and born of the magic of Gitana san Kovichi, the Ancient One, and given unto the Druswids for some purpose of their own; this, she knew. But there was more—much more—to it than that; there simply had to be! And gradually, as she worked, reading and scribbling copious notes to herself until long after she heard the chapel angelus ringing Lauds, Ileana started, she thought, to see the pieces of the puzzle clearly.

She remembered what she had been taught over the years and what she had read, too, in *The Book of Laws,* one of the many volumes that comprised the extensive collection known as *The Teachings of the Mont Sects.* She could see the first law in her mind even now: *For every force in the universe, there is an equal and opposite force.* Because it would not have been written therein if it were not true, the girl could not dispute the veracity of the statement. It gave her much upon which to reflect.

If she accepted that her joining with Cain had been so vital that the High Priestess Sharai had betrayed her to bring it about, then Ileana could not help but conclude that in some significant way, she and her husband balanced each other so the symmetry of the cosmos was maintained. She felt that somehow this was the key that would unlock all the other secrets she wished to know. But how?

If she, who was called Ileana, had been Chosen by the Light, as her name implied, did Cain, then, belong to the Darkness? Was that why there was within him that place where she feared to look?

Nay, she thought instantly, rejecting the notion.

He was a Druswid, which meant he had passed the Trial of the Light—and not once, but twice. Had he been a minion of the Foul Enslaver, he would not have been able to survive the test of the blinding, burning crystal sphere; he would have been slain by the High Priest Kokudza, who no doubt had wielded the captured ray of the Light. But then, if she were the Light and Cain were not the Darkness, how did he fit in?

The paradox bewildered her, and Ileana decided there must be something she was missing. There was nothing to do but start again, sift more finely with her mind's sieve the pages of her books, journals, and grimoire. She could have wept with despair at the hours wasted; but then, unraveling a tangled skein was seldom easy—nor had she expected it to be. The answers to her questions were there somewhere, buried in the maze of volumes spread open before her —and perhaps in her subconscious as well. She had only to look hard enough to find them.

Somehow, Ileana reflected, they were tied to whatever was happening on the far side of the planet, as well as to her LifePath and Cain's. But how? What was there, lying in wait for the unsuspecting, the unwary, in The Unknown? Was it a giant sea monster, as some had claimed?

She closed her eyes, remembering that summer during her childhood when the body of the old High King Lord Gwalchmei had died and her father, the Lord Balthasar, had been crowned the High King of all Tintagel. They had journeyed to Vikanglia for the coronation, she recalled, and during the voyage, someone had spied a few broken pieces of wood floating on the waves of the Mistral Ocean. The captain of the PT *Mystic Rose* had ordered the sails furled and the anchor weighed so a dinghy could be lowered over the side of the galley to fetch the planks. Once aboard, they'd been soberly examined by the captain, the first mate, and her father, who'd realized the pieces of wood had once been part of a lifeboat belonging to the CV *Far Explorer*, a vessel that had been dispatched to the other half of the world by the continental government of Vikanglia. At this discovery, the planks had been wrapped in an unused length of canvas, taken to the captain's quarters, and locked in his sea chest.

Even now, Ileana could feel the evil that had emanated from the sail-encased pieces of wood, the Power that had leaped to life within her in response to the Darkness she had sensed streaming from the planks. Taken unaware, she had not been able to control the fearsome force, had not even recognized it for what it was. Had she not fallen and struck her head against a capstan, knocking herself unconscious, she would have inadvertently destroyed the ship and

all aboard it with the violent energy that had burst forth
from within her, causing the wind to roar and the sea to
madden.

But before she'd blacked out, Ileana recollected, a blurred
image had taken shape in her mind, a gruesome, macabre
thing like nothing she had ever before seen. Now she
shivered at the thought of it, wondering again, as she had so
many times before, what it had been and why she'd envisioned it.

Had it been a part of the Darkness? Was it still? Was she
somehow to do battle with it in Time Future? She trembled
at the notion. If this were her destiny, indeed, she did not
want to know it.

Since that time, Ileana knew, pieces of other lifeboats had
been found, and strange, twisted skeletons, believed nevertheless to be Kind, had washed up on the shores of the
continents, evidence, the Druswids insisted, that the Darkness had once more awakened to stretch Its hand out over
the slowly rebirthing land and seize it in Its grasp.

The girl shuddered at the idea. If this were true, then Its
Minion Chaos, Its Demon Fear, and the rest of Its corrupt
followers might even now be heading toward the known-
inhabited continents.

But if this were so, would not the Druswids know it?
Would not they have seen such signs of the things to come?

Yea, Ileana thought, *and they would have taken steps to
gird themselves against the Foul Enslaver and those who
serve It, for that is what I would have done had I looked into
the fires and mists and seen such portents.*

But what if the omens had been dreadful, like nothing her
eyes had ever before beheld? she asked herself slowly. What
if they had been but shapes and shadows of Time Future,
ill-defined and unclear, so the form the Darkness would
take could not be determined, only Its strength and power
felt—and that so awesome as to be utterly terrifying—as
the image she had seen aboard the *Mystic Rose* had been?
What would she have done then?

The answer came suddenly to Ileana with startling clarity,
and she knew instinctively that it was true. She would have
performed the Ritual of Choosing to call forth a Defender
of the Light, one who would be vested with the Power of the

Elements, for that was the greatest force one who had been Chosen might wield.

Quickly, she leafed through the papyrus pages of her grimoire to find the description of the ceremony. She had little knowledge of how the rite itself was conducted, for such instructions were handed down from the Ancient Ones only to the High Priest and the High Priestess of the Mont Sects. The two rare and ancient books in which the necessary summonses and spells to cast the ritual were set forth were closely guarded, for if ever they fell into the wrong hands, the results would be catastrophic. The Power invoked by the ceremony was so intense, a novice—or even a lesser-ranked Druswid—would not be able to control it; and one who served the Foul Enslaver would twist and taint the rite, using it to produce an overwhelming, diabolical force. Thus the dark secrets of the ritual must remain a mystery to Ileana. Still, the account contained in her grimoire provided enough information for her purposes, and with that, she was content.

It was extremely difficult to execute, she read, for in order for its magic to succeed, the stars and planets must be favorably aligned in the heavens, a rare circumstance. Further, the officiant must have great power, strength, knowledge, and skill, as the rite was both physically and mentally draining and fraught with peril, the Spirits called forth from the Far Beyond capable of turning on and destroying the one who had summoned them. Thus, conducting the ritual was to be considered only in the most dire of instances, when the Darkness lay upon the land. If such a need arose, it was recommended that the officiant seek to bring forth a male child, as one so Chosen would be physically stronger than his female counterpart, presumably an advantage against the Foul Enslaver.

Slowly, Ileana closed her grimoire, struck by the possibilities the passage now caused her to contemplate. *A male child.* Cain was older than she. Was it logical, given her suspicions, to assume he, too, had been conceived and born of the Ritual of Choosing? Was that why they were inexplicably bound together? Had the Ancient Ones who had performed the ceremonies woven about her and Cain a web of incantations and spells from which they could not escape? Yea, perhaps. But why? Ileana wondered. They were SoulMates. There was no need for them to be drawn together by magic.

But then, she reflected, SoulMates were often reborn centuries and worlds apart, and even when they managed somehow to come together, they did not always recognize each other, for one's physical shell changed with each LifePath. One must search instead for a special look or a certain gesture that stirred one's memory and made one recall the other. Yet she and Cain had both been reborn in the same time and place, and she had seen him in her dreams even before he had come to her in the flesh.

Now Ileana thought this was no peculiar accident of fate, as she had once believed. If Cain, too, had been conceived and born of the Ritual of Choosing, as she surmised, then she had been deliberately—not randomly—Chosen, for the odds of two separate ceremonies eleven years apart producing SoulMates were astronomical. Somehow she had been brought here specifically because she *was* Cain's SoulMate.

The Druswids must have needed SoulMates for their purpose, then. But why? She could think of only one reason: because they had believed the Darkness that was to come would prove so powerful that only two who had once been one could defeat it!

The girl went cold and sick with terror at the revelation. Heaven's Light! What could be so horrible, so vile? She did not know.

She was even more puzzled now, too, by the wariness and suspicion that she sensed Cain felt toward her and that, if she were honest with herself, she must admit she returned. If they were both needed to defend the land against the Foul Enslaver, it did not make sense for this tension to exist between them. Yet exist it did. Why?

For every force in the universe. . . . A significant balance. . . . The symmetry of the cosmos. . . . An equal and opposite force. . . . The Power. . . . The key . . .

What did it mean? What did it mean?

Over and over, the question echoed in Ileana's mind. Then, suddenly, her heart plummeted to her belly, as though the earth had dropped from beneath her feet. Now she knew the answer. Now she recognized the shadow that stood between her and Cain: It was knowledge—knowledge that one of them might forsake the Light and turn to the left hand of the Darkness . . .

Nay! That must not be, for then the Power of the Elements that had been given unto that one by the Ritual of Choosing would be used not for the Light, whence it had come, but *against* the Immortal Guardian and all It had created! Then, unless stopped, that one would ravage all Tintagel! Only the other, who had likewise been conceived and born of the Ritual of Choosing and gifted with the Power of the Elements, would possess a force equal but opposite to its twin. Only each would stand in the other's way.

SoulMates. A balance of power . . .

She cursed them. Oh, how she cursed them, those Ancient Ones, their bodies long since ashes scattered to the elements, those two who had gambled with her LifePath and Cain's by masterminding such a scheme. Yet she could not help but see the wisdom of it and admire their cleverness.

No wonder her husband spoke no word of love to her. He dared not. Loving her might someday prove a fatal weakness, for if ever the Foul Enslaver consumed one of them, each would have to destroy the other!

Ah, that cut like a two-edged sword, Ileana thought with a sinking heart, for now she realized she could not let herself love Cain any more than he could let himself love her, lest she become as vulnerable to him as he would be to her. She might hesitate, then, to do her duty. Even now, memories of what they had shared in Time Past haunted her; and she did not know, if it ever became necessary, whether she would be able to slay the man she had once called beloved, for surely, it was he who would turn to the Darkness! Had she not sensed something deep inside him that frightened her?

Now Ileana realized what a debt she owed the High Priestess Sharai, who had drugged her so she would be willing in Cain's arms that Beltane eve when they had lain together beneath the RingStones. The love she had felt for him in so many LifePaths past had been subjugated by her fear of him. Had she fought him, had she unleashed the force that was hers against him, she would have wakened that which slept within him. And he . . . perhaps he would have crushed her, for his strength and power had been greater than hers then.

O Reverend Mother, I didn't know. I didn't know, Ileana wept silently.

Since then, only some instinct of self-preservation had kept her from pitting herself against Cain, unsure, as she had been, of the outcome. And he . . . what of him? He, too, must be uncertain of triumph, or he would have made some attempt to probe the limits of her abilities.

Cain knew, then, what she had only just now guessed. But if he did, then he must know, as well, that they must recapture the love they had once shared; it was all that would save them. Why, then, did he hesitate? Ileana did not know, any more than she knew how a beast of the Darkness —for surely, that was what it was—had come to be within him or why. For these questions alone, she had found no answers.

Tired, she buried her head in her hands, wishing now that she had never sought to learn what had been concealed from her—and rightfully so.

Before, in her ignorance, no doubt she would have tried to win Cain's love, and perhaps she would have succeeded. Now, the Demon Fear had got its hooks securely in her, and she was afraid. She must conquer her fright, Ileana knew. She must think of the Light, think only of the Light. . . .

A fleeting memory from her childhood stirred within her, a memory of when she had faced for the first time the crystal sphere, blinded and burning alive. An essence had touched hers then, a warm, comforting spirit . . . Cain. It had been Cain, she thought. He cared. Deep down inside, he still cared for her—if only a little. He was not yet a minion of the Foul Enslaver.

An ember of hope flickered to life within her and began to blaze steadily, a tiny flame—but there just the same. Ileana knew now what she must do. She must open her heart to him and somehow rekindle his love for her before it was too late! It was the only way.

Otherwise, they were surely doomed—and all Tintagel with them.

Chapter 18

I dare not let myself love my wife, knowing, as I do, that it may one day prove fatal to me. Yet even so, with each passing day, my resolve to hold myself aloof from her grows harder and harder to maintain. Words I yearn to say to her tumble to my lips, and I must bite my tongue to keep them from spilling out and hurting us both with visions of what cannot be.

What a difficult task has been laid upon me: to spurn she who is my SoulMate and whom, in so many LifePaths past, I have loved. In truth, I have never known a more beautiful woman. Her eyes are like candles on a dark, wintry eve, aglow with a warmth that dispels the gloom. Her smile illuminates her face so it seems as though the Light Itself shines upon her.

Still, it is not just her fair countenance that attracts me, but her inner spirit as well: her wisdom and honor, her compassion and caring, her sense of justice and humor. Already she has won a place in the hearts of those who flock to the Lesser Court—and carved a niche for herself in my own, too, I fear.

If only I could take her in my arms and tell her how I feel! If only I could speak to her of the doubts that plague me, could put right what is wrong between us! But I cannot.

At night, I dream, and in my dreams, I see myself standing at the edge of a deep, dark, yawning chasm. I know that if I do not back away from it, the ground beneath my feet will give way and I will pitch forward into the divide. But still, I cannot seem to move.

From far below, like a lover, Ileana beckons to me, her eyes veiled and mysterious, a smile curving her lips. Against my will, I reach out to her, step toward her, and the earth crumbles beneath me. Then I am falling, falling. . . . But I do not care. I have but one thought in my mind: Will Ileana catch me? Or will she stand by, watching and laughing, while I plunge to my death?

I do not know.

Ah, Heaven's Light, how I wish I knew the answer.

—Thus it is Written—
in
The Private Journals
of the High Prince Lord Cain I

WITH A START, THE LORD CAIN SIN KHALI SUL ARIEL REALIZED guiltily that he had not been attending the discussion taking place in the assembly hall at Ariel Heights, where, a fortnight ago, the High Council had convened for a special session. Covertly, he glanced about the circular chamber to see whether anyone had observed his lack of interest—but no one had. Even Ileana, who sat at his side, had her eyes fixed unwaveringly on the High Minister Radomil, who currently had the floor.

From beneath half-closed lids, Cain studied his wife intently, wondering what she was thinking. Though she hid it well, ever since the scroll-bearing messenger-hawk dispatched by the High King Lord Balthasar's order had arrived at Khali Keep and they had learned of the gathering of the High Council, she had been tense and upset.

But why? Cain wondered. Cygnus was her birthplace, Ariel Heights, the home of her family. And yet she had not wanted to come here, he thought. Indeed, it had seemed almost as though she'd been *afraid* to come here. Why? What did she know that he did not?

Cain's black eyes narrowed speculatively as this question crossed his mind. Abruptly, feeling that whatever was decided at this meeting might prove important to him, he turned his attention to the matter at hand.

"More than a twelvemonth has passed since the brave windjammer known as the *Storm Chaser* departed from the harbor at Astra," the High Minister Radomil was saying, "and since that time, we have received no word as to its fate. Much to my sorrow, I think we now have no choice but to assume that like so many of its unfortunate predecessors, the gallant ship has been lost." The High Minister paused respectfully for a moment to allow the impact of this statement to be absorbed. Then he continued gravely, "It is, therefore, with a heavy heart that I submit we have no alternative but to follow our original plan of sending the second vessel, the *Moon Raker,* in search of its sister.

"My fellow councillors, I do not make this suggestion lightly," Radomil insisted. "No one knows better than I how many valiant crews have set sail from our continents over the past years never to be seen again; and I am well aware we may be condemning yet another to such an uncertain destiny by our decision. But if, as the High Priest Kokudza and the High Priestess Sharai have warned us, the Time of the Prophecy is at hand, if the Darkness has awakened and once more cast Its shadow over the land, I do not see how we can sit idly by and wait for Its malevolent force to crush us! We dare not, lest we become as the Old Ones did during the Time of the Wars of the Kind and the Apocalypse, when the worlds went mad and the Foul Enslaver and Its Demons annihilated almost every single one. We must instead dispatch another craft to The Unknown to discover at all costs exactly what is happening on the far side of our planet. Only when we have some inkling of what we are up against can we begin to make adequate preparations to defend ourselves from whatever is to come!"

"Hear, hear!" several of the listeners concurred, cheering and applauding the High Minister's decisive, invigorating speech.

His words had made a great deal of sense. Though knowledge of the Darkness was as yet confined to the High Council and to those few guild members who, of necessity, had been informed, it was only a matter of time until the common folk, too, learned of the matter. Already they sensed a wrongness in the land and were uneasy. If they were to discover what was amiss, perhaps there would be panic in the streets, as there had been in the Time Before, for at the left hand of the Foul Enslaver sat Its Minion Chaos. If pandemonium ensued, it would take precious days, weeks, perhaps even months to restore order and to build defenses, and by then, it might be too late. Radomil was right. The High Council dared not delay taking action.

"Hear, hear!" the councillors continued to shout, their enthusiastic display shaking the rafters of the assembly hall.

Satisfied he had made his point, the High Minister resumed his place upon the tiered crystal benches that encircled the chamber, and the High Electress Elysabeth, his successor, rose. She waited until the High King Lord Balthasar had indicated his approval of her. Then she walked gracefully to the center of the crystalline floor and held up one hand to silence the noisemakers.

"Most worthy Lords and Ladies," she began, the gleaming gills on the sides of her neck pulsing, a certain sign of emotional agitation in a Loreleish, "good Ministers and Ministresses, I, too, am deeply saddened by the loss of the mighty windjammer *Storm Chaser*, which we all thought so magnificent and so invincible. Its failure to return—or even to contact us by means of one of the messenger-hawks it was carrying—is indeed a terrible blow to us all.

"Nevertheless, I cannot help but agree with my most esteemed superior"—Elysabeth indicated the High Minister Radomil, whom she admired immensely—"for I also am highly concerned about our lack of knowledge in this matter, our desperate need to learn what defenses will prove most effective against the Darkness that threatens us all. As Master Radomil does, I feel that to·do nothing while the Foul Enslaver and Its Demons may even now be marching toward us is the height of folly!

"Therefore, I take great pride in demonstrating my confidence in Master Radomil's proposal by seconding it before the High Council!"

Once more, the assembly hall erupted with a roar.

"Let's put it to a vote!" several of the councillors urged loudly. "Let's put it to a vote!"

Flushed with pride at how well she had carried out her duty, and knowing from the smile of approval on his face how pleased the High Minister Radomil was with her performance, the High Electress took her seat.

"Order!" The High King Lord Balthasar pounded his heavy, ornate gold scepter upon the dais, where his High Throne had been placed earlier. "Order!"

Gradually, at his command, the chamber quieted. But before Balthasar could speak again, the Lady Pualani sin Gingiber, the Queen of Tamarind, a rank she had held for many years, stood slowly, her imperious pose an obvious demand for recognition. Wearily resigned to the fact that despite the call for a vote, there was instead to be further discussion, the High King acknowledged her, and Pualani took the floor.

"My fellow councillors," she intoned in her mellifluous voice, "I do not believe anyone here would champion a cause of wait-and-see when we know the Darkness may soon come upon us. Therefore, I, too, am in agreement with the proposal put forth by Master Radomil and Mistress Elysabeth to send the *Moon Raker* to The Unknown. It is indeed imperative that we discover just what is occurring on the other half of our world. But"—she raised one hand regally, evidence that she was accustomed to giving orders and having them obeyed—"I myself must urge that we proceed with both care and caution in the matter and that we rethink our attitude toward the expedition we are currently contemplating." Pualani paused to let this penetrate, then went on.

"We know from the Records that survived from the Time Before that once there were four more continents on the far side of Tintagel: Montano, Botanica, Aerie, and Verdante. Over the past years, both the planetary and continental governments of the known-inhabited continents have dispatched ships to The Unknown for the purpose of exploring these remaining four continents—if they still exist—and of establishing contact with any tribes that may have escaped annihilation during the Time of the Wars of the Kind and the Apocalypse. Thus, in addition to their crews, these vessels have been staffed with civilian envoys: linguists, anthropologists, botanists, archaeologists, historians, and the like.

"Only in light of the strange—and almost certainly

violent—disappearance without a trace of these crafts do I dare to suggest that perhaps we have been mistaken in peopling them with such peaceful representatives; that perhaps we have been mistaken, as well, in our belief that during the Time of the Rebirth and the Enlightenment, Faith, the Keeper of the Flame, appeared to all those who wielded the Swords of Truth, Righteousness, and Honor against the Darkness in the Time Before—"

At that, a horrendous outburst ensued as, shocked and horrified, those gathered in the assembly hall gasped. The High Priest Kokudza, the High Priestess Sharai, and several of the other councillors leaped angrily to their feet. Strident accusations of blasphemy were hurled through the air; and for one terrible moment, those of the High Council feared they were about to witness the Queen's arrest, as once Master Stiggur, the shipbuilder who had suggested the two windjammers then under consideration be powered by mechanical devices, had been taken into custody.

But Pualani was not a commoner and a mere guild member; she was of the Royal Blood and the supreme, undisputed head of the Royal House of Gingiber. Her green eyes blazing, her breasts heaving, she faced unflinchingly those who would have denounced her.

"Wait!" she thundered, lifting one hand emphatically. "Hear me out! I still have the floor, do I not?" She glanced to Balthasar for confirmation of this, and he nodded curtly. "Very well, then. Let no one try to take it from me, for I promise ye I shall not easily relinquish it! I mean to have my say; and though it be heresy, ye dare not close your eyes and ears to me, for the *Moon Raker* may be our last chance, our only hope of vanquishing the Darkness that threatens us all! Would ye few who are so quick to judge condemn us all to the Foul Enslaver because of your refusal to listen? If that is the case, then by the Blue Moon, I curse ye!" Pualani's cutting words lashed them.

At last, still muttering heatedly to one another, the High Priest Kokudza and the rest sank slowly to their seats, indicating their reluctant willingness to hear the Queen's words. She eyed them all sharply for a long, uncomfortable minute, then continued.

"As I was saying before I was so . . . abruptly interrupted,

I think we must examine the possibility that the Keeper Faith's appearance was not a universal—or even a planetary—event; that perhaps only a few of the Tribes were selected to spread the Word, as only a few persons are Chosen to be blessed with more than the five senses.

"If this is so, then it may be that any tribes on the four remaining continents are unaware of the existence of the Light."

At this, the High Priest Kokudza, the High Priestess Sharai, and several of the councillors again sprang from their seats. But as before, Pualani refused to be quelled. She drew herself up proudly, once more silencing them with a fierce, haughty stare and a sternly upraised hand; and those who would have repudiated her thought better of it. Grumbling to one another, they sat down; and she resumed speaking as though no lapse had occurred.

"In their ignorance, such tribes may still follow the paths of the Old Ones, which led to the disruption of the harmony of the universe in the Time Before, to famine, plague, war, and death. Such tribes may, in fact, be rife with the Darkness.

"If this is the case, then in Time Past, we have sent many good men and women into the very jaws of the Foul Enslaver, unprepared for what they would face, defenseless against whatever they found. This was wrong of us, and we dare not do it again lest we imperil our immortal souls by our actions. If the *Moon Raker* fails, as those ships before it have failed, to come back from The Unknown, there may not be enough time to assemble another expedition to travel to the far side of the planet. Then we, too, shall be crippled by our ignorance of the Darkness, for we will not know what measures to take against It, and thus we will be virtually helpless when It invades our shores—as It surely shall!

"Therefore, I say that we, who have been taught to live in peace, must, in the Name of the Light, put aside our scruples and do whatever is necessary to ensure that the second windjammer survives its journey and safely returns to us. We must see that it is manned with commanders and captains who are trained to lead, to assess situations quickly, and to make snap decisions. We must see that they are followed by warriors who know their duty, who will stand fast in the face of adversity and meet their challengers head on. We must see that the ship is armed with weapons that will stave off attack and be capable of vigorous assault as well. And finally, we must see that it is accompanied by Druswids who can look into Time Future and advise those aboard of the lures and snares of the Foul Enslaver.

"I, the Lady Pualani sin Gingiber, say that if we do not do these things, we need not look for the vessel to come back to us, for surely, it will not!"

With that chilling prediction, the Queen flung her head back arrogantly and marched to her bench, as though daring anyone present to question her right to do so. Nobody did. Instead, those gathered in the assembly hall were still, stunned and appalled by her words but recognizing their wisdom nevertheless.

Surreptitiously, the High Priest Kokudza gazed about the chamber to gauge the expressions on the councillors' faces. A secretive, smug smile curved his lips as he saw that despite their initial opposition to her, most of those present now appeared to be seriously—if somewhat hesitantly —considering Pualani's suggestions.

'Tis just as well I did not press for her arrest, Kokudza thought, *for she was right in pointing out our narrow-mindedness, our refusal to examine ideas contrary to our beliefs. In such a manner did the Old Ones produce the Fanatics and the Terrorists who could not see beyond their noses, so blinded, as they were, by the Demons Fear, Ignorance, Hate, and Prejudice. We dare not allow ourselves to become as they were, more righteous than the Immortal Guardian Itself. That way lies madness. We are not bigots who are too stupid to see that though they preach their sermons in the Name of the Light, in reality, they serve not It, but the Foul Enslaver.*

Though I doubt she knows it, Pualani has done the Druswids quite a favor. I shall have to make a mental note to repay her. Perhaps a copy of some treasured manuscript. . . .

Kokudza's eyes met those of the High Priestess Sharai, and he saw that they both thought as one. He nodded to her, then turned away, pleased they were in agreement.

From the High Throne, the High King Lord Balthasar surveyed the assembly hall. It had been a long two weeks, and he would be glad when this session had ended. He sighed. Thank the heavens, it did not seem as though anyone else wished to speak. Perhaps now he could call for a vote, and the High Council could be dismissed. But even as the thought crossed his mind, Balthasar observed the Lord Tobolsk sin Tovaritch, the King of Iglacia, lumber to his feet, hefting the belt he wore with his gallibiya up around his immense girth. Inwardly, Balthasar groaned; but he motioned for Tobolsk to take the floor anyway, and the King did so.

"Most worthy Lords and Ladies," he addressed his fellow councillors, "good Ministers and Ministresses, I think we can all now perceive the reasons why the Queen Lady Pualani was able to emerge victorious from the Royal Low Games held to determine the successor to Tamarind's Royal Throne. In the face of overwhelming opposition and the threat of arrest as well, she spoke eloquently, with both courage and conviction, and dared not only to remind us of our responsibilities, but to point out to us our flaws and fears. I personally feel she should be applauded—not condemned—and so it is with a great deal of pride that I salute her."

With that, Tobolsk turned and, striking his heart with his right fist, bowed to the Queen, the highest honor one of equal rank could bestow. An appreciative cheer rose from the onlookers, for even if they were not in complete accord with the King, they admired and respected his honesty and spirit. With a gracious nod, Pualani acknowledged his accolade.

Once the applause had died down, Tobolsk spoke again.

"I agree with Master Radomil and Mistress Elysabeth," he declared soberly, "in that we must indeed dispatch the windjammer known as the *Moon Raker* to the far side of Tintagel as soon as possible. But"—he paused and lifted one hand for emphasis—"I also say unto ye that if the ship is not refitted and manned in the manner in which the Queen Lady Pualani has proposed, ye may as well sink it in the harbor at Astra, for it is surely doomed!"

Another quarrelsome debate followed this announcement, but the King was unperturbed. He was used to the outrage and protestations of his own advisers and soldiers at his uttering such bald, provocative statements, and he paid the High Council no more heed than he would have done his own Royal Court.

Like one of the massive polar bears of his homeland, he trudged to his seat, where he motioned for one of the pages to bring him something to eat. After selecting a ripe red apple from the silver bowl of fruit proffered for his inspection, he polished it on the sleeve of his gallibiya, then bit into it lustily, munching contentedly.

"Order!" Balthasar bellowed, glaring about the assembly hall—particularly at Tobolsk—with annoyance. "Order!" Wrathfully, the High King thumped his scepter up and down strenuously upon the dais. "I will have order in this chamber, or I shall bring this session of the High Council to an immediate close," he warned.

Abruptly, with the exception of a few of the bolder councillors, who went on arguing softly with one another, those in the assembly hall fell silent.

The Light be praised! Balthasar thought triumphantly. *Perhaps now I can finally call for a vote!*

But to his dismay, before he could open his mouth, the High Prince Lord Cain, at a subtle signal from the High Priest Kokudza, stood. Curbing his impatience, Balthasar granted Cain the floor, and the High Prince strode to the center of it.

Once he had got his opening remarks out of the way, he chose his words carefully.

"I know some of ye are reluctant to commit yourselves to the plan that has been suggested by the Queen Lady Pualani and endorsed by the King Lord Tobolsk," Cain said, "and with good reason. We know from the Records in our Archives the kind of violence warmongers are capable of inciting." He paused, then went on. "But I do not believe anyone here is guilty of that. I think we all do but seek to defend the Light and our planet.

"My fellow councillors, I say unto ye that this will not be possible unless we are indeed willing to take up our swords and shields!" he asserted firmly.

"Did not the Prophet Joella warn: 'For everything the Immortal Guardian created, there is a purpose, thus were the Swords of Truth, Righteousness, and Honor given unto the Kind to wield against the Darkness.'? Yea, for it is so written in *The Word and The Way.*

"Did not the Immortal Guardian Itself smite the planets during the Time of the Cataclysms, when the Darkness lay upon the land? Did not the Light Itself bid Ishtar, the Keeper of the Stars, to slash her powerful sword across the heavens so they would rain fire upon the worlds? Did not It bid Ōkeanos, the Keeper of the Seas, to cast his massive trident into the oceans so they would overflow their boundaries and flood the land? Did not It bid Ceridwen, the Keeper of the Earth, to swing her mighty sickle over the land so it would divide and upheave? And did not It bid Vāti, the Keeper of the Winds, to blow his breath through his great horn so the air would sweep away all before it? Yea.

"And why did the Immortal Guardian do all this, I ask ye? So there would no hiding place for the Foul Enslaver and Its Minions upon that which the Light created!" Cain's voice rang out authoritatively through the assembly hall.

"Can we, who are Its image, do any less than the Being who gifted us with Its immortal essence? Nay, I think not.

"My fellow councillors, the Queen Lady Pualani has called for commanders, warriors, and Druswids to be aboard the *Moon Raker* when it sets sail for The Unknown. I submit to ye that I am a proven leader, trained in the arts of battle, and a twelfth-ranked priest besides. Therefore, I offer the High Council my services and ask to be appointed head of the forthcoming expedition."

Yet another disruptive diatribe greeted this request.

"Nay!" the Lord Faolan sin Lothian, the King of Vikanglia, exclaimed above the clamor, jumping up from his bench. "Why, the very idea is unthinkable!"

"Do ye dare to suggest, Lord"—the Lady Nenet sin Khali, the Queen of Bedoui, bolted to her feet in response, shaking with rage, her black eyes shooting sparks—"that a member of the Royal House of Khali should shrink from his bounden duty?"

"Nay, nay, I—I meant no such insult." Faolan swallowed hard, for Nenet's temper was infamous. "'Tis only that . . . er . . . well, we have already lost the Lord Yhudhah to the wasting sickness, Lady. Do ye—do ye . . . er . . . think it wise that the Lord Cain risk journeying to the other half of the world? After all, he *is* the High Prince. Dare we chance losing him, too?"

"Ye shall find no one qualified to take his place," the High Priest Kokudza averred, rising and gripping the crystal rail before him tightly in an effort to restrain the Power that was surging through his body.

"Nor none better than I to follow him." Ileana spoke for the first time as, at the High Priestess Sharai's barely discernible nod, she moved to stand at Cain's side. "I also am accustomed to dealing with difficulties, and I am a seventh-ranked priestess as well. If my husband chooses to travel to the far side of Tintagel, I shall go with him."

"Lady, I protest." The Lord Xenos sin Ariel, the King of Cygnus, rejected the notion stoutly. "Ye are the High Princess. 'Tis bad enough to hazard the High Prince's life in such a reckless manner. We dare not gamble with yours, too!"

"And why not?" Ileana asked tersely. "If the Lord Cain does not return from The Unknown, then I will no longer be the High Princess in any event." She shrugged. "What will my fate matter then?"

"The Lady Ileana does have a point," the Lord Lionel sin Morgant, the King of Lorelei, noted logically. "I say we should let them both go if that is what they want. If they don't come back, we're probably all doomed anyway!"

This glum remark provoked yet another outcry, and the chamber once more disintegrated into chaos.

This time, after the High King Lord Balthasar had managed to reestablish order, he did not wait for anyone else to stand, seeking the floor, but called immediately for a vote. The list of councillors was read aloud by one of the heralds, and each member of the High Council responded either yea or nay. In the end, the majority ruled that as soon as the *Moon Raker* had been refitted and manned in accordance with the Queen Lady Pualani's suggestions, the windjammer would be dispatched to the other half of the world. Cain and Ileana were to be in charge of the expedition.

"This is madness!" the Lord Xenos expostulated upon hearing the decision. "Indeed, the Darkness is already upon us! To send both the High Prince and the High Princess to the far side of Tintagel, not knowing whether or not they will return—"

"One of us shall come back, Lord, I promise ye," Ileana vowed fervently. "One way or another, one of us shall come back."

Cain, startled by the words, glanced at his wife sharply, wondering how she could make such a statement.

And then he knew.

She knew! he thought suddenly, his eyes narrowing with suspicion. *That is why she did not want to come here! She knew we would be chosen to journey to The Unknown, while I, who am a twelfth-ranked priest, had no inkling of it! What else has she seen in the fires and mists that I have not? What makes her so certain one of us will return? And which one of us does she believe it will be? Herself? Yea, else she would not have volunteered to go. Ah, Ileana, ye whom I once called beloved, is what I have seen in my dreams true then? Shall ye seek to destroy me after all?*

At the thought, without warning, something dark and hideous that lay deep inside Cain stirred, like a somnolent, fiery beast, disturbed but not fully roused from slumber, that had raised its horned head and flicked its spiny tail, sending a terrible shudder down his spine. It was like nothing he had ever felt before; it racked his entire body, twisting his insides into knots. In response, the Power sprang so fiercely to life within him, it was all he could do to control it, to keep it from bursting forth and wreaking havoc upon the assembly hall.

The High Priest Kokudza, the High Priestess Sharai, and Ileana, sensing the energy he forcibly suppressed, stared at him, aghast. The girl trembled uncontrollably as she gazed into her husband's eyes. For one nightmarish instant, it was as though the Darkness Itself looked back at her slyly.

"Cain," she whispered, stricken. "Oh, Cain . . ."

She would have stretched out one hand to touch him, but he jerked away from her as though she had stabbed him, sick comprehension and horror etched on his face.

Ah, Ileana, beloved, I can see your heart in your eyes. Heaven's Light! What a fool I have been! Ye sense the Darkness within me, and still ye reach out to me. Ye care. Ye still care.

But she must not, Cain realized suddenly with a sinking heart. The Darkness had but stirred within him, and he had felt Its awesome strength and power—greater, perhaps, than his own. If ever It awakened, It would coil about him like a serpent strangling Its prey; and if he fought It and lost, It would swallow him whole. It would not be Ileana, then, who destroyed him, but he her! And she, loving him, might hesitate to defend herself against him!

Ah, beloved, for your own sake, I must teach ye to hate me, body, mind, and soul, as I must learn to hate ye, lest my love for ye somehow be used by the Foul Enslaver and Its Demons to deceive and destroy ye. . . .

"This special session of the High Council is at an end," the High King Lord Balthasar announced, banging his scepter down peremptorily upon the dais and exhaling a sigh of relief. "Go with the Light."

Neither Cain nor Ileana heard the words. He was already striding toward the doors of the assembly hall, and she —she just sat there, her heart slowly shattering within her.

THREE-QUARTER MOON

The Darkness

Chapter 19

PSALM EIGHTY-THREE
Against the Enemies of Tintagel

O Immortal Guardian, do not remain silent;
Do not be unmoved, O Light, or unresponsive!
See how your enemies are stirring;
See how those who hate ye rear their horned heads,
Weaving a plot against your people.

Conspiring against those ye protect, they say,
"Come, we will finish them as a world;
The name of Tintagel shall be forgotten!"

Unanimous in their plot,
They seal a treaty against ye:
The lairs of Fear, Ignorance, and Prejudice,
Hate, Greed, and Apathy,
Rage, Sloth, and Jealousy,
Vanity and Lust;
And now unnatural Gluttony has joined them,
To reinforce the Minions of the Foul Enslaver.

Treat them like Bohdan and Márek,
Like Sipâtu at the River Orchid;
Wiped out at Jerusha,
They served to dung the ground.

237

Treat their commanders like Hádiya and Dukker,
Their captains like Ódinum and Zoheret,
Those who once said, "Let us take for ourselves
Possession of the cloisters of the Light!"

O Immortal Guardian, bowl them along like
    tumbleweeds,
Like chaff at the mercy of the wind;
As fire devours the forest,
As flame licks up the mountains,
Drive them on with your khamsin;
Rout them with your maelstrom;
Cover their scaly faces with shame,
Until they seek your name, O Light.

Famine and plague be always theirs,
War and death; and let them know this:
Ye alone bear the name the Light,
Immortal Guardian of all things Ceaseless and
    Universal.

—Thus it is Written—
in
The Word and The Way
The Book of Prayers, Psalm Eighty-Three

The Zephyr Ocean, Tintagel, 7271.9.34

THE DARKNESS WAS GROWING STRONGER NOW. THE LORD
Jaroslav sin Tovaritch could feel It dimming the Light in his
soul, eating away the brightness that had once been his.

Soon. Soon it would be over and he would be gone like the
others, all two hundred and forty-nine of those who had
been aboard the *Storm Chaser*, which had been attacked
and sunk off the coast of the continent of Aerie. Only a few
dozen had managed to make it to shore; only seven had
escaped the fate that had awaited them on the other half of
the world. But even they had been too late. The Foul
Enslaver and Its Demons had already been among
them. . . .

With excruciating effort, Jaroslav glanced down at himself, seeing through the strange red film that covered his swollen eyes the hideous remains of his body, now pathetically wasted and almost totally paralyzed. He was not afraid. He had seen it happen before—at close range—to the other six.

How long had the boat been drifting upon the waves, its single sail battered to shreds by the elements, its mast broken in two, its oars ripped from their locks and washed overboard? He didn't know. He had lost track of time. It didn't matter. His body was going to die anyway.

There had been food enough. Jaroslav's mouth twisted in a grim caricature of a smile at the thought, for it filled him with loathing and repugnance to remember what he and the rest had eaten. And there had been fresh water, too, for it had rained now and then, and they had caught in a bucket what droplets they could. But there had been nothing they could do about the brilliance of the daylight and the searing intensity of the summer heat, just now cooling with the first chill of autumn. They had not known what would happen to them; they had not been prepared for it. And so, in the end, the sun, Sorcha, watched over by Ishtar, the Keeper of the Stars, had finished them—one by one. He, Jaroslav, was the last.

He would be glad when he died. He was an Iglacian, and the Iglacians were a proud race, too proud to survive as what he had become.

Still, there was one last thing he must do before death claimed him: He must destroy the small, crude dinghy he and the others had fashioned to make good their escape from the far side of Tintagel. Only then would the known-inhabited continents of his people be safe. If he failed— Nay, he would not think of that. Doubt was fatal. It opened the mind to the Demon Fear, who ate away the courage in one's soul. To be a man who lacked bravery was a shame no Iglacian would bear.

The thought gave Jaroslav strength. He struggled valiantly to rise, to reach the horn cup that had once belonged to the Lady Amalasand sin Lothian, whom he had once loved. He had tried to take it from her before, knowing it was their only hope. But suspecting what he'd intended, she had held on to it fiercely, fighting him tooth and nail for possession of it; and too sickened and disheartened by the sight of what she, who had once been so beautiful, had become, Jaroslav had not pressed her for it. Amalasand would have killed him rather than let him wrest it from her. Only now that she was gone was there a chance for him to make use of it.

Like a precious jewel, the cup lured him, the curved, polished horn of which it had been carved gleaming with a soft, burnished glow, the delicate blown glass set into its generous mouth reflecting the sun's rays like the Crystal Mountains of his homeland. If only he could get his hands on it! He could use the glass to bend the sun and set the wooden craft on fire.

Slowly, tortuously, his fingers leaving a trail of blood behind him, Jaroslav began to pull himself along the plank bench against which he'd been uncomfortably sprawled, having previously lacked the will or energy to move. A sudden wave caught the bobbing boat, heaving it up from the waves. He was thrown off balance; his shoulder slammed agonizingly into one rough side of the dinghy. Splinters gouged his skin; but though he would have given much to be able to feel them, Jaroslav did not. That was impossible now. As the crest peaked and the craft lurched downward, he was painfully tossed about again. This time, he rolled across the bottom of the boat, striking his head against one of the slabs of teak that served as seats. Jaroslav crumpled to the floor, his body, aching horribly, lying some distance from his goal.

He groaned faintly, knowing the Darkness was watching him, laughing at his futile attempts at movement, eagerly awaiting the death of the physical shell It had once thought to distort and to warp to Its command.

Think of the Light! Jaroslav warned himself sharply. *Think only of the Light, or the Foul Enslaver will know what ye mean to do and It will tighten Its grip on ye before ye can succeed. . . .*

Determined, he gritted his teeth against the pain and, deliberately, painfully, started to haul himself forward once more with his left arm. The appendage was withered and weak from the creeping disability by which he had been beset. Desperately, Jaroslav prayed the limb would not go completely numb, as his right one had done some time ago, before he reached the horn cup. For that was the harbinger of death—the palsy in the left arm. Seconds after the appendage became incapacitated, his heart would burst; his chest would explode—

Don't think about it! Think only of the Light!

The Darkness tittered in his ear, a terrible, mirthless hissing sound. Inwardly, Jaroslav shuddered, forcing himself to ignore the macabre chuckling. With difficulty, he focused his misted red eyes on the horn cup. There wasn't much time left, and he was the last hope of the dinghy's destruction. The six before him had failed: Amalasand, Thanasis, Liliha, and the others. The Foul Enslaver had crushed them in Its fist, and they had not known how to fight It, how to free themselves from Its cruel grasp. Their world had not prepared them for such a monstrosity. They had been shocked by Its evil, driven mad by Its horror. Even now, Jaroslav could feel the final remnants of his ragged sanity unraveling at their tattered edges. He could feel the Darkness swirling up to engulf him—

Don't think about it! Think only of the Light!

He gasped for air. Sweat beaded his brow, then trickled down into his eyes, blinding him. Frenzied, heedless of his spattering blood, he clawed at the bottom of the craft, dementedly dragging his paralyzed bulk forward. From sly, crazed eyes, the Foul Enslaver watched him with grudging admiration. Jaroslav had lasted a long time, far longer than the rest. And he had been clever, emptying his mind of its chaotic thoughts, willing it into blankness, filling it with the Light. But the embryo of the Darkness within him was strong, too—and growing steadily more powerful, despite the waning of his body.

Spurred on by his torment, Jaroslav shifted himself inch by inch toward his goal. The tips of his fingers just brushed the glass rim of the horn cup.

Without warning, his left arm went numb. He gasped once more, then choked violently as a seizure shook his entire body. His heart beat sickeningly in his breast, pounding harder and harder, as though it would burst.

Somehow, with the sheer tenacity of his will, Jaroslav forced himself to breathe slowly and deeply, to concentrate on retarding the vital organ's frantic pace. Gradually, to his great relief, the furious thrumming of his heart lessened and his nerves ceased to race.

Thank ye, O Light, he sent a mental prayer to the Immortal Guardian before, mercifully, he sank into oblivion, the horn cup lying just beyond his reach, forlorn and forgotten.

The Foul Enslaver smiled with wicked glee. Jaroslav was indeed a worthy foe. Somehow he had managed to survive what the other six had not. Perhaps there was hope for him yet.

At the thought, the Darkness giggled to Itself victoriously, then fell silent.

Chapter 20

I am beyond ecstasy! In truth, with the exception of being named a mistress shipbuilder, nothing so exciting has ever happened to me in this LifePath. I can scarcely believe I am really here aboard the Moon Raker, which I designed! Sometimes, I have to pinch myself to be certain that I am not dreaming, that I will not presently awaken and find myself still in my bed in my small cell at Spindrift Hall.

Imagine me, Mistress Halcyone set Astra, a common, Houseless bastard, being singled out for such attention!

My every wildest fantasy, the ones for which I'd often mocked myself in Time Past, had already come true the day GuildMaster Demothi had summoned me to appear before the High Council, and the councillors had voted to construct the ships whose plans I'd drawn up. Of course, I'd known I would achieve the rank of mistress for that. Even old HallMaster Erasmios, the head of Spindrift Hall, could not dare to blackball me after that—as he had so often in Time Past. And I'd been so thrilled and overjoyed at my success, I'd thought myself at the height of my glory. I never dreamed it would prove but the beginning of my upward climb.

I must admit I was frightened initially when I received the message from the High Princess Lady Ileana, requesting my presence at Ariel Heights. It is rumored she is a powerful sorceress, and at first, I was afraid she had somehow discovered how it was that I had come to conceive the idea for the windjammers.

Naturally, I never told anyone the truth about that, for I would surely have been arrested and confined to solitary, where I would have been forced to undergo extensive counseling to redirect my misguided spirit. That, I felt, was unnecessary, for I cannot help but think some of the laws laid down by the Druswids and the High Council are just the slightest bit silly.

After all, what harm did I do by my actions? None that I can see. The councillors got their vessels, didn't they? And I got my rank. A pretty good deal for all concerned, if I do say so myself.

So what was the big crime if I found something that, in Time Past, had belonged to the Old Ones, and I didn't report it? It wasn't as though it were an infernal machine or anything. It was only a bottle—the likes of which I'd never seen before, to be sure—but just a bottle all the same.

I don't know how it ever survived the Time of the Wars of the Kind and the Apocalypse intact, but somehow it did. I found it by sheerest chance one day, half buried in the earth outside the city walls of Astra. I don't know why no one ever discovered it before I did. I like to think it was because Ōkeanos, the Keeper of the Seas, meant it for me.

At any rate, it was a beautiful glass bottle mounted on an elegant wooden base. Inside was a model ship. I don't know how the vessel ever got in there, for the mouth of the bottle was no bigger than a nykel, and the craft filled the whole of the bottle's insides.

It was a magnificent ship! I'd never seen the like, but the moment I saw it, I knew how strong and swift it must have been. There was a brass plaque attached to the base that said: Shooting Star, and then the date. Beneath that, it read: The greatest windjammer ever to sail the seas.

I knew at once that I could re-create it, but I was afraid to copy it sail for sail and line for line, for HallMaster Erasmios—who, even if it wasn't the Way,

*never did like me because I was a Houseless bastard
with no family to enrich Spindrift Hall's coffers—was
bound to be suspicious of how I had managed to come
up with such a design. So I made it smaller and took
out one of the masts and initiated some other changes,
too, for I'll admit I didn't quite understand how
everything on the vessel in the bottle operated. I hated
to smash the glass and take the ship inside apart, for I
was afraid I wouldn't be able to put it back together
again, and certainly, I knew there was no way I could
get it into another bottle.*

*Still, I was fairly sure my reconstruction of it, even
though it was crude and not quite accurate, would work
all the same—and so was HallMaster Erasmios when
he saw my sketches and my own model, which I'd built
to help demonstrate them. Oh, he sniffed and stuck his
nose up in the air and said my windjammer (I kept the
name on the brass plaque; after all, who would know
where the word had come from?) would no doubt prove
highly impractical. But he couldn't wait to show it to
GuildMaster Demothi anyway, which, in the end, was
how I came to the attention of the High Princess Lady
Ileana.*

*As I said before, her note scared me stiff, for I
thought she'd somehow found out about the Old Ones'
bottle with the vessel inside and meant to interrogate
me herself before turning me over to the Common
High Guard.*

*But instead, she said that she'd had a vision in which
she'd seen me standing beside her on the deck of the
Moon Raker, journeying to the far side of Tintagel,
and that I should get my affairs in order so I could
accompany the windjammer when it set sail for The
Unknown.*

*At first, I almost wished she had called the Guard
and had me taken into custody, for I didn't relish the
thought of venturing to the other half of the world,
particularly when so many before me had never returned from it. But then I reckoned that if the High
Princess Lady Ileana were as powerful a sorceress as
some claimed, she wouldn't be going herself if she*

*hadn't foreseen she'd be coming back; and I figured
that since it had been me she'd dreamed of standing
alongside her, I had a good chance of making it home,
too. Besides, I could hardly refuse to obey her, even
though she'd made her command seem like a request.*

*And so that was how I, a common, Houseless bas-
tard, came to be aboard the* Moon Raker, *looking
forward to finding fame and fortune on the far side of
the planet and entertaining aspirations way above my
station in this LifePath.*

—Thus it is Written—
in
The Private Journals
of the Shipbuilder Halcyone set Astra

"NAY, YE DAMNED FOOLS, FURL THE MAINSAIL FIRST!" HALCY-
one yelled through her cupped hands above the roar of the
wind and the sea. *"Then* take in the flying jib, the topgall-
ants, and the topgallant staysails! By the moons! Captain!"
She turned desperately to Captain Zesiro, who was in
charge of the *Moon Raker's* crew. "If they don't get the
bloody mainsail down, we're liable to be driven straight
underwater to the bottom of the ocean!"

"For the Light's sake! Do as she says!" he hollered, seeing
that the situation was critical. "She designed the damned
ship, didn't she?"

Though they had been at sea for several long weeks now,
the crew was still as yet barely accustomed to the names of
all the sails, much less how they functioned. Nevertheless,
to Halcyone's vast relief, the bewildered sailors at last
hurriedly scrambled toward the mainmast to grapple with
the lines that would furl the proper canvas; and within
moments, the wildly pitching vessel had regained a portion
of its equilibrium.

The tempest that held them in its throes had descended
upon them suddenly, taking them, for the most part,
unaware. They'd been sailing blind, relying only on the
windjammer's compass for direction, for the day had
started off dark and dreary and a low, thick mist had lain
over the ocean, obscuring their view. Though Captain

Zesiro had suggested they weigh anchor and wait for the fog to lift, the commander of the expedition, the High Prince Lord Cain, had insisted on pressing on.

Their supplies, he'd said, were limited. Who knew when they would reach land to obtain more? A wasted day might prove fatal later on.

Worriedly shaking his head and eyeing Cain thoughtfully, the captain had reluctantly ordered the crew to assume their posts and carry out their duties.

By late morning, it had begun to drizzle and a gust had arisen, causing the haze to shift intermittently so it had seemed as though a flotilla of ghosts had sailed about the ship, their moans soughing plaintively with each breath of air. It had been only the wind, of course, and the creaking of the masts and spars, but it had been enough to make the crew star themselves for protection and mutter soft prayers to Ōkeanos, the Keeper of the Seas.

Still, nothing worse had occurred, and Captain Zesiro had exhaled a sigh of relief, thinking perhaps they would soon be free of the clinging damp.

Instead, like a snake striking, the storm had fallen upon them, the bloated heavens opening abruptly to spew forth their contents, the gale descending upon them with a thunderous cry, as though to sweep them from its path.

Now the captain estimated the speed of the wind was fifty knots or more, and the waves of the maddened ocean were so high, they were crashing over the rails of the windjammer to swamp its top deck. The sailors were nearly waist deep in water and clutching the lifelines fiercely as they staggered beneath the cruel lash of the squall that whipped them unmercifully.

Only the commander of the expedition, Cain, appeared unmoved by the torrent that pelted them savagely. As a great fist of lightning spread its fingers across the darkened firmament, the captain could see him standing upon the forecastle, gripping the rail tightly and staring off into the distance.

"Bloody priest!" Captain Zesiro swore.

He had never liked the idea of having Druswids aboard a vessel. They made the crew, who were generally plain common folk, nervous; and any unusual incident was viewed with mistrust, for no one knew for sure what powers those belonging to the Mont Sects possessed—or how they might employ them. Even now, the captain half suspected Cain of having somehow brought about the maelstrom with which they'd been afflicted—but for what purpose, he could not fathom. He would have been very surprised to learn that Ileana, watching Cain from where she stood upon the top deck, harbored the same doubts and suspicions.

Ever since they'd set sail from the city of Astra, Cain had grown increasingly more brooding and silent, until it had seemed as though he were a complete stranger to her. Now, as she gazed at him, it did not seem possible that he was her SoulMate, that she had loved him in Time Past—and loved him still.

He was dressed in an aba of unrelieved black, whose wet folds flapped about him wildly in the wind, making him appear like an ominous bird of prey. His shaggy ebony hair was streaming back from his dark, hawklike visage, and his eyes were locked on the far western horizon, as though he could see it clearly through the blinding rain. Well, he was a twelfth-ranked priest, so perhaps he could.

What did he see? Ileana wondered. She had no answer to her question. He kept his thoughts shielded from her as closely as she guarded hers from him.

He seemed not to feel the brutal downpour, the chilling sting of each gust, or the violent heaving of the *Moon Raker* upon the turbulent, whitecapped waves.

Holding on to one of the lifelines securely, her head bent against the buffeting gale, Ileana began to make her way slowly toward her husband, gasping with shock as she was drenched by yet another cold, foamy crest breaking over the starboard rail of the windjammer.

"Furl the upper topsails!" she heard Halcyone shriek above the cacophony and confusion. "And drop the outer jib!"

Thank the Light that I saw her in my dreams, Ileana thought, *and insisted on her accompanying us, for we would surely have been lost without her! Perhaps this is what happened to the* Storm Chaser. *Mayhap it encountered just such a squall, and its frightened crew didn't have enough experience to strike the canvas in the proper order. At least we have a chance of surviving. I shudder to think what our fate would have been had we been aboard a mere galley. No doubt we would already have capsized. . . .*

Ileana stumbled on, hauling herself forward inch by inch along the lifeline, feeling the water churn around her, as though it meant to grab hold of her and hurl her overboard. High above her, she could see sailors clinging desperately to the rigging as they attempted to free snagged canvas and rope so Halcyone's orders could be carried out. Ileana thought the crew members must be out of their minds. She didn't know how they were managing to hang on, for surely, their hands must be even more numb than hers, and she could barely maintain her grip on the lifeline.

The ship beat to windward, its headway scant as it reared and bucked upon the roiling sea. Lightning flashed, its crackling shards splitting the slate-grey heavens so they looked like a mirror shattering. Moments later, thunder clapped, as though Ishtar, the Keeper of the Stars, had struck her mighty sword against a massive shield. The rain ravaged the vessel; the wind pillaged the sails, making them flog uncontrollably. Some were already tattered shreds. But still, somehow, the masts stood firm.

With one hand, Ileana pushed her sodden hair from her face and tried to wipe the streaming water from her eyes. But it was useless. Sheer instinct kept her going in the right direction.

"Lady!" Captain Zesiro shouted, stricken, as he spied her. "What are ye doing here? Ye must get below to your cabin at once!"

"Nay." She shook her head. "I must reach my husband!" She pointed to Cain.

Then, before the captain, who would doubtless feel duty-bound to stop her, could do so, she pressed on. At last, she stood before the ladder leading up to the forecastle. Determinedly, she began to climb, praying she would not be washed away by a wave in the process. When, finally, she had gained the top, she made her way to Cain's side and laid one hand upon his arm.

"Cain!" Ileana called in his ear. "Cain!" He turned to her then, his face hidden in the shadows. "Are ye mad that ye dare to challenge the Power of the Elements? Come away

249

before the sea claims ye! We've got to get below to our quarters!"

Just then, an eerie light shot out from the foremast to dance along the rigging. The green fire illuminated Cain's countenance clearly, causing Ileana to gasp involuntarily and recoil from him in horror. His eyes were glazed over and veined with red; narrowed to slits, they raked her slyly, as though the Darkness Itself peered out at her. His lips were twisted in a grim caricature of a smile that frightened her beyond measure; and his hands, when he reached for her, seemed like talons, his fingers curled, his nails sharp as claws in the turbid light.

The fiery beast within him is stirring, she thought. *Perhaps, even now, it has come fully awake.*

She shivered as he touched her. But to her relief, he did nothing further; it was as though he were tranced, watching her but not wholly cognizant of her presence. Warily, carefully, she forced herself to give him a gentle shake.

"Cain." She spoke again. "Cain."

A few moments later, whatever had looked out at her from her husband's eyes was gone and he was once more himself.

"Ileana," he said, startled. For the first time, he seemed to become aware of the horrendous storm and of the fact that he was soaked to the skin. "I—I—" He broke off abruptly and shook his head as though to clear it. "Why aren't ye below?" he asked sharply. "Come. I'll help ye to the cabin."

They had managed to clamber down the forecastle ladder and grope their way across a portion of the top deck when one of the sailors working frantically to untangle the canvas and rope suddenly lost his footing on the rigging and fell. With a loud scream, he splashed into the high water swirling over the deck, and as the vessel rocked crazily from the impact of yet another giant wave, he was swept overboard. There was nothing anyone could do to rescue him. All were too intent on saving themselves.

The wind was now blowing at a speed greater than sixty knots. Captain Zesiro had lashed himself tightly to the ship's wheel, and under Halcyone's shrill directions, the large foresail and the inner jib were being furled. Hastily, the two crew members still in the rigging finished cutting through the snarled canvas and rope, and the heavy, wet mainsail the sailors had been struggling to free came crashing down, narrowly missing Cain and Ileana.

He caught her wrist with one hand, dragging her behind him as he pulled himself along one of the lifelines toward the hatch leading to the lower decks. She was grateful for his sheer physical strength, which alone enabled them to triumph over the elements to reach their quarters.

Just as they achieved their goal, they heard a loud cracking noise sound above the brutal tattoo of the rain and the whining of the wind, followed by the deafening impact of splintering wood.

"By the Blue Moon!" Cain cursed. "One of the bloody masts has gone!" He opened the door to their cabin and roughly thrust Ileana inside. "The Foul Enslaver Itself couldn't have conjured a worse storm. We'll all be lucky if we don't drown! How came ye to be up on deck like that, endangering yourself? Where is Sir Husein?"

"Assisting the crew. I gave him permission to do so, for every hand was needed. Indeed, we ought to be up there now, I guess—"

"Nay. There's nothing anyone can do now but ride out this tempest and hope the weather clears before we're all consigned to the bottom of the ocean," Cain declared firmly. "Get out of those clothes, Ileana; they're sopping wet. Then get into the bunk. You'll be warmer and safer there. I dare not light the brazier; the way we're bouncing about, the coal's liable to fly out and set the ship on fire. Well, what are ye waiting for? Do as I told ye!"

Setting her teeth to keep them from chattering, the girl hastily undressed, then climbed into the bed. Drawing the covers up around her to take some of the chill from her body, she studied Cain intently in the dark grey light that filtered dimly through the lead-glass lozenge panes of the cabin's unshuttered windows. Briefly, she remembered her earlier suspicion that her husband had somehow invoked the sudden squall, and she wondered if he meant to drown them all. Then, somewhat ashamed, she recognized that the thought was unjust. There was no way he could have called forth his power without her realizing it.

Even now, she could sense the internal struggle taking

place within him as he fought to hold the Darkness at bay. Lightning flared; thunder boomed. The rain beat ominously against the windows, and the wind screeched an unKind cry. The sea swelled and dipped sickeningly, wreaking havoc upon the ship that battled so valiantly, timbers groaning as it fought to hold itself together and stay afloat. In determined counterpoint to the violent melody of the storm, Cain's power surged and eddied within him, sparring with the beast of the Foul Enslaver that lay coiled in the darkest chasms of his soul, now and then rousing itself to rear its horned head or flick its spiny tail.

How long could he hold out against it? Ileana wondered. Twice now she had seen it staring out at her through his eyes. Would there come a day when the beast prevailed and Cain himself no longer returned to her? She shivered at the thought. Now she realized more clearly than ever that she must do whatever she could to bind him fast to her so he would not be defeated by the Darkness.

Slowly, Ileana laid one hand upon his chest and rested her head on his broad shoulder.

"Lord, for all that I am a priestess, I do not know if we shall see another tomorrow in this LifePath," she whispered. "I do not want this body I now inhabit to die without knowing your touch one last time. All that we ever shared in Time Past, I would find again this eve and hold on to it till morning—or death—comes. Take me in your arms, Cain. Please. Love me as though I will never feel ye beside me and within me again. For all that we've ever been to each other—then and now—do this for me . . . beloved."

Tears stung Cain's eyes at her words, and with difficulty, he choked down the lump that had risen in his throat. How could he ever have doubted her? How could he ever have thought for even one second that she would seek to destroy him? She had seen the Foul Enslaver in his eyes, and still, she had not turned away from him.

How had It come to be within him, Cain wondered, the Darkness that even now fed upon him slowly, inexorably? He was a Druswid, a Defender of the Light. He would not willingly be turned to Its antithesis.

By the moons! he wanted to shout. *Am I not to be given a choice after all, then?*

He did not know. He could only trust in Brother Ottah's words to him that night so long ago in the Hallowed Hall of Mont Saint Christopher. Now they echoed in his mind, along with so many others.

She is called Ileana. Do ye know its meaning, sirrah?

Yea. It means "Chosen by the Light."

Think about that, and remember what ye have been taught.

CAIN/'kan/ n [Bd Qayin, fr. OBd Qanah]: "One who is given a choice. . . ."

Do this for me . . . beloved.

Slowly, Cain drew Ileana into his embrace and closed his eyes. This one time, he thought, he would let himself love her as he so yearned to do; and he would remember it, no matter what became of him in Time Future, no matter if, as he feared, the Foul Enslaver proved stronger and more powerful than he.

"I love ye, Ileana . . . Chimene . . . Raizel . . . and all the other names I have ever called ye in Time Past," he murmured. "But I will not make love with ye as though it were the last time, a time of joy and sadness and memories that belong to the winter of one's years. Instead, I shall love ye as a young man loves in the spring of his first LifePath, when all is new and tender and sweet, as yet untouched by the pain and shadows that scar one's soul, as a patina mars old pewter, leaving it more beautiful with age. Let us pretend, then, that this is only the beginning for us, that we have all the time in this world—and the next—to grow old together and to learn those things that, when they are gone, linger on in our memories, now and always, forever cherished in the heart."

Gently, with one hand, Cain tilted her face up to his. His breath brushed her lips lightly, an exquisite prelude to their lovemaking that made Ileana inhale sharply, as though she were taking into herself the Breath of Life that was his, warm and vibrant and filled with the essence of him, before his mouth closed over hers tenderly in the blackness of the night that now saturated the cabin.

In the beginning, it was a tentative kiss, filled with longing and expectancy; and it was as he had said, as though they were eager young lovers coming together for the first time, discovering slowly and with delight the pleasures that awaited them.

He kissed her as a butterfly does a flower, softly, quickly, his lips touching hers like the fluttering of gossamer wings before coming to light and stilling, his tongue darting forth to probe the nectar of her mouth. Deeply, he tasted her; and it was as though time had ceased, as though they had no past, no future, only this moment, bittersweet.

As though he were blind and seeing her with his hands for the first time, Cain caressed Ileana's face. His fingertips swept across her silken eyebrows, traced the hollows of her delicate lids, and brushed her feathery lashes. His palms stroked the planes and angles of her velvet countenance. His thumbs followed the outline of her trembling lips before he kissed them again, and then again, his tongue once more parting her pliant, yielding mouth to explore the softness within. Every moist, concealed crevice opened to him invitingly; her tongue grazed the edge of his, making Cain quiver like a taut leather bowstring. Deliberately, he captured her tongue with his so they intertwined in a tangle of passion before he withdrew, his lips trailing kisses across the slant of her cheek to her temple.

There, he buried his dark visage in the damp silver strands of Ileana's hair, inhaling deeply the sweet scents that clung to her satin tresses: the fresh smell of autumn rain and the fragrant hyacinth perfume she used always, this wintry woman-child, as graceful as the flower she had taken for hers, the violet blossom that, despite its fragility, bloomed while the snow yet lay upon the ground. He murmured words of love in her ear, his breath warm upon her skin, and nibbled her lobe before letting his mouth slide down the nape of her neck to that sensitive place where it joined her shoulder. Languidly, he teased the spot with his tongue, causing a tiny shower of sparks to erupt in her body, fanning the embers of her desire for him—and his for her.

His hands roamed heatedly over her flesh; she felt his palms cup her breasts, glide lingeringly across her nipples, taunting them so they stiffened and strained against him.

Of their own volition, her arms crept around his back, drawing him nearer. She reveled in the feel of him: the softness of his hair as she burrowed through it with her fingers, then slowly pulled them free to stroke the long, ragged ends that curled against his nape; the smoothness of his skin as her hands slipped down to tighten upon his back; the way in which his powerful, corded muscles bunched and rippled beneath her palms as she clutched him to her, hungry for what he offered.

She knew him so well, and yet in this LifePath, she knew him not at all, this man who aroused her so intimately, so unerringly, draining the very life from her body and pouring it back in. The sheer power and masculinity of him overwhelmed her; she had never known a man such as this. In all the LifePaths she had ever lived, no one had ever made her feel as Cain did. Ileana wanted to go on embracing him forever, wanted to go on feeling his strong arms wrapped about her, taking possession of her, protecting her from the world and whatever it might hold.

His lips were like molten ore when they claimed her breasts; his tongue laved her nipples, sending rivers of fire coursing through her body. Deep within the secret core of her womanhood, a burning ache flickered into being to become a blaze of wanting as he nurtured its flames.

Unable to think, only to feel, Ileana drifted on a tide of sensation, letting it carry her where it willed. She did not know how long she floated in the timeless void she had entered. She did not care. Nothing mattered but Cain and the love they knew as mouths and tongues and hands met flesh and melded.

Outside, a jagged bolt of lightning illuminated the night sky; thunder echoed in response. The rain pounded against the window as savagely as Cain's heart thrummed against Ileana's when he suddenly pressed her down and took her, her low cry of surrender lost amid the howling of the wind. The ship beneath them thrust up from the waves, then plunged back down into the ocean in a rhythm the two lovers shared and at last surpassed as they shuddered with release and clung together feverishly.

When it was over, they lay quietly, damp with sweat and sated; and as though it had somehow been appeased by their lovemaking, the fury of the storm abated, too. In the hush that fell over the sea, Cain drew Ileana into the cradle of his arms, where she nestled her head against his shoulder.

This is where I belong, she thought, *where I have always belonged. We are one, Cain and I, and nothing shall take that from us—not even the Darkness! I shall fight It with my body's last, dying breath; this, I swear!*

Sudden tears of mingled joy and sadness for all they had ever known and might never know again pricked her eyes, and she let them fall, her love for Cain filling her to overflowing as, wordlessly, hearing the thoughts that cried out to him from her heart, he gently kissed the glittering droplets from her cheeks in the silence.

Chapter 21

*Verily do I say unto ye that the Foul Enslaver wears
many faces, and even one who is wise may be deceived
by them. Therefore, if ye would know those who are
Defenders of the Light, look not upon their countenances, for such are but masks that may be easily
assumed. Look instead into their hearts, for therein is
where the truth lies.*

—Thus it is Written—
in
The Word and The Way
The Book of Ahren, Chapter Eight, Verse Twelve

MORNING CAME SOFTLY, THE SUN STEALING OVER THE EASTERN
horizon as though not quite certain the tempest had ended,
and the world awakened to a pale, hazy rose dawn tinged
with a warm golden glow when the mist lifted to reveal the
sky. The sea was calm, its gently rippling waves untouched
by a single fleck of foam; the slightest of breezes stirred,
causing the *Moon Raker*'s lone line of unfurled sails to
billow like white clouds drifting across the firmament.

While those aboard the windjammer, most of whom were
now gathered on its top deck, were relieved the day promised to be clear, the thought did little to brighten their glum
faces as they surveyed the damage done to the ship. The
mizzenmast had snapped in two; the tip of its upper
portion, still partially attached to the lower by a large
splinter of wood, was trailing over the port side of the

257

vessel. What canvas remained had taken a stiff beating; though the sails taken in early on were fairly intact, tattered remnants of several others fluttered like streamers from the spars. One of the lifeboats was missing, another, badly battered. Most of the cages of live chickens meant to supply fresh fowl and eggs had washed overboard; a few dead hens lay scattered among the tangled ropes, seaweed, and other debris that littered the deck. The BeastMaster reported that several of the swift messenger-hawks had been lost and that two goats and one cow in the hold had suffered broken legs and had had to be destroyed. The steady thumping of the pumps in the bilge punctuated the morning quiet, making those aboard the windjammer painfully aware of the fact that though the squall had ceased, there was still the chance it had fatally crippled them.

Captain Zesiro sighed tiredly, for he had been up most of the night and he knew there would be no rest for him this day.

"All right," he barked gruffly to the downcast crew. "There's no sense in standing around here bemoaning our fate. What's done is done, and we'll just have to make the best of it, that's all. Thank the Light that we survived the storm and that we've got a spare mast and plenty of canvas stored below. Somehow we'll manage to effect repairs here at sea. We are indeed fortunate that Mistress Halcyone, who designed the ship, is aboard. She shall prove a great help to us, I'm sure. Now divide yourself up into groups, and let's start cleaning up this mess."

Once the sailors had set about their duties, the captain turned to Cain, who was waiting for his report. He enumerated the difficulties they faced, not the least of which was the fact that the vessel had clearly been blown many leagues off course.

"I cannot be certain of our exact position, Lord," Captain Zesiro stated, "for the storm was so violent, it caused the compass needle to spin uselessly in circles, and I had no means of navigation. However, I feel quite sure we are no longer upon the Zephyr Ocean, but are now crossing the Monsoon Ocean."

"I see," Cain said. "Then, according to the Records in the Archives, from which our maps were copied, we aren't heading toward the continent of Aerie anymore, but the continent of Verdante. In that case, Captain, we must take care we do not inadvertently stray into the Forbidden Waters."

"Yea, Lord," Captain Zesiro agreed soberly.

The Forbidden Waters were so named because the southern polar cap, Janus, was thought to be unstable and it was considered extremely dangerous to venture too close to the continent. It was not unusual for glaciers to crack suddenly into massive chunks that broke away explosively from the frozen land, causing horrendous ice floes and giant tidal waves that made the surrounding oceans shudder and churn. Blizzards accompanied by bitterly cold, biting winds scoured the continent constantly, making it uninhabitable. No trace of life had ever been found there—no tribes, no animals, no plants. If those aboard the ship should somehow become marooned on the southern polar cap, they would be doomed.

"Still," the captain continued, "for all that we are off course, Lord, I do not think we have passed the Point of No Return. If that is so, we should be fairly safe from Janus."

"How far from Verdante do ye estimate we are, Captain?" Cain asked.

Captain Zesiro shook his head.

"As to that, I don't know," he admitted, squinting his eyes against the morning sun as he gazed intently across the ocean. It was as though he could see a faraway shore and were trying to gauge its distance. "'Tis hard to say. If I could pinpoint our current location, I could judge more clearly. As it is, I can only guess a month's journey—or more, no doubt, now that 'twill be necessary to wait until the ship is repaired before we can make any real headway." He sighed. "'Twas bad luck, that storm blowing up like that."

"Yea." Cain nodded, then glanced at the sky, as though half expecting it to begin clouding over once more. "We must hope it was not a portent of the future."

Later, Ileana was to remember his words and to wonder if they had been prophetic. But at the time, she thought nothing of them, for she had seen naught in the mist that had presaged the tempest, nor had she felt anything but the awesome, natural power of the elements that had lashed the windjammer. Had the squall been fraught with an evil force, surely, she would have sensed it.

"Cap'n!" the lookout posted in the crow's nest suddenly cried, startling Ileana from her reverie. "There's something floating off to starboard!"

Immediately, Captain Zesiro called for his spyglass. Once it had been brought from his quarters, he opened the brass telescope and peered through its eyepiece.

"I don't know what to make of it, Lord," he said as he passed the spyglass to Cain. "It looks like the remains of a small craft, and there seems to be some sort of creature clinging to one of the broken planks. It—it appears to be Kind, Lord—but I've never seen the like before."

"Nor have I, Captain. Nor have I," Cain repeated slowly, his brow knitted as he collapsed the telescope. "Still, if it is Kind, it must be rescued. If it is still alive, perhaps we can save it. If not, it must have a proper funeral. Send a boat to investigate, Captain, but be sure it is accompanied by armed warriors. The creature seems to be dead, but there is no point in taking any unnecessary risks."

"Yea. By your command, Lord."

At once, Captain Zesiro turned away to start issuing orders to the crew, and presently, one of the undamaged lifeboats was lowered over the side of the vessel. Then two sailors and four soldiers descended the rope ladder that had been dropped over the starboard rail. After they were firmly seated in the gently bobbing dinghy, the two crew members began to row toward the creature that was hanging on to a piece of wood drifting with the waves.

Once they had reached it, the sailors pulled in the oars. One of the warriors lifted his long iron javelin and, with its sharp tip, hesitantly prodded the creature experimentally. It didn't stir, but the soldier wasn't taking any chances. Laying aside his spear, he fashioned a running noose in the rope he carried slung over one shoulder. Then, deftly, he tossed the resulting large loop over the creature's head and the splintered plank upon which its body was draped. Gradually, he eased the coil beneath the ends of the wood, then drew the hemp tight around the creature's waist.

At his signal, the two crew members once more took up their oars. Towing the creature behind them slowly, they rowed the lifeboat back to the *Moon Raker*. There, after the creature had been carefully hauled aboard, it was laid upon the deck. No one made an attempt to examine it. Instead, Cain, Ileana, and the rest who crowded about to get a look at it stared at the creature silently, shocked and horrified by its appearance. None of them had ever seen anything like it, and though they felt certain, from its basic body structure, that it was Kind, they had difficulty accepting that fact.

From head to toe, the creature was totally and absolutely black—not just the dark, coffee-colored hue of many Tamarinders, but as black as the night sea when the moons did not shine and the stars were obscured by mist. Though its body topped six feet in length, its head seemed too large for its torso, as though the flesh covering its cranium had somehow swelled all out of proportion. It was completely bald, its forehead ridged at the center with two vertical, knobby protuberances that seemed to be like eyebrows, then swept up into short, hornlike protrusions that jutted from the top front half of its bulging head. The bottom ends of the ridges continued down its face, melding and forming what appeared to be the creature's broad, flat nose. On either side of this, wide-set, were its shuttered eyes. They were like slits, devoid of lashes. Its mouth was a grim black slash; its long, square jaw narrowed to a small, triangular chin that was almost nonexistent as it disappeared into a throat fan. Its ears were tiny and pressed close to its head.

The creature's body was naked; and although it seemed as though once, it might have been well formed, muscular, and extremely powerful, now it was pathetically wasted and its limbs were withered. The fingers of its hands and the toes of its feet were shrunken, too; but their nails resembled fat talons, long and curved, with sharp, pointed tips that made Ileana shiver as she studied them with morbid fascination. At the place where its navel appeared to be, a short umbilical cord hung; it seemed somehow retracted into the creature's torso. The creature did not appear to possess any visible external genitalia, so Ileana assumed it was female. A truncated tail jutted from the base of its spine.

Still, all of this would not have been so gruesome had the creature's skin not been reptilian in appearance. It was hard and tough, like a hide, and covered with thick, rough barklike scales. Now it was dry and cracked from exposure to the elements and encrusted with brine from the ocean.

Ileana shuddered with revulsion, recoiling from the creature. It reminded her of a slithering heloderma or a crested dragon, though it didn't begin to approach the giant saurians' size. It ought never to have been brought aboard, she thought. There was something . . . unnatural about it, a—a . . . wrongness—yea, that was it!—that she couldn't quite put her finger on. She fervently hoped the creature were dead.

At last, Cain and Captain Zesiro bent to examine it. Cain called for a small mirror, and after it had been brought, he held the looking glass to the creature's nose and mouth to see if it still breathed. It did. The faintest trace of mist clouded the mirror.

"It's still alive," Cain said. "Sir Ahmed, Sir Husein, help me get it to sickbay."

"Nay!" Ileana burst out, startling those gathered around the creature. "'Tis evil, a minion of the Foul Enslaver; I feel it! Throw it back whence it came!"

"Lady, we do not know that," Cain rejoined censuringly. "If it be Kind, then 'tis our bounden duty to offer it succor."

"'Tis a vile thing, I tell ye!" Ileana averred. "The Immortal Guardian never fashioned something so repellent!"

"It created lizards, did It not? This creature is not so very different," Cain pointed out. "Perhaps it is only more highly evolved, as we were once anthropoids before the Light gifted us with Its essence. Would ye have us commit murder simply because we don't care for the saurian's looks? If it does not belong to the Darkness, as ye suggest, we would imperil our immortal souls by such an action!"

There was nothing Ileana could say to that. The creature was wicked; she knew it was, and she could not understand why Cain was championing its cause. It was almost as though he were glad they had found the thing. His eyes were glowing with a fervid light, and he could not seem to tear them away from the creature. He was actually touching it, examining it for injuries, his hands running over it as expertly as a healer's. Ileana felt cold and sick with fear; her stomach roiled. Only last night, those same hands had been caressing her. She would not relinquish her husband so easily to the foul thing.

"Then I insist the creature be locked in the ship's hold and guarded day and night," she declared vehemently, "a wise precaution, surely, under the circumstances. Perhaps the *Storm Chaser* and the other vessels that sailed from the known-inhabited continents to the other half of the world also took aboard their crafts such saurians, as ye would call the thing; and what of the strange skeletons that washed up on our shores? Might they have belonged to creatures such as this one?"

"Yea," Captain Zesiro chimed in. "The High Princess Lady Ileana is right, Lord. Until we know more about it, we dare not take any chances."

"Very well," Cain conceded finally. "Let us lock it in the hold, then."

Once the unconscious reptile, who still had not stirred, had been carried below and shut up in one of the storerooms without mishap, Ileana began to breathe a little easier. Still, she could not shake off the terrible sense of trepidation that enveloped her; and for a long time after the creature had been taken away, she pondered going down to the hold herself and slaying the thing's body. She was, in fact, so riddled with apprehension, she actually went so far as to venture below and peer through the mesh grill set into the storeroom door at the black shape huddled on the straw. Its chest rose and fell so shallowly, so erratically, the movement was barely discernible. The light from Ileana's lamp had no effect whatsoever on the saurian; it was oblivious of her presence.

"Do ye wish to go in, Lady?" one of the guards asked.

"Nay," she replied at last, shaking her head and turning away.

The reptile could do nothing in its present state—or so she hoped.

> *Ah, woe is me, woe is me.*
> *I have taken a serpent*
> *Unto the bosom of my house*
> *And nourished it at my breast.*

—Thus it is Written—
in
The Rape of Gwenhwyvar
by the Bard Alsandair set Windestun

The physicians aboard the windjammer did not know how to treat the creature; they were not even certain what ailed it, although they agreed that it and its small craft must have been at sea when the storm had struck and that the saurian had suffered exposure to the elements. Every so often, they spooned a little water down its throat; but that was all. So in the end, it was perhaps not so much a testament to the healers' talents as it was to the reptile's strength and willpower that it survived.

It was three days later that it finally stirred and showed faint signs of recovery. After that, it got swiftly stronger with every passing day, though it refused to eat the nourishing soup that was left in a dish, morning and night, in the storeroom. Soon the physicians thought the creature might be well enough to eat some bread and cheese; but this, too, it ignored. At last, hoping to find something to tempt its palate, they asked the cooks to save the table scraps left over from meals. But nothing appealed to the saurian.

"It must eat," Cain insisted when the healers reported its lack of appetite. "Surely, it does not live on water alone."

"It doesn't," Ileana responded, sick and shuddering, as she entered their quarters in time to hear her husband's remarks. "It consumes raw flesh!"

The others in the cabin stared at her, speechless with shock, for only savage animals ate uncooked meat, and even the physicians had reached the conclusion that the reptile was Kind.

"How do ye know?" Cain questioned sharply. "Do ye have proof of this?"

"I saw it," Ileana told him, blanching, for ever since the creature had roused, she had made a habit of going below to check on its progress. She did not trust it, and now, more than ever, she was convinced it was evil. "'Tis eating the—the rats in the hold. 'Tis—'tis swallowing them . . . alive," she uttered, stifling the urge to vomit as she remembered how the saurian had opened its jaws and slowly devoured the squirming rat, whose tail it had held fast in one hand.

"Nay!" Cain choked out, horrified. "Nay!"

"I tell ye, I saw it! Now will ye listen to me? 'Tis not Kind, but a—a reptile—even worse! A reptile that looks Kind! An abominable, deceptive thing! 'Tis unnatural, I tell ye, and therefore a minion of the Foul Enslaver. Throw it overboard, Lord. Please. Throw it overboard before 'tis too late!"

For a moment, Ileana thought Cain would do as she begged. But then, horribly, she saw the beast within him look out of his eyes, and she knew he would refuse to get rid of the creature.

"Just because it's carnivorous doesn't make it wicked, Ileana," he stated coolly. "Perhaps it is simply not as highly evolved as we are. Besides, it seems harmless enough. It has displayed no hostility toward us."

"Nay, not yet. But that does not mean it won't!"

"Nevertheless, I think ye are forgetting the purpose of this expedition, which is not just to explore the far side of the planet, but to discover what form the Darkness has assumed in Its encroachment upon the land. If the saurian belongs to the Foul Enslaver as ye claim—and we still don't know that to be true—'twould be wise if we kept it and studied it at close range. 'Tis only a single reptile. What can it possibly do against a shipload of two hundred and fifty Tintagelese, the majority of whom are trained soldiers?"

Ileana had no answer to that, nor did anyone else in the cabin. In fact, two of Cain's advisers from the Lesser Court, who had volunteered to accompany him on the journey, were nodding in agreement.

Can they not see he is not himself? Ileana wondered desperately. *Can they not feel the struggle taking place inside him between his power and that beast whose breath is the fire of death, that beast who belongs to the Darkness? Ah, Heaven's Light! Perhaps they cannot. Mayhap only I, a priestess, can sense these things. O Immortal Guardian! Help me. Help me. Little by little, I am losing him! I know I am. He fights that which is within him; with every last ounce of*

*his strength, he fights it. But it is draining him, and I do not
know how much longer he can hold out against it. He looks
so weary, my heart aches for him. Oh, beloved . . .*

So none would see the tears that stung her eyes, Ileana
turned and, murmuring some excuse, hurriedly left the
cabin.

Feeling in need of some fresh air, she made her way to the
top deck, where she climbed the ladder to the forecastle,
noticing, as she did so, that the repairs to the ship were
almost finished. The new mizzenmast was firmly entrenched near the vessel's stern; all the sails had been
mended or replaced and were billowing gaily from the spars.
The deck itself had been cleared of debris and neatly
swabbed, then scrubbed with holystones to smooth the
rough patches splintered by the storm. Only a few minor
details still needed to be corrected. Otherwise, the windjammer was now making excellent headway, the day being
pleasant, if cool, for it was spring here in the southern
hemisphere.

Ileana gripped the forecastle rail tightly, forcing herself to
bring her tumultuous emotions under control. If she were to
save her husband, she could not afford to lose her objectivi-
ty in the matter. She must remember the things she had
been taught at Mont Saint Mikhaela, what she had read in
its library, and what she had guessed during her nights of
study at Khali Keep. Somehow she must remain calm and
discover a way to compel Cain to pitch the creature overboard before it regained its full strength.

To Ileana's despair, before she could take any real action
toward her goal, however, the following afternoon, her last
hope of persuading her husband to rid them of the saurian's
presence was destroyed. Although the idea appalled her,
together with the physicians, she and Cain went below to
take the reptile a dish of raw meat from a freshly slain
rabbit. The creature fell upon the uncooked flesh ravenous-
ly, its sharp teeth tearing large, bloody chunks from the
bones in such a voracious manner, Ileana couldn't bring
herself to watch.

She turned away until it had finished consuming the
repugnant meal and licked its chops. Then, to her utter
horror, the saurian spoke.

"Thank ye . . . ssso much," it rasped weakly in perfect Tintagelese, its hoarse, sibilant voice sending chills down her spine. "Ye sssaved . . . my life, and I am . . . mossst grateful. Had ye not come along and . . . ressscued me, I would sssurely have . . . perisssshed."

"Ye can talk," Ileana breathed, stunned.

"But . . . of course. Do not . . . all the Kind . . . ssspeak?"

"Yea," Cain said, shooting his wife a smirk of triumph and satisfaction she knew belonged to the beast within him. "Where are ye from?" he queried eagerly. "Do ye have a name? Are there others of your tribe who survived the Time of the Wars of the Kind and the Apocalypse?"

"Pleassse. I am . . . very tired," the reptile hissed, closing its peculiar eyes, which, except for their black pupils, were totally red. "I mussst . . . ressst. But I ssshall . . . ansssswer your quesssstionsss later, I . . . promissse."

But later never came, for just then, without warning, the ship suddenly groaned and shuddered, then heaved wildly upon the waves, lurching violently to one side. Ileana and the rest, taken unaware, were thrown to the floor of the storeroom, where they rolled like marbles hit by a taw, slamming into the walls and one another. One of the young healers, Doctor York, fell unavoidably atop the creature. Ileana heard an odd, sharp *whoosh,* and then the physician cried out, as though injured. Still, when he managed to stagger to his feet, he appeared unharmed and assured the others it had been only the impact of the blow knocking the wind from him.

They accepted his explanation without question, for one of the lanterns they'd carried into the hold had been overturned by the vessel's tossing upon the waves. The glass chimney had shattered, and oil had run out from the brass base, setting the pile of straw on the storeroom floor ablaze.

"Guards!" Cain shouted. "Guards!"

Immediately, the door was flung open wide, and the two warriors stationed outside appeared, their swords held at the ready.

"Put those away," Cain ordered, gesturing at the weapons, "and fetch buckets of water to douse this fire. Quickly! Quickly!"

The soldiers raced away, while the others grabbed the blankets that had been provided for the saurian and began to beat frantically at the flames now licking their way up the storeroom walls. Acrid smoke filled the air, blinding them, making them cough and gag as they fought for breath. The reptile did nothing to help. It cowered in one corner, hissing as though terrified. The windjammer continued to pitch crazily. Wails of terror could be heard from above, and from other parts of the hold came the shrieks of the beasts aboard the *Moon Raker*.

"Get this fire out!" Cain yelled to the warriors, who had now returned and, with the pails they carried, were casting water onto the flames. "I've got to find out what's happening on deck."

He grabbed Ileana's hand, hauling her behind him roughly as he stumbled through the passages of the hold, then up the ladders to the top deck.

"By the Blue Moon!" Cain swore as he saw the chaos that reigned above. "This bloody ship is accursed! Heaven's Light!" He inhaled sharply and Ileana screamed involuntarily as they spied the cause of the ship's distress.

The vessel was caught in the throes of a horrendous sea monster, an immense black octopus, its tentacles spanning some seventy-five feet or more. Without warning, it had risen from the sea to attack the windjammer, wrapping three of its massive tentacles about the ship, its suckers leeching tightly to the *Moon Raker*'s deck and sides.

Ileana had never before seen anything like it. The monster was grotesque, as though deformed. Its thick, rubberlike flesh was partially covered with patches of unnatural scales and ridges, as though encrusted with layers of barnacles or kelp. Its huge, saccular body was grossly distorted, one side much larger than the other, knobby, and ill-formed. Its eyes, gleaming with an odd, murky orange light, bulged from the top of its head. When it opened its mouth to tear at the vessel, Ileana gasped as she observed a pair of pointed, horny beaks and a daggerlike radula before the gaping orifice snapped shut, puncturing a portion of the forecastle. With a sickening crunch, wood shattered and splintered, pieces flying in every direction.

Several of the soldiers, dying or already dead, lay scattered upon the deck. Others slipped and slid in the dark, inky, slowly paralyzing substance the octopus had ejected from its body, as, with their blades, they hacked frantically at the giant tentacle sprawled across the bow. But Ileana could see that the warriors were having little success at loosing the arm. Others manned the catapults, ballistas, and mangonels that were secured on deck just behind the windjammer's rails. Even now, a barrage of sharp iron spikes and heavy stones aimed at the monster's ballooning sack was released; but these, too, barely scathed it.

The ship bucked and rolled as the octopus shook it brutally; great waves broke over its sides, swamping the deck and washing soldiers and sailors alike overboard. Ileana saw one of the monster's tentacles pluck one man from the ocean and hurl him into the distance.

The crew grappled desperately with lines and sails, trying to maintain some control over the vessel. Dangling ropes cracked like whips from the spars; canvas flogged as though buffeted by a blustering gale. The wheel of the windjammer spun uselessly. Timbers strained, creaking and whining in protest at the brutal assault.

"Cain, we've got to do something!" Ileana cried as she lunged across the reeling deck.

At her command, the Power sprang to life within her, coursing through her limbs. She lifted her hands and stretched them out before her. Blue fire blazed from her fingertips. The flames seared the octopus's arm. A shrill, unKind shriek split the air as the monster squealed with pain. Its tentacle writhed, sweeping across the deck, lashing the warriors who slashed at it with their swords and knocking them over the smashed rails of the vessel. The arm lifted and slapped back down hard, punching a jagged hole in the deck. Several of the soldiers and sailors lost their balance and disappeared into the chasm, their screams piercing Ileana's ears.

Again the blue fire leaped from her fingertips, scorching the octopus's tentacle. With a loud *whoosh,* its suckers yanked free, ripping up half the deck and causing shards of wood to spiral hazardously through the air.

From the corner of one eye, Ileana saw her husband dash forward, tightly gripping his shield, which his manservant, Mehtar, had hastily fetched from his cabin. Deftly, Cain maneuvered the buckler to protect himself from the poisonous ink the monster spewed forth vehemently as he edged toward it and lifted his left hand to send blue fire shooting into one of its bulging orange eyes. The orb exploded in a burst of flames, spraying blood and pulp in all directions. The octopus howled with agony, its enormous tentacles flailing spastically. One slammed savagely into the windjammer's hull, bursting through its copper sheath and splitting the wood beneath. With a deafening roar, the sea gushed into the aperture, and the high-pitched screams of the men and women on the lower decks and the cries of the terrified beasts in the hold rang out pathetically over the ocean. Another of the monster's arms struck the foremast, cracking it in two and sending the top section flying like a loosed spear.

Smoke billowed from the stern of the ship, and Ileana realized dimly that the two guards had not been able to put out the fire in the storeroom. It had eaten a path through the lower decks.

"Cain!" she yelled hoarsely, pointing at the flames even now licking their way up the mizzenmast. "Cain!"

His face was horrible to see, seized by an unholy light, his mouth twisted in a gruesome grin of exultation. Still, some sane part of him recognized their danger, and he nodded to her curtly before turning back to blast the octopus's remaining eye from its socket. Once more, the monster keened with anguish, its jaws agape so its throat loomed before them like a dark, forbidding void, its horny beaks like pikes about to impale them, its radula poised to strike.

One last time, Cain raised his left hand. Blue fire burned its way down the octopus's throat before its jaws clamped shut convulsively, then opened again to reveal its charred inner tissues as it spouted smoke and screamed soundlessly. Then, gradually, defeated, it released the vessel from its ravaging clinch and glided slowly beneath the ocean's surface.

"Man the lifeboats!" Cain hollered above the pandemonium that prevailed on the now rapidly sinking windjammer. "All hands, man the bloody lifeboats!"

Those who had heard and were able to do so moved quickly to carry out his orders. Others ran to their quarters to salvage what they could; Mehtar bravely raced away to save the most important of Cain's and Ileana's belongings. Soon what was left of the top deck was filled with warriors and crew members scrambling to get off the ship. Regardless of sex or rank, the youngest of those aboard went first until, finally, only the commanders—Cain, Ileana, Sir Ahmed, Sir Husein, and Captain Zesiro—remained. They dropped into the last dinghy and found places alongside Halcyone set Astra, the mistress shipbuilder; Doctor York, the young physician; Charis, Ileana's handmaiden, and Mehtar, Cain's manservant, all of whom had survived.

Moments later, with a loud, sucking noise, the magnificent *Moon Raker* vanished into the dark blue depths of the Monsoon Ocean, leaving behind it four ill-equipped lifeboats, which bobbed forlornly on the waves. Slowly, unable to believe more of her companions had not managed to escape, Ileana counted those who were left. There were forty-seven of them. Forty-seven out of the two hundred and fifty who had set sail from the city of Astra.

The only thing that mitigated her deep feeling of devastation was that the unnatural saurian creature was not one of them.

CORNUCOPIA

Map by Rebecca Brandewyne

Chapter 22

We are the Watchers of the Grapevine Coast,
Pledged to guard its verdant shore.
No Worms! No Worms! Cybele, hear our cry.
Keep our apples safe forevermore.

—Thus it is Written—
in
The Battle Cry of Plumthicket
by the Bard Greenleaf of Cornucopia

FOR DAYS THEY ROWED AND DRIFTED, ENDLESSLY, IT SEEMED, with only the sun and the stars to guide them. Cool spring rain fell now and then, so they did not thirst; and with their swords and javelins, Cain and the soldiers were sometimes fortunate or skillful enough to spear a fish or two, which were eaten raw, there being no means of cooking the catch. At first, Ileana's stomach rejected the revolting fare; but since there was no other, she soon learned to adapt and, along with the rest, greedily consumed her portion, trying hard not to think of the reptile's long, sharp teeth and claws as it had gnawed the dead rabbit's raw flesh from its bones. Unlike her, Cain ate his fish with relish, displaying no apparent qualms, and Ileana realized the hold of the beast within him was growing stronger.

She was worried, too, about Doctor York. He did not look well, and once or twice, she noticed him staring covertly at the others in a peculiar, disturbing fashion. Everyone was suffering from the ill effects of exposure to the elements, but

273

York's symptoms seemed worse than the others'. Some of his hair had fallen out in clumps, and to Ileana, it appeared his skin was drying and flaking more than the others'. His fingernails badly needed trimming as well. She hoped he were not coming down with some sickness, for he was the only physician they had left.

"Lord, look!" Sir Ahmed cried suddenly to Cain, startling the girl from her reverie. "Do my eyes deceive me, or are those birds I spy off yonder?"

Scarcely daring to hope, they all turned to where Sir Ahmed pointed. There, in the distance, a flock of sea gulls dipped and soared against the pale blue sky.

"Land!" Ileana breathed. "We must be close to land!"

"Yea," Cain agreed. "Ahoy," he called through his cupped hands to the other three dinghies. "Ahoy." He indicated the birds. "Land ho! Land ho!"

Their spirits rising, their vigor renewed, those in the small crafts set their backs to the oars and began to row feverishly toward the western horizon. By early afternoon, the continent of Verdante was in sight.

It was easy to see why it was so called, for it sprawled before them like an emerald-green paradise. Towering hills covered with vegetation rose sharply, then fell away to level ground below, where a dense jungle reminiscent of Tamarind filled the sweeping terrain. Tall, leaf-crowned palm trees lined the golden beach.

To the weary travelers, it was a welcome haven, beautiful and beckoning. It was only when they drew near to the shore that they saw how it was flawed, for a small army bristling with weapons was waiting to receive them.

Involuntarily, Ileana gasped as the leader of the group stepped forward from the shadow of the trees into the bright sunlight. A dwarf, he stood barely four feet tall, if that, though he was stocky and muscular. A tall, peaked broad-brimmed brown hat adorned with a single green feather perched jauntily upon his fat, round head. He was dressed in a green, short-sleeved shirt and a brown cotton vest decorated with embroidered designs. Baggy green leggings hugged his sturdy calves; brown hemp boots covered his feet. In one hand he carried a stout wooden shaft as big as he was; a keen-edged triangle of flint had been affixed with resinous fiber to its tip.

The dwarf was shouting and gesturing at them menacingly, his meaning plain, although none could understand his language.

"He doesn't want us to land," Ileana said.

"Well, that's just too damned bad," Cain growled. "I didn't come all this way to be driven back by a dwarf." He turned to the other lifeboats and hailed those within. "Keep rowing!" he commanded grimly, hastily stripping off his white kurta.

This, he held aloft, waving it like a flag. But the dwarf went on yelling and shaking his spear at them threateningly.

"Damn!" Cain cursed, running one hand through his ragged hair. "Either he doesn't understand the planetary peace signal, or he just plain doesn't intend to honor it. Well, *I* don't intend to be kept from landing. Keep rowing!" he yelled to those in the other dinghies.

At that, the rest of the figures standing among the trees on the beach stepped forward to line up beside their leader.

"Why, they're all dwarfs!" Ileana exclaimed, startled.

"They're probably a tribe that somehow mutated after the Wars of the Kind and the Apocalypse," Cain speculated. "'Tis unimportant. What matters is that they're obviously hostile."

He had no sooner got the words out of his mouth than the dwarfs loosed a barrage of javelins at them; and although the Tintagelese warriors immediately raised their shields, one of the missiles struck Captain Zesiro, piercing his throat and killing him instantly. Blood spurted from the fatal wound, spraying warm and wet and sticky upon Ileana and the others.

"May the Blue Moon fill ye with a thousand sorrows!" Cain cried to the dwarfs, and before anyone could stop him, he jumped to his feet, his hands burning with the blue fire of the Druswids.

He raked the shore with the flames, setting two of the dwarfs ablaze and singeing several others. The two who were badly hit fell to the ground and began to roll, while the rest rushed over and started flinging sand on them to put out the fire. The dwarfs quickly got the flames doused. Then, casting fearful glances in Cain's direction, they hurriedly lifted their injured fellows to their shoulders and marched away as fast as they could, vanishing into the rain forest.

"Well, I guess that takes care of that," Cain asserted as he sat back down in the lifeboat.

"Yea, those damned dwarfs got what they bloody well deserved!" Doctor York hissed in agreement, his eyes gleaming.

No one else spoke. They were all too shocked by what had occurred. War was not the Way, and they were stunned and appalled that Cain had made no further peaceful entreaties before responding to the dwarfs' unwarranted attack. Ileana stared at her husband, knowing what was happening to him; but she was unable to explain to the rest. Biting her lip, she turned away, glancing with concern at York. What was the matter with him? He had actually approved of Cain's actions. Had the healer somehow been infected by the Darkness within Cain? By the Light, if that were so, what was going to become of them all?

They reached Verdante at last. There, they discovered that five of those in the other dinghies had been killed by the dwarfs; three more had been wounded. Doctor York treated the injured, while Cain divided the rest into groups. He ordered half the remaining warriors to scout the surrounding area; the rest were to stand guard. Ileana offered to take Charis, Halcyone, and some of the rest to gather coconuts and fruit, with which the trees were abundant, and deadwood to build a fire so the bodies of the slain might be properly cremated. After that, all moved to carry out their assigned tasks.

Once the travelers had repeated the Prayer of Passing for the souls of their departed fellows and feasted hungrily on the bounty yielded by the jungle, they dragged their small crafts into the rain forest and carefully concealed them beneath some brush. By that time, the scouts had returned to report they had found a nearby village inhabited by the dwarfs. Cain, having fed and rested, was, to Ileana's relief, once more himself and in control of the situation.

"Then, by all means, let us proceed there at once," he

said. "I doubt that they'll give us any further trouble, and it is important we make contact with the natives. Perhaps we may learn something from them."

Thus the party set out on foot for the village, hacking their way through the jungle. It was toward sundown when they finally came upon the large glade in the rain forest that the dwarfs had cleared in order to construct their village. The maze of gnarled trees, tangled shrubs, and twisted undergrowth had been painstakingly cut away and removed to expose the soft, mossy ground. The dwarfs had left standing one enormous, ancient banyan, which they had divested of its lower branches so there was plenty of room to walk around underneath. In the remaining limbs of the tree, the dwarfs had built their homes.

These were made of wood and so well fashioned that at first, it was difficult to see them, for they appeared to be part of the banyan itself, following the shape and curve of its many trunks and branches. It was apparent the rooms in the houses were all on different levels, for each dwelling boasted several thatched green roofs of varying heights. None of the buildings had any visible means of access to and from the ground, so Ileana assumed ladders were used for such and, after the incident on the beach, had been drawn up to prevent invasion.

At the heart of the clearing, where the main trunk of the gigantic tree had once stood, was a wooden statue of a woman. Around the banyan itself was a large, deep trench that Ileana initially thought was a moat. However, when she observed that it was filled with wood instead of water, she decided she must be mistaken. From the corner of one eye, she noticed a barely discernible movement, and she realized guards were posted in the branches directly above the inner perimeter of the glade; no other dwarfs were in sight.

Slowly, motioning for the others to stay behind, Cain advanced toward the clearing, his aura glowing. Ileana knew he was using it as a shield to protect him from the dwarfs' spears.

"Hail the Tribe of the Dwarfs," he called in Tintagelese, his palms upturned and spread wide to show their emptiness, although, remembering how the blue fire had leaped earlier from his fingertips, Ileana thought this could hardly prove reassuring. "I am the Lord Cain sin Khali sul Ariel, the High Prince of all Tintagel. I bring ye greetings from the six known Tribes of our world. I, and those who accompany me, come in peace. We mean ye no harm. We want only to talk to ye." He paused to let this be absorbed, but the jungle was silent.

"I say again: We come in peace," Cain said. "We mean ye no harm. It was ye who attacked us, ignoring our white flag, which is our truce symbol. We did but defend ourselves against ye. We are a peaceful people; we do not want to fight ye. Please, send your leader forth to speak to me. He shall not be assaulted, I swear it!"

Still, there was no answer, and Ileana saw Cain's self-control begin to slip.

"Who is your leader?" he continued more loudly, his voice now goading rather than placating. "Let that one show himself—unless he be a coward!"

At that, Ileana heard an excited babbling in the branches of the banyan. It was abruptly stilled, and for a moment, she thought the dwarfs, who had obviously got the gist of Cain's insult, would let it pass unprotested. But presently, through a window of what appeared to be a very large house, she spied the edge of a trapdoor as it was slowly raised, and then a rope ladder with wooden rungs was tossed through the hole in the floor. Clattering against the trunk of the tree, the ladder unrolled until, finally, it dangled freely. After that, two dwarfs began to descend to the ground. Eyeing Cain warily, they hesitantly approached him, stopping just short of the trench surrounding the glade. Ileana saw that one of the dwarfs was the leader of the army who'd attacked them from the beach. But it was the other who spoke.

"Hail, Lord Cain sin Khali sul Ariel," the dwarf greeted Cain in halting, strangely accented Tintagelese. Although Ileana had some difficulty understanding him, she recognized the fact that he did not acknowledge her husband as the High Prince of all Tintagel. "I am Bergren Birchbark, Elder of the village of Plumthicket," he went on, "and this is Tom Thorn, Head Elder. He does not speak your language, so I am to act as interpreter. What is it ye wish of us, Lord?"

"Only what I said: merely to talk," Cain replied. "Over

the past years, my people have dispatched many ships to this side of Tintagel. None of these vessels—nor those aboard them—have ever returned. We want to know what became of them. The Druswids, our . . . spiritual leaders, have sensed a wrongness in the land. We think perhaps the Darkness, a . . . great evil force such as was loosed during the Time Before, has once more awakened to cast Its shadow upon us. We believe this has something to do with the disappearance without a trace of those who preceded us."

Bergren Birchbark turned to Tom Thorn and, gesturing to emphasize his words, spoke to him rapidly in the dwarfs' language.

"They are from the far side of Tintagel," Bergren Birchbark uttered to his leader. "They search for the others of their tribes who came before them. They say they mean us no harm. They seem friendly enough, and after all, none of their ilk has ever offered us injury before. I think 'twould be wise to admit them to our village, Head Elder. Their leader has powerful magic, as we have seen. It may be that if we refuse to speak with them, he will turn on us and set our village on fire."

Tom Thorn nodded soberly.

"Very well, Bergren," he said. "Bid them be welcome to Plumthicket, then. But be certain there are no Worms among them. We know *they* are warmongers and not to be trusted!"

"This is so," Bergren Birchbark agreed. He turned to address Cain once more. "Have your people step forward so we can see them," he demanded.

Puzzled but seeing no reason not to acquiesce to the request, Cain motioned for Ileana and the others to show themselves. It seemed the two dwarfs exhaled a sigh of relief, and then a smile that did not quite reach his worried eyes split Bergren Birchbark's apple-cheeked visage.

"Be welcome to our village, Lord," he declared. "Come."

At that, with a great deal of nervous laughter and prattle, all the dwarfs descended from their houses. Some of them carried wide wooden planks, which they laid across the trench so Cain and the others could pass over it into the circle. Then, still chattering, the dwarfs crowded about them curiously, if a trifle shyly, *ooh*ing and *aah*ing.

Other than their small stature, their prominent noses, and their pronounced cheeks, the dwarfs had little in common with one another, though all the men had mustaches and long, wavy beards. The dwarfs came in every shape—some thin, some fat, though most tended to be in between. The color of their hair and eyes ran the gamut of shades, which Ileana found fascinating. She was just as interested in them as they were in her.

Finally, Bergren Birchbark shooed his people away. Then he motioned for Cain and Ileana to follow him and Tom Thorn to the large house, which he called the Cranberry Inn.

After they had ascended the ladder into the inn, Ileana was surprised to discover how spacious, neat, and cheerful the place was. Once inside, Cain had to duck his head, for the roof was much lower than those to which he was accustomed. He also chose to sit cross-legged on the bare floor rather than risk seating himself on one of the stools or benches ranged around the tables, for though the chairs were stout, he was not certain they would bear his weight.

"This is Apple Annie," Bergren Birchbark introduced Cain and Ileana to the plump, comely barmaid, who nodded and beamed, then bustled about fetching refreshments and making sure they were comfortable.

Once they had eaten the excellent meal of fruit, vegetables, and bread and were downing their second cup of fine cranberry wine, Tom Thorn and Bergren Birchbark settled back on their stools, producing beautifully carved pipes from the pockets of their vests. They filled the pipes with tobacco from their pouches, then lit the wooden bowls, puffing contentedly as they drew on the stems.

After a moment's silence, Bergren Birchbark spoke again.

"We wish to apologize for the manner in which we attacked ye and the rest on the beach, Lord." He spoke gruffly. "We understand that six of your party were killed and three more wounded, and for that, we are both deeply sorry and aggrieved. Had we known from the outset who ye were, we would not have assaulted ye. But we could not be certain, at that distance, that ye did not have any of the Worms with ye."

"The Worms?" Cain queried, perplexed.

"Yea, the devils of Mastiphal, the UnEarth One. They are hideous creatures who have invaded our land, Cornucopia, and waged war against our people. Many of us have been taken prisoner or slain. My own wife and child were captured three months ago." Bergren Birchbark's voice was grim, and his clear blue eyes were filled with sorrow.

"I'm sorry," Cain said, and Ileana was glad he had managed thus far, since the incident on the beach, to suppress the beast within him.

The inn was momentarily still. Then the dwarf continued his tale.

"That is why we are so quick to defend ourselves against all strangers and the reason, too, why we have dug such a deep trench around Plumthicket. Ye may have noticed it and the fact that 'tis filled with wood. Each night, those among us who are the Tenders set it afire to keep the Worms at bay, for the creatures are afraid of the flames. During the day, our Watchers guard our shores and our Hunters search for the Worms. The creatures seem to prefer the darkness and may often be caught napping during the daylight hours. When one is so discovered, the Hunters, who have much courage, build a fire about it and burn it alive. That is the only way we have found of killing them. Their hides are so tough, our spears have proved useless against them."

"These . . . Worms—what do they look like?" Ileana asked, an icy tingle of foreboding suddenly chasing down her spine.

"They are dreadful creatures," Bergren Birchbark averred. "Scaly black things with horns and tails—"

The girl inhaled sharply at his words.

"We have seen one," she told him. "We spied it floating on a broken plank in the ocean and took it aboard our ship, the *Moon Raker*, which was lost at sea. It spoke to us. It called itself Kind. I never trusted it," Ileana disclosed. "And when our vessel was assailed by a giant octopus and sank, the creature drowned."

"Be glad," the dwarf stated firmly. "It would have tried to

befriend ye, and then, once it had lulled ye into a false sense of security, it would have turned on ye! So did the Worms deceive the people of Cornucopia in the beginning."

"I knew I was right not to trust it!" Ileana said fiercely, gazing hard at her husband.

"Perhaps so," Cain conceded slowly. "But nevertheless, there is much we might have learned from it had it survived."

"Perhaps, perhaps not," Bergen Birchbank said. He paused, then continued. "That monster, the octopus, some of my people have seen, too," he announced. "Like the Worms, it is the work of Mastiphal. There have been similarly malformed creatures sighted in the rain forest. Fortunately, since we are not game hunters or fisher folk, we have had little reason to fear them. But I have heard the octopus has attacked many boats, some of your own people's among them."

"Then we are not the first of our tribes to come here?" Cain leaned forward eagerly, and for a moment, Ileana was afraid the beast within him would rouse. But to her relief, it did not.

"Nay." The dwarf shook his head. "There have been others like ye. That is how I learned to speak your tongue."

"I wondered about that," Ileana remarked.

"Yea." Bergren Birchbark nodded. "They came here to Plumthicket, just as ye have come. One of them, a young man from a place known as Aethling, a . . . city, he called it, taught me your language many years ago. I have a good ear," the dwarf boasted, "and I've had a few opportunities to practice, too, so I've not forgotten what I learned. Some of your people stayed for a while, though others remained only a few days." He drew on his pipe, then shrugged. "Always, in the end, they moved on. I do not know what became of them. None of them ever returned."

"I see," Cain said thoughtfully. "Do ye know where they might have gone?"

"North, to other lands, to Nomad and Gallow, I suppose. Farther than that, I cannot say. I have not ventured beyond the town of Barterville myself. We Cornucopians are not explorers. We prefer to keep to ourselves. Cybele provides for all our needs, and we are content."

"Cybele?" Ileana inquired.

"The Earth One," Bergren Birchbark elucidated. "She whom we worship. That is her statue ye saw in the middle of our village. The young man from Aethling insisted her name was Ceridwen and said she was only a Keeper, which I gathered was some sort of servant to your god and not a goddess at all." The dwarf seemed very put out by this. "He kept talking about the Light. In fact, all your people have mentioned this Light. Do ye not know the sun was set in the sky by Cybele to bring life to the earth?"

"The Light is not the sun," Ileana explained. "It is the Being who created all that ever was and ever shall be. It is the Immortal Guardian who blessed us with the gift of Its essence and bestowed upon us that which is known as Free Will, so we might choose our own LifePaths and destinies. Do ye not have Records in your Archives of the Time Before?" she queried, hoping to learn more than she already knew about the Prophecy—and the Sword of Ishtar, of which the legend spoke.

Before Ileana had left Astra, she had been informed by the High Priestess Sharai that the Holy Relic must at all costs be found. According to legend, if the Time of the Prophecy were indeed at hand, as the Druswids believed, the sword would be revealed to the Chosen One so it might be carried into battle against the Darkness. Without the blade, the Druswids feared the Foul Enslaver could not be defeated. Over the years, they had searched all the known-inhabited continents for the weapon, but to no avail.

"Ye are our only hope, Ileana," the High Priestess had told her. "If ye are not the Chosen One . . ." Sharai's voice had trailed away as she'd gripped the girls' shoulders tightly. "Ye *must* find the Sword of Ishtar, Ileana! Ye must claim it as yours! 'Tis said it will magnify its wielder's power tenfold. Without it, we are all surely doomed."

Now, emerging from her reverie, Ileana glanced eagerly at Bergren Birchbark, waiting for him to speak.

"The others of your tribes asked this question, too," he disclosed. "But, nay. We have no written . . . Records or . . . Archives, as ye say." He dashed her hopes, hesitating over the words of the Tintagelese tongue. "We know little beyond the history of Cornucopia, which has been handed down to us by the bards. Once, aeons ago, the land was destroyed by a great war; this, we know. There are still ancient ruins in the jungle from that time. But who fought this terrible battle—or why—we do not know or care. We are a peaceful people—or were until the Worms invaded Cornucopia."

"And when did that happen?" Cain asked.

"Several years ago," the dwarf replied. "At first, there were only a few, and we befriended them, for they seemed harmless enough. But then, gradually, more and more came, and we learned of their wickedness, their warlike nature. We have been battling them ever since."

Just then, they were interrupted by the arrival of another dwarf, whom Cain and Ileana had met previously. His name was Jiro Juniper. He waited until he received permission to speak, then addressed Tom Thorn briefly. The Head Elder then said something to Bergren Birchbark, and the dwarf resumed speaking.

"The Tenders have ignited the trench fire," he translated. "Also, though I must apologize for the act, it was necessary to burn your boats. They attract the Worms. We do not know why the creatures want them, but since they do, we destroy all boats that land upon our shores."

Ileana, remembering the bits and pieces of lifeboats her people had found over the years and the strange skeletons that had washed up on the coasts of Tamarind and Bedoui, thought she knew the answer to this. The Worms, as the dwarfs called them, were attempting to reach the known-inhabited continents! She shivered at the notion. From what Bergren Birchbark had said, it was evident the Worms were warmongers, and she herself knew they ate raw flesh. Ileana was now more certain than ever that the creatures were minions of the Foul Enslaver. Surreptitiously, she glanced at Cain, and she saw he, too, had at last come to this conclusion.

"We must go north, as the others of our tribes did," he informed the dwarf. "We must find out what became of our people and learn more about these saurians, the Worms, as ye call them. If they are the form the Darkness has assumed for Its evil work, then they must be destroyed before they can spread throughout the world. Will ye accompany us,

Bergren Birchbark?" Cain inquired. "Will ye guide us through Cornucopia?"

The dwarf was silent for a minute. Then he turned and spoke to Tom Thorn at some length. The Head Elder's expression was grave as he listened and occasionally interjected a sentence or two. But finally, he nodded, and Bergren Birchbark addressed Cain again.

"Very well," he consented. "I will take ye as far north as Barterville. If the Worms are your enemies, then ye are counted among the friends of Cornucopia."

The remainder of the evening was spent making plans for the long journey. Bright and early the following morning, preparations for the trip got under way.

Laughing and talking excitedly, proud to contribute in some way to the forthcoming expedition, the dwarf women gathered tall grasses, which they cut and wove tightly into flasks that were sealed with sap and left to dry in the sun. Once they had baked solid, the containers were filled with water and wine and plugged with corks. Baskets with long rope handles, to be slung over one shoulder, were crammed to bursting with dried fruit and vegetables and hard bread that would keep for many weeks.

From the silkworms and cotton plants cultivated by the dwarfs came fine material and thread, with which Ileana, assisted by Charis, Halcyone, and several of the dwarf women, sewed new garments for herself, Cain, and the rest of their party, their own clothes being ragged from their travails. In addition to an etek, a kurta, and a pair of shaksheer for everyday wear, Ileana made herself an abayeh, as well as a priestess's chasuble and cap.

After that, from a stout branch she chopped from the trunk of an ancient oak, she fashioned a staff that could also serve as a wand, for her own seven wands and the caskets in which she'd kept them, as well as her cards and rune stones, had been lost when the *Moon Raker* had sunk. She created new rune stones from pebbles she found upon the beach; but her cards were not so easily replaced, and at last, she was forced to reconcile herself to their loss.

The warriors were busy honing their swords and polishing their shields, breastplates, and helmets. The dwarf men carved ash spears tipped with sharp flints and made certain, too, that there were plenty of resinous wood torches, which they had found to be the only truly effective weapon against Worms.

Finally, a few weeks later, the travelers were ready to depart from Plumthicket, and they said goodbye to the dwarfs who had befriended them. Then, along with Bergren Birchbark and Jiro Juniper, who had volunteered to accompany them, they set out on foot toward the village of Cherryvale, which lay near the northern border of Cornucopia.

Chapter 23

*I was in much better spirits than I had been for many
a day when we left Plumthicket, for it seemed to me
that during the time we had spent among the gregarious dwarfs, Cain had regained a great portion of his
strength and power, of which the beast within him had
slowly been draining him. I had not seen the thing I
feared look out of his eyes for some time now, and
though I knew it yet lay coiled deep inside him, I dared
to hope perhaps he were winning the battle they waged
for control of his immortal soul.*

*But alas, this was not the case, as, sick at heart, I was
soon to discover.*

—Thus it is Written—
in
The Private Journals
of the High Princess Lady Ileana I

THE EXPEDITION'S PROGRESS WAS SLOW, FOR THE STEAMING
jungle was a massive maze of intertwining branches, and
many times, it was necessary for the soldiers to clear a path
with their swords so the travelers might pass. Still, Bergren
Birchbark, who marched at the head of the procession, did
not appear to be disturbed by this, guiding them unhesitat-
ingly through the labyrinth of vegetation.

Over the passing days, they skirted the base of the high
Walnut Hills just north of Plumthicket and several towering
volcanoes to the west that thrust up defiantly from the midst

of the splendorous rain forest. As they trudged along, Ileana marveled at the sights around her.

Some of the trees were so tall, she could not even see their tops, which soared above the thick, luxuriant canopy woven by their lower, leaf-laden limbs. Other trees were so small, they stood scarcely higher than the dwarfs. Never before had Ileana seen so many different species clustered together. Growing so close to one another, they seemed to form one giant, spreading tree, like the banyan of Plumthicket. Vines and moss hung from their branches and climbed their trunks; trailing ends swung from tree to tree so it appeared as though the gorgeous multicolored orchids and other flowers with which the dangling plants were burdened bloomed in midair.

The jungle teemed with animals, too. Hordes of blood-sucking mosquitoes and small black flies rose in swarms when disturbed, buzzing angrily and biting mercilessly those unfortunate enough to have roused them. Stinging bees, hornets, and wasps posed a hazard also, as did the deceptively colored, sleek-skinned snakes that slithered from the trees to coil about their victims, crushing them to death.

Tiny lizards that reminded Ileana of the reptile aboard the *Moon Raker* darted along the dark, rich, spongy ground crawling with ants, ticks, beetles, termites, centipedes, spiders, cockroaches, and scorpions. Prehensile-tailed porcupines, silky anteaters, and tough-shelled armadillos waddled through the undergrowth, where coatis and ratlike agoutis scampered, their noses twitching as they sniffed the air. Dêor and perytons crashed recklessly through the brush, alarmed by the weird, womanlike screams of prowling smilodons, the high squeals of tapirs, and the deep grunts of peccaries. Monkeys cheeped and chattered in the trees, swinging from limb to limb, stirring up birds and bats alike, though the sloths continued to hang undisturbed from the branches, changing positions so infrequently that algae actually grew on their fur.

Here and there, the companions spied the ruins of which Bergren Birchbark had spoken that first night in Plumthicket. It was evident some of the ancient buildings had once risen many, many stories above the ground, for portions of several of the burned-out, blackened structures still stood, reaching dizzying heights. Now vines and other encroaching vegetation filled their floors and clambered up their sides; animals scurried along empty halls and between the crevices of the rubble formed by collapsed rooms. An eerie scent of death and decay that made Ileana shudder hung over the once sprawling, industrious cities of the Time Before. She starred herself for protection and hurried on, glad the relentless, eroding effects of time and the diligent labor of her own people over the centuries had removed all traces of such blights from the six known-inhabited continents.

When they reached the River Corn, Ileana was astounded and delighted by the thousands of beautiful, gossamer-winged butterflies that fluttered along the flower-strewn banks, where graceful, elegant, long-necked herons, flamingos, swans, and marabou storks mingled with sun bitterns and cormorants. Ducks and geese paddled in the water, their loud quacking a counterpoint to the discordant melody of calling curassows, brilliantly plumed tanagers, untidy hoatzins, funny-faced cotingas, big-billed toucans, and gaudy macaws. Tiny hummingbirds hovered and flew endlessly from blossom to blossom.

At night, when the travelers made camp, Ileana watched the fireflies flit from bush to bush and listened to the droning of the cicadas and the croaking of the frogs and toads. It seemed as though the darkness were alive, and sometimes a prickle of fear would raise the hairs on her nape, for it felt as though the expedition were being stealthily stalked by unseen creatures who were only waiting for the right opportunity to pounce upon her and the rest.

Early one morning, while the others still slept, she rose to find her husband and Bergren Birchbark talking soberly together a short distance from where the guards kept watch over the camp. Their voices were low, their faces, grave. After Ileana had poured herself a cup of coffee from the clay pot upon the fire, she approached them and spoke of her growing apprehension. She was dismayed to discover they shared her trepidation.

"I, too, have felt uneasy," Cain admitted. "'Tis as though we are being studied, our strengths and weaknesses assessed. I think it is only a matter of time before we are set upon by whatever is watching us."

"'Tis the Worms!" Bergren Birchbark asserted stoutly, his voice rising. "'Tis the Worms! They mean to attack us, capture us, and force us to become their slaves!"

"Shhhhh! Keep your voice down!" Cain hissed warningly, glancing at the others, who slumbered on, though a few stirred restlessly before resuming their snoring.

"Sorry," the dwarf apologized softly, flushing. "But 'tis true, I tell ye!"

"But why would the Worms want to do that? Take us prisoner, I mean?" Ileana asked, perplexed. "Do they have cities or castles, then, or fields or mines, that they have need of manual laborers?"

"I do not know," Bergren Birchbark confessed. "I do not fully understand what these things of which ye speak are." Then his jaw set adamantly. "But what other purpose could the Worms have for taking captives? They do not hold them hostage for ransom."

Ileana had no reply to this, nor did Cain. Yet the girl felt somehow that the answer lay before her—if only she could see it.

Later that afternoon, as they continued to follow the River Corn northward through the rain forest, they spied one of the misshapen creatures about which Bergren Birchbark had told them that first evening at Plumthicket. Intent on digging for roots, the wild boar was unaware of them, so they had ample opportunity to study it without fear. Its head was ridged and deformed, one cheek swollen all out of proportion to the other, its snout twisted and missing one sharp, curved tusk. Its back was peculiarly humped and scraggly, having lost a great many bristles. Large, scabby patches covered its thick, rough skin; its cloven hooves were strangely distorted. Its sides heaved as it grunted laboriously, then began to masticate the gnarled tuber it had uncovered beneath the loosened soil.

"It is the work of Mastiphal, the UnEarth One," Bergren Birchbark insisted grimly, and Ileana could not help but think he was right.

That night, when they made camp, she observed that her husband had doubled the number of sentries normally posted and that the fire was larger than usual. Turning from its flames, she stared intently into the darkness, wondering what was out there. Involuntarily, she shuddered, wishing herself safe within the boundaries of the trench at Plumthicket, ensconced in a treehouse, the ladder pulled up behind her.

As she continued to gaze about warily, Ileana saw that the others appeared to be on edge, too. As though they sensed that the blaze burning steadily at the heart of camp might offer them some protection, Charis and Halcyone huddled before it, as did the few sailors who had survived the assault on the *Moon Raker*. The soldiers who were not on guard duty had congregated near the flames as well, feeding them constantly with wood that had been gathered before sundown and stacked near the center of camp. In sharp contrast to the rest, Doctor York sat a good distance from the fire; earlier, he had complained that the light bothered his eyes. Ileana noticed he kept rubbing his arms as though they itched or he were cold. Perhaps this latter were the case, she mused, for once or twice, she saw his body twitch uncontrollably, as though he were shivering. He looked tired, she thought, and worried, too. The gills on the sides of his neck were fluttering rapidly. Her eyes strayed to his drawn face. A few wisps of hair, which was still coming out in clumps, hung limply over his sparse eyebrows.

"Nerves," York had told her when she'd mentioned her concern about his shedding. "No doubt I'll wind up as bald as some of those old Druswids!" Then, realizing what he'd said and to whom, he'd blushed to the roots of what hair he had left and added, "The priests, I mean; no offense intended, Lady."

"None taken," Ileana had replied, smiling. "They shave their heads, ye know, most of the bald ones. They have some idea that hair interferes with the flow of cosmic energy, though we priestesses have yet to find this to be so."

Now, recalling the conversation, the girl shook her head. Poor York. He was a physician, not a warrior. He simply wasn't cut out to be trekking across the world. She wondered why he had volunteered for the task when he obviously would have been better off remaining in Lorelei, his homeland. She didn't know. But then, she didn't remember

him as a fidgety man before the *Moon Raker* had sunk.
Perhaps he just hadn't realized how difficult the journey
would be, she speculated. Certainly, what they had endured
would have tried the soul of even the strongest Kind.

Ileana's own nerves felt considerably frazzled, although
she was able to calm them with deep breathing and medita-
tion.

In the distance, she could hear the roar of the Rye Rapids,
where the River Corn joined the Rivers Wheat and Oat at
the head of the Pumpkin Hills. The village of Cherryvale lay
just beyond, Bergren Birchbark had said. The sound of the
rushing waters was soothing, and after lying down upon the
gaily patterned blanket Apple Annie had given her, Ileana
finally managed to doze off.

Sometime later, she awoke with a start, her heart pounding in her throat. She had been dreaming, and in her dream,
she had seen the hideous, blurred image that had come to
her so often in the past. Only this time when it had taken
shape in her mind, she had been able to see it clearly, and
she had recognized the unnatural saurian creature they had
rescued from the ocean.

"High Princessssss," it had hissed, grinning at her slyly,
"do ye not know me? Your husssband doesss."

Now, remembering, Ileana buried her face in her hands,
horrified. Her shoulders shook as she wept silently so the
others of the expedition would not hear her. Then, her keen
ears suddenly discerning a subtle, alien whisper, she abruptly stilled her tears and lifted her head to listen to the noises
of the night. One by one, she identified and eliminated the
sounds: the sonorous splashing of the Rye Rapids in the
hills, the plaintive soughing of the faint breeze, the gentle
rustling of the leaves, the soft swaying of the tall grass, the
monotonous hum of the locusts, the intermittent croaking
of the frogs, the rhythmic chirping of the crickets, the
startled skittering of some small animal through the brush,
and then—nothing. Silence. Eerie and foreboding.

Gooseflesh prickled Ileana's arms as a low, wicked hiss
faded into the sudden hush. Too late, she cried out a
warning as the black shadows, which moments before had
seemed one with the trees, emerged from the jungle to fall
upon the travelers.

By the light of Tintagel's three moons, the girl could see the reptiles clearly: their scaly, horned heads; their pointed teeth gleaming, canines dripping saliva; their black, barklike skin; their hands curled like talons, and their nails as sharp as claws. Each of them sported an array of weapons: swords, shields, spears, and daggers mostly, though a couple wielded spiked morning stars, which *whooshed* sickeningly through the air as, with a snarl, the creatures rushed forward to assault the nearest guards. Fiercely, courageously, the warriors shouted their own long-unused battle cries and met steel with steel.

The clash of blades rang out through the jungle, sending a river of terror coursing through the land; and it was as though the rain forest itself held its breath, paralyzed by fear, as the first wave of the onslaught was greeted with a determined defense. Swords crashed upon shields as devilish thrusts were turned aside by deft parries. Dirks flew through the air, and the heavens rained javelins as Bergren Birchbark and Jiro Juniper tossed one shaft after another. The saurians were hardly slowed by the barrage of weapons they encountered. They used their shields to push their opponents back and knock them savagely to the ground. Once they were down, the unfortunate victims were rendered unconscious, then dragged into the brush. Ileana saw one reptile deflect a blade with his naked, upraised arm. Missiles struck their marks, only to bounce uselessly off the creatures' impervious bodies.

The saurians employed their own weapons primarily to disarm their opponents, then seized them with sharp teeth and claws, viciously tearing out the jugular veins of those who could not be subdued. The soldiers struggled bravely, but it was obvious they were no match for the carnivorous creatures. Even the valiant dwarfs, who had seen such atrocities before, flinched in the face of this adversity.

Blue fire erupted from Ileana's fingertips, only to close upon a force it had never felt before as it slammed into the thick, tough armorlike flesh of one of the gruesome saurians, singeing it—but little more. The reptile hissed and smirked, a terrible grin, and came on. Horrified, the girl called up her power as she had never summoned it before, and for a moment, it roiled so violently within her, she thought she would not be able to control it. Gritting her teeth, she fought to master the waves of energy that emanated from her body. Her aura blazed frighteningly, shooting sparks in every direction. The flying embers burned friends and foes alike before at last she managed to channel the awesome force and direct it at her enemy.

She aimed at the creature's face. The blue fire burst from her hands, flaring straight into the saurian's glowing red eyes. As the orbs ruptured, leaving their sockets hollow and rimmed with cinders, the reptile gave a shrill cry of anguish that sent shivers down Ileana's spine, for she knew, sickened unto death, that the scream had been Kind.

At the realization, the Power abruptly lurched within her, as though she had been slapped a stunning blow. Her breath caught in her throat, choking her; deliberately, she expelled it, slowly willing the Power to steady its suddenly erratic flow inside her. She lifted her hands again. Blue fire stabbed the now blind, reeling creature, blasting its head from its shoulders. Aflame, the disembodied thing sailed through the air, then hit the ground, rolling, to come to rest at Ileana's feet.

She gasped, stricken, as she stared at what she had wrought; the fiery head gazed back at her sightlessly, turning gradually to ash. Ileana doubled over, vomiting onto the earth. For an instant, she could have sworn she'd seen a Tamarinder's dark visage looking up at her from the flames. But no one who followed the Way could ever have been so malevolent. Then, before her very eyes, the face had changed, become racked with pain, begged her pitifully for assistance.

Help me. Help me, the mouth had seemed to cry, the empty eyesockets had seemed to beseech; and instinctively, her heart unable to deny the wrenching plea, Ileana had reached out to the thing before she'd realized what it was. . . .

A trick of the moonlight. 'Twas only a trick of the moonlight—nothing more, she told herself firmly and shoved the thought from her mind.

Once more, dizzily, the girl felt the Power stagger within her, and she realized—horribly—that it was rebelling against the use to which she had turned it. She had been

Chosen by the Light, and the Power of the Elements had been bestowed upon her, through Gitana san Kovichi, by the Immortal Guardian Itself. Her gift had not been intended for this purpose. Ileana dared not continue to wield it against the saurians; she did not know what might happen to her if she did.

Dazed, she got shakily to her feet, wondering dimly if Cain had been affected in the same manner.

To her utter horror, she saw he had not. His eyes were gleaming with a dreadful, fervid light, and his mouth was distorted cruelly in an unholy grin of triumph and satisfaction as blue fire blazed from his fingertips, destroying one reptile after another.

Shrieks of agony split the night as the bodies of the creatures were ignited by his fearsome force. The pungent, nauseating smell of roasting flesh filled the air, making Ileana retch until there was nothing left to come up. The dying screams of the saurians dinned in her ears as, their bodies irrevocably inflamed, their hearts began to explode in their chests, ripping open their torsos so blood and pulp spewed forth in every direction, spattering in equal measure their own kind and those who defended the camp. Ileana gasped as globules of odious icor splashed upon her shaksheer.

But even more revolting to the girl were Cain's hoarse, unnatural howls of glee as he watched the reptiles erupt into blazing chunks of matter. Even the warriors, hardened by their years of training and now fighting for their very lives, faltered as they heard the terrifying sounds of his twisted mirth.

The dead and dying lay scattered about the camp, but still, the creatures advanced, several of them dragging away hapless prisoners—some of whom were screaming hysterically—while other saurians kept Cain, the warriors, and the two dwarfs engaged. Ileana inhaled sharply as she saw one of the ugly reptiles, crawling along on its belly, slither toward Charis and Halcyone. Without even thinking, the girl called up her power—not to blast the grotesque black face with its hate-filled eyes, for her instincts warned her against this, but to surround the two women with a shield of fire so they would be safe from the creature's encroaching fingers. The saurian reached out for the two women, then snatched its hand away quickly as it was seared by the wall of bright blue incandescence Ileana erected.

Hissing angrily, the reptile turned to focus its attention on her, sensing she had caused the flames. But the creature could do nothing to her; her aura prevented it from touching her. As she grasped this fact, Ileana realized suddenly that she was not helpless against the saurians, as she had thought. She could use her power against them—just not in the way she had originally sought to do.

She closed her eyes and summoned her strength; her body began to shimmer even more brilliantly until she was enveloped by a halo of dazzling, white-hot light. Slowly, she let the luminescence flow from her being to curl like mist around the soldiers and the two dwarfs, making them immune to the reptiles who assailed them.

Enraged, the creatures vigorously increased their attack; but it soon became evident they could make no further headway against their opponents. Little by little, the saurians began to fall back before the renewed fervor of the warriors and the dwarfs, who now harried them mercilessly. Spears cast by Bergren Birchbark and Jiro Juniper pierced the red eyes of several of the reptiles, this being their only apparent vulnerability. The lighted torches the soldiers had grabbed and now swung before them menacingly helped to drive the repulsive creatures away from camp.

At last, tossing their captives over their shoulders and dragging two of the dead warriors behind them, the defeated saurians retreated as swiftly as they had appeared, melting into the jungle and the blackness of the night.

Chapter 24

*Though the well of the Power within one who has
been Chosen may be deep, it is not unlimited; therefore, the one who would draw upon it must take care
not to drain it dry. Such a one must exercise both
judgment and restraint when summoning the Power,
calling forth only what is needed for the task at hand,
for only a fool would use a lightning bolt to singe a fly.*

*After the Power has been released, the one who is
wise will rest; and if the reservoir of the Power has been
emptied, such a one must eat and sleep and give it time
to replenish itself. Otherwise, that one's mind and body
will grow too weary to control the Power summoned
—or to call it forth at all; and the Power itself,
exhausted, may fail that one during a time of dire
need.*

—Thus it is Written—
in
The Gift of the Power
by the Sorceress Saint Sidi
san Bel-Abbes set Mosheh

THE REPTILES LEFT BEHIND THEM A CAMP DEVASTATED BY THE
battle. The dead soldiers lay where they had fallen, their
sightless eyes glazed over and, in most cases, filled with
shock, their faces contorted from the rending pain that had
accompanied their Time of Passing. Bits and pieces of the
creatures themselves were scattered all over the place,

dismembered torsos lying yards from ragged limbs. Swords that had been courageously wielded now gathered dirt upon the ground, while dented shields, blackened firebrands, and shattered spears silently told their somber stories. The grass was dark and sticky with the blood that had been spilled and was now congealing beneath the moonlight. Cain was nowhere in sight, and Sir Ahmed, too, had vanished.

Realizing this at last as her aura gradually faded, Ileana forced her numb mind and body to take charge of the dazed expedition, recognizing that everyone else, having observed Cain's absence, as she had, was looking at her expectantly.

"York, see to our wounded," the girl directed the healer, who was staring off into the distance strangely, as though he intended to chase after the saurians, Ileana thought, her brow knitted with puzzlement. "Doctor York!" she barked again, more sharply. Slowly, he turned toward her, and for a moment, Ileana could have sworn something sly and evil looked out of his eyes. But then he blinked, and she decided she must have been mistaken. "See to our wounded," she repeated, breathing a sigh of relief as he moved to carry out her orders.

"Charis, Halcyone, stoke up the fire," she went on. "Then assist Doctor York with the injured." Seeing the two sobbing women attempt to stifle their tears, then rise and start, puppetlike, toward the woodpile, Ileana turned to Sir Husein, who now stood at her side. "How bad is it?" she asked gravely, for she knew the answer would not prove pleasant.

"Bad, Lady," he reported grimly, knowing she did not wish to be spared the truth. "Seventeen warriors are dead. Six more are wounded. Two are missing, as are the four crew members who survived the *Moon Raker*'s sinking." He paused, then continued soberly: "The Lord Cain has disappeared, too, Lady, as has Sir Ahmed."

"The missing soldiers are dead," Ileana said brusquely, trying hard not to dwell on what had become of her husband. "I saw the reptiles haul them away."

"But . . . why would they want the corpses, Lady?" Sir Husein asked, frowning. "I don't understand—"

"Neither do I." Ileana cut him off abruptly. "I can only guess what the creatures intended to do with them, and I pray to the Immortal Guardian that my supposition is wrong, for if 'tis not, then the saurians are even more depraved than I feared," she asserted, shuddering at what she suspected would happen to the bodies. Deliberately, she forced the horrifying notion from her mind and went on. "The four sailors were taken prisoner. The Light only knows what shall happen to them, for 'twas obvious the reptiles wished them taken alive."

"Do ye—do ye think they mean to torture them, Lady?" Sir Husein queried, appalled.

Ileana blanched, for this was a concept so alien to her people that the thought had never even crossed her mind.

"Oh, Husein," she breathed, stricken, "I hope not. What earthly purpose could that serve?"

He shook his head.

"I don't know, Lady. But the Records in our Archives contain many entries detailing such treatment of captives —usually to gain information from them, although 'tis written that there were once those who derived considerable sadistic enjoyment from watching their victims suffer before murdering them. Perhaps the saurians are such creatures, for they obviously have a propensity for violence and a liking for corpses, though the reason for *that* still eludes me—"

"They're carnivorous, Husein," Ileana uttered quietly. He studied her confusedly for a moment, then inhaled sharply. "Say nothing to the others," the girl instructed as she saw he had grasped her line of thinking. "They have been subjected to enough horror for one evening. Now find Sir Ahmed, and let's get this camp cleaned up. I want the bodies of our warriors cremated and the Prayer of Passing said for their souls as soon as possible."

"By your command, Lady." Sir Husein bowed, then walked off in search of Sir Ahmed.

"Ah, Bergren Birchbark"—Ileana turned to the dwarf, who had joined her silently—"do ye and Jiro Juniper not have some shovels in your packs?"

"Yea, Lady," he replied, nodding.

"Get them. I don't want the reptiles touched. Have the four uninjured soldiers and Cain's manservant, Mehtar, help ye scoop up the creatures' remains and pitch them into the fire."

"Yea, Lady." Motioning to Jiro Juniper, the dwarf moved away.

After that, grabbing an unused torch and lighting it from the fire, Ileana slipped reluctantly from camp, wondering, when she managed to find Cain, if he would still be the man she knew.

The decaying leaves and twigs that formed the rich, fertile loam of the rain forest crunched softly beneath her booted feet as she wended her way through the trees and brush, hoping she would not become lost in the labyrinth. Overhead, intermittently, through the intertwining branches of the deciduous trees, she could see the three moons of Tintagel hanging low in the black-velvet sky and the silver stars glittering like diamonds. The torch flickered in her hand, lighting her path as she continued forward, her heart filled with fear.

Even before she saw him, Ileana could sense her husband's presence; and as the tide of unbearable anguish that poured forth from his being washed over her in the darkness, a lump constricted her throat, threatening to choke her. She ached for him in every way a woman can ache for her man, and she wished fervently that she could take his hurt into herself so he would no longer be torn apart by the beast within him. She would willingly have given herself to save him, so deeply did she love him.

She found him standing at the edge of the riverbank, his arms pressed rigidly against a tree trunk, his head hanging between them, and his sides heaving, as though he were laboring to get his breath. From the corner of one eye, Ileana spied Sir Ahmed some distance away, waiting respectfully in the shadows. Behind him stood Sir Husein. The two warriors saw her at once, and wordlessly, with one hand, she waved them away, though she suspected they would not go far. It was their bounden duty to protect her and Cain, and this they would do with their bodies' last, dying breath.

Slowly, the girl approached her husband. Such was his grief that he did not hear her footsteps or sense her nearness, and when she laid her hand gently upon his shoulder, he jumped, startled, and whirled to face her as though she were an enemy, his sword swiftly drawn and held at the ready.

"Ileana!" he said, relief evident in his voice as he sheathed his blade. "What are ye doing here?"

"I—I was worried about ye," she explained, her eyes searching his ravaged face.

The beast was still there, watching her, and for a moment, she was afraid. Then, determinedly, she pushed her fear to the back of her mind. This man was her husband. Whatever he had done, whatever he had become, she loved him still; and she could not believe there was no trace of he whom she had once called beloved remaining in his soul. Abruptly, as though Cain sensed what was in her heart and rejected it, he shook off her arm and turned away.

"Go back to camp, Lady." He spoke curtly, in a tone calculated to hurt her, but Ileana paid no heed.

"Nay. I will not leave ye alone out here," she declared. "Cain, please, don't shut me out like this. Tell me what is in your heart and mind. I love ye. I have always loved ye—"

"Ye fool!" he snarled, whirling around and advancing toward her wrathfully, as though he would strike her. "Ye are a priestess! Do ye not know what is happening to me inside? Do ye not sense how the Darkness preys upon my soul? Every day, It grows stronger, while I—I am diminished in like measure." His words were bitter. "Soon I shall no longer be able to fight It. Then, Ileana, my brave, beautiful wife, will ye still be able to look into my eyes and say ye care?"

"Yea," she vowed fervently, "for I have more faith than ye. If only ye would return my love, Cain, together, we could defeat that which seeks to destroy ye; I know it!"

He laughed harshly, the ugly sound sending chills up her spine.

"Ye know nothing! *Nothing!*" he spat. "Ye are like the Light Itself, pure and holy, while I—I am not fit to walk upon the ground ye have trodden. If ye knew what I knew, had seen what I saw tonight— Ah, Immortal Guardian! Even now, they haunt me—those faces, those pathetically pleading faces . . . *Kind* faces, Ileana, where the saurians' ought to have been. Some trick of the Foul Enslaver, I thought. But I did not know that for sure, and still, I killed their bodies. And I enjoyed it! I *gloried* in it! I felt more powerful than I have ever before felt in this LifePath, as though I were invincible. *And I wanted to go on slaying them!*"

The girl could not help herself. She cringed at Cain's terrible words, wishing he had never spoken them.

O Sharai! her heart cried out to the old High Priestess who had foreseen, in part, what was to come. *Ye were right. Ye were so right. There are indeed things that are better left unknown. . . .*

A trick of the moonlight, Ileana had thought, that Tamarinder's sightless eyes, filled with agony, that she had seen staring up at her. Yet Cain had seen Kind faces, too. What did it mean? What did it mean?

"It was as ye said." Ileana forced herself to speak normally. "A trick! Only a wicked trick! They are not Kind, those hideous creatures. They are minions of the Foul Enslaver!"

Yet she remembered how her power had rebelled at killing the saurian, and her confidence in her words was shaken.

"Ye don't believe that, Lady, any more than I do," Cain averred. "I saw what happened to your power, priestess! Ye, who were Chosen by the Light, could not kill the reptiles, for ye knew them to be Kind. But I—who belong to the Darkness, who knew also that they were Kind—I *wanted* to slay them, and I did. Ah, Heaven's Light, I did! Go back to camp, Ileana—as fast as ye can, before I destroy ye, too! I am more Kind than the saurians. Your power will be useless against me also. Can't ye understand that? I'm being eaten alive by the Darkness, and once it consumes me, I'll kill ye. Ye won't be able to stop me!"

"I don't believe ye will do that, Cain," the girl said quietly, praying she were right. "I don't believe ye can. Ye love me; I know ye do, whether ye admit it or nay. Open your heart to me, beloved! Together, we can fight that which is within ye!"

If only we could, beloved, he thought sadly. *But I dare not let ye stand at my side. 'Tis my battle—and mine alone. I must best it before it does me, or else . . . Ah, beloved, I*

*could not bear knowing I destroyed ye. Hate me, Ileana!
Hate me with all your heart!*

"So ye want to fight the beast that lies coiled inside me, do
ye?" he asked, his voice deliberately hard and mocking as,
inexorably, he moved toward her, like a smilodon stalking
its prey. "Very well, since that is your wish, Lady. . . ."

Cain smiled—a terrible, mirthless grin—and before
Ileana realized what he intended, he yanked her to him,
enfolding her in a ruthless embrace. His lips swooped down
to capture hers savagely, and horribly, she knew it was not
he who kissed her but the beast within him. She could feel
its overwhelming strength and power as it plundered her
mouth, brutally compelled her lips to part, to yield beneath
the onslaught of its encroaching tongue. Her head spun
dizzily as the Darkness rushed up to engulf her. She
couldn't breathe. *She couldn't breathe!*

She felt the beast's hands tearing at her etek, and she
began to struggle violently against it. But she was no match
for it; she was not physically strong enough to oppose it, and
her power had been exhausted by the battle with the
unnatural saurian creatures. Now, though she summoned it
with every last ounce of her will, it failed her.

The girl shivered as the beast ripped open her kurta to
expose her breasts to its hungry, raking gaze, and the cool
night air of spring touched them, kissed them. She could
feel the beast's hands upon her, caressing her, as it muttered
dreadful things in her ear. She cried out, wondering dimly if
Sir Husein and Sir Ahmed still watched from the shadows;
and somehow that made it all seem even uglier. . . .

Then, without warning, as suddenly as it had seized her in
its grasp, the beast released her. Ileana stumbled back,
clutching the sides of her torn kurta and etek together as she
stared at the beast, scarcely daring to believe it had let her
go. It leered back at her with Cain's eyes, jeered at her with
Cain's mouth—

She turned and ran, blindly, tears streaming down her
cheeks. With one hand, she wiped her lips, scrubbed them
fiercely, as though she could somehow cleanse them of the
beast's touch, its taste. But still, she felt as though her
mouth would never be clean again. She could hear the
beast's laughter ringing in her ears, taunting her. She raced

on, faster and faster, heedless of the branches of the trees that slapped at her face, grabbed at her clothes.

At the edge of the riverbank, the beast stood motionless, making no move to give chase. After a time, it snickered smugly to itself, pleased at the fear it had wrought in Ileana.

But the part of it that was Cain's heart broke wrenchingly in the darkness just the same.

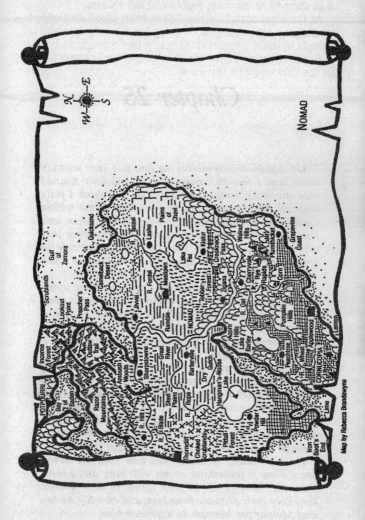

Map by Rebecca Brandewyne

Chapter 25

My hands are trembling so badly, I can scarcely write, and I fear this page shall be indelibly stained with my tears. Until last night, I do not think I fully realized the strength and power of the beast within Cain. Now my faith has been unspeakably shaken, and I no longer know if he is capable of conquering that which is inside him. Its hold on him has become so great, it has turned him against me; and I do not know if my love alone is strong enough for both of us.

Hope is all I have left to me now, hope that somehow, some way, there is still a part of Cain that is sane. How horrible to believe the man one loves is mad. I close my eyes at the thought, and still, the word leaps out at me boldly from the page. Yet I cannot strike it out, for I fear it is the truth.

He has withdrawn into himself like a sick animal, and I do not know if my attempts to reach him are doing any good at all or if I am only wasting my time. He watches me continually, slyly, and sometimes I feel as though he is laughing at me, as he did last night. The idea is frightening. Yet I know if I stop trying to get through to him, we are lost and Tintagel is doomed.

He is so tense, so silent that now even the others sense there is something wrong with him; and I think they, too, have begun to grow afraid of him. Warily, they keep their distance from him, and even Sir Ahmed and Mehtar are hesitant to approach him.

We marched all day at a frantic pace and through

pouring rain, but no one complained. We could not put behind us fast enough that place where the reptiles attacked us and so many of our number were slain or taken prisoner.

This last still disturbs me, for try as I might, I cannot imagine what the creatures do with their captives, and I have reluctantly come to the sickening conclusion that Sir Husein is right: The saurians torture their poor victims to death for sport. How horrible if that be true. But the only other explanation that has come to me is so unspeakable, I cannot even bring myself to write of it.

Yet time and again, my eyes stray to Doctor York, and I remember the reptiles' faces last eve, and my dreams are haunted by what I suspect—what I fear.

This night, I shall force myself to eat and sleep, for I dare not allow my power to be drained from me again. I shall need it desperately in the coming days, I think.

We reached the Cornucopian village of Cherryvale at sunset, and the news the dwarfs here imparted to us is alarming. Over the past several weeks, they have seen large numbers of the Worms, as they call the creatures, on the move. The Cherryvale dwarfs report that the saurians appear to be gathering en masse and marching north to some unknown destination for some equally mysterious—but I fear ominous—purpose. The Cherryvale dwarfs are terrified.

I, too, am afraid, for if there are enough of the reptiles, I believe they could launch a massive invasion of both the continents of Aerie and Verdante—and do so with every expectation of success. If this is the creatures' horrendous plan, it must at all costs be stopped before it can be brought to fruition, for if the far side of the planet falls, it will be only a matter of time before the entire world is overrun by the saurians and Tintagel, as I know and love it, is no more.

The thought fills me with despair, and it is all I can do to hearten myself and to hope the Ancient Ones' faith in Cain and me was not misplaced, for though I do not know how the reptiles came into being or where they originated on our planet, I feel beyond a shadow of a doubt that it was their coming the Druswids foresaw in the fires and mists so long ago—a Darkness so vile, Gitana san Kovichi and Takis san Baruch gave their very lives to protect us from It, as I have learned from Cain.

Truly, the Time of the Prophecy is upon us; and if this is so, according to legend, the Sword of Ishtar shall reappear, taken from the secret Holy Place by one who has been Chosen by the Light.

I feel in my heart and soul that I am that one, as the Reverend Mother hoped. But I have no inkling of where the sword lies or how it may be warded. What will it do to me if I am not the Chosen One? I do not know. Yet if I cannot find the blade, if I am not the one meant to bring it forth, I shudder to think what will become of us all.

Time and again, I summon the fires and mists, and cast the crude rune stones I fashioned at Plumthicket. But I see nothing save the Foul Enslaver, growing ever stronger and more powerful—and laughing at me with my husband's mouth.

—Thus it is Written—
in
The Private Journals
of the High Princess Lady Ileana I

THE FOLLOWING MORNING, THE CHERRYVALE DWARFS GUIDED the weary travelers through the Crookneck Pass, which lay to the north of the sprawling Walnut Hills. Then, with rafts they kept carefully concealed in caches when not in use, they ferried the companions across the Great River Ramble to its far shore, a land called Nomad. From there, after thanking the Cherryvale dwarfs for their hospitality and their help, those of the expedition continued on alone, trekking westward until they reached the small town of Zigana, which lay in a sheltered green hollow in the hills bordering the northern bank of the river.

Zigana was only a trading post, really, for as Bergren Birchbark explained to the others, the Nomads were gypsies. They lived in gaily painted caravans with high, rimmed wheels, traveling from place to place as the mood struck them.

"You'd best be on your guard," the dwarf warned the rest, "for most of them are either beggars or thieves, and they prey on unsuspecting strangers. They're wise to their own kind and thus not as apt to deceive one another, for they're a hot-tempered tribe, too, as quick to take a knife to one another as they are to fleece a poor, dumb sheep for its wool. They're not likely to assist us, but we shall see."

The town edifices—the trading post, inn, and tavern, as well as a few scattered shops and huts—were all built of logs and constructed in a ramshackle manner, as though intended for temporary use. Some of their walls were higher than others, which made their uneven thatched roofs sag. The spaces between the logs had been chinked with clay, but poorly, and Ileana could see several gaps in the walls. Here and there, doors and windows had been irregularly cut into the logs. Dilapidated shutters banged in the slight breeze, as did the hinged shingles, their paint peeling, that swung from the signposts stuck in the ground before the three main buildings. On the outskirts of town stood a couple of caravans. Tethered nearby, grazing contentedly, were several horses—animals distantly related to the Bedouin faesthorses—and a pair of unicorns. Other beasts, their tails flicking at flies, were tied to hitching rails in front of the trading post, inn, and tavern.

Bergren Birchbark motioned toward the latter, whose sign he translated for the others. THE GREEN DRAGON, it read.

"It's there we shall learn any news," the dwarf said.

Warily, uncertain of their welcome, the travelers pushed open the door and went inside. Abruptly, the alehouse, which contained several customers and the talk, laughter, and music usual in such a place, fell silent, and all eyes turned curiously—and a trifle suspiciously—to the newcomers.

As Ileana glanced about, she saw that the tavern's interior was no better than its exterior. The common room was big and square, the far wall boasting a large stone fireplace with a scarred mahogany mantel that was decidedly unlevel. The hearth itself was grimy with soot and ashes, as though following its last use, it had never been cleaned. Haphazardly stacked to one side of the fireplace was a pile of wood, most of which was not yet properly seasoned.

To Ileana's right was the bar, huge and crude, fashioned of rough planks and tilting slightly at one end. Along its bottom ran a wooden rail, deeply gouged and splintered. Above the bar hung a crazed mirror, before which were shelves lined with an ill assortment of mugs, glasses, and plates, some pewter, others colored cut glass. There were even a few fine crystal goblets, looking very much out of place among the rest. Beneath the shelves, atop a long counter, perched wooden cradles holding casks of wine and ale.

The room itself was filled with tables, chairs, and benches, all of which had seen better days and were as mismatched as the barware. The tables were stained and marred. Some of the chair legs looked as though they might collapse at any moment, having obviously been poorly glued to begin with. One of the benches was so rickety, Ileana wondered how anyone dared to sit on it.

The floor was as unkempt as everything else, dangerously warped in places and badly in need of polishing. It was slick with grease in spots, remnants, no doubt, Ileana thought, of the unpalatable stew whose pungent aroma wafted from the kitchen to mingle with the thick cloud of tobacco smoke that hung in the air.

Upon spying the travelers, a man at once stepped forward from behind the bar. He was big and beefy, his skin swarthy and none too clean, his brownish black hair oily, streaked with grey, and flowing like a mane. Thick brows swooped above his glittering black eyes. A large nose jutted over his bushy, drooping mustache heavy with wax. Beneath his firm, fleshy lips was a full beard that, combined with his long hair, gave him a lionlike appearance. A diamond stud earring twinkled in one lobe. He was dressed in a white silk kurta, open at the throat to reveal the numerous gold chains that hung from his neck to rest upon his broad, matted chest. Over the sweat-stained shirt, he wore a once beautifully embroidered woolen cepken, now bedraggled. The vest only partially concealed the jewel-encrusted dagger stuck into a tattered red satin hizaam wrapped around his considerable girth. Garish striped silk chalwar, patched here and there, and worn black leather boots hugged his corded legs. His outstretched hands flashed with rings.

"Welcome to the Green Dragon, strangers," he greeted the party in Nomad. "I am Tesio, the owner of this humble establishment. What can I do for ye?"

Fortunately, Bergren Birchbark did indeed have an ear for sounds and knew the Nomad language.

"I am Bergren Birchbark, Elder of the village of Plumthicket in Cornucopia," the dwarf replied in the gypsy's tongue, "and this is the Lord Cain sin Khali sul Ariel, the High Prince of the six Eastern Tribes of Tintagel, and his wife, the High Princess Lady Ileana. The rest are members of our expedition. We seek both refreshment and information. As I recall, the last time I was in Zigana, the Green Dragon served a cold tankard of fine ale—"

"And still does," Tesio bragged, beaming. "Pray, be seated, my good man—and the others, too." He indicated a couple of empty tables. Then he raised one hand and snapped his fingers at a dark, fat but comely woman behind the bar. "Durva," he called to his wife, "bring a round of ale for our guests." She nodded and smiled, the anxious expression in her eyes fading; and Tesio turned back to the now seated travelers. Without waiting for an invitation, he pulled out a chair and sat down beside them.

"So," he addressed Bergren Birchbark again, "if ye have come from the village of Plumthicket, ye have journeyed far. Yet most of ye dwarfs seldom venture beyond the borders of Cornucopia—unless it is to do a little business. But ye have not the look of a trader about ye." Tesio's dark eyes gleamed inquisitively.

"That is because I am not," Bergren Birchbark responded. "I am acting as a guide for the Lord Cain and his people. They come from the far side of Tintagel and search for others of their tribes who may have passed this way. They also look for the Worms, the lizardlike warmongers who have invaded our land, Cornucopia. Perhaps ye have seen them?" the dwarf suggested.

"Bah!" Tesio growled, then spat upon the floor. "Devils in snakeskin is what they be! Yea, I have seen them—and so have many others of my tribe. Several caravans have been attacked; many gypsies have been killed or taken prisoner."

"'Tis the same in Cornucopia," Bergren Birchbark announced, pulling his pipe and pouch from his vest pocket. After filling and lighting the burnished wooden bowl, he drew on the stem slowly, then continued. "My people in the village of Cherryvale reported to us that they have recently seen large numbers of the Worms on the move. They appear to be marching northward. The Lord Cain and the Lady Ileana fear the Worms may be gathering an army with which to assault and conquer us and our land. He and the rest of his party mean to meet the Worms in battle and destroy them."

"Bah!" the gypsy snorted again. "That is impossible! The creatures are invincible! They cannot be slain!"

"So my people thought in the beginning," the dwarf stated, "till we learned the Worms are afraid of fire. We have killed several of them by waiting until they slept, then building large bonfires around them."

"Perhaps that is true," Tesio conceded, "but even so, how will ye burn up an entire army if what ye say is so and the creatures are massing, preparing for a large-scale invasion of the continents? Nay." He shook his head. "If that is the case, we can do naught but take to the hills and hide, as many of my people have already done, or travel to Mestipen, where the King of the gypsies, Lord Roldan, keeps a great stone castle that may be easily defended."

"Even so, the Worms would but besiege ye," Bergren Birchbark pointed out logically, not quite certain what a castle was, but reasoning that it must be some sort of stronghold, "and in the end, ye would be forced to surrender or starve. Nay. I prefer to take my chances with the Lord Cain. He is a sorcerer with much power. He can slay the Worms with his bare hands—with which he commands a strange blue fire—as does his wife, the Lady Ileana, a sorceress in her own right, who used her magic to protect us from the Worms. I, Bergren Birchbark, saw this when we were set upon by the Worms during our journey here to Zigana. Many of them were killed, and those who were not fled in fear."

At that, the gypsy's eyes slid with interest to Cain and Ileana. Then he grunted.

"He is still but a man, she, a mere woman; and I do not

see how they can hope to prevail over an entire army! There is an odd look in the Lord's eyes I find disturbing. I think he must be crazy in the head! Go home, dwarf. Only a fool would follow a madman!"

Though privately Bergren Birchbark had told himself these same things, the gypsy's comments both angered and annoyed him, and stubbornly, he rejected them.

"I am many things, Tesio Tavernkeeper," the dwarf uttered loftily, "but I am not a fool. Over the passing weeks, I have come to believe the Lord Cain is our only hope. Scoff if ye will, but I have seen none other with his power —except for his wife, of course, and she has been naught save kind to us all."

"Well, it is your neck, Bergren Birchbark," Tesio asserted, shrugging. "But others of these six Eastern Tribes of which ye spoke, the Tribes of which ye claim the Lord is High Prince, have passed through Zigana before, and none of them has ever returned. Frankly, I do not think this time shall prove any different."

"In which direction did they travel?" the dwarf asked, pointedly ignoring the gypsy's skepticism.

"West—toward the land of Gallow. But many seasons have passed since I saw them. The Worms, too, as ye call them, seem to be heading that way. But I cannot say for sure. I, Tesio"—the gypsy struck his chest with one hand —"am not such an idiot as to follow them!"

With that parting remark, he pushed back his chair and returned to tending his bar. Shooting him a disgusted glance, Bergren Birchbark blew the foam off the tankard of ale Durva had set before him. Then, grimacing, he took a sip of the stout brew before turning to address Cain. Softly, the dwarf translated the conversation.

Cain listened silently. Once Bergren Birchbark had finished, the High Prince shrugged.

"What the gypsy thinks is unimportant," he declared. "We have learned what we wish to know, and that is all that matters. We shall stay overnight at the inn here, then continue on our way tomorrow. How far from Zigana is this land called Gallow?"

"Several days' journey, Lord," the dwarf reported. "'Twould be easiest, I think, if we traveled north through the Tobbar Forest, then west across the plains southeast of Mestipen, which is another Nomad town. It has apparently grown in size since last I saw it, for previously, it was mostly old stone ruins. There, from what Tesio Tavernkeeper told me, the King of the gypsies, Lord Roldan, is in possession of a—a . . . castle, whatever that may be." Once more, Bergren Birchbark pondered the unfamiliar word. "I gathered it is some kind of defensible stronghold. At least we might be able to find refuge there, should it become necessary." The dwarf's voice was grim. "The gypsy confirmed what the villagers of Cherryvale told us, Lord—that many of the Worms are on the move. So we had best be on our guard.

"If we have no trouble, we will eventually come again to the Great River Ramble. The land of Gallow lies on its western side. At the place where the Great River Ramble joins the River Rope is the town of Barterville. We should be able to replenish our supplies there."

Cain nodded thoughtfully; but before he could speak, the door of the alehouse opened and two men walked in. At their entrance, the room once more fell silent as those present assessed the newcomers.

It was evident at first glance that they were not gypsies, for one of them was a giant of a man, standing well over seven feet tall and massively built. He had flaming-red hair, a mustache, and a long, bushy beard, which he stroked absently as his narrow blue eyes surveyed the tavern intently. He was garbed in a short-sleeved, knee-length brown leather tunic, girded at the waist with a wide leather belt from which dangled a huge battle-ax and a morning star. A short blue wool cape hung from his shoulders; leather sandals that laced up to the knee adorned his feet.

The smaller man, who just topped six feet, was lithe but muscular. His face was lean, all sharp angles and planes, and he was clean-shaven. His skin was fair, in sharp contrast to his hair, black as a raven's wing, and his one eye, which was a startling shade of emerald green. The other was covered by a black patch, from which a jagged scar ran down his cheek. Even so, he was still a handsome man, Ileana thought as she studied him. He was clothed in a black silk shirt with long, full sleeves; a black leather jerkin; and a pair of thigh-length, slashed and puffed black satin breeches. Close-fitting black chausses encased his legs; high, wide-cuffed black leather boots clung to his calves. Atop his head, perched at a jaunty angle, was a black velvet cap with a tight headband and a wide, flat circular crown draped to one side and bedecked with a black plume. The man carried a sheathed broadsword at his waist; the hilt of a dirk protruded from the cuff of one of his boots.

His eyes swept the room, lingering on Ileana before he and the giant moved to take seats at an empty table. Immediately, those in the tavern resumed their conversations. As he had done previously, Tesio hurried from behind the bar to take the newcomers' order. Then, swishing her gaudy, flounced skirts provocatively, a young, black-haired, black-eyed gypsy girl whom Ileana had noticed earlier in one corner sashayed over to the two men and sat down beside them.

Resting her elbows on the table, she leaned forward enticingly so the tops of her breasts swelled above the low neck of her ruffled blouse. She studied the men from beneath her half-closed lids; her tongue darted out to moisten her pouting scarlet lips.

"I am Syeira," she murmured in Nomad to the slender, scarred man. "For a piece of silver, I will tell your fortune, stranger."

The man settled back in his chair, smiling faintly with amusement as he eyed the girl appraisingly. It was obvious he had understood Syeira's words, for after a moment, he took a silver coin from the pocket of his jerkin and tossed it upon the table. Then the giant said something to him in a strange language, and the man laughed.

"Do ye speak Tintagelese?" he inquired of Syeira in flawless Nomad. "My friend would like to hear my future also."

"Yea . . . stranger," she answered haltingly in the common tongue. "I speak it—a little. Many of my people did—once. Some have remembered and taught others." Her hand closed over the piece of silver on the table. She picked the coin up, bit it, then slowly tucked it between her breasts, which were straining against the thin fabric of her blouse. Then she smiled. "Let me see your palm, stranger," she commanded throatily, holding both of hers out invitingly.

As Ileana heard the poorly spoken Tintagelese, she turned in her chair to get a better look at the gypsy and the giant and his companion. She saw the handsome man lay his hand in the girl's cupped palms, then watched as the gypsy began to examine it with a great show of concentration, turning it this way and that, her thumbs rubbing it sensuously.

"Ye are a man who must work for a living." The girl spoke, causing Ileana to shake her head imperceptibly with wry amusement and faint contempt, for even a child could have surmised this from his calluses. "And in order to survive, ye have sometimes been forced to take dangerous risks." Well, that much was obvious from the scar on the man's face, Ileana thought scornfully. "This makes ye very attractive to women," the girl went on seductively, "and ye have known many. Yet always ye have moved on, for ye live by the sword—and perhaps shall die by it."

At that, Ileana almost snorted aloud, now certain the gypsy had no real power to speak of. The man was both good-looking and armed—and a traveler as well. He was perhaps in his early thirties, so it was only natural to assume he had had his share of females. He spoke, from what Ileana had heard, at least three languages fluently—proof that he had journeyed far and wide, seldom remaining in one place for very long, no doubt. His sword was worn, though well cared for, indicating it was not merely for show. From that, anyone could have deduced that it might, in the end, prove the death of him.

Thoroughly disgusted, Ileana was about to turn away when she realized the man had observed her interest and was now looking at her speculatively, one eyebrow cocked.

"What say ye, Lady?" he asked her, to her surprise. "Do ye think I shall die as the gypsy has foretold?"

Ileana shrugged.

"Perhaps," she replied. "But I would not be too concerned about it if I were ye. The girl only guesses. Ye should make her return your money, for 'twas taken under false pretenses."

"Ye lie!" Syeira cried irately, leaping to her feet, her black

316

eyes flashing. "My power is great. Beware, Lady, that I do not curse ye for your interference!" She shook her fist threateningly at Ileana.

Ileana smiled wryly.

"Your power is limited to a *very* slight sentience and an extremely shrewd, calculating nature," she stated calmly. "Ye cannot harm me."

Syeira gasped, then sputtered with rage. Once more, silence descended upon the tavern as all eyes turned to the two women, those present holding their breath expectantly, the gypsies grinning with anticipation at the idea of a cat fight, Tesio rolling his eyes and swearing softly at his eldest daughter's impetuosity. He spoke a little Tintagelese and thus had got the gist of the conversation. For Heaven's sake! Why couldn't the girl be more like her younger sisters, Beti and Orlinde, who had married well and did not cause trouble? he wondered. He could not afford to have his customers berated; it was bad for business. Still, he did not want to listen to his daughter's sharp, castigating tongue the rest of the day either, and these particular travelers were not likely to pass this way again. . . .

As the thought crossed his mind, Tesio suddenly remembered what Bergren Birchbark had said about the two foreigners and their magic, and the gypsy hastened from behind the bar. Much as he disapproved of his bad-tempered daughter, he did not want her burned to a cinder by the Lady Ileana's crazy husband should he take offense at the manner in which his wife had been insulted and threatened.

"Now, Syeira," Tesio began placatingly in rapid Nomad, "there is no need for such rude behavior. I'm certain the High Princess Lady Ileana did not mean to disparage ye with her remarks. She is a stranger to our land and unfamiliar with our ways. Also, she claims some power herself and perhaps felt some resentment toward ye because of it. No doubt yours is much greater than hers, daughter," Tesio flattered Syeira outrageously, knowing she did not, in truth, possess any real ability to foretell the future, but relied on her natural instincts about men and her considerable beauty and charm to dupe them into believing her.

"Is this true?" Syeira turned to Ileana, addressing her in

Tintagelese. "That ye have some power yourself?" The gypsy looked Ileana up and down scornfully, then laughed shortly. "Frankly, I do not believe it. But if 'tis so, then perhaps ye would care to prove it?"

Ileana shrugged, then glanced questioningly at the handsome, scarred stranger.

"Be my guest," he invited, proffering his hand.

After a quick glance at Cain, who said nothing, she rose from her chair to take a seat beside the one-eyed man. Then, much as Syeira had done earlier, Ileana held his hand in hers, though she made no attempt to examine his palm. Instead, calling forth her power, she looked deeply into his mind. His skin was warm—she could feel the Blood of Life flowing within him—and his thoughts were dark and complex, as though he had kept them to himself for a long time.

Slowly, she began to speak.

"Ye are a stranger in a strange land," she intoned, causing Syeira to snicker and lift her eyes skyward as though anyone might have known this. The other gypsies laughed appreciatively, but Ileana only ignored them and continued softly. "The name by which ye are now called is not yours. Ye assumed it out of defiance—to remind ye of that which caused ye to take it, and also to spare your family pain." At that, the stranger started and stiffened visibly, his one eye narrowing warily; and a tense hush enveloped the alehouse as those within suddenly realized they were not about to hear a sly tale consisting of general platitudes and mere guesses.

"Once ye were a prince among your people, beloved by all save one," Ileana went on. "But this one was in a position to do ye much harm. He arranged for the murder of a man close to ye, a kinsman, perhaps, then falsely accused ye of the deed. Because ye did not know of his treachery, ye could offer no defense. But because ye were a prince and beloved, ye were not hanged for the crime, but banished from your land.

"Since that time, ye have wandered far and wide, searching for some means of clearing your name, but ye have found none; and the one who unjustly imputed your honor has sought to slay ye so ye can never return home to expose him. The scar ye bear is from a battle many seasons past, when ye were set upon by this one's henchmen."

"Who is he?" the stranger asked hoarsely, gripping Ileana's hand tightly in his. *"Who is he?"*

She shook her head.

"I do not know for certain, for a shadow lies between ye. But 'twas someone who stood to gain much by your removal, a crown and a throne, perhaps, if your people follow the ways of the Old Ones. This much I can tell ye, however: He who would see your body dead wears a strange ring shaped like a serpent—"

"Nay!" the stranger burst out. "Nay! I do not believe ye!"

Ileana shrugged.

"I do but speak what I see," she said, then let go of his hand. "There is nothing more I can add, Garrote the Dispossessed."

Chapter 26

Purchased from the gypsies in the town of Zigana, of Nomad:

> *Three horses and one unicorn at a cost of five platinas, one ruby ring*
> *Two ponies at a cost of one platina, one silbar*
> *Six saddles at a cost of two platinas, one bronzot*
> *One pair of matched unicorns at a cost of two platinas, one golden*
> *One gypsy caravan at a cost of three platinas, one golden, two bronzots, one emerald ring*
> *One leather harness at a cost of two bronzots, one nykel*
> *Assorted foodstuffs at a cost of one golden, one silbar, three bronzots, two cuprums, one isarn, one peltro*

How I thank the heavens that Mehtar, my manservant, had the presence of mind to salvage my purse and Ileana's from our cabin before the Moon Raker sank. Only because of this was I able to give Tesio Tavernkeeper hard currency, in addition to the two rings he also demanded as payment for the above-listed items. Had I lacked the money, the thief would surely have insisted on having mine and Ileana's wedding bands and keys, and the Druswidic collars that are the symbols of our rank; and with these things, we could never have parted.

*If we manage somehow to return to Khali Keep, I
shall see that Mehtar is generously rewarded for his
assistance. He is a good man and has always served me
well.*

—Thus it is Written—
in
The Private Journals
of the High Prince Lord Cain I

HOLDING HER BREATH FOR FEAR SHE WOULD BE DISCOVERED AND
summarily dispatched to her room, Syeira tiptoed across
the green spring grass, cool and damp with morning dew,
that edged the west wall of the tavern. Once she had reached
the north end of the alehouse, she paused, listening intently.
Then, carefully, she peeked around the corner to the front of
the building, where the foreigners were just concluding their
business with her father. Syeira's heart pounded as she
clutched her small bundle of meager possessions tightly,
wondering for the umpteenth time if she was doing the right
thing. Her father would be so angry and her mother so sad
when they found the note she had left pinned to her pillow
on her bed in the attic.

Still, Syeira thought, she was withering away here in this
ramshackle tavern, this sleepy hollow in the hills. Already
she had known eighteen years and had yet to find a
husband, while Beti and Orlinde, her sisters, had both been
married for some time. It just wasn't fair!

The fact that she had imperiously rejected several would-
be suitors, Syeira conveniently thrust from her mind. She
had considered them all beneath her, and indeed, they *had*
been lacking in some manner, or they would have pursued
her harder instead of being intimidated by her snapping
eyes and sharp tongue.

Before, it had not mattered. There had been plenty of
men passing through Zigana, and all of them had gravitated
to the alehouse. Syeira had been certain that sooner or later,
she would find one who pleased her. Now there was little
chance of that. Most of the gypsies, terrified of the strange,
lizardlike creatures who had invaded the land, were either
hiding in the hills or had taken refuge in Lord Roldan's

castle in Mestipen. Travelers were few and far between, most of them foreigners, as the ones last night had been, though Nicabar and his band had stopped in, hoping to glean what news they could before joining the others in the hills.

Only her father—stubborn old man!—had refused to budge. He had built Zigana himself, he'd said, and nothing was going to drive him away. He would close the shutters securely at night and lock them; the creatures were seldom seen during the day, so there was little to fear then.

Though a gypsy born and bred, Tesio had not a drop of wanderlust in his blood. Many years before, he had insisted he would not go chasing about in a caravan, risking his neck stealing, when he could make twice as much money running the tavern. To her disgust, the rest of Syeira's family had agreed with him. Beti and her husband now managed the inn, and Orlinde and her husband were in charge of the trading post. The others in the band worked as artisans, producing crafts to be sold or bartered at the trading post.

But with this, Syeira was no longer content. Until last eve, she had been proud of her skill as a fortune-teller. Though she knew she had no real talent for predicting the future, she had made an art of studying people—their speech, mannerisms, clothes, and so forth—and most of the time, she'd proved clever enough to fool them. But last night, *she'd* been made to look the fool—and before her father's band and Nicabar's, too! The gypsies were a gregarious people. Soon everyone in her tribe would know how she'd been exposed for a charlatan and shamed. She would never be able to hold her head up again! That is . . . unless she were to acquire the power to perform real magic—like the High Princess Lady Ileana.

Syeira was not so proud now. She would beg if need be, but she must learn the Lady's secrets! Besides, Garrote the Dispossessed had not looked like a man who was easily intimidated; and even if he were a prince, as the Lady had said, he had been banished from his homeland. Now he was just an Outcast, and perhaps, Syeira mused, she would find favor in his one good eye.

She tossed her head, set her jaw determinedly, and

slipped like a wraith after the travelers now leaving the
Green Dragon behind. Her family and the rest of her band
might wish to remain in Zigana, but she did not. Soon
perhaps no one would come to the alehouse—no one but
the lizardlike creatures, that is, and Syeira did not intend to
fall prey to them!

*We are making better time now that Cain was able
to purchase mounts for us from the gypsy Tesio
Tavernkeeper. I was touched that my husband chose for
me a dapple-grey unicorn, so like my own alaecorn,
Ketti, who was left behind at Khali Keep, as Cain's own
faesthors, Ramessah, was, for we did not want to risk
bringing the beasts with us, not knowing what we
would face in The Unknown. Though, at the time, I
was saddened by my parting from my faithful Ketti,
now I am glad she did not come with me, for she would
surely have drowned as the other animals did when the
Moon Raker sank.*

*Our party, which shrank in size considerably after
the slaying of the nineteen warriors by the saurians
and the capture of the four sailors, has grown again.
Garrote the Dispossessed, the Outcast, and his friend,
the giant, Ulthor, who is from a land called Borealis,
have joined us. They were traveling in the same
direction we were, they said, and volunteered to accompany us, there being safety in numbers. They, too, have
seen the reptiles and recognized the danger the creatures pose to the land. In addition, they told us the land
of Gallow is rife with Outcasts, most of whom have
turned outlaw and will murder a man for a few alumes.*

*'Tis obvious both Garrote and Ulthor are no strang-
ers to battle, and so I am glad of their presence. They
have proved themselves worthwhile companions, quick
to lend a hand when needed; and Cain has been more
himself since they became a part of the expedition, for
which I am most grateful. I think Cain senses Garrote
is a kindred spirit, maligned through no fault of his
own yet determined to prevail against the odds by
which he has been beset. It is so hard to watch my*

*husband's inner struggle and know that there is noth-
ing I can do to help him, that this is a battle he must
fight alone.*

*I curse the beast within him who would take him
from me; and at night, when Cain lies sleeping, I hold
him close and kiss him softly so he will not awaken,
and I pray my love can somehow draw him back from
the edge of the dark chasm that threatens to engulf
him.*

*I watch Doctor York, too, for I am certain he is
hiding something from us, something terrible. He
traded a hizaam for a hat from one of the gypsies at the
Green Dragon, and he has taken to wearing it constantly, pulled down low over his forehead so we cannot see
his face. He claims it is because the sunlight hurts his
eyes. At night, he keeps his distance from us, remaining
in the shadows to occlude his features.*

*I fear my worst suspicions are true, yet even now, I
hesitate to write of them, hoping desperately that I am
wrong.*

—Thus it is Written—
in
The Private Journals
of the High Princess Lady Ileana I

"Oho! What have we here!" Ulthor roared, his voice
booming with laughter as he carried a squirming, shrieking
figure from behind one of the many trees in the Tobbar
Forest. "It looks to me as though I've caught myself a pretty
gypsy wench!"

As he tossed her upon the soft grass in the sylvan glade
where the expedition had temporarily paused for respite,
Syeira rolled over, sat up, and glared at him, rubbing her
posterior, feigning injury.

"How dare ye?" she spat. "Ye had no right to treat me in
such a fashion. My father is a very important man—head of
his own band!"

"Yea, and a more thieving lot I've yet to see," Ulthor
insisted with mock indignation. "Why, imagine charging

five dimeks for a tankard of ale! 'Twas sheer road robbery, that's what!"

Before Syeira could repudiate this statement, Cain spoke coldly.

"What are ye doing here, girl?" he asked. "Spying on us for your father and his band? Perhaps they are planning to set upon us in the woods to steal back that for which they have already fleeced us most thoroughly!"

"That's a lie!" the gypsy hissed as she got to her feet, her black eyes shooting sparks. "I—I— " She broke off abruptly, biting her lip.

Things were not going at all as Syeira had planned. She had thought Garrote the Dispossessed would step forward to defend her, would beg her pardon for treating her so shabbily last night at the Green Dragon, and would sweep her up before him onto his horse, claiming her beauty had bewitched him. Instead, he was only gazing at her as coolly and remotely as the Lord Cain, the disapproval plain upon his face.

"My father doesn't even know where I am," the gypsy confessed sullenly.

"Then I repeat: What are ye doing here, girl?" Cain questioned sharply.

"I—I want to go with ye!" Syeira shot a quick glance at Ileana. "Your wife has much power. I—I want her to teach me her magic so I can become a real fortuneteller and redeem myself in the eyes of my people."

Cain shook his head, grimacing at the gypsy's foolishness.

"She can't do that, girl," he told Syeira tersely, irritated. "One is either Chosen—born with the Power—or not. Unfortunately for ye, my wife was right: Ye have almost none, and even if ye did, we could not be bothered with ye just now. We must defend the land from the Darkness that has come upon it. Ye shall have to return to the Green Dragon at once!"

"Nay!" the gypsy cried. "I won't go back—and ye can't make me!"

"As ye wish, then," Cain declared, shrugging. "'Tis up to ye whether ye want to remain alone here in the forest, for ye certainly shall not be allowed to accompany us. We must travel swiftly, and we cannot be held back by a spoiled, impetuous child prone to temper tantrums."

Syeira blanched, a wild, scared look in her eyes. The idea that those of the expedition, upon discovering she was following them, would leave her behind had never crossed her mind. She was accustomed to getting her own way and had thought that by simply refusing to go home, she could force the companions to accept her as one of them. Now it seemed this was not to be the case. It was evident that the Lord Cain was in charge of the party and that if he ordered the others to have nothing to do with her, they would indeed march on without so much as a backward glance in her direction.

"Ye can't leave me here," the gypsy wailed. "'Twill be dark soon, and—and those dreadful creatures who look like lizards will get me!"

"She's right, Cain," Ileana pointed out quietly.

He studied his wife for a moment. Then he nodded curtly.

"Very well, then," he said to Syeira. "But you're to cause no trouble, girl, or we'll leave ye in the next town we reach. Get in the wagon with Damsel Charis and Mistress Halcyone."

With that, he turned his back, mounted his horse, and trotted off to begin issuing orders to the soldiers. Quickly, the others started preparing to move on, securing their flasks to the pommels of their saddles, tightening girths, and checking weapons.

"I would prefer to ride with Garrote," the gypsy announced as though to no one in particular; but all the same, from beneath half-closed lids, she slanted a look at the Outcast to see if he was listening.

Now that she was certain the travelers intended to take her along with them, some of Syeira's fear had receded.

"Oho! So that's the way the wind blows, is it?" Ulthor, who had discerned the remark, inquired bluntly, hauling the gypsy up before him onto his massive horse before she had a chance to protest. "Forget it, my girl. Outcast or nay, Garrote's still a prince and not for the likes of ye."

"Put me down!" Syeira demanded angrily, trying to twist

away from the giant's grip on her waist. "I told ye: I want to ride with Garrote!"

"Too late. He's already ridden on," Ulthor observed, chuckling, guessing his friend had also heard the gypsy's pointed comment and had cantered off as rapidly as possible so as not to be saddled with her. "You'll have to be content with me, I'm afraid."

"Why should I be?" Syeira snapped. "You're only a common giant!"

"Yea, that's true," Ulthor agreed placidly. "But then, I don't have to worry about marrying a princess, and I'm more than big enough to handle a fiery little wench like ye. And that, my beauty, is a statement I'll bet no other man in your life has ever been able to make!"

The gypsy tossed her head arrogantly, but the giant noticed she slowly ceased her struggles all the same. Beginning to whistle a merry tune, he tightened his hold on her imperceptibly, in no particular hurry to catch up with the others.

It was just shortly after sundown when some of the warriors, who had been scouting on foot, ran back to inform Cain they had spied a group of the reptiles farther on in the woods. At once, the High Prince signaled a halt. Then he, Garrote, Ulthor, Bergren Birchbark, and Sir Ahmed rode forward stealthily to investigate the situation. What they discovered both sickened and horrified them.

The creatures, who had obviously been marching all day beneath the shade of the trees, had stopped and pitched camp in a small clearing. Several of the saurians were busy with their duties, the most unspeakable of which was the butchering of four dead bodies, pieces of which were then distributed among the reptiles and eaten raw. The men crouched in the forest, whitened with shock as they took in the grisly scene. Reeling, remembering his wife and child, who had been taken captive by the creatures, Bergren Birchbark turned away to vomit quietly into the bushes. Never before had the men watching from the trees witnessed such evil. Truly, the saurians had been totally corrupted by the Foul Enslaver!

At the center of the glade were three large wooden cages

mounted on wheels, within two of which were several prisoners.

One of the pens was filled with people from numerous tribes, but Cain had never before seen anything like them. They all looked as though they were in the advanced stages of some hideous, disfiguring disease. They were totally bald and naked, their heads grossly swollen, their foreheads distorted with ridges. Their eyes had turned colors; some were pale pink, some a deep rose, others a vivid blood red. Their cheeks bulged at the bridge of their noses so these appeared broad and flat; their lips were thinned to gruesome slashes in their faces. Huge, scaly black patches covered their entire bodies and seemed to be thickening, hardening, and spreading, so it was impossible to differentiate between men and women. Their navels had distended and were hanging like cords from their abdomens, some long, some short, depending upon the state of retraction.

In sharp contrast to this, the nude captives in the second cage all looked normal, though it was obvious they were terrified. Now, as Cain and his companions continued to stare silently, stunned and disbelieving, incapable of action, two of the reptiles opened the door of the pen and roughly removed one of the prisoners. They dragged the screaming woman across the glade, where they forced her to stand upright before a third creature. Before Cain even realized what this saurian intended to do, quick as a flash, with a soft *whoosh,* its umbilical cord lashed forth to stab the woman in the stomach. She cried out again, more from shock and fear than pain, Cain thought. Then the two reptiles who were holding her hauled her over to the third, unoccupied, pen, thrust her inside, and locked the door, while two more creatures yanked another victim forward.

"Great God Daeggawode!" Ulthor breathed in sudden, awful understanding. "That thing is infecting those poor people with something that will turn them into atrocities like itself! Good Goddess Friduric preserve us! Those wicked spawn of Zaebos are BodySnatchers!"

"Worse than that," Cain intoned grimly, stricken to the very core of his being as, horribly, he realized at last what the saurians really were. "They're SoulEaters. *SoulEaters!*

They're defiling the very essence of those people, befouling it with the Darkness. Now those wretched spirits will never be able to become One with the Immortal Guardian in the End, as has been promised to all those who believe. By the Light! *By the Light!*"

Cain rose, his aura blazing, his hands aflame with the blue fire of the Druswids. Now he understood everything—the beast within him, why it was there—*everything!* The reptiles were not Kind, but they were not beasts either. They were . . . *UnKind!*—creatures who had once been Kind but were no longer. Ileana could not destroy them because she had been Chosen by the Light. She sensed within them the traces of their Kind essence, that which had been One in the Beginning with the Immortal Guardian, and she could not turn her power against them. But he, Cain, had been instilled with the Darkness. He felt the vestiges of the Light's essence in the SoulEaters, and he *wanted* to destroy it! It was the antithesis of the beast inside him.

Now it was as though some madness suddenly seized him in its fist. He raked the clearing with blue fire and watched the creatures explode, their blood and guts spewing forth, their heads and limbs flying through the air, their dismembered torsos exploding; and he laughed mirthlessly. The eerie images of the Kind faces they had once had, screaming noiselessly with agony as death claimed them, only spurred him on. They could not touch him. His was a Darkness greater than theirs.

When every last one of the saurians lay in bits and pieces on the ground, he turned the blue fire on the diseased bodies in the first cage, and the anguished wails of these, their metamorphosis not yet complete, were even more dreadful to hear. But they were music in Cain's ears.

He slew the body of the woman in the third pen, infected before his very eyes. Her soul was yet part of the Light, barely tainted by the rottenness that would have putrefied it. She screamed and screamed as the blue fire consumed her, for her body had not even begun to reach the stage where her heart would burst within her.

At last, Cain's hands swept to the second cage, to those who had not yet been infected by the creatures. Gripped by frenzy, he wanted to kill them, too. But some sane part of him yet survived, and it fought with its all might to subdue the beast within him.

Slowly . . . slowly . . . slowly, with the greatest of difficulty, he compelled himself to lower his hands, to sheathe his power, to let his aura fade.

Quickly, as though they feared he might change his mind, Garrote and Ulthor ran to the pen and released the petrified prisoners. In shock, they rushed blindly through the forest, as horrified by their benefactor as they had been by the saurians themselves.

"Lord." Sir Ahmed laid one hand tentatively upon Cain's arm, remembering how Ileana had done so after the battle in the Cornucopian jungle. "Lord, 'tis over," he said softly. "'Tis over."

To the soldier's vast relief, gradually, the dreadful light in his master's eyes dimmed, and he shook himself a little, as though coming to his senses.

"I—I—" Cain's voice broke off abruptly as he stared at the carnage he had wrought, sickened and mortified. "Burn them, Ahmed," he whispered hoarsely. "Burn every last, accursed one of them!"

Then he strode to his horse, untied the animal, mounted it, and galloped away as though the Foul Enslaver Itself were pursuing him.

FULL MOON

The Sword of Ishtar

Map by Rebecca Brandewyne

Chapter 27

Doctor York's body is dead. Cain killed it. He had to. The healer had been infected by the reptile aboard the Moon Raker, and it was only a matter of weeks, perhaps days, before the metamorphosis would have been complete and York would have turned on us all.

I was, of course, as horrified as the others to learn what the creatures truly were—are—but I cannot really say I was shocked, for I had already begun to suspect this some time ago, despite the fact that I hoped I were wrong.

UnKind. SoulEaters.

The words ring even now in my mind, like a hammer upon an anvil, making me feel as though I have been dealt a stunning blow and sent reeling. This is a Darkness so vile, so evil, it surpasses all others.

The Foul Enslaver has been with us since the Beginning; but because of the Immortal Guardian's gift to the Kind—the Tree of Life and Knowledge upon which blooms the Fruit of Free Will—we have always before been given a choice to determine the paths we follow, the destinies we meet, whether we shall honor, serve, and defend the Light or the Darkness.

But the saurians have taken away this freedom to choose—not just in this LifePath, but forever, for once the soul has been so foully corrupted by the Foul Enslaver, it can never return to the Immortal Guardian; it is beyond all salvation, all redemption, all forgiveness, and the Way to become One with the Light in the End is eternally lost.

The reptiles have been clever, taking prisoners, allowing no one to see what becomes of them, for otherwise, those evidencing the initial signs of the disease would be slain by those not yet infected, and the Darkness would be unable to spread, to devour our planet. Only the creature aboard the Moon Raker, *startled when York fell upon it, reacted instinctively, lashing out at him with its umbilical cord.*

So much more has been made clear to me now, why that beast I fear so deeply lies within Cain. He is becoming the Darkness, a Darkness more vicious than that of the saurians. Only in this manner can he destroy them and, in doing so, serve the Light. But what a terrible risk Takis san Baruch, the Ancient One who performed the Ritual of Choosing from which Cain was conceived and born, as I have learned from my husband, took in imbuing him with that beast. For if ever there comes a time when Cain is unable to regain control of it, he will become a threat greater even than the UnKind themselves. How will I fight him, then, when my power is useless against him? Surely, this, the Druswids did not foresee! I only hope it will not prove a fatal error.

I lie awake at night and wonder how all this will end, and the words Syeira spoke to me one day after we crossed the Great River Ramble into the land of Gallow echo in my mind.

Teach me your magic, Lady, she said, *and in return, I will make ye a love potion, for ye have trouble with your man—yea?*

Yea, it is true—but not so simple as Syeira, who is yet a child in that she sees only black and white, believes. Would that I did have a potion to recapture Cain's love for me. But I know in my heart it is not that easy. There are too many forces at work, and until I understand them all, I dare take no action one way or another, not knowing the outcome.

The answer is there, within me, if I can but find it.

*Until then, I can do naught but go on searching—and
hope and pray.*

*How I wish the High Priestess Sharai and Sister
Amineh were here to guide me. But they are not; and
though, three times, I have projected myself astrally to
reach them, the distance was far and I was weary, so
their images were blurred and I do not know if they
understood my TelePath. I will try again when I am
stronger, when I no longer have this ominous feeling
that I must conserve every ounce of my power, that
soon I shall need it all to prevent Cain from destroying
me and Tintagel.*

—Thus it is Written—
in
The Private Journals
of the High Princess Lady Ileana I

The Ambush Woods, Gallow, 7273.5.28

JUST WEST OF SHARPSTOWNE, IN THE LAND OF GALLOW, WAS A
bridge that spanned the River Hilt and marked the beginning of what was known as the Outlaw Trail. This road
wended its way through the Ambush Woods and the Razor
Mountains, and was so called because it was rife with
murderers, reivers, and other criminals who obeyed no laws
but their own. It was this road, Garrote the Dispossessed
informed the rest of the expedition, that they must follow if
they were to continue their pursuit of the UnKind, the
SoulEaters who appeared to be making their way ever
northward.

Both Garrote and Ulthor, well known in Sharpstowne,
had visited an often frequented tavern there to glean the
latest news. Now they reported that even the outlaws, who
had seen the UnKind, as so many others had, feared the
reptiles and had gravitated toward the towns of Gallow,
where they felt safer.

Nevertheless, Garrote, as a precaution, Ulthor said, had
recounted to those in the alehouse the story of the expedition's battle with the SoulEaters in the Tobbar Forest of
Nomad. The two were certain the tale would spread rapidly.

"I do not think"—Ulthor smiled grimly—"that anyone will then be too eager to waylay and rob us on the Outlaw Trail. Garrote's description of the Lord Cain's power was . . . most detailed."

Ileana shuddered at the thought, surprised that despite what they had seen and knew of her husband, Garrote and Ulthor—and the two dwarfs as well—had chosen to continue to accompany the expedition. Ever since Bergren Birchbark had learned what the UnKind did to their captives, he had determined to do what he could to help destroy them, knowing they had turned his wife and child into creatures such as they. After reaching Barterville several days ago, he had decided not to go back to Cornucopia, and the quiet but dedicated Jiro Juniper had elected to remain with him.

Now the hooves of the animals and the wheels of the gypsy caravan clattered upon the old wooden planks of Blackjack's Bridge. Soon the thick Ambush Woods, which reminded Ileana of the Melantha Forest of Cygnus, closed around them and they were on their way through the multitude of deciduous trees and evergreen pines that had—with good reason—been given their ominous name.

Still, the companions journeyed northward for several weeks without incident, and Ileana began to relax slightly, certain the story Garrote had told in Sharpstowne had done its work. The others presumed as much also; and tired from the long, difficult trip, their fear of the SoulEaters having turned to a numb acceptance of the horrifying danger the saurians posed, the travelers were less vigilant than they should have been. Thus they were taken unaware when, just south of Preacher's Pass, they were attacked by a band of reivers who had either missed or discounted Garrote's tale of Cain's power.

With blades, morning stars, and cudgels, the filthy group set upon the companions and were met with like weapons as Cain, Garrote, Ulthor, and the rest formed a defensive circle about the women and the caravan that held most of the expedition's supplies. The clash of steel upon steel echoed through the mountains as the grim battle —punctuated by shouts, grunts, and moans—ensued.

It would have ended in moments had Cain cast away his sword and shield to blast the outlaws with the blue fire of the Druswids; but to Ileana's relief, he did not. The reivers were thieves—and no doubt murderers, too—and they would pay for their crimes in their next LifePath or be condemned to the Darkness. But even so, there still remained the chance, however remote, that those who had not already been irrevocably corrupted by the Foul Enslaver might yet repent their wicked deeds and return to the Way. More important than this was the fact that whatever else the outlaws might be, they were still Kind. It was only right that Cain use no more force than was necessary to defend himself and those who looked to him for protection.

The fact that he did not call forth his power told Ileana there was still a part of him that was untainted by the Darkness, that still adhered to the Light and Its teachings, which were the Druswidic laws. The thought gave her much joy; and after the brief skirmish had ended and the reivers who were still alive had fled, no match for those who had opposed them, she ran to her husband's side.

For a fleeting instant when Cain turned to her, Ileana could have sworn there was love and concern for her in his eyes. Then, slowly, like shutters drawn across a window, the look faded to be replaced by one of coldness.

"See to the wounded, Lady," he said brusquely. Then he pivoted on his heel to begin issuing orders to the rest of the party.

Ileana bit her lip, hurt, wondering what had caused his abrupt change of mood.

He does love me! she thought fiercely. *I know he does! Why must he pretend he does not? It's almost as though he's afraid to love me, to let himself grow too attached to me. But if that is the case, it can mean only that he believes that, eventually, he will have to face me, to fight me, and he will end by destroying me because I cannot use my power against him!*

The girl shivered at the notion, hoping it were not true. But she could see no other reason why Cain would deliberately turn away from her when she was certain he loved her still. It did not matter what she did; Ileana understood that now and was filled with despair at the realization. Cain was determined not to open his heart to her, to admit his love for her. That night aboard the *Moon Raker* was all he ever meant her to have, just a memory of all they had ever shared and lost. He would offer nothing more; he dared not; and if that were so, she would indeed be forced to do battle with him in the end, despite her power's rebellion at such a use and no matter the outcome. She would have no other choice, for she was pledged to honor, serve, and defend the Light, while he—he turned ever more to the left hand of the Darkness. Soon there would no longer be even these small moments when she felt sure a part of him was yet hers.

With a heavy heart, Ileana mounted her dapple-grey mare, wondering why Cain had purchased her a unicorn so similar to her alaecorn, Ketti, if he did not care.

I don't know how much longer I can bear the wounded expression in Ileana's eyes when she looks at me. What is even worse is that I don't know how much longer I shall have to.

I have fought the beast within me with every last ounce of my strength and power—but to no avail. The Darkness grows ever stronger inside me, and soon, very soon, I know I shall be totally consumed by It.

I live in horror of that day.

When I remember the battle in the Tobbar Forest of Nomad, I am sickened unto death by the realization that I almost murdered—yea, murdered!—those poor, terrified, innocent people who had not yet fallen prey to the UnKind, the SoulEaters.

Everything within me that is good and decent rebelled at turning my power on those people; but still, the Foul Enslaver's grip upon me was so strong, I don't know how I managed to break free of it in time. If Sir Ahmed had not recalled me fully to my senses, I shudder to think what would have happened.

Perhaps next time, I shall not be so lucky. Perhaps next time, I shall commit murder—and mayhap the victim will be Ileana.

The thought preys on my heart and mind and soul. How can I let myself care for her—as I so yearn to do—when I know what a hold the Darkness has on me and how It may use my deep love for her to destroy her?

Ah, Heaven's Light. 'Tis like a madness that eats at

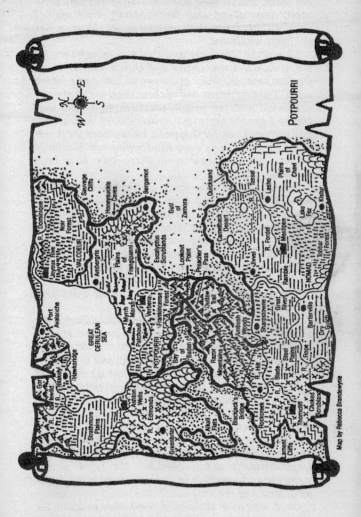

Map by Rebecca Brandewyne

my brain, and as time goes on, I know my periods of sanity grow fewer and further apart. Each day, I wonder if 'tis I who shall awaken in the morning—or the beast within me.

I know the others are afraid of me, though they try not to show it. Even Garrote and Ulthor, who seem like fearless men, are wary of me—and how can I blame them? I am surprised any of them continue to journey northward with me, to take orders from me. But they believe I am the key to the destruction of the UnKind; and perhaps I am, for it appears I alone have the power to kill the SoulEaters' once Kind bodies, now hideously warped by the disease with which they have been infected.

Where did it come from, I wonder, this terrible malady that eats the bodies and minds—the very essence—of the Kind? Perhaps it is something left over from the Time of the Wars of the Kind and the Apocalypse, something that has lain sleeping ever since, waiting for its chance to strike. I do not know, and no doubt it is unimportant. It is here, and there is nothing at present that can be done to change that.

I must worry instead about those of the expedition and their welfare.

The days are short and cold now, for after passing Lookout Point in the Razor Mountains, we left the continent of Verdante behind and entered the land of Potpourri upon the continent of Aerie; and it is winter here in the northern hemisphere. We are all weary and chilled to the bone, for we lack the proper accoutrements for the weather. Garrote has assured me we can purchase these, as well as other supplies, in the Potpourrian city of Verbena. The bodies of the reivers we slew at Preacher's Pass in the Razor Mountains bore purses rich with money and jewels, so we are no longer virtually destitute—thank the Light! It has stung my pride sorely to be unable to provide any better for Ileana and the rest.

Once we reach Verbena, I hope, too, to learn the latest news. I must discover the place to which the UnKind are marching, converging, and destroy them

*before they begin a massive invasion of the land, as I
fear is their intent. Otherwise, the SoulEaters shall
overrun Tintagel, and its tribes will be no more.*

—Thus it is Written—
in
The Private Journals
of the High Prince Lord Cain I

At midday, the travelers left behind the last of the
mountains and, once upon flatter terrain, entered what
Garrote called the Frankincense Forest, named for the trees
that grew in abundance there. Ileana thought it must be a
lovely place during the summer, when the branches of the
slender trees were heavy with leaves and flowers. Even now,
the fragrant aroma of the coarse bark lingered in the cold,
frost-tinged air and brought memories of Mont Saint
Mikhaela back to her, for the cloister had often been filled
with the pungent scent.

Yet the forest, like that of Cygnus, was beautiful in winter.
Snow lay thick and heavy upon the earth and the naked
branches of the trees. Icicles clung like frozen tears to the
limbs and encrusted smaller bushes with webs of gossamer
rime. Above, the sky was a pale, misty grey. Sometimes,
here and there, a white dēor or peryton bounded nimbly
through the woods, startled by the companions, and an
occasional snowshoe rabbit hopped across the ground.

Ileana shivered as an icy breath of wind touched her
cheeks; she was glad of her etek, though the knee-length
jacket did little to ward off winter's chill. She hoped they
would reach Verbena soon.

But many long days of riding passed before the party at
last sighted the high walls of the city. Ileana was surprised to
see such an obviously large, well-built, and fortified settle-
ment, for during the course of the expedition's journey, it
had seemed to her that the western half of Tintagel was
much less advanced than its eastern counterpart.

So far, she and the rest had yet to discover evidence that
the people here had salvaged any of the Records of the Old
Ones, much less established any Archives; thus they knew
almost nothing of the Time Before, except that there had

once been a great war. The people themselves, except for the more civilized dwarfs, bordered on the barbaric. Religion was diverse; the Light was not recognized as the creator of all things. The Power was looked upon as some mysterious, mystical thing at best; at worst, Cain was believed to be a warlock and Ileana, a witch. Few could grasp the fact that it was only that their senses were more highly developed than those of others who had not been Chosen to receive such a gift. Only Cornucopia appeared to have any real form of government, and that was fairly primitive. This side of the planet, Ileana thought, must have been far more devastated during the Time of the Wars of the Kind and the Apocalypse than the other half of the world had been.

But Verbena, though very different from what Cain and Ileana were accustomed to, was a city in every sense of the word, as the entire party saw when, after thoroughly inspecting them and requesting that they state their business within, the guards permitted them to pass through its iron gates.

Ileana was astonished by her surroundings, for the entire city was constructed of petrified wood that blended in so naturally with the trees that encompassed it that it seemed a part of the forest. The only color that punctuated the yellowish brown hue of the petrified wood was green. Everywhere, there were green signs, green doors, green shutters, and green roofs. Like the cities of the known-inhabited continents, Verbena had been built with a care for nature. The narrow cobbled streets twisted among the towering trees; the edifices themselves sat upon patches of grass and dormant wintry flowers. Even the air was filled with the fragrance of dried blossoms and leaves, herbs and spices, and scented oils.

There were houses and shops, vendors hawking their wares, and noise, lots of noise, which those of the expedition found comforting as they rode along. They gawked at displays and passersby, who gaped with like curiosity at them; and Ileana guessed there were relatively few strangers seen in the city nowadays, it being so dangerous to travel.

The people of Verbena fascinated her and the others as much as they did the Potpourrians, for the latter were all of slightly smaller stature than normal and slender, with a willow's grace. Their features were sharp, though handsome, and their ears were pointed.

"Why, they're all elves!" Syeira, seated before Ulthor on his mighty horse, exclaimed loudly, staring.

"Girl, don't ye know 'tis rude to shout so about people's appearance," the giant rebuked the gypsy sternly but fondly. "The Potpourrians are a highly intelligent tribe—and very well educated, too, I might add. They know things about history that nobody else on the entire continents of Aerie and Verdante does!"

"Is that true?" Cain, who had overheard this conversation, asked Garrote the Dispossessed.

"Yea." The one-eyed man nodded, then announced, "I think it would be wise if we were to go at once to the castle. I'm sure the King Lord Coriander will want to meet ye, and 'tis there we shall best learn what is happening anyway."

"Why should the King grant us an audience?" Cain inquired, quirking one eyebrow.

"Because I—I . . . know him," Garrote admitted at last. "I was . . . once betrothed to his daughter."

Though the others, even Ulthor, were bursting at the seams with curiosity upon hearing this confession, no one said anything further. Even Syeira, who had parted her lips to speak, couldn't manage a word, since Ulthor instantly clapped his hand over her mouth to silence her.

"Garrote's past is his own business," the giant hissed in the gypsy's ear. "Ye would do well to remember that, little spitfire!" Then he ruffled the hair on the top of her head.

Ileana thought Syeira would surely box Ulthor's ears; but instead, she actually seemed pleased by the giant's rough treatment of her. She sighed and nodded, then settled back happily into the cradle of his strong arms, shrugging and smiling.

With Garrote leading the way, the travelers continued along the slush-filled streets of Verbena, eventually coming to the fortress, which had been built along the north wall of the city. Garrote spoke briefly to one of the watchmen at the open portcullis, who gave him a sharp, appraising glance before motioning for them to pass; and presently, they found themselves in a large courtyard. There, Garrote dismounted and again muttered something to one of the guards, then handed the man a ring. Staring at the gold seal with disbelief, the sentry disappeared hurriedly into the keep. Sometime later, a beautiful, fair-haired, blue-eyed girl came running breathlessly down the snowy steps, her long skirts caught up in her hands, her piquant face alight with hope.

She stopped short upon seeing those gathered in the courtyard; her eyes roamed over them eagerly. Then, suddenly, she cried out and flung herself into Garrote's arms.

"Gerard, oh, Gerard, oh, Gerard," she sobbed over and over in perfect Tintagelese.

Heedless of the rest, Garrote hugged the elfin girl as though he would never let her go, kissing her, murmuring endearments in one of her delicate pointed ears, and stroking her long blond hair.

"Rosemary, oh, Rosemary, after all this time, I—I hardly dared to hope—" He broke off abruptly, swallowing hard, still seemingly unaware of the others looking on avidly, Syeira with an expression of resignation on her face, Ulthor grinning hugely.

It was the giant who finally intruded upon the joyful reunion.

"Gerard, is it?" His hearty voice, filled with laughter, rang out over the courtyard. "Hmmmmm. Methinks Garrote suits your face much better, man."

Garrote—Gerard—glanced up sheepishly, a faint blush staining his cheeks.

"Yea, no doubt," he confessed. Then, drawing a little away from the elfin girl, he made the necessary introductions. "Rosemary, these are my friends," he said, naming them simply, with heartfelt sincerity. "We have journeyed long and far together. My friends, this is the Princess Lady Rosemary of Potpourri—and I gather from my enthusiastic reception, despite all that has happened, still somehow my betrothed."

Rosemary smiled at them tremulously, her eyes filled with tears of happiness.

"Be welcome in my father's castle," she greeted them warmly, holding on to Gerard's arm tightly, as though she still could not quite believe he was real. "Please, won't ye come inside?"

After the companions had dismounted and their animals had been led away by the guards, they followed the Lady Rosemary into the fortress, Ulthor, Syeira, and the two dwarfs staring around with wide-eyed wonder. Cain and Ileana merely noted the keep was well furnished and well kept, and they chalked up a mark in the elves' favor.

"This place reminds me of home somehow," Ileana whispered to her husband as they traversed the corridors of the castle.

"Yea, it does me, too," he replied. "Garrote—Gerard —said the elves had Records and Archives. Perhaps we will learn something here that will help us."

Of its own volition, Ileana's heart leaped at his words. *Us,* he had said. Just a little slip, after all, but one that meant the world to her. She smiled, feeling much as she suspected the Lady Rosemary had felt moments ago in the courtyard, and her hopes rose. Perhaps here she would discover the whereabouts of the Sword of Ishtar, which she *must* have if the Time of the Prophecy were truly upon them.

"Perhaps we will," she agreed with her husband. "Perhaps we will, beloved."

But this last word she spoke very softly, so Cain would not hear it and remember to shut her out of his heart.

Chapter 28

Hear ye, hear ye. It is hereby proclaimed that the Prince Lord Tarragon of Potpourri and his sister, the Princess Lady Rosemary, have joined the expedition commanded by the Lord Cain sin Khali sul Ariel, the High Prince of the six Eastern Tribes, who has pledged to destroy the UnKind, the SoulEaters who have invaded our land to infect us with their disease.

Let whosoever shall henceforth have cause to offer succor to this expedition do so at once or suffer the penalty of banishment forever from the land of Potpourri.

Further, let whosoever shall willingly waylay this expedition and thereby cause it to suffer loss or delay be hanged by the neck until dead.

With my own hand have I affixed my official seal hereto.

—Thus it is Written—
in
A Proclamation
issued by the King
Lord Coriander IV of Potpourri

"THE UNKIND ARE MASSING HERE, IN THE HOLLOW HILLS JUST west of the Strathmore Plains, in Finisterre," the King Lord Coriander announced to the travelers gathered in his privy chamber this late evening. He jabbed his finger upon the old yellow map spread open on the table before him. "'Tis where I would begin if I were intent on invading both the continents of Aerie and Verdante.

"As ye can see, this starting point will enable one half of the SoulEaters' army to march northeast around the Great Cerulean Sea into Borealis. From there, it can continue south into Valcoeur, then move southwest directly into Potpourri. Meanwhile, the remainder of the army can travel southeast across Finisterre, then head east into Potpourri. The two halves can then converge here, in Verbena, and journey south to sweep across Verdante, following, in the opposite direction, much the same route ye yourselves took from Cornucopia. If the UnKind have sufficient numbers, the land and the people will be helpless against them." Coriander's face was grave.

The elf was in his early fifties, a distinguished-looking man with thinning grey hair and keen, pale blue eyes that shone with a wealth of wisdom and concern. A bejeweled gold crown sat regally upon his head. He wore a long blue tunic trimmed with ermine; satin shoes with pointed toes that curled up at the ends peeked from beneath the hem of the garment. A heavy gold chain bearing a large medallion hung about his neck; rings bedecked his fingers.

Ever since becoming aware of the SoulEaters, he now went on to explain, he and his advisers had been studying —as well as fighting—them. Some months ago, they had learned what the UnKind truly were and had taken what steps they could to prevent their people from falling victim to the reptiles.

The King had decreed that all Potpourrians were to remain in the cities, which were now vigilantly defended with catapults and ballistas that fired flaming missiles, and mangonels that hurled heavy stones that had been rolled in pitch and set ablaze. With these tactics, the elves had managed to stave off several attacks, and recently, it was thought the SoulEaters had given up and left the land. Then scouts reported vast numbers of the UnKind on the move, heading east toward the land of Finisterre. As Cain had done, Coriander had come to the conclusion that the creatures, having infected enough people to swell their ranks, were now assembling for a massive invasion of the two continents.

"'Tis imperative they be stopped on both fronts," he stated soberly, "at the River Idlewild and at Ashton Wells, here and here." He pointed out the river and the city on the map. "Since surmising the SoulEaters' intent, I have been in constant contact with the Lord Gerard's father, the King Lord Arundel of Finisterre. He, too, realizes the terrible danger of the situation, and he has informed me both the city and the castle there have already begun preparations for battle.

"With your permission"—he glanced at Cain—"I shall notify him of your arrival here and tell him to expect ye at Ashton Wells, along with a force of Potpourrian soldiers, sometime in the near future. From what Gerard has said, ye have great power, Lord; but I do not think ye will reject a little assistance—eh?"

"Nay." Cain shook his head, his visage grim. "If there are as many of the UnKind as ye say, we shall indeed need a like army to defeat them."

"Very well." The King nodded, then turned to Gerard. "As for ye, young man," he began, "as Rosemary has no doubt told ye, both your father and I have been searching for ye for months. It is now known that ye were unjustly accused of your brother the Prince Lord Niles's murder, and your banishment has been lifted."

Gerard started visibly. "But I still don't understand how ye found out—"

"Your father learned the truth of the affair when he overheard your brother the Prince Lord Parrish babbling to himself one night in a drunken stupor. 'Twas he who killed Niles, Gerard, and made it appear as though ye had done the foul deed," Coriander declared.

"I know," Gerard rejoined, not as surprised by this last as the King had thought he would be. "I did not want to believe it at first, but the Lady Ileana was kind enough to read my palm one evening and, in doing so, divined enough of my past that I knew it could only be Parrish who had slain Niles. Parrish ever coveted the throne, and with both Niles and me out of the way, he stood next in line to inherit."

"Yea," Coriander said. "That was the way of it. But he

has been duly punished for his crimes—and in a way not even ye, I'm sure, Gerard, would wish. During the last skirmish between your father's people and the SoulEaters, Parrish was taken prisoner by the UnKind."

Gerard blanched.

"You're right, Lord," he agreed quietly. "Not even I would have wished him such a cruel end."

"I shall inform your father you'll be arriving home shortly, and of course, I'm sure Rosemary has already told ye the two of ye are still betrothed." The King looked fondly at his daughter. "That is . . . if ye still want her, the minx!"

Gerard smiled and hugged his prospective bride.

"Was there ever any doubt of that, Lord?" he asked. "Indeed, I was afraid 'twould be the other way around. I'm not the same man I was when I left Finisterre. I've—I've lost my eye and—and—"

"Oh, Gerard. I told ye that didn't matter," Rosemary insisted, her love for him lighting up her countenance. "In fact, I think that black patch makes ye look rather dashing."

Everyone in the privy chamber laughed at that, whereupon, once more, Coriander's face grew solemn.

"I shall hate to lose ye again so soon, Gerard," he averred, "but I fear the matter of the SoulEaters will not wait. However, both Rosemary and her brother, Tarragon, will be accompanying ye, for my headstrong daughter has vowed nothing will part her from ye again—she never stopped believing in your innocence, ye know—and my son shall lead the Potpourrian warriors. Now I reluctantly suggest we get on with our plans for the impending battle. Otherwise, I'm very much afraid there shall be no one left in the land to dance at your wedding."

The Sword of Ishtar was brought to Tintagel by a mighty lord of Time Past. Made of metal fallen from the stars, it was twice forged and thus invincible, and for many centuries, it was used to defend the Light.

During the Time of the Wars of the Kind and the Apocalypse, however, the Foul Enslaver and Its Minions reigned supreme, and the True Defenders of the

Light were few. Because of this, it was feared that the sword would somehow fall into the hands of those who served the Darkness and thus would be turned against the Light.

So this would not come to pass, the sword was taken secretly to the Holy Place in the Citadel of False Colors, which the Custodians—those who in the Time Before had been given the Power—had caused to come into existence. There, the sword was vested with magic and laid into the altar for safekeeping, never to be wielded again until the Time of the Prophecy, when, once more, the Light will dim and two who once were one will come forth to meet the challenge of the Darkness.

Then, the one Chosen by the Light shall enter the Citadel and take the sword from its resting place. All others who would seek to do so will perish in the crystal flames of truth.

—Thus it is Written—
in
**Fragments of *The Book of Lore*
from the Records in the Potpourrian Archives**

Careful to touch as little as possible the torn, crumbling yellow page she had just finished reading, Ileana handed it back reverently to the head librarian, Sage, who was in charge of the Potpourrian Archives.

"Is there nothing more?" she asked quietly, glancing up at him, a note of despair in her voice.

"Nay, Lady," the elf replied, shaking his head. "I'm sorry, but as ye know, much was lost during the Wars of the Kind and the Apocalypse, for the Old Ones recorded most of their data on disks, which no one has ever been able to transcribe. Of the books that survived, only a few are intact; the majority are in some way damaged. Of some, like *The Book of Lore*, we have, sadly, only fragments."

"I understand," Ileana uttered regretfully. "The Archives of my homeland, too, are in like condition—and for like reasons. Still, I wish there were something more, no matter how little, that might be of use to me."

Sage cocked his head and scratched one of his pointed ears as he thought for a moment.

"Well, now that you mention it, it *does* seem to me as though I recall reading something else once, something about a strange citadel. . . ." His voice trailed off, and he frowned in concentration. "Let me see now." The elf drifted away, searching the shelves of the Archives. A few minutes later, he reappeared, bearing a book in his hands. He opened the volume and began to leaf through its pages. "Ah, yea." He nodded with satisfaction, pleased that his memory had served him well. "Here is the entry I recollected, though, truthfully, I doubt that 'twill do ye much good, Lady. As ye can see, 'tis only a poem—a song really—and quite a cryptic one at that. I don't even know if the citadel to which it refers is the one wherein the Sword of Ishtar is said to lie."

"Nevertheless, under the circumstances, I must leave no stone unturned," Ileana asserted, taking the heavy tome the librarian handed her.

She laid it upon the table before her. Then, eagerly, she began to read the words written therein:

CANTICLE OF THE CITADEL

Time was
when the world was new and unscarred
by the trespasses of the Kind who
turned from the Light to the Darkness,
unheeding of the Word.
But then the Way to the Immortal Guardian was lost,
and Tintagel was cast into
the arms of Chaos,
who sits at the left hand
of the Foul Enslaver;
and the wars and the cataclysms came.

Violently,
the winds of change swept across the land.
Disease and death followed in their wake;
and naught was as it had been.
Ah, woe unto the world!

A cloud enshrouds the sun,
and there are rings around the moons.

Yet—on a distant shore of cliff and tree,
mind triumphed over matter,
and the gift of the Power
was given unto these,
who now looked into Time Future
with farseeing eyes
and shuddered at the shape of things to come.
Like a Phoenix,
they rose to answer the call,
a flame of hope,
blessed by the Keepers.

From the elements, those who became the Custodians
fashioned a citadel;
and in the Holy Place within,
they laid that which was their greatest treasure—
and the Kind's salvation.
Then, with what had been bestowed upon them,
they warded what they had made.

In the heart of the vale, the Citadel stands,
silent now, as it was in the Beginning,
with only the whisper of the Custodians' passing
to stir the air and lift the dust
that lies otherwise undisturbed in the twisting halls,
the intricate mazes none has trodden,
lo, these many ages past—and more.
Long forgotten,
only the Citadel remembers its purpose
and waits for the Chosen One to come,
as the Prophecy has ordained.

Ever listening, even in its slumber,
the Citadel dreams in chameleonic colors,
and the images move in light and shadow,
amorphous things, unreal, phantasms that yet form
reality in the eyes of the beholder,
who cannot see
that nothing is ever what it appears to be.

Through the night and a dusky dawn,
a quester rides toward golden gates.
Will this one hold the key
to unlock them?
Through a swirl of mist,
a quester walks toward ancient doors.
Will this one know the answers
to the riddles behind them?
Many have entered therein,
but they are only scattered ashes now.
Thus does the Citadel defend its prize.

Beware!
Ye who would breach what beckons from a crooked sky.
Destiny lurks in that enchanted spire
of prepotent puzzle;
and only one who has been Chosen by the Light
may reach through the crystal flames of truth
to seize a fallen star.

Slowly, Ileana closed the book and returned it to Sage, her heart heavy. Much of the strange canticle eluded her. Still, she had felt the Power stir within her as she'd read the words, and now this led her to believe they held some special significance for her.

"I'm sorry, Lady," the librarian said as he observed her downcast expression. "I *do* wish I could be of further help, but there simply isn't anything else—at least, not to my knowledge."

"That's all right. Even though the canticle is obscure, I feel somehow that it contains what I need. If I study it more closely, perhaps I can make some sense of it. Would ye be willing to allow me to have a copy of it, Sage?" Ileana inquired.

"Of course." The elf agreed to her request more readily than he normally would have done. The Records in the Potpourrian Archives were greatly prized and closely guarded; copies of manuscripts were given unto very few. But with his much publicized decree, the King Lord Coriander had made it clear that no one was to stand in the way of those who opposed the terrible saurian creatures that had invaded the land. "I'll put Hibiscus, Vetiver, and Neroli to work on it right away. They're the most highly skilled illuminators we have."

"Thank ye," Ileana said, rising. "I would appreciate it if ye would have the finished copy delivered to my chamber as soon as possible."

"By your command, Lady." The librarian bowed respectfully.

Some hours later, after her receipt of the copy of the canticle, Ileana was still no closer to fathoming its mysterious meaning than she had been before, and now she was filled with dejection. If the Time of the Prophecy were indeed at hand, as she feared, then the Sword of Ishtar *must* be found and carried into battle against the Darkness—and time was running out.

Yawning, she stood and stretched, then rubbed the back of her neck, which was knotted from bending over the table at which she was working. She reached for her cup of coffee, only to find it was nearly empty, so she grasped the coffeepot that sat upon the small burning brazier on the table and poured herself another cup. Slowly, she sipped the hot, strong black liquid, savoring its unusual, slightly bitter taste. It was made with chicory, the elfin handmaiden who had brought it to her had said. After a few moments, feeling much revived, Ileana resumed her chair and began again to study the pages of the canticle that lay before her.

It was evident the two opening stanzas were nothing more than a brief retelling of the Time Before, so the girl wasted no time with these, already familiar with her world's past. The third stanza, she felt, spoke of those who had been Chosen, though she was certain they had not been Druswids, for the Mont Sects had not been established until after the Time of the Rebirth and the Enlightenment. It was these unknown Chosen, Ileana surmised from the fourth stanza, who had built the Citadel and placed within it their greatest treasure. This, she believed, was the Sword of Ishtar. It was the remaining stanzas of the canticle that puzzled her. Obviously, the Citadel was protected by magic. But what kind of spells had been used to ward it? And —even more important—where *was* the Citadel?

Sighing, the girl glanced at the small, ornate clock that sat upon the mantel over the blazing hearth. Though the hour was late, Cain had not yet returned to their room. He must still be closeted in the privy chamber with the King Lord Coriander and the rest, she thought. Frowning, she gathered up the pages of the canticle and rose. She would join the others, she decided, and share with them what she had discovered. Perhaps they could shed some additional light on the subject.

Ileana hoped so. She desperately needed a ray of encouragement right now—no matter how slender or faint. Every time she read the canticle, the Power surged more forcefully within her in response to the words; and now she felt in her bones that she and the others must not march into battle without the Sword of Ishtar at their side.

Chapter 29

RECIPE FOR DRAGONBANE

Ingredients:
One forked tongue of a lizard
One dried snakeskin
One dragon claw
Three mistletoe berries
One cup of deadly nightshade juice
Two spoonfuls of toadstool powder
One pinch of bat guano

Implements:
A mortar and pestle
A small black iron cauldron
An oak staff or wand
A clay jar fashioned from marsh mud
A cork for jar
A fire

Directions: *With mortar and pestle, grind lizard tongue, snakeskin, and dragon claw until finely pulverized. Add mistletoe berries and mash until mixture is pasty in texture; then set mortar aside and let mixture stand.*

Pour deadly nightshade juice into cauldron and heat over fire until boiling. Stir in mixture of lizard tongue, snakeskin, dragon claw, and mistletoe berries. Keep stirring until liquid thickens to syrup. Add toadstool powder and bat guano.

Walk three times around fire, reciting the following
verse:

> Power of deadly reptiles three
> In this mixture hither be.
> Make this poison strong with pain,
> Enough to prove a dragon's bane.

Wave staff or wand over top of cauldron. Then
remove mixture from fire and pour into jar. Seal
container tightly with cork.

—Thus it is Written—
in
The Grimoire
of the Witch Belladonna set Myrrh Marsh

AFTER SEVERAL HOURS OF DISCUSSION, THE COMPANIONS HAD
reluctantly decided to split up into three groups. The Prince
Lord Tarragon, the Princess Lady Rosemary, the Prince
Lord Gerard, and Sir Husein were to lead the elfin army, as
well as the soldiers of Cain's party, to Ashton Wells in
Finisterre, where they would meet with Gerard's father, the
King Lord Arundel, and oversee the preparations for the
forthcoming battle. Ulthor, Syeira, and three elfin warriors
were to sail across the Great Cerulean Sea to Port Ava-
lanche, in Borealis, where they would seek an audience with
the Lord Erek, who was the chieftain of Ulthor's clan, to ask
for the assistance of the giants in the fight against the
SoulEaters. Lastly, in search of the Sword of Ishtar, Cain
and Ileana, along with Sir Ahmed, Mehtar, Charis,
Halcyone, the two dwarfs, and two elfin guides, Mace and
Dill, were to journey to the high, thickly wooded land of
Valcoeur, whose name, translated into the common
Tintagelese, meant "Heartvale."

Based on the canticle's third and fifth stanzas, this was
the only clue to the location of the Citadel of False Colors.
None knew if it had any merit, but as no other suggestion
had been put forth, it was all they had.

Now, after crossing a frozen patch of the River Patchouli
and carefully skirting the eastern edge of Myrrh Marsh,
Mace led the travelers over the flat, snow-covered Plains of

Frangipanni. The moors were beautiful in the spring and summer, he said, when the delicate pink-, red-, and purple-blossomed shrubs that had given them their name were in bloom. But now the bushes were bare, brown, and scraggly, like the tumbleweeds Ileana had seen in Gallow. Still, the hoarfrost and icicles with which the shrubs were draped gave them an ethereal loveliness all the same, making them appear like spun sugar.

Had it not been for the uncertain outcome of their quest, Ileana would have delighted in her environs. Instead, her cape drawn closely about her, she huddled miserably upon her unicorn, wondering if she had done the right thing, after all, in telling Cain about the Sword of Ishtar. Ever since he had read the canticle, he had been like a Fanatic of the Time Before, his mind focused monomaniacally on obtaining the weapon.

'Tis the beast within him that wants it, Ileana thought, dismayed. *But why? To turn the blade to the hand of the Darkness?* She shivered at the notion. *I must not let him get hold of the sword. I do not know what magic it might possess or how the beast within him means to use it.*

But still, she remembered what she had seen in the frozen pond that winter of her childhood, and a terrible sense of foreboding suddenly clutched her tightly in its fist. Cain —with the Sword of Ishtar in his hand. . . .

Nay! I will not let it happen! the girl vowed fiercely. *I cannot!*

But the image haunted her; she could not put it from her mind. Fright and despair taking their toll on her, she rode on silently through the swirling grey mist, watching Cain surreptitiously, her heart filled with trepidation.

The beasts' hooves crunched upon the snow and ice. The high wheels of the caravan rolled roughly over the hard ground, leaving uneven, parallel lines in the fine layer of snow that lay upon the earth. Mingled with these were the tracks of the animals as they plodded on, heads hanging, nostrils blowing white clouds into the air.

Through the wraithlike wisps of mist, Ileana could see some distance in every direction, and as she had so long ago in Vikanglia, she experienced an uneasiness at being so totally exposed on the flat, open land. But except for an occasional small creature skittering through the brush, nothing moved. It was as though their party were all alone in the world.

Unnerved by the idea, she quickly pushed it from her mind, chilled to the bone as, from nowhere, it seemed, a low, eerie moan echoed across the plains.

"What was that?" she asked softly as, simultaneously, all drew to a halt and glanced about anxiously.

"'Tis Belladonna," Mace whispered, "the witch of the marsh. I had hoped to avoid her. She's usually asleep at this early hour, but our passing must have wakened her. Hurry! Let's move on, and perhaps we can still escape from her."

But even before the words had left his mouth, the mist parted to reveal the ugliest hag Ileana had ever seen.

From the top of her tall, conical hat, with its bent peak and flat brim, to the tips of her stout leather hobnail boots, the crone was garbed completely in black. Strands of unkempt black hair streaked with grey, from which her large, pointed ears protruded prominently, straggled down her back; thick, swooping black brows accentuated her piercing, deep-set black eyes, which were strangely clouded with white. Her narrow, beaked nose hooked crookedly over thin, tobacco-stained lips and a sharp chin with an unsightly wart, from which coarse black hairs grew. Sunken, wrinkled cheeks cast into relief her high cheekbones and angular jawline. The wide sleeves of her ragged cloak billowed over aged, clawlike hands knotted with blue veins. Her knobby, skeletal fingers, with their long, sickle-shaped nails, curled like talons around the gnarled staff she leaned upon heavily for support. An enormous, long-haired black cat, wearing around its neck a silver collar adorned with a tiny silver bell, rubbed itself caressingly against the hem of the witch's gown, mewing and hissing, its back arched, its tail bushed out and twitching.

"Be quiet, Hemlock!" Belladonna snapped crossly to the beast. "And stop that pacing before ye trip me!"

Immediately, the cat sat, its slanted yellow-green eyes gazing unblinkingly at Ileana and the others for a moment before, its disdain for them evident, it lifted one paw and, spreading its pads wide, began furiously to clean it. Satisfied that the cat was no longer hovering about her knees, the harridan turned her attention to the companions. She stared at them steadily, much as the cat had done, and with a start, Ileana realized the witch was stone-blind.

"Travelers," she addressed them, her voice croaking, "listen to me. I know who ye are and what ye seek. But the Sword of Ishtar shall never be yours—not unless ye have my help."

"Begone, wicked old bat!" Mace cried, making the ancient sign against evil. "We want none of the foul spells or obnoxious potions ye use to rob the vain and the foolish of their will and possessions!"

"So ye say now," Belladonna rejoined, unruffled. Then, her face sly, she crooned throatily, "But mark me: I have looked into Time Future, and there will come a day when ye shall have need of what I offer."

"And what is that?" Cain inquired coldly. "The eye of a newt? The tail of a lizard?"

"Nay," she muttered scornfully. Then, as though amused, she gave a short cackle. "My power is much greater than that, Lord. I will give ye a poison, the most potent poison on earth. Dragonbane, 'tis called, for 'twill kill even that mightest of creatures within moments."

"And what need would we have for such?" Mace asked sharply. "There are no dragons in Potpourri. I say again: Begone, wicked old bat! Go peddle your putrid brew to someone else!"

"I have always had a fondness for bold men, Mace of Verbena; but ye, sir, are beginning to annoy me. Now silence your tongue before I do it for ye!" The beldam advanced on him threateningly. Warily, once more making the ancient sign, Mace nudged his stag back a few paces, and the hag laughed again harshly. "So ye are not so brave after all, are ye, young man? Ye know I speak the truth when I tell ye I have much magic at my command! Well"—she turned back to Cain—"do ye want the dragonbane or not, Lord?"

"That depends," he replied, "on what ye want in return for it."

"Ah, that." Belladonna smiled, revealing blackened, toothless gums. "Why, 'tis only a small thing, Lord, such a tiny favor—and little enough payment for a poison as powerful as the dragonbane, I promise ye. I merely want to borrow the body of one of your companions for a moment, that I may see through eyes undimmed, as mine are, by the shadows of night."

"Don't do it, Lord!" Mace spat. "'Tis a trick!"

Cain gave him a quelling stare.

"*I* am the commander of this expedition, Mace," he reminded the elf. "I will decide what shall and shall not be done." His eyes, gleaming with that strange, fervid light Ileana had come to dread, slid once more to Belladonna. "Show me the dragonbane, witch," he demanded.

"As ye wish, Lord."

After fumbling briefly at the leather belt she wore beneath the folds of her cloak, the crone withdrew a drawstring pouch. This she opened to reveal a fat brownish-black clay jar fashioned of marsh mud and sealed with a thick, wide cork. Cain snorted contemptuously at the sight.

"Do ye take me for a fool, witch?" he queried curtly. "How do I know the jar is not empty?"

"Come." Belladonna beckoned with one age-spotted hand. "See for yourself, Lord."

Slowly, Cain dismounted and walked toward the harridan. Once he had reached her, she rested her staff in the crook of her elbow and carefully uncorked the jar, then thrust it toward him. Instantly, acrid green fumes billowed from the container and a vile, nauseating stench filled the crisp morning air. His head reeling slightly, Cain staggered back from the jar. Chortling, Belladonna restoppered the container.

"Well, Lord, is it a bargain or nay?" she asked.

"Yea." He nodded. "Give me the dragonbane, witch."

"Not so fast," she chided, smiling smugly, quickly removing the jar from his reach and dropping it back into the leather bag. Then she firmly retied the pouch to the belt at her waist. "There is one more condition to which ye must consent before I relinquish the poison to ye."

"I *told* ye 'twas a trick, Lord!" Mace insisted angrily. "She's not to be trusted—I warn ye!"

"Silence!" Cain hissed, throwing the elf a sharp glance. Then he addressed Belladonna once more. "What more would ye have, witch?"

"Only this: I must be allowed to choose the body I will briefly inhabit."

"And is that all?"

"Yea, Lord."

"Very well, witch. I agree to your terms," Cain said, much to Ileana's consternation.

But she knew it was the beast within him that had spoken, and arguing would do nothing to prevent its bargain with the beldam. Mace had already proved that. For some reason, the beast wanted the dragonbane. Still, the girl felt that the elf was right: The hag was not to be trusted.

"The witch may use my body," Ileana offered, knowing she would be in a far better position than any of the others to combat any trickery Belladonna might intend.

"Nay." The crone shook her head. "I sense that another's eyes are more to my liking." She raised her staff, and as though it were a divining rod, it quivered a moment, then pointed directly at Charis. "That one. I choose that one," the harridan stated firmly.

"Well, what are ye waiting for, damsel?" Cain snapped to the now petrified handmaiden sitting upon the seat of the caravan. "Climb down from there at once! There is naught to fear."

Nevertheless, sensing otherwise, Charis hesitated and cast a frightened glance at her mistress. But Ileana only shook her head warningly, motioning for the handmaiden to do as she was bidden. Slowly, Charis descended from the wagon, moving timidly to stand before the witch. Before anyone had grasped how rapidly the transference would take place, Belladonna mumbled a few words, then waved her staff. Almost immediately, her body slumped to the ground, and the handmaiden's head jerked up like a marionette's whose strings have been pulled too roughly.

"Ahhhhh," the beldam sighed with Charis's voice. "To see again! Ye fools!" she gloated exultantly. "Now ye shall be powerless against me!"

Then, before any of them realized what she meant to do, she snatched up her staff, forced the handmaiden's legs into a run, and began racing toward the marsh.

"Heaven's Light!" Ileana screamed. "She's trying to steal

362

Charis's body. Cain, stop her! She's trying to steal Charis's body!"

To her relief, Cain tackled the witch-cum-handmaiden, knocking her to the snow-laden ground, where they rolled over and over together, struggling furiously with each other, Belladonna's essence having fueled Charis's slender body with an unnatural strength. Ileana and the rest, having by now dismounted, stood by helplessly, frozen with shock, horrified by the gruesomely twisted faces and bared teeth of the two viciously snarling combatants. They looked like maddened beasts as each clawed brutally at the other's throat. Seeing no way to use her power to intervene lest she accidentally injure Cain in the process, Ileana could only watch and pray that her husband would prevail.

Finally, he managed to gain the upper hand, and straddling the witch-cum-handmaiden, he grasped her shoulders and shook her savagely, pounding her head violently against the wet earth.

"Get out of Charis's body, ye wicked old bat!" He unconsciously employed Mace's name for the witch. *"Now!* Or I'll slit your scurvy throat!" He yanked his dagger from its sheath inside his left boot and pressed it against the side of her neck.

"If ye do, you'll condemn the maid as well," Belladonna pointed out, distorting Charis's voice so it grated gutturally. "Her essence is still here—with me—inside this physical shell."

Grasping the situation at once and realizing they needed some means of forcing the hag from Charis's body, Ileana made a sudden leap for Hemlock, who was sitting silently nearby, his eyes—their black pupils narrowed to slits—taking everything in. The cat mewed and hissed angrily as Ileana seized it by the ruff, causing its tiny silver bell to clatter shrilly.

"Dill, get a bag!" the girl cried, scarcely able to maintain her grip on the now wildly contorting animal, which spat and clawed at her devilishly. "Mace, take care of Belladonna's body before she can get back into it!"

Without hesitation, Dill ran to the caravan, flung open the door, and scrambled inside. As rapidly as he'd vanished, he reappeared with an empty burlap sack. Together, he and Ileana stuffed the howling cat inside and tied the bag shut with a stout piece of rope hastily furnished by Bergren Birchbark. Meanwhile, Mace picked up the crone's staff, which she had dropped during her fight with Cain. With the stout branch, the elf struck her body a resounding whack over the head. Then, as though not quite certain he'd knocked her unconscious, he hit her again. After that, tossing the staff aside, he bent and ripped from the witch's belt the pouch containing the dragon-bane.

"Now"—Ileana spoke through gritted teeth to the witch-cum-handmaiden—"ye get back in your own body, or so help me, we'll slay your evil cat!"

Minutes later, her essence once more inside her own physical shell, Belladonna moaned and stirred, and Cain assisted a shaking, sobbing Charis to her feet.

"Damsel, are ye all right?" he inquired, his eyes still alight with an odd glow. Wordlessly, she nodded. "Mehtar, Halcyone," he called grimly. "Help her back to the wagon. The rest of ye mount up," he went on as his manservant and the mistress shipbuilder rushed forward just in time to catch Charis as she swayed on her feet, then collapsed. "Ileana, bring the cat."

"Nay . . . nay . . ." the witch groaned, rubbing her bruised head. She groped for her fallen staff and attempted to rise. "Not Hemlock . . . not Hemlock . . ."

"Don't try to follow us," Cain warned, "or we'll drown him in the nearest river! And just in case ye think to try any more of your tricks . . ." He raised his left hand; blue fire shot from his fingertips, burning the harridan's staff to a cinder. "There. That should keep ye more honest for a while." He turned to the others. "Move out!" he commanded.

The questers needed no further urging. In moments, they were galloping across the plains, eager to put as much distance as possible between themselves and the groggy Belladonna before she could recover her senses.

It was not until nearly three hours later, when they were certain they had eluded the awful witch, that they remembered the cat. The travelers paused to rest, and after fetching the sack from the back of the wagon, they opened it up to set Hemlock free.

"Why, he's changed colors!" Ileana exclaimed, startled, as an enraged white ball of fur shot out of the bag like a comet, sneezing violently and trailing a cloud of what looked like fine snowflakes behind him.

"Nay, Lady." Dill grinned, holding up the empty sack. "'Tis flour. I only hope those couple of cracks Mace dealt her didn't addle Belladonna too badly. Otherwise, she's liable to turn that powder puff into a toad before she realizes her mistake!"

At that, everyone—even Charis—began to laugh, nervously at first, then harder and more naturally the more they thought of Mace bravely bashing the hatchet-faced witch on the head, not once, but twice—and with her own staff to boot! It wasn't really funny, but it cheered them nevertheless. With considerably lighter hearts, they rode on toward Valcoeur.

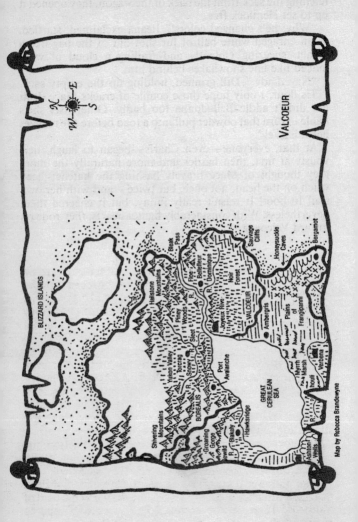

Map by Rebecca Brandewyne

Chapter 30

ᛒᛗᛈᚠᚱᛗ

ᚠᛏᛏ ᚠᛗ ᛈᚼᛈ ᚦᚹᚿᛈᚼ ᛗᚠᚱᛗ ᛏᚠ ᛏᚱᛗᚼᚼᚠᚼᚼ ᚻᛗᚱᛗ

—Thus it is Written—
on
The Rune Stone of Warning
at the Citadel of False Colors

AT LAST, AFTER SEVERAL WEEKS OF TRAVEL BLESSEDLY FREE OF further unpleasant events, the companions reached the elfin city of Ambergris, near the northern border of Potpourri. There, they stopped overnight to rest and to learn what they could from the city's inhabitants. But other than the fact that they, too, had seen large numbers of the SoulEaters on the move—heading south—the townspeople had little to report; and as the Records in the Archives here were in even poorer condition than those in Verbena, the travelers discovered little to assist them with their quest. An ancient, faded map, showing two Valcoeurian cities, one of which —named Joyeux Rive—was marked with the symbol for a stronghold, was all they found.

The next morning, seeing no better course of action, the companions set out toward the stronghold, hoping it still existed and were the citadel for which they searched.

They followed the eastern shore of the Great Cerulean Sea until, after many days of riding, they came to the land of Valcoeur. There, at the border, Mace lifted one hand to signal a halt.

"Beyond lies Valcoeur." He pointed to the north.

367

"How do ye know?" Ileana asked, glancing about curiously.

The Plains of Frangipanni still stretched before them in a blanket of white, and she could spy no discernible landmark that would distinguish the border between the two countries.

Mace shrugged in response to her question and shook his head.

"I don't know," he told her. "I just sense it. The land feels different somehow."

"Yea. I feel it, too," Jiro Juniper chimed in, having by now learned enough Tintagelese to converse with them. "There's something odd about it."

"Yea." Dill nodded solemnly. "No Potpourrian ever comes here if he can help it. That is why so little is known about the place."

"Why do the elves avoid it?" Ileana queried.

"Because . . . well . . ." Dill hesitated. Then, reluctantly, he explained, "There are many peculiar tales told of the Valcoeurians, Lady, and there are too many travelers who have journeyed to this land never to return from it."

"I see," Ileana uttered quietly, her brow puckering into a thoughtful frown. Perhaps it was here, then, that many of her people had disappeared. "In that case, we had best be on our guard."

"Yea," Cain agreed, staring off into the distance as though he too perceived the strangeness of the country. "Ride close together—and keep your weapons at the ready."

"By your command, Lord," Mace said, then dug his spurs into his stag's sides.

The majestic beast leaped forward, the others hard on its heels as they left Potpourri behind.

For nearly two hours the plains continued, lifeless and barren beneath winter's mantle. Then gradually the moors began to give way to a densely wooded region that was marked on the map as Noir Forest. Here, tall stands of fringed evergreen trees—pines, spruces, cedars, firs, junipers, and cypresses—grew alongside trees that had lost their leaves and looked naked and forlorn next to their handsomely clothed brothers. Bushes of holly and mistletoe bright with berries formed an intricate maze around the trunks of the trees. Delicate snowdrops and other fragile winter flowers bloomed amid the fallen cones and decaying matter that lay upon the ground. Here and there, patches of rich black loam showed at the base of the trees, whose branches had shielded the earth from the snow.

The forest was hushed and still, with only the occasional hoot of an owl or the cry of a snowbird to break the silence. The companions saw no one. Yet it was here, nevertheless, that Ileana was first assailed by a faint but undeniable twinge of disquiet. It was nothing she could definitely put her finger on—just an odd sense of perturbation, as though she were being watched. She knew Cain felt it, too, for she observed that his left hand never strayed too far from the hilt of his sword, and once or twice, he reached inside his cloak to be certain the pouch containing the dragonbane was still securely fastened to his belt.

She wished Mace had never taken the poison from Belladonna's inert body. Over the past months, Ileana had come to realize the strength and power of the beast within Cain waxed and waned according to the amount of evil to which it was exposed; and she thought that somehow the presence of the dragonbane was keeping the beast inside her husband aroused.

Periodically, it looked out at her through Cain's eyes, making her shiver; and her heart grew cold and sick with terror when she thought of how strong and powerful the beast would become with the wickedness of an UnKind army to feed it. She was very much afraid that then Cain would no longer be able to regain control of it, and it would seek to destroy her.

There must be some way to prevent that from happening, Ileana reflected, deeply disturbed. She did not want to do battle with Cain; her power would rebel against her turning it against him, perhaps would fail her completely. Besides, she did not even know if she *could* bring herself to fight him, even though she knew the fate of the world would hang on her decision. Nay, there simply must be another way. There just *had* to be! But though she felt the answer lay within her grasp, it still eluded her, leaving her feeling more anguished than ever.

By the Passion Moon! her heart cried out silently to the forest. *What must I do? What must I do?*

To the girl's utter shock, without warning, a strange, unfamiliar essence touched her mind in reply.

Do not fear, Child of Winter, it murmured. *When the time comes, ye will know what must be done.*

Who—who are ye? Ileana's mind asked hesitantly.

One who would help ye, came the response. *Follow the trees at the edge of the sea. They will lead ye to what ye seek. Afterward, remember what ye have been taught—and have courage, Child of Winter. We who each in time become the Custodians are with ye. We will see ye safely through the woods.*

Then, as suddenly as it had come, the essence withdrew, leaving Ileana alone again with her thoughts.

"Mace," she called abruptly. "Stay in the forest, but keep within sight of the sea."

"By your command, Lady," he said, glancing at her curiously.

But he did not question her order—nor did she enlighten him as to the reasons behind it.

The essence that had so briefly brushed her mind never spoke to Ileana again. Nevertheless, for the remainder of the trip, she was conscious of it—and others—watching her, and every now and then, she thought she caught a glimpse of a small, slender form—no bigger than a child—gliding swiftly, gracefully, through the forest. It seemed the figure had long moss-green tresses and skin as brown as an oak tree. Yet along the shore, Ileana could have sworn she spied quick flashes of hair that was the blue of the Great Cerulean Sea and flesh as golden as the sand that stretched to the waves.

Fairies, the girl thought. *They are fairies—sprites, dryads, nymphs, and the like. Over the ages, their minds have so highly evolved that their bodies have diminished in equal measure. The Power must indeed be strong within them. That is why they were Chosen to serve as the Custodians. We have guessed right! The Citadel of False Colors is here! I know it!*

And when, at long last, the questers came to a place where a cascade of breathtaking purple mountains rose in crooked majesty against the sky and a glorious, snowy vale spread its splendor across the land, they realized instinctively that they had reached their journey's end.

A city, Joyeux Rive, had stood here once. Now there remained only ruins. But some distance beyond, in the heart of the vale, an enchanted spire pierced the dusky dawn and beckoned the travelers forward. Like magnets to steel, they were drawn to the sweeping hollow. In respectful silence, they passed the ruins of the city, then began to wend their way down the dirt road that led to the stronghold.

They were halfway there when, without warning, a wall of what at first Ileana thought was mist appeared, blocking their path. Startled, she and the others drew up short, uncertain what the strange silver fog portended. It hovered before them, drifting and shifting in shape and shadow; and though it did not seem in any way threatening, still, none of them wished to ride on through it. They glanced at one another uneasily. Before they could determine upon a course of action, however, the cold, clammy cloud that had so mysteriously formed began slowly to dissolve as, one by one, anguished, distorted faces with thin, elongated torsos started to detach themselves from the haze. Finally, it was no more.

Only then did Ileana recognize the amorphous figures for what they really were: Weeping Wraiths—the pure ethereal essence of those whose bodies had died but who, having experienced their passing before it had been time, were still bound to the earth, their LifePaths as yet unfinished.

Go back. Go back, the Wraiths soughed plaintively, their silent voices like wind moaning in the minds of the travelers. *Once we were as ye, but the Citadel proved our undoing. Now we must pay the price for our sins. Go back. Go back.*

Then they vanished as suddenly as they had materialized. Ileana and the rest looked at one another wordlessly, fear enveloping them like a shroud. They had been warned —and by those who had gone before them into the stronghold.

"We have no choice," the girl said, determinedly breaking the stillness, though her voice quavered a little. "We must go on. Without the Sword of Ishtar, we are doomed; I know it!"

Without waiting for a response, she urged her dapple-grey mare forward, her chin held high, her shoulders squared, though her heart beat too quickly in her breast. Reluctantly, the others followed, only Cain still undaunted.

A few paces from the stronghold's golden gates, the companions came to a halt and, of one accord, dismounted. Then, awed by the magnificence before them, they stood speechlessly staring at the Citadel of False Colors.

It towered above them imposingly, like nothing they had ever before seen. They could not even begin to guess how it had been constructed, for its steep, high, circular walls and tall, conical roofs were totally sheathed in silver. It was this, Ileana thought, that must have given the stronghold its name, for the gleaming metal reflected all that encompassed it—the leaden dawn sky; the silvery blues and dark greens of the pines and the browns of their trunks; the deep purples, pale pinks, and bright yellows of the winter flowers that bloomed amid the powdery white snow—so, like a kaleidoscope, it seemed as though the Citadel shimmered in a swirl of ever-changing colors, none of them its own.

Yet for all its massiveness and grandeur, it was delicately fashioned, without watchtowers or battlements or any other visible defenses. Instead, it was crowned with a single spire and guarded only by the set of golden gates, topped with heavily ornamented spikes, which barred the entrance to the surrounding courtyard. The stronghold was five stories high, with each floor smaller than the last, so that except for randomly placed, graceful turrets, the Citadel resembled a cone. Strangest of all was the fact that except for the stained-glass panes of the tower capped by the spire, the stronghold had no windows; a pair of enormous doors was the only apparent means of entry or exit. Set into one of the giant silver pillars from which the gates hung was a weathered grey stone into which runes had been chiseled.

Upon seeing this, Ileana stepped nearer to decipher the symbols written thereon:

BEWARE
ALL YE WHO WOULD DARE TO TRESPASS HERE

Despite the warning, she pushed tentatively against the gates. They were locked fast. Yet oddly enough, a large gold key dangled from a chain hanging around one of the spikes above her. Frowning, Ileana started to reach for the key; but before she touched it, some instinct warned her to stay her hand.

. . . nothing is ever what it appears to be.

The words from the canticle echoed in her mind, and now Ileana recognized that gaining entry to the Citadel could not be so simple. While the others watched curiously in silence, she began to examine the ornamentation on the gates, her palms running cautiously over the intricate designs, probing, pressing. At last, as her hand swept across the head of a dragon, a soft click sounded, releasing the latch on the gates. Slowly, noiselessly, they swung open; and a smile of satisfaction curved Ileana's lips. She had passed the first barrier! But there would be others, she knew, and she suspected they would become progressively more difficult to overcome. Her smile faded at the thought.

Soberly, motioning for the rest to follow, Ileana led her now skittishly prancing unicorn into the silver-paved courtyard. Hesitantly, one by one, the others passed through the gates, Cain bringing up the rear, pausing to inspect the lock. After he, too, had entered the courtyard, the portals closed behind him as soundlessly as they had opened. Instantly, hearing the click of the latch, Cain pivoted. But he was too late. The gates were closed fast and refused to budge, no matter how hard he pushed on the head of the dragon. Finally, shrugging, he gave up the attempt and turned to address the questers.

"The latch was rigged," he informed them gravely. "If Ileana had used the key, it would have triggered some sort of a mechanism, releasing a dart—poisoned, no doubt—that would have pierced her heart. Be on your guard. There is no telling what other traps may lurk within."

The rest nodded, their eyes wide and troubled. Then they gazed around the courtyard warily, as though expecting to see further obstacles. But there was nothing that immediately captured their attention. Still, they shivered and drew their cloaks more closely about them. It had begun to snow again, and now a chill, bitter wind swept through the vale, causing the flakes to dance in misty flurries.

Moving more quickly now in order to keep warm, they explored the courtyard, but the enclosure that circled the Citadel revealed nothing. There was naught between the outer wall and the stronghold itself—no other buildings, not even a stable. Scattering upon the ground a bale of hay from the caravan, then leaving the animals to fend for themselves, the travelers slowly approached the wide steps to the ponderous doors of the Citadel. There, like sentries, two life-sized silver smilodons sat on either side of the portal, their sightless eyes seeming to watch every move the companions made.

Suddenly, to Ileana's horror, the colossal cats began to change color. Even as she watched, their fur turned to its natural tawny shade and their eyes glowed amber in the winter light. Then, horribly, unbelievably, they lunged toward her. Their powerful muscles bunched and quivered as they bounded down the stairs to crouch before her, spitting and hissing, their tails twitching. Their pitiless eyes warning that her body was only a heartbeat from death, the beasts sprang at her, their ferocious teeth bared, their scythelike claws unsheathed. Someone screamed—Charis, Ileana thought—and then the elves' crossbows thrummed as they sent their quarrels flying. Blood gushed from the gaping wounds made as the sharp stone arrowheads tore through flesh to embed themselves in the animals' entrails. But still, snarling viciously, the smilodons came on. The spears of the dwarfs hummed; two more shafts struck the big cats—to little avail. Then Cain's and Sir Ahmed's swords were glinting beneath the sullen sky as the two men drew their weapons to slash brutally at the savage beasts. Finally, the animals collapsed upon the crimson-stained snow. Moments later, no trace of them remained; and when Ileana glanced toward the doors of the stronghold, she saw that, incredibly, the once-more silver smilodons were again sitting motionlessly before the portal. The arrows and javelins of the elves and dwarfs lay scattered on the ground; not a single drop of blood dripped from Cain's and Sir Ahmed's blades.

"'Twas all in our minds," the girl whispered, stunned. "'Twas all only in our minds—an illusion."

Yet she knew that if the men had not reacted so swiftly, they would all be dead now—*because they had believed the cats were real.*

Once more, the words of the canticle rose to haunt her:

Ever listening, even in its slumber/the Citadel dreams in chameleonic colors/and the images move in light and shadow/amorphous things, unreal, phantasms that yet form/ reality in the eyes of the beholder . . .

Now it all began to make sense, and at the realization, Ileana buried her face in her hands, her shoulders shaking with silent sobs. Now she knew how the Custodians had warded the Citadel. They had gifted it with their essence. Through them, the stronghold saw, it heard, it dreamed —and *it deceived! Everything* here was a deception! That was the real reason for the Citadel's name, Ileana thought.

What stabbed her to the very core, however, filling her with terrible uncertainty and dread, was the fact that the Power here was overwhelming—perhaps greater than hers and Cain's, for even she and her husband had not recognized that the beasts were illusions. Surely, she thought, she had brought herself and the rest to their deaths! Soon they would join those who had gone before them—the Weeping Wraiths now bound to the vale so they might warn others of their folly.

Nay! Ileana could not let that happen! She must manage somehow to pull herself together! It was too late now to go back. It was as she had pointed out earlier: They had no choice. They must go on.

Summoning her courage, the girl drew herself up proudly, and it was as though she had never faltered. Defiantly, she walked up the steps, past the now still cats, to the ancient doors of the stronghold. Above them, chiseled into a long, weathered grey stone spanning their width, were more runes, which read: THE CITADEL OF FALSE COLORS. Taking a deep breath, she pushed firmly against the portals. To her surprise, they opened easily at her touch.

Once inside, Ileana found herself in a large, round silver hall lighted by torches. It was hushed and layered with dust, as though no one had trodden here for many years. All along the walls, slightly darker argent ribs rose to the vaulted ceiling, where they diverged like the rays of a fan to form decorative tracery. In the center of the room stood a silver pedestal that was shaped like a column but was only three feet high. Its base was set upon a plain square plinth and was formed by upper and lower tori, between which was a layer of scotia. Its shaft was fluted and filleted, its capital sculpted with hills in bas-relief. On its top reposed a beautifully carved wood rose. Directly behind the pedestal was another set of doors. They, too, were huge; but unlike the others, these were fashioned of oak. Above them was a rune stone similar to its immediate predecessor. THE HALL OF EARTH, it proclaimed.

As the rest of the questers filed inside, Ileana moved to study the closed oak portals. They were locked, but it was obvious they were meant to be opened with the rose. Still, remembering the key hanging temptingly on the gates outside, she hesitated. Perhaps this, too, was only a trick. Nevertheless, after thoroughly scrutinizing the doors and finding no other means to spring the latch, Ileana returned to the pedestal, picked up the rose, and tentatively inserted it into the lock. Immediately, the portals parted to reveal a long, dark, winding corridor.

"Each of ye grab a torch," she instructed the others.

Then, taking one of the firebrands, she stepped into the passage that loomed before her. Instantly, the icy chill of winter was melted from her bones by the gentle heat of the earth and her nostrils were assaulted by the fresh, rich scents of fertile loam and dew-kissed grass. Mingled with this were the fragrant smells of flowers, herbs, spices, and oils. Yet there was nothing apparent to account for either the warmth or the aromas. By the light of the torches, Ileana could see that this hall, too, was made entirely of silver and, initially at least, appeared to be empty. Cautiously, the companions set out to explore it.

It wasn't long before they realized that it was an intricate maze and, worse, that they were hopelessly lost. Further, the walls of the seemingly endless hall were engraved with tableaux of the earth, and from these were born hideous illusions. Silver beasts, which seemed to change to their natural colors and come alive as the smilodons outside had done, attacked the questers mercilessly; and despite the fact that they knew the animals were deceptions, they were forced to combat them, lest, horribly, one of the creatures somehow turned out to be real. Monstrous trees reached out like the stranglers of rain forests to crush the life from the companions' bodies. Distorted flowers, weeds, and vines entangled their limbs, as though to hold them prisoner; and Cain and Sir Ahmed were kept busy as, with their swords, they hacked ceaselessly at the encroaching plants. There were places where, beneath the questers' feet, the floor seemed to shake and shudder ominously before, violently, it cracked apart to expose great, yawning fissures that made the companions cling tightly to the walls.

Constantly, with their essence, Cain and Ileana reached out to the minds of the others, reassuring them, repeating over and over that the dreadful scenes were untruths, tricks to deceive them.

But not all was unreal. Here and there were dangerous snares like the one at the gates, concealed mechanisms that when touched or trod upon fired missiles, released poisonous gases, dropped nets, or opened trapdoors in the floor. These hazards, however, Cain, Ileana, and the two elves, who had sharper physical senses than the rest, deftly avoided, for the gleam of argent in such places was just the slightest bit darker and duller than the remainder of the hall, as though worn from countless years of being triggered and reset. But Bergren Birchbark accidentally activated a rope that snapped down like a whip from the ceiling to coil tightly about his neck before retracting, jerking him up off the floor and nearly choking him to death before the others managed to cut him down. They shuddered to think what would have happened to him had he been alone. From then on, Cain brought up the rear so he could be certain no one else made a fatal misstep.

Aeons later, it seemed, when the torches gave out, he and Ileana called forth the blue fire they commanded and lighted the questers' way.

Finally, just when Ileana was beginning to think they would never manage to escape from the nightmarish hall, they lurched into a large, circular chamber whose walls were lined with blazing torches. By the flickering yellow-orange flames, the companions could perceive that at long last, they had reached the end of the awful maze; and gratefully, their breathing labored, they sank to the floor.

Tired, they uncorked the flasks they carried and opened their small packs, which contained dried provisions. Then, after quenching their thirst and filling their bellies, they rose to examine their surroundings.

To Ileana's relief, she saw that the walls here were devoid of engravings; nor did she spy any hidden pitfalls. Instead, ornate ribs and fan tracery adorned the walls and vaulted ceiling. Because of this, she surmised that this chamber, like the first room, served as a sanctuary for those fortunate enough to attain it.

At its center stood a silver pedestal almost identical to the one before the doors to the Hall of Earth. This one's capital, however, bore a raised design of waves. A starfish sat on its top. Directly behind the column was an argent spiral staircase.

Upon observing these things, the questers realized another ordeal lay before them, and after much discussion, they decided to rest a little longer before venturing on. Their heavy eyelids drooped, and presently, they dozed. A while later, they abruptly awoke, startled that they had drifted into slumber and wondering how long they had slept. Since there were no windows in the Citadel, they had no way of knowing.

They were disinclined to leave the sanctuary; but recognizing that they could not remain here forever, they gathered their belongings quietly, talking in whispers, as though the Citadel were alive and could hear them. After that, each seized a firebrand from the silver holders in the walls, surprised to see that the torches were still burning as though new. Ileana took the starfish from the pedestal. Then, slowly, the companions climbed the steps to the second story.

There, they found themselves before another set of portals. These, however, were constructed of seashells and pearls. Above them was another rune stone, which announced: THE HALL OF WATER. Ileana pressed the starfish into the lock, and the doors swung open to unveil another long, dark, winding corridor. It, too, was made of silver and proved to be a maze, though, eventually, the questers discovered it was shorter than its predecessor.

As they entered the passage, they were struck by the tangy coolness of the ocean. The salty scent of spindrift pervaded their nostrils, and when they moved, it seemed as though they were buoyed by waves. But as before, they discovered no explanation for the odd sensations.

Again the walls were engraved—this time with pictures of the sea—and the companions did not need to observe the giant eel bearing down on them from nowhere to know what sort of illusions awaited them in the Hall of Water. Collectively taking a deep breath, they plunged forward, and once more, the nightmares began.

Time passed. The questers did not know how much, but it seemed like forever as, with gaping jaws and pointed teeth, killer whales and great white sharks pursued them fathoms deep beneath the ocean's surface. They struggled furiously for breath as titanic octopuses and squids clutched them with sucking tentacles and sprayed them with inky fluid that blinded their eyes and paralyzed their bodies. Kelp wrapped around their arms and legs, dragging them down to the depths of the sea. Horrendous tidal waves knocked them to their knees, and sheets of pouring rain pelted them relentlessly.

Cain and Ileana did what they could to protect the minds of the others, relieved that Halcyone, at least, faced these deceptions fearlessly. But Charis screamed with terror as she slammed herself brutally against the floor, snatched beneath the ocean's surface—or so she thought—by a raging whirlpool. There, she rolled helplessly over a concealed mechanism, and only Sir Ahmed's yanking her rapidly to one side prevented her from being speared by an iron trident abruptly ejected from the ceiling.

The end of the maze came none too soon for the companions, who felt as though they had been spewed through its egress by a tremendous, white-crested breaker. Wearily, they staggered into the sanctuary beyond, where, again, brightly flaming firebrands provided a much appreciated welcome. As quickly as possible after making sure the chamber was the haven it appeared, the questers relieved themselves of their packs, then sprawled upon the floor.

"I cannot walk another step!" Jiro Juniper cried. "If ye go on, ye must go without me!"

"And me!" Charis squeaked, still terrified by her narrow escape in the hall.

"I think we all could use some sleep," Ileana observed, gazing at the drawn, frightened faces of her companions. Only her husband appeared unaffected by what they had been through, though even he had dark mauve rings under his eyes. "There is no telling how long we have been in the Citadel—hours, no doubt. Perhaps even days. We are safe here. I suggest we get some rest."

Her proposal was scarcely agreed upon before everyone, including Cain, was deep in slumber; and so it was that none of them heard, sometime later, the light footfalls that echoed in the halls of the Citadel, the gentle voices that chimed like the tinkling of bells in the passages until they reached the room at the end of the Hall of Water.

"The questers have come halfway," one of the voices noted softly so as not to disturb the companions who slept in the sanctuary, oblivious of the childlike intruders. "No one else has managed to accomplish that for many years now."

"That is true," another voice affirmed. Then it added, "But there are still two more halls they must overcome —and the Choice as well—before they are admitted into the Hall of Truth; and even there, they may fail."

"Yea," the first voice sighed, as though troubled by the thought. "Still, the Child of Winter has much power, and her heart is filled with love. Perhaps she is indeed the one Chosen by the Light. Perhaps she will succeed."

"Perhaps," the second voice responded noncommittally. "Come. We must hurry. They will awaken soon."

Quickly, the two who in time would become Custodians leaned against the walls the wooden ladders they bore. Then, one by one, from the silver holders, they removed and extinguished the torches that had burned low. These, they replaced with fresh firebrands, which they lit with blazing fagots. After that, gathering up the ladders and used torches, then glancing about to be certain they had left nothing else undone, they exited the room as silently as they had entered it.

Shortly thereafter, Ileana stirred and stretched. Yawning, she turned over, trying to find a more comfortable position. Then, abruptly, feeling the cold silver floor beneath her, she awoke, coming fully to her senses. Cain was already up, she saw, though the others slept on.

"Good morning," she greeted her husband quietly, yearning suddenly to be enfolded in his arms, to feel his lips upon hers.

She took a tentative step toward him. Then, sadly, she reminded herself he was not likely to welcome her advances, and she paused, bending down to pick up her possessions —and to hide the tears that had started without warning in her lavender eyes.

"Or good afternoon, as the case may be," Cain rejoined, his heart aching and filled with anger that he dared not let himself love her as he so longed to do, for he had not missed the expression on her face. "Who can say? I know time has passed, yet the firebrands seem to have burned down not at all."

"Yea," Ileana said tremulously, frowning as she turned from him to observe that this was indeed so. "Perhaps they have been vested with magic."

"Perhaps—and yet . . . I could have sworn I heard someone moving around in here earlier." Cain shook his head and shrugged. "But then, mayhap 'twas only my imagination after all. Go. Rouse the rest. I know they are exhausted, but we dare not linger here any longer. Each moment we delay puts us that much further behind schedule, and we must reach Ashton Wells before 'tis too late!"

Incredibly, Ileana had got so caught up in the dreamlike quality of the Citadel that she had almost forgotten they had an urgent purpose for entering it: They must obtain the Sword of Ishtar! Now she hurried to waken the others. Talking little, the questers broke their fast, washing their hasty meal down with water and wine from their flasks. Then they once more surveyed the chamber.

Like those before it, it was round and silver; its walls were ribbed; its ceiling was vaulted and embellished with fan tracery. At the center of the room was a pedestal that, except for the swirls of wind chiseled on its capital, matched its predecessors. On its top lay a single snow-white plume, its delicate edges fluttering gently, as though ruffled by a breeze, though there was none. Another spiral staircase wound its way upward behind the column.

Sighing, suspecting what lay ahead, Ileana grabbed a torch and the feather and began to ascend the steps to the third story. Resignedly, the rest of the companions followed, Cain giving one last look around the sanctuary to be certain they hadn't left anything behind.

At the head of the stairs was yet another set of doors, but they were like nothing the questers had ever before seen. The portals were woven of a strange white cloudlike fabric stretched over a clear frame of some unfamiliar material that resembled glass but was unshatterable. The rune stone above read: THE HALL OF AIR. Ileana fitted the plume into the lock, and the doors glided open with a whisper to expose another long corridor. It twined and twisted before the companions, seeming even darker and more forbidding than the previous two halls had been. When the questers stepped inside, they were greeted by a cold, biting wind that caused the flames of the firebrands to waver wildly, casting elongated shadows on the engraved silver walls and making the tableaux thereon shift and shimmer eerily. The air was thin and moist; all except Ileana and Charis, accustomed to high altitudes, had difficulty breathing.

Slowly, the companions started down the passage. They had not gone far when they were set upon by a flock of immense vultures, whose beaks and talons tore at them viciously. Shouting the battle cry of the Royal House of Khali, Cain and Sir Ahmed met the attack head on, their swords flashing in the torchlight. Yet when the fight was done, not a single drop of blood or even a stray feather lay upon the floor.

"More illusions," Ileana said, relieved, and pressed on.

She had barely got the words out of her mouth when three shrieking rocs, their mammoth wings beating furiously, appeared from nowhere to chase the questers through the Hall. After that, large, fierce eagles swooped from the ceiling to pluck them from the floor, bearing them aloft, only to send them plummeting crazily through the air. Wisps of distorted clouds and mist billowed about them, freezing and smothering them. Hurricanes and cyclones swept them away into nothingness. Mehtar tripped and fell against a wall, setting off a hidden mechanism that smashed a bottle to emit a fog of sickly green gas that nearly asphyxiated them all before, coughing and gasping for breath, they managed to escape from it, Ileana protecting them with her aura.

Thankfully, the companions soon learned that this maze was shorter than the last. As though buffeted there by violent winds, they stumbled into the sanctuary at its end. Yet as before, once the questers entered the round silver chamber with its aesthetic ribs and fan tracery, the nightmares ceased.

Again the companions rested and refreshed themselves, then made a closer inspection of their environs. Another argent pedestal, its capital tooled with flames, stood in the center of the room. A brass taper, wick burning, rested on its top. Behind this, another spiral staircase led to the fourth floor.

Driven now by a strange sense of urgency—as though she and the others, dazed and tranced, had already lingered too long in the Citadel—Ileana seized a torch from the walls. Then, taking the taper as well, she started up the steps, the others hard on her heels. At the head of the stairs, they were greeted by a pair of hammered-copper doors, above which was inset another grey rune stone. THE HALL OF FIRE, it stated.

"This must be the last one," the girl commented, as though talking to herself. "There are no other elements save ether—and that belongs only to the Immortal Guardian."

"Yea," Cain agreed. "Let us proceed then, for surely we are near the end of our quest—and we must get the sword!"

Ileana nodded. Then, carefully, she pushed the taper into the brass lock. The latch clicked audibly. Creaking forebodingly on their brass hinges, the copper portals divided. Instantly, a blast of heat smote the questers and the acrid smell of smoke permeated their nostrils.

"I don't like it," Dill muttered uneasily as they gazed into the shadowy corridor that stretched before them. "It seems different from the others."

Ileana thought so, too. Nevertheless, she crept forward into the passage. The rest of the companions, bunched closely together, followed. By the light of the torches, they could see that this hall, too, was silver; its walls were engraved with flames—but oddly, Ileana thought, nothing else. Nor, strangely enough, could she discern any duller spots of argent here and there to indicate concealed mechanisms. At the realization that no snares seemed to lurk in the hall, a prickle of fear tingled down her spine, causing the fine hairs on her nape to stand on end.

"There *is* something different here," she murmured, "something terrible. . . ."

"Let me go first, then," Cain demanded.

His sword and shield in hand, he moved to stand protectively before his wife. But she saw that his eyes were shining with that peculiar light, and she knew the beast within him sensed evil in the maze.

Apprehensively, the questers advanced down the corridor. It was as though they walked through fire, yet they had no sensation of being burned as they traversed the labyrinthine passage. Instead, like ghosts, they seemed to pass through the unreal flames unscathed.

"What was that?" Mace asked sharply, his elfin ears attuned to every nuance of sound.

Immediately, the companions drew to a halt, their bodies taut and poised for flight, their breathing stilled as they listened intently to the silence. Ileana could not be certain, but she thought she heard a faint slithering noise somewhere in the distance ahead—then, nothing. It was as though whatever lay beyond them now stood as tensed and hushed as they did, waiting.

Cain inhaled deeply, his nostrils twitching as he detected a unique, slimy sulphuric odor he had smelled before in the past—in the Haghar Desert and the Raokhshna Bluffs of Bedoui. Not a heloderma, but something very like it. . . .

"A dragon," he breathed. "By the Blue Moon—go back!" he yelled to the others. "Go back! *Run!*"

The companions did not hesitate, but turned and raced back in the direction whence they had come, only to watch in horror as the copper doors of the maze abruptly slammed shut before they could reach them. Too late, the questers realized their mistake: The entire hall was a silver trap, and they were caught fast in its deadly jaws!

They had no sooner grasped this fact than, hissing and venting fire, the perilous dragon was upon them. Numb with shock and fear, they stared at it incredulously, unable to believe their eyes. Even Cain, who had seen the rare beasts before, was awed by the size of the creature.

It was gargantuan, standing nearly fifteen feet high at the shoulders. Its huge, horned head, crocodilian-looking and set upon a long, thick neck, towered five feet above that. Its massive wings were partially folded, for there was not room in the corridor for the reptile to spread them wide, but even so, Ileana could tell its wingspan was enormous. Except for its golden throat, belly, and the underside of its spiny tail, which ended in a sharp triangular point, the dragon's whole body glistened with armorlike scales that shone blood-red in the torchlight. Its front legs were short and seemed relatively harmless in comparison to the rest of its monstrous torso, but Ileana knew their appearance was deceptive, for the dragon's skeletal feet were tipped with wickedly curved claws. Its powerful hind legs were ponderous; its long, flat feet were studded with talons. Most terrifying of all were the beast's glowing golden eyes with their slitted black pupils that seemed to pierce right through the companions, rooting them to the floor.

The creature hissed again, emitting flames that came from a special organ in its body, where internal acids and gases combined and ignited to be expelled through a second trachea, evolved specifically for this purpose. The reptile's neck rippled as it bent its head toward them, razorlike teeth bared. Its tail swished, cracking like a whip against one wall.

Charis and Halcyone screamed. Instantly, because she did not know whether the dragon was real, Ileana summoned her power. Her aura blazed forth, a haze of white-hot light, to envelop the questers, warding them against the beast. The elves' crossbows twanged, and the dwarfs' spears sang, but the shafts bounced off the reptile's skin.

"That is useless!" Cain cried. "Stay back! Don't try to help me! It drains Ileana's power to shield ye and let your weapons pass through the barrier at the same time."

Yea, that is so, the girl thought, remembering how, in the jungle of Cornucopia, she had protected the others while they'd fought the band of SoulEaters. Afterward, when she had needed it, her power had failed her. Only a meal and sleep had restored it.

She must not let that happen now! The water, wine, and dried provisions the companions carried were running low, and there would be no rest for her—not so long as they were trapped in the Hall of Fire with the crimson dragon. Somehow they must overcome it, even if it were only an illusion; otherwise, the bodies of some, their minds unable to believe fully Ileana's reassurances that the beast was unreal, would surely die.

From one corner of her eye, as she watched the creature warily, the girl saw Cain, beyond her circle of warding, slowly kneel, his aura burning about him. Keeping one eye on the reptile, he yanked from his belt the leather pouch that held the jar of dragonbane. Carefully, he pulled the cork from the container, wincing slightly, his eyes burning, as he inhaled the acrid green fumes that wafted from the jar. Then, laying his sword upon the floor and taking care to ensure none of the poison touched him, he began to pour the thick black liquid upon the blade.

As though scenting danger, the dragon sidled back a little; but still, it taunted the questers, seeming to derive considerable enjoyment from tormenting them. It stared at them intently, the incessant motion of its head and its unblinking amber eyes hynotic, like those of a snake before striking. Every now and then, it lunged toward them, its vile, forked tongue spitting fire, its claws raking the air, its tail undulating savagely. But then, as though it knew it could not penetrate the barrier around the companions, the beast drew back, watching, waiting, its gaping maw seeming to laugh at them.

At last, Cain stood. He had slain a dragon once before, but then he had had several warriors to help him. Now he must face this creature alone, knowing that if he failed to kill it, Ileana and the rest would fall prey to its fury. If it were only an illusion, his wife would no doubt survive —and perhaps some of the others as well. But if it were real . . .

Nay! It must *be a deception—like those of the other halls!*
Cain thought.

Then, grimly, he realized he dared not take that chance.
Ileana was already exerting a great deal of her strength and
power; she could not continue to do so forever. Then, if the
reptile were real, it would tear her and the rest to shreds, for
Cain knew his own strength and power would be sorely
taxed by the impending battle. He would be unable to
defend his wife and the others. He might even, he recognized with a sinking heart, be unable to defend himself
—not only against the dragon, but against the beast within
him, already feeding upon the vermilion creature's malevo-
lence and straining to break free of the invisible chains with
which he kept it bound.

Cautiously, his now poisoned sword held at the ready,
Cain approached the fire-breathing reptile, the sheer force
of his will counteracting the peculiar, mesmerizing effect of
the dragon's glittering eyes. The beast reared its ugly head;
once more, its sibilant voice issued from its jaws and flames
erupted from its throat. The blaze singed the hazy edges of
Cain's aura, sending sparks showering through the passage.
Ileana's heart lurched sickeningly in her breast as her
husband faltered, startled, his power ebbing and flowing
briefly before he managed to regain control of it. Then,
crouched low, his mouth set in a thin, tight line, he crept
toward the creature, his sword and shield poised for combat. Despite her husband's height and muscular build,
Ileana could not help thinking how small and insignificant
he appeared compared to the behemoth dragon that towered over him menacingly.

Warily, man and beast stalked each other, lunging and
feinting, each watching closely for any sign of weakness in
the other's defense. The reptile was hampered by its size in
the relatively narrow hall. But Cain was equally disadvan-
taged by the fact that he must constantly shift his aura,
creating gaps through which to wield his blade. It was for
this reason that he employed his shield—to cover the
resulting cracks in the circle of warding that encompassed
him.

Suddenly, bounding forward with a surprising rapidity

for a creature of its proportions, the dragon lashed out with its forelegs, one of which slipped through a chink in Cain's aura. He cringed and cried out, stumbling as the reptile tore away one sleeve of his kurta, leaving five dark trails of blood wealing from his shoulder to his elbow.

Cain!

With difficulty, Ileana stifled the scream that rose to her throat, knowing she must do nothing to distract her husband lest she break his concentration, thereby disrupting the smooth current of his power. Already her own was wavering, made erratic by her lack of attention; and breathing slowly, she forced her mind to focus on guarding the others. Still, her eyes remained locked on Cain's dark figure; her heart prayed silently for the man she loved.

Quickly regaining his balance, Cain struck back with unexpected swiftness, his sword biting deeply into one of the beast's thick haunches. The dragon shrieked hoarsely with pain as blood welled from the wound, spraying the silver floor with flecks of red foam. Enraged, the creature charged, its claws scrambling for purchase on the now slick surface beneath its feet. It slid and skidded wildly. For an instant, it seemed as though the reptile would smash right into Cain. But at the last minute, it managed to recover and swerved to one side to avoid encountering his aura. Even so, the beast could not withdraw fast enough to escape being burned by the perimeter of the blue barrier. Jagged bolts of fire exploded in the corridor; the nauseating smell of roasting flesh filled the air.

Its voice grating with agony and anger, the dragon fell back, dragging its now smoldering, blackened wing. Again Cain's blade swept out, delivering another brutal blow to the creature, nearly slicing off one of its forelegs. Roaring flames, the reptile pivoted protectively; its tail pierced a crevice in Cain's aura and whipped violently across his chest, flinging him against the wall and knocking his weapons from his grasp. His circle of warding flickered and flashed like lightning, shooting stars spewing crazily from its boundaries. Stunned by the impact, Cain sprawled upon the floor, his aura winking as his power surged and recoiled within him. Then, abruptly, the blue barrier vanished.

Ileana gasped, stricken with fear for her husband as she

saw him lying helpless and exposed, his sword and shield some distance away. Her own aura fluttered, its white-hot light darkening to violet as, hurriedly weighing the consequences, she compelled the flow of her power to divide and channel itself in her mind.

Sluggishly, blinking its eyes and shaking its head as though dazed, the dragon turned to study the damage it had done. It lurched forward, then paused; and to her vast relief, for she had begun to doubt its efficacy, Ileana realized the poison on Cain's blade had started to affect the beast. It was no longer thinking clearly.

Quickly, before the reptile could recover to attack again, Ileana concentrated the bulk of her power on Cain's weapons. Inexorably, the sword and shield began to slide across the floor. Hearing them scrape along the silver surface, the injured creature cried out irately and staggered toward them. Its tail caught the buckler, flipping it over, then pounding it viciously. The shield bounced several times; then, clattering and clanging, it skittered down the hall. After that, its head lolling, the dragon leaned warily toward the blade. Catching a whiff of the poison, it drew back, its now glazed eyes darting to Cain. Seeing the beast's attention hone in on her stirring husband, Ileana hazardously, recklessly, relinquished her hold on the aura that protected her and the others.

"Cain!" she screamed, her power welding to grip the sword and send it flying through the air. "Cain!"

At the girl's anguished wail, the reptile wheeled about, its eyes glaring at her evilly, its mouth seeming to grin superciliously. Without warning, the creature's horned head swooped straight toward her, smoke and flames billowing from its yawning maw. She had a fleeting impression of a long, dark tunnel filled with fire and vicious, pointed teeth closing in on her. . . .

In one swift, lithe movement, as the weapon came hurtling toward him, Cain caught the hilt of his blade, sprang to his feet, and brought the sword down hard, like an ax, upon the dragon's scaly, serpentine neck, almost severing it in two. Blood gushed like a fountain from the terrible gash as the beast stumbled, then slowly toppled with a crash to the floor, its head slithering to rest just inches from Ileana's trembling body. To her utter horror, she saw the reptile's mouth gape and realized the creature was still alive. Mercifully, its wounds, combined with the dragonbane that had entered its system, rapidly proved too much for it, however. It swallowed convulsively, smoke wafting from its nostrils in a final, sighing breath, before at last it shuddered and lay still.

Ileana stared at the crumpled creature, shocked as it began to shimmer brightly, then fade until it disappeared entirely. It had been an illusion, only an illusion—like everything else! Yet it had seemed so real. . . .

"Are ye all right?" Cain rasped, panting, as he sheathed his sword and came to stand beside her, the fervid light in his eyes dimming now that the scarlet dragon had been vanquished.

Wordlessly, Ileana nodded, her eyes taking in the fact that his shirtsleeve was no longer ripped, his arm no longer injured. These, too, had been only deceptions, placed in the minds of the companions by the Custodians who guarded the Citadel. Even she, a sorceress, had been fooled, her love for Cain clouding her mind's eye. She should have realized —if Belladonna had spoken truly—that the poison ought to have killed its intended victim within moments if the dragon were real.

What more lies in store for us? she wondered, once more shaken and dismayed. *Now, when both Cain and I are weak, our power drained, what lurks ahead to assault us, to entrap us? Haven't we yet proved ourselves worthy of claiming the Sword of Ishtar? I know the Citadel must exact a costly toll of those who dare to enter it. But surely we have already paid twice over the price of admission. . . .*

"Come," her husband said, interrupting her reverie. To her surprise, he put his arms around her and pulled her close. One hand caressed her cheek as he lifted her face to his. "I know ye are suffering from both hunger and fatigue, Ileana. But we cannot stay here. We dare not—not while we are both sapped of our strength. Who knows what else may lie in wait in this hall? We must reach the sanctuary chamber—and quickly."

"Yea, ye are right, Lord."

But still she clung to him, reluctant to leave the warmth of his embrace. How long had it been since he had held her thus? Too long. Even now, she knew it was only because he was too worn out to conceal his emotions and grateful that she had saved his life that he cradled her so. But Ileana did not want his gratitude; she wanted his love. And somewhere deep down inside, she clung to the hope that despite all the evidence to the contrary, he still cared for her. He must. Otherwise, she had nothing—nothing at all.

So was there nothing before the Immortal Guardian brought forth the Light into the Darkness, a voice echoed softly in her head, startling her. *Hold fast to your hope, Child of Winter, for it is the hope of the world as well. Therein does the answer lie. Go now. The Hall of Fire is empty—ye have prevailed over its only pitfall—and your final test awaits.*

Before Ileana could reply, the voice was gone. For a moment, she could not even be certain she had heard it. But its words rang in the chasms of her mind, and she knew that she must not forget them, that somehow they were the key. . . .

"Let us go," she said to her husband. "There is naught else in this hall, and I feel that the Sword of Ishtar is near."

Silently, the companions wound their way through the passage until they reached the circular room at its end. This sanctuary was identical to those before it—with one exception: It boasted two pedestals instead of one, and their capitals were bare of ornamentation. Atop one of the silver columns, piled high, was a large heap of gold coins and jewelry whose precious, many-colored gems sparkled enticingly in the torchlight. In sharp contrast to this, the top of the second pedestal boasted nothing but an old, rusty key. Behind the two columns, a spiral staircase curved its way up to the fifth floor.

"By the Passion Moon, will ye look at that!" Halcyone breathed, her eyes wide with awe as she approached the glittering treasure. "Do my eyes deceive me—again!—or is that really a damned fortune lying there? Heaven's Light preserve us! We're rich! *We're all bloody rich!*"

"Nay!" Ileana cried, some instinct warning her. "Don't touch it! Don't touch so much as a single coin!"

"But why not?" Halcyone asked curiously, frowning. "It *is* real, isn't it? It's there for the taking, isn't it?"

"Yea." Ileana nodded, feeling certain this was so—and thus suspecting a trap. "But I promise ye if ye touch it, something dreadful will happen. I sense it! 'Tis meant for those who serve the Demon Greed. Come!" she uttered sharply. "We came for the sword; that is all we shall take. Heed my words, or like the Weeping Wraiths of the vale, ye shall pay the price for your folly!"

Determinedly, the girl snatched up the key and began to climb the steps to the fifth floor. More unwilling than Ileana simply to throw away a fortune, the others followed in single file, dragging their feet and glancing back wistfully at the small mountain of gold and jewelry they left behind. Still, none dared to return to purloin even a ring, for Cain stood at the foot of the stairs to guard against this. Finally, when the last quester was partway up the staircase, he, too, started to ascend it.

At the head of the steps, the companions came to a standstill, their breath catching in their throats as they gazed at the magnificent set of doors before them. Beautifully wrought of pure, clear crystal, the portals shone like thousands of brilliant stars, reflecting every nuance of light and shadow cast upon the silver walls and nearly blinding the questers who stared at them speechlessly, overwhelmed by their splendor. Above the doors was a rune stone that read: THE HALL OF TRUTH.

Slowly, her heart pounding, Ileana turned the key in the lock and the portals parted. She gasped at what they divulged, for nowhere had she ever beheld such breathtaking loveliness, such glorious radiance. Truly, Ishtar herself had blessed this dazzling tower. No wonder it had been deemed a Holy Place. It was round, as the sanctuary chambers had been, and its ceiling was vaulted and silver. But there, the room's resemblance to the rest ended, for the walls of the Hall of Truth were composed entirely of stained glass.

Outside, dawn had broken over the horizon, and the rays of the winter sun streamed through the windows, turning the tower into a kaleidoscope. Ribands and ribands of colors filled the chamber, twisting and intertwining, colors that were like mist—without substance, illusory. Yet here was the real truth of the Citadel, for now Ileana could see that like a tapestry, the scenes depicted in the stained glass told the history of the Sword of Ishtar: how, fallen from the stars, it had been forged by the fires of heaven, then forged again by the fires of a distant earth. How it had then been brought to Tintagel by a great lord and handed down through the generations to the True Defenders of the Light. How, during the Wars of the Kind and the Apocalypse, the Custodians had feared for its safety and had built the Citadel to ward it against the Darkness.

Now, at the very heart of the chamber, Ileana observed the diamondlike crystal altar wherein the sword had been laid; and inexorably, she approached it, feeling as though her destiny waited there—had awaited her coming a millennium or more.

Her companions watched in silence, unmoving, as though some unseen force held them back. But it was nothing more than their own fear and awe, for suddenly, it seemed to them that Ileana had become a stranger, a force vested with and blessed by the Light, a power greater than any they had ever imagined. It was as though time stood still and they dreamed, as the Citadel dreamed—the same dream, in which Ileana appeared to float like a wraith through a swirl of chameleonic color and they were but amorphous figures on the fringes of her reality, unimportant, forgotten. Even Cain felt diminished, as though his body were fading into nothingness, while at the same time, Ileana's seemed to grow brighter and brighter, blinding him as once the crystal sphere of the Druswids had blinded him. But now, as then, the sensation was only in his mind.

Unaware of his thoughts or those of the others, Ileana reached the altar and knelt reverently before it, starring herself and murmuring a prayer to the Immortal Guardian. Then, seeming to know instinctively what she must do, she stretched out her hands and placed them on top of the crystal. There, the Sword of Ishtar was embedded, only its raised outline visible upon the surface of the altar. The crystal was bitterly cold to her touch, so cold, it seemed to burn her hands; but she, who was a child of winter, paid no heed to the searing chill. She was Ileana—Chosen by the Light. She felt nothing, heard nothing, saw nothing as, slowly, she closed her senses to the world and, breathing deeply, called up her power.

At last, with the wild, rapturous cry of the Keepers roaring in her ears, she felt that which she had summoned burst forth from within her. Incandescent blue fire shot from her fingertips to travel like jagged lightning up the hilt of the sword to its point. Gradually, the blade began to glow, to pulsate with iridescent light—the magic of countless Custodians, their bodies long since ashes scattered to the elements, awakening, joining with Ileana's own to become crystal flames of truth that pierced the very core of her being, ferreting out the innermost secrets of her heart. Purples, blues, greens, yellows, reds . . . a swirl of painfully intense multicolored lights blinded her as, little by little, sensing she was indeed the Chosen One, the altar melted away like ice to expose the Sword of Ishtar. Then, suddenly, the shimmering aura that encompassed the girl turned white-hot and the weapon lay bare before her, its iron blade gleaming like molten ore, its solid gold hilt shining, the many precious jewels set therein glittering as though they had absorbed the colors of the blazing luminescence.

As though in a trance, Ileana reached out to grasp the hilt of the sword. The blade was ancient, aeons old, and heavy, heavier than she had ever dreamed possible, weighted with power. She could barely lift it. Yet inch by inch, she began to pull it from the crystal until at last, without warning, it was free. For a moment, it shone like a beacon in her hands. Then, abruptly, its glow vanished, leaving it cold and dark and still, and briefly, she wondered if it, too, were but an illusion. But, nay. The hilt about which her fingers tightened was real enough, strong and solid and worn with age.

Marveling, she studied the sword. Now it looked no different from any other. But she had seen its magic; she had felt its power. It was an awesome weapon—the greatest on Tintagel. Surely, it would drive back the Darkness that threatened the world! Clutching the blade triumphantly to her breast, she rose.

Her quest was ended. The Sword of Ishtar was hers.

Map by Rebecca Brandewyne

Chapter 31

*My heart is filled with the most bitter of sorrows, for I
have been deceived by my beloved.*

—Thus it is Written—
in
The Private Journals
of the High Princess Lady Ileana I

AFTER ILEANA TOOK THE SWORD FROM THE CRYSTAL
altar, a door opened in the floor of the Hall of Truth to
reveal a dark, winding, gradually descending orifice down
which she and the rest slid until they reached the bottom
level of the Citadel. There, they were ejected through the
tunnel's cleverly concealed egress at the back of the stronghold on to the silver paving blocks of the courtyard. Now,
slightly dazed and vastly relieved that they were apparently
free to go, the questers set off in search of their mounts,
certain the beasts were dead. To their amazement, however,
they discovered that in their absence, the animals had
been well cared for and were ready and waiting for them
just beyond the Citadel's golden gates, which stood wide
open.

Not bothering to question why this was so, the companions hurried through the portal, feeling as though they'd
abruptly awakened from a long, dream-filled sleep. Immediately after they left the courtyard, the gates swung closed
behind them, the latch clicking firmly into place; and the
Citadel resumed its eerie air of watchfulness and forebod-

ing, its enchanted spire gleaming dully in the grey early morning light.

"How long do ye suppose we were in there?" Jiro Juniper asked, staring back at the stronghold as though he could not believe they had escaped from it alive.

"A week at least," Mace replied. "Maybe longer." He glanced worriedly at the leaden sky. "By my reckoning, 'tis nearly the dead of winter, and we've months of travel ahead of us. We'll never get to Ashton Wells in time!"

"We must!" Cain insisted grimly. "Otherwise, our journey here will all have been for naught, and Tintagel will be doomed to the Darkness!"

"How much time would we save," inquired Ileana, standing quietly to one side with the Sword of Ishtar in her hands, "if we sailed across the Great Cerulean Sea instead of trekking overland?"

"That would be impossible, Lady," Mace stated flatly. "We don't have a boat."

"We could build one," she asserted, smiling at Halcyone, whose eyes had begun to sparkle with understanding and excitement. "Nothing grand, to be sure, but a boat just the same. What do ye say, mistress?" She turned to the young shipbuilder from Astra. "Could we do it?"

"Yea, Lady." Halcyone nodded eagerly, the wheels in her mind whirling furiously. "I know we could construct a big raft at least . . . and if we had something to use as a sail . . . we could piece one together from odds and ends, I suppose. Why, we could even dismantle the caravan! It could serve as a shelter for us."

"Let us get started right away, then," Cain interrupted impatiently, having already decided to proceed with the proposed plan. "We have not a moment to lose!"

Desirous of putting as much distance as possible between themselves and the Citadel, whose spell still seemed to hang over them like a pall, the questers needed no further urging. Hurriedly, they mounted up and started down the road that would take them from the vale to the sea. Once upon the beach, they set about searching the sandy shores for driftwood, having no way to chop down the tall trees of the forest and Ileana feeling strongly that the land's strange, childlike inhabitants would not permit this in any event.

She knew the Valcoeurians were still watching them, for oddly enough, the questers had no difficulty finding on the beach several long, sturdy pieces of driftwood ideally suited to their purpose. Though Ileana said nothing to the others, she felt certain the fairies were somehow responsible for this.

Within the next few days, with some stout hemp they'd discovered among their supplies in the caravan, the companions lashed together, under Halcyone's direction, a crude but serviceable raft. Then they removed the wheels from the wagon, and with wooden pegs carved by Bergren Birchbark and Jiro Juniper, secured the vehicle to the raft. Ileana and Charis sewed several light woolen horse blankets together to fashion an inelegant sail; and from some rope, pegs, and a few scraps of wood, Halcyone managed to contrive a rather awkward rudder. Aboard this unlikely contraption, after turning the animals loose in the forest, certain the Valcoeurians would care for them, the travelers embarked on their journey to Finisterre.

The Great Cerulean Sea was often rough and stormy, and twice the companions felt sure they had been blown off course, though they couldn't be certain, for they had difficulty navigating. The closer they got to the center of the sea, the more strongly some force seemed to take possession of Mace's compass, making it spin wildly. Most of the time, the firmament was gloomy and overcast, sullen clouds obscuring the sun by day and the stars by night. Sometimes mist hung so low and thick over the water, the travelers could scarcely see, and it both rained and snowed, further adding to their misery. Those not on duty huddled about the brazier inside the caravan, trying to warm their chapped faces and numb hands and feet, and listening to the howl of the icy wind that cut them like a sharp knife and set their teeth to chattering. Still, there being no other choice, the companions sailed on as best they could; and some weeks later, much to their relief, they spied the tall watchtowers of Ashton Wells in the distance.

Once they reached the eastern shore of Finisterre, the travelers wearily dragged their raft through the freezing water up onto the snowy beach. Then, abandoning the craft, they marched toward the castle as quickly as possible, chilled to the bone and dull-eyed with hunger and exhaustion.

They were welcomed with both surprise and joy at the fortress, where a hot meal and a happy, tearful reunion with Gerard, Ulthor, and the others did much to restore their flagging spirits.

"We thought ye lost for sure," Gerard claimed as he came running to greet the companions, Rosemary clinging lovingly to his arm, and Ulthor and Syeira following hard on his heels, shouting and laughing. Hands were clasped tightly and shoulders hugged all the way around. Then Gerard motioned for everyone to be seated at the trestle tables in the great hall. "Bring food and drink for our guests! Quickly! Quickly!" he called to the handmaidens who served the keep. Then he turned to his friends, his face growing grave as he thought of the news he had to impart to them.

They listened soberly while he described the vast army the UnKind had indeed assembled in Finisterre, as they had feared, and that was even now camped in the Hollow Hills beyond the Strathmore Plains, waiting for an opportune moment to send hordes of invaders throughout the continents of Aerie and Verdante.

"There are hundreds of them, perhaps thousands," Gerard spoke tiredly, for he had slept little since coming to the castle to help his father, the King Lord Arundel, oversee preparations for the forthcoming battle. "Given the slow progress of the disease, it must have taken the SoulEaters years to infect so many people secretly, so none would guess what had become of them. And mayhap there were many who did not survive. . . ." His voice trailed away, and he shook his head. "I don't know. It is like a nightmare, one from which I am afraid we shall not awaken."

The travelers told him, then, of the success of their quest, recounting their trials and tribulations in obtaining the Sword of Ishtar; and they saw that Gerard and the rest were cheered by the victory. Then Ulthor spoke of his and Syeira's journey to Borealis to meet with his clan's chieftain, the Lord Erek. The giants were even now marching toward Ashton Wells, Ulthor said. After that, having at last been greeted by the King Lord Arundel, who'd looked as worried and fatigued as his son, the newcomers were shown to the chambers that had been made ready for them. There, knowing themselves safe behind the high walls of the fortress, they fell into a deep sleep for the first time in months.

The following morning, they rose, feeling greatly refreshed, and flung themselves wholeheartedly into the frenzied work being done to fortify the keep. All along the ramparts, Ileana saw that catapults, ballistas, and mangonels had been erected and braced upon the walkways. Beside them, in neat, pyramidal piles, were rows of ammunition: arrows, torches, scrap iron, and stones. Here and there were large cauldrons of pitch and oil and stacks of wood that would be used to heat them. Barrels of water had been set out, with buckets placed near at hand for dousing fires. Below, in the courtyard, hammers rang upon anvils as blades and javelins were forged; and men and women scurried to and fro, securing livestock and granaries and making certain the larders were full. Inside the castle itself, pallets for the warriors had been spread wherever there was space; and dried plants and herbs with medicinal properties, as well as jars of healing balm, had been brought from storerooms to the great hall, which was to serve as an infirmary. Daily, men, women, and children from the town arrived, frightened and seeking sanctuary; others, fearing the fortress would fall before the onslaught of the UnKind, gathered what possessions they could carry and fled south in search of hiding places.

Cain and Ileana labored as diligently as the rest, doing whatever job was needed, no matter how hard or dirty. Still, most people kept their distance from Cain, afraid of the strange, mad look they saw in his eyes whenever he stared out across the Strathmore Plains to the Hollow Hills beyond and spied the SoulEaters massed there. Ileana, however, was a welcome sight. All had heard the tale of the mighty Sword of Ishtar, which she now carried in a sheath slung across her back, and the weapon had come to represent a symbol of hope for those who would do battle with the UnKind.

The girl never let the blade leave her protection; she even slept with it beneath her, for she knew Cain wanted it —desperately. He lusted for it with the same monomaniacal fever that had driven him to lead the expedition into

Valcoeur to obtain it. Ever since Ileana had freed it from the crystal altar, he had watched her like a hawk, constantly, waiting for her to lower her guard so he might take the sword from her.

Even now, silently, in the spacious room they had been assigned upon their arrival at the keep, he studied her covertly, his eyes half closed so she could not read his thoughts as she gazed at his reflection in the mirror before her. What was he thinking? Was he even now plotting how to steal the sword from her? He dared not challenge her for it; as long as it was in her possession, she was stronger and more powerful than he. This, they both knew.

Biting her lip, Ileana averted her eyes, pretending to be absorbed by the crystal flacons of scent and clay jars of dried petals arrayed on the dressing table before which she sat, brushing the tangles from her long silver hair.

Wordlessly, Cain continued to contemplate her, noting the way in which the candlelight and firelight illuminated her tresses and beautiful face so it was as though a halo glowed about her head and the Light Itself shone upon her delicate countenance.

She is so lovely, and tomorrow, I may destroy her, a small, sane part of him thought bitterly, filled with anger and grief at the notion.

Restless, he rose from his chair and moved to the windows set into the north wall of the room. Through the lead-glass lozenge panes, he could see by the diffuse light of the wintry moons of Tintagel the Strathmore Plains in the distance, the hideous black shapes silhouetted against the far horizon.

There were hundreds of them, perhaps thousands, as Gerard had said. Cain knew. He had been watching them now for nearly a fortnight, waiting, as they had watched and waited. But for what, no one knew. Then, this morning, a SoulEater so immense as to be utterly terrifying had joined the throng. Ulthor had recognized the reptile at once.

" 'Tis Woden," he had muttered uneasily, "a giant from Borealis. He is, of course, much changed; but I would know that limp anywhere, for I was the cause of it. He must have been taken captive by the UnKind. But then again, perhaps he was not. He was already so evil, maybe he *wanted* to become one of the SoulEaters, thinking it would make him invincible. He was ever possessed of a warped mind and spirit."

" 'Tis he for whom the saurians have been watching and waiting," Cain had said, somehow sure this was so. "*He* is their leader, Ulthor. *He* is the one who must be defeated at all costs."

After the coming of Woden, Cain had realized something else: Tomorrow was the winter solstice, the shortest day of the year—the longest night. And the SoulEaters were nocturnal creatures. Tomorrow evening, he knew with certainty, they would attack.

Before then, he needed something: the Sword of Ishtar. The beast inside him had told him so. Still, he knew in his heart that if he asked Ileana to give it to him, she would refuse. It was a sacred weapon; it belonged to the Light. She would not relinquish it to him, who was tainted by the Darkness.

Yea, it was so. Cain could feel the Foul Enslaver in the very marrow of his bones. He was mad with It. And Ileana knew it. He could see it in her eyes when he turned to look at her again.

Don't be afraid! he wanted to cry out to her, to comfort her.

But the beast within him would not relent. Now, at long last, it was stronger than he. And it needed the sword, the blade Ileana had taken from the Holy Place and now kept so carefully from his reach.

Ye love her—and she loves ye, the beast hissed in Cain's ear. *Ye can persuade her to lower her guard. Use her love for ye to make her lay aside the sword. I need it! I must have it! It will strengthen my power tenfold!*

There it was—the thing Cain had most feared: that the Darkness would twist his and Ileana's love for each other and use it to deceive and destroy her.

He shut his eyes tightly and, with all his might, willed the beast inside him to be silent. But still, it went on whispering to him, and of its own volition, his mind listened. To his horror, he felt his lips move as though they had a will of their own.

"Ileana," he breathed hoarsely, seductively; and though it was his voice she heard, it was not he who called out to her. "Ileana, come here."

As though in a trance, hypnotized by his dark, gleaming eyes, she stood and walked toward him slowly, trembling a little with fear. She loved Cain, her husband; but the man before her was not he. The Darkness had devoured him, leaving Its beast in his place, and she was unsure what she should do. Should she try to call him back? Nay. It was too late now for that. He was what he must be in order to destroy the UnKind, the SoulEaters who threatened all Tintagel. Ileana could only go on loving him—and pray that was enough.

She quivered when he touched her, drew her close, for she saw, then, what he intended; but she did not protest. Some part of her wanted this, wanted to feel his arms around her one last time before tomorrow—tomorrow, when the Un-Kind would begin their assault upon the castle and Cain must go out and face them alone, a minion of the Darkness more terrible than they. She even understood why it must be so. But it didn't help. For all his strength and power, he was mortal; his body could die, perhaps *would* die—even as hers might meet a like fate. Ileana could not bear the thought of that happening—not until they had grown old and grey together, when they would welcome their Time of Passing, the releasing of their essence from their aged physical shells. But not now, when death would prove such a painful parting of their hearts, their minds, their souls. Was that what was to be? She did not know. She knew only that if it were, she wanted to feel Cain's arms around her one last time, his mouth upon hers, for no matter what he had become, she loved him still.

He threaded his hands through her hair and lifted her face to his. His eyes were closed, and Ileana knew she didn't want to see what was in them. If she did not see them, she could pretend it really *was* Cain who held her in his strong embrace, whose lips sought hers and claimed them gently, tenderly at first. How strange that it should be so. It was not what she had expected. But then, that was the way of the Foul Enslaver, was it not? To cast Its lures in honeyed tones and velvet raiment? She wanted to laugh and to cry at the same time. She was being seduced. Expertly. By a beast she called her husband.

Ah, beloved, her heart cried out to him silently. *Not like this. Not like this!*

But if he heard the pleading thought, he gave no sign.

His arms tightened around her. His tongue darted forth to trace the outline of her mouth, vulnerable and tremulous as it parted for him of its own accord, yielded to his kisses that burned like a fever, leaving her hot and breathless, although she shivered as though chilled. Her head spun, too, as though she were dazed or delirious, and fleetingly, she wondered if it was more than just his lovemaking at work upon her senses, if he had perhaps drugged the wine they had shared earlier. Fool that she was, she had not even thought of this until now. Mentally, she cursed herself. She should have passed her ring around the rim of the chalice. . . .

The thought slipped away as Cain's tongue plunged between her lips, seeking the sweet moistness within, like nectar and ambrosia all rolled into one. Lingeringly, he savored it, felt it melting on his tongue, warm and rich with the flavor of her.

Ah, Heaven's Light, Ileana. I never meant it to be like this.

Cain had assumed the beast would be savage, cruel, would make her despise him; he had hoped it would be so. But it was not.

Desperately, he tried to curl his hands into talons, to dig his nails like claws into her tender skin and hurt her. But his body seemed to have a will all its own, and he could not make it obey. His palms glided like feathers along her shoulders, pushing aside her abayeh so it slipped down to reveal one full, ripe breast, divided from its twin by the leather strap of the sheath in which she carried the Sword of Ishtar. If his fingers had touched the thong, Ileana would have drawn back, suspecting treachery. But instead, Cain's hand closed possessively over her breast, squeezing softly, eliciting a tiny moan of pleasure from her.

His mouth slid along her slender neck. Groaning, he buried his face in the hollow at the base of the pearly pillar of perfection. He could feel the pulse that fluttered there, and his loins tightened and began to throb with a like rhythm of desire.

She is yours, the beast rasped horribly in his ear. *Take her. Take her! Get the sword!*

Cain tried not to do as he was commanded—but to no avail. His love for Ileana, his longing for her . . . these were his enemies now, and they were stronger and more powerful than he. His lips left a trail of fire down her chest; his mouth seared her nipple, branded it as his.

Somehow her abayeh floated to the floor, like twilight mist descending upon the land. His own garments followed; Cain couldn't remember how or when. Then he and Ileana, too, lay upon the floor, naked and intertwined upon a thick, fur rug, breast to breast, thigh to thigh, a mass of sensation. Touch, taste, texture . . . all these things they felt, and more, for they had been Chosen; their senses were beyond those of mere mortals, honed to a fine edge of perception, sharp and piercing.

Their bodies molded together, flesh clinging to flesh, damp with sweat that glistened like evening dew in the soft glow of the candlelight and firelight, the wintry silver shimmer of the starlight that streamed in through the windows. Tintagel's moons climbed higher in the ebony night sky, but Cain and Ileana were oblivious of the passing of time. It had no meaning for them. Their awareness was keenly narrowed, focused acutely, almost painfully, on here and now.

Slowly, exquisitely, he buried himself in her, felt her warm, wet softness envelop him, suck him down into it like a whirlpool of dark fire. He drowned. He burned. She cried out, her hands gripping his smooth, broad back tightly as she shuddered and writhed beneath him, somewhere far beyond his reach now in a moment hers alone, though he had brought her to it and gloried in it when it came. Then he, too, was soaring higher and higher. Passion burst within him, spilled into her, draining him, filling her, life-giving rain falling upon fertile earth.

And then, like the hush that follows a storm, they rested quietly together.

Gently, Cain drew Ileana's head against his shoulder, pushed the strands of damp hair from her face, then kissed her lips. Drowsily, she basked in the golden afterglow of their lovemaking. Something stirred at the edges of her slowly fading consciousness; but not wanting this moment spoiled by the troubles of the world, the girl sighed and thrust the disturbing thought from her mind. There would be time enough tomorrow for the burdens that weighed so heavily on her small shoulders. Sated and content, she drifted into a deep, peaceful sleep such as she had not known for many nights—and dreamed of loving Cain. . . .

Some hours later, Ileana awoke with a start, her body cold and aching from lying upon the hard stone floor. The room was still cast in shadow, and for a moment, she could think of nothing except that it was not yet light. Then, without warning, everything came flooding back to her—clearest of all the uneasy feeling that she had earlier pushed away. Stricken now, she knew, even before she felt it pressing softly against her back, that the leather sheath encasing the Sword of Ishtar was empty. The blade was gone.

She sat up and drew the fur rug about her for warmth as a tight, icy fist of dread grabbed her stomach and began to twist it into knots; fingers of hurt clawed through her body, making her shudder like a wounded animal huddled upon the floor. A ragged sob caught in her throat. She had been used—tricked by the beast within Cain—*and she had let it happen!* She, a priestess, had shirked her duty—and for nothing more than a night of passion! Ileana felt sick and ashamed. How could she, the High Princess, have been so foolish? How could she, a sorceress, have been so deceived?

She didn't know. She had no excuse. She had held the world in her hands—and she had thrown it away for Cain! *Nay!* Her mouth opened to cry out in protest; but the only sound that issued from her throat was a strangled gasp of agony and horror as she suddenly spied her husband standing before the dying embers of the hearth, naked and savage, a barbaric stranger she did not know—did not want to know.

His black eyes burned with the fire of the beast within him. A malevolent, exultant grin distorted his dark, handsome visage as, slowly, chillingly, he caressed the sharp iron blade of the sword he gripped triumphantly in his sinister left hand.

Chapter 32

Ye must be ever vigilant, for the Darkness is like a Carnivorous Beast. When Its belly is full, It slumbers in Its lair and Its Cubs lie close at hand. But when It hungers, It stalks the land to prey upon the Kind, and Its Cubs follow in Its footsteps.

Therefore, if ye are wise, ye will walk always on the path of the Light and carry the Swords of Truth, Righteousness, and Honor at your side, that ye may strike down the ravaging Beast and Its Cubs, who would spring upon ye and, with sharp teeth and claws, tear ye to shreds and devour ye.

Smite first the Cubs, for they are dangerous, and the unnatural Beast will sacrifice them to save Itself. Cut their heads and hearts from their bodies; but let no drop of their foul blood touch ye, for it is poisonous and fatal. Then slay the Beast Itself in like fashion. After that, cause all to be consumed by fire, and the winds to scatter the ashes to the land and the seas.

Ye who would hesitate to do battle in this manner are lost, for though the Immortal Guardian, in Its infinite wisdom, bids ye to live in peace, the Foul Enslaver, Its antithesis, follows not this Commandment and so is the Light's enemy and must be destroyed.

—Thus it is Written—
in
The Word and the Way
The Book of Joella, Chapter Thirteen

THE FIRST MOON HAD RISEN SOME TIME BEFORE, AND SHORTLY thereafter the Blue Moon had joined its sister in the black-velvet sky. Now the deep lilac Passion Moon was beginning its inevitable ascent into the heavens. The stars glittered like silver ice against the firmament, bathing the ground far below with a pale, shadowed light that for some unknown reason had an unnatural cast, as though it were touched by the hand of the Darkness. The snow that blanketed the barren Strathmore Plains gleamed white as death; beneath it, a hard frost encrusted the earth, making the dormant grass slick and treacherous. The wind soughed plaintively, bitterly cold and foul with the putrid stench that was the breath of the UnKind.

It was the longest night, the dead of winter. The SoulEaters had timed their invasion well. There would be no grass fires to stop their advance upon the land. In fact, there would be nothing but Cain, Ileana, and a handful of determined soldiers and frightened townspeople to stand between them and the two continents they coveted.

From where she stood upon the ramparts of the castle at Ashton Wells, Ileana could hear the horrible hissing of the reptiles and the stealthy slither of their feet across the frozen ground as they began to pour from the Hollow Hills like black, oozing slime to besmirch the Strathmore Plains.

There, a dark, solitary figure waited to meet them—a man even more corrupt than they, a madman who fed off their evil and was in turn consumed by it until all he had once been was vanquished and in its place stood a beast—a beast whose very breath was the fire of death, a beast who was Cain.

Her heart in her throat, Ileana watched as the creatures surged forward to begin their attack, swarming over the heath like army ants, hundreds upon hundreds of them, their teeth snapping like mandibles, their taloned fingers waving like pincers, their scaly bodies glistening in the moonlight. But the lone man did not flinch as, snarling and drooling, they ran toward him.

What is he waiting for? Ileana wondered anxiously. *Why hasn't he called up his power? By the moons! Has it—has it failed him?*

The terrifying notion had no sooner occurred to her than, to her horror, Cain was swallowed by the terrible ranks of the saurians. The girl gasped, stricken. Surely, she thought, he could not have survived that onslaught. Surely, even now, his body was being torn limb from limb—that hard, muscular body that had pressed hers down only last night and made love to her with such exquisite finesse. . . . Nay! She must not think about that now! She had failed to do her duty once; she must not do so again!

Yet she could not tear her eyes from the place where the tall, lithe man had stood alone to meet that fearsome charge. He was her husband, and, ah, Heaven's Light, in spite of everything, she loved him still!

Ye are a fool, Ileana! she told herself scathingly.

But her heart did not care. It leaped and quivered in her breast with disbelief and joy as she saw that, incredibly, Cain still lived. At the last moment, he had summoned his vast power and brutally unleashed it. The resulting explosion had devastated the reptiles. Bits and pieces of a multitude of UnKind bodies lay scattered in every direction; blood seeped into the ground, staining the snow scarlet. Other creatures, stunned by the violent blast, milled about aimlessly, as though they had lost their wits. But those saurians that had been far enough away to escape injury came on, whipped to a slavering frenzy by the fate of their vanguard.

Now, his aura blazing, illuminating his form, Cain lunged forward to engage the reptiles who bore down on him relentlessly. Shouting the battle cry of the Royal House of Khali, he brandished wildly the Sword of Ishtar, which he gripped tightly in his left hand. The girl's breath caught in her throat as she watched the Holy Relic begin to flicker erratically as, forcibly, inexorably, Cain bent it to his dreadful will, joining his power to the Custodians' magic. Suddenly, a vile, sickly yellow-green light erupted from the weapon; fractured veins of electricity shot out from its tip, piercing the torsos of the nearest creatures. They howled and writhed in agony as the chartreuse rays penetrated their hearts, then abruptly burst like fireballs to envelop their bodies, setting them afire. Ileana clapped her hands to her mouth, certain she was going to vomit as, without warning, the vital organs of the saurians ruptured and their torsos exploded.

Cain did not even check his stride as the flesh and blood flew, but went on slashing methodically, again and again —like an automaton of the Time Before—at the black tide that threatened to engulf him.

How can he murder them so? Ileana wondered, sick unto death at the carnage he wrought. *How can he?*

She knew the answer; she just did not want to believe it. At long last, the beast within him had come fully awake. At long last, it had devoured him.

There is nothing ye can do for him, the girl told herself sternly. *Ye are not of the Darkness, but of the Light. Ye cannot fight alongside him. Ye can but defend yourself and the others. Ye must think of the world, not of Cain. . . .*

But still, Ileana's heart cried out in protest as, slowly, she forced herself to breathe deeply, rhythmically, and deliberately shut her mind to the sights and sounds of the battle far below. Finally, her arms spread wide and lifted to the night sky, her oak staff clutched firmly in her right hand, she called up her power—the Power of the Elements with which she had been vested. As though the heavens themselves heard her silent cry, thin, jagged tridents of lightning such as none had ever before seen cracked across the firmament in every direction, seeming to shatter the ebony void as they hurtled toward her staff. A shower of dazzling sparks shot up from its tip; and as it had once before, the wild, glorious cry of the Keepers rang out in Ileana's mind and swelled to a roar, like a crescendo of harps and flutes. White-hot flashes of color burst before her eyes like shooting stars as that which she had summoned suddenly erupted from within her and exploded across the plains with a blinding magnificence that struck fear and awe into all who saw it.

The very earth seemed to quake, the sea to madden, the wind to shriek as aura after aura ignited and flared until at last a towering wall of brilliant blue fire stretched along the banks of the River Idlewild and the edge of the forest bounding the north of the moors, preventing the UnKind from marching into the woods and the Majestic Mountains of Finisterre, across the Groaning Gorge into the land of

Borealis. To the west lay the Hollow Hills and, beyond, the Harmattan Ocean, now churning as though caught in the grip of a horrendous hurricane. To the east, the Great Cerulean Sea roiled and eddied, thunderous whitecaps spewing violently onto the shore. To the south was the fortress itself, a beacon of blue fire that seemed to spiral up to the very heavens.

The virulent waves of black bodies that flowed across the heaths broke and ebbed from the impact of the incandescent reefs that had abruptly dammed their current; those reptiles who did not retreat quickly enough were burned alive as the blazing barrier engulfed them. For a moment, Ileana's power wavered wildly as the piteous images of those who had once been Kind rose to haunt her, beseeching her to stop their suffering and torment. Resolutely, she compelled herself to ignore the soundlessly screaming faces, to strengthen and steady her power. She had not meant to destroy the creatures; she had not forgotten how doing so had affected her once before. She was therefore much relieved when, growling their rage, the saurians fell back. Even Woden, their leader, could not force them to breach the walls she had flung up in defense against them, for the reptiles feared fire. It was this that had prevented them from conquering Cain.

Now, the plains awash with the light of her vast aura, Ileana could see her husband clearly; and once more, her heart lurched with terror for him as she watched row after row of the UnKind hurl themselves at him, brandishing their weapons purposefully in their sharply clawed hands, baring their pointed white teeth between lips twisted in macabre sneers. But still, Cain did not falter; and silently, Ileana gave thanks to the Immortal Guardian for this, though she knew why it was so—and what it would mean to her in the end.

Hissing and dribbling saliva, as though deranged, the SoulEaters shot arrows and pitched spears at Cain crazily, only to see them eaten up by his aura. Their swords and morning stars were useless against him, the blades and spiked balls melting from the intense heat of the energy he radiated. Flames danced eerily up the creatures' weapons, like green fire climbing the rigging of a ship at sea, to set their bodies ablaze; and they contorted and squealed with pain as they were consumed by a Darkness more evil than their own. Hundreds of them perished as Cain plowed his way through their ranks, cutting them down. His aura burned like wildfire around him; the Sword of Ishtar glowed with that malignant yellow-green light that seared the UnKind mercilessly as it sliced their heads from their shoulders and stabbed through their hearts. The sound of the saurians' vital organs rupturing, their bodies fulminating, shook the plains ceaselessly, lashing the SoulEaters into a maniacal state. They were infuriated by their inability to overcome a single man. The night reverberated with their screams of rage. The gnashing of their ferocious teeth sounded like a horde of cockroaches being crunched underfoot; the scrape of their daggerlike nails against metal as they flung away their fruitless weapons and set upon Cain like mad dogs sent chills down Ileana's spine.

The rasping vociferations of the angry reptiles dinned in her ears; but even so, she could still hear the agonized screams of those whose bodies were dying, the soundless cries that issued from the creatures' awful, gaping mouths. She could see the deceptively pleading images of the once Kind faces that lingered briefly on their hideous visages before their bloodred eyes glazed over to stare up her accusingly. She knew Cain could hear and see them, too, those vestiges of Kind essence irrevocably corrupted by the Foul Enslaver, those rancid spirits turned to the Darkness —to which, now freed from their physical shells, they forever escaped, strengthening It, feeding Its power.

Ileana thanked the Light that the others, those who defended the keep, lacked the heightened senses that would have allowed them to hear the silent, anguished wails, to see the tortured, unreal countenances as she and Cain did.

Think of the Light. Think only of the Light, the girl repeated over and over to herself as she closed her mind to the wrenching sounds and sights.

Beside her, Bergren Birchbark's and Jiro Juniper's flaming spears whined as they sailed into the ranks of the saurians, singeing thick black hides, puncturing crimson eyes. The crossbows of the elfin soldiers vibrated; from the corner of one eye, Ileana could see the Prince Lord Tarragon gesturing sharply as he issued orders, his fair hair streaked with grime, his handsome face grim. Farther along the ramparts, Gerard commanded his father's warriors, who manned the catapults, ballistas, and mangonels. At his side, the Princess Lady Rosemary expertly jammed ammunition into one of the war devices. Ulthor loaded stones into another as easily as though the massive rocks were marbles. Even Syeira was helping by setting a torch to the missiles that were dipped in tar before being launched.

It seemed as though the heavens rained fire, as though mighty Ishtar herself rode among the stars, her great sword in hand, carving chunks of the celestial bodies to fall upon the earth and scorch it irreparably. The night was afire, as though the whole world were coming to an end, as the Keepers and the Prophets had foretold. It was a nightmare, like the Time of the Wars of the Kind and the Apocalypse all over again, the Minions of the Darkness marching on the land, the Defenders of the Light standing fast against all odds.

Hour after hour, the battle raged, and still, the reptiles came on, trampling over their fallen cohorts' maimed and decapitated bodies, which littered the ground like rubble. Strips of scaly black flesh lay everywhere; blood stained the snow crimson, running in rivulets to form slick red pools where there were indentations in the earth. Acrid smoke and the rotten odor of death filled the air. The snarls of the UnKind split the night as, searching for some way to penetrate it, they prowled and paced wrathfully before the wall of blue fire warding the keep. Upon impact with the aura, their arrows and spears burned to cinders; their grappling hooks and ropes disintegrated to ashes; their battering rams crumbled to charred stumps. Only an occasional quarrel or javelin managed to enter the gaps through which the defenders sent their own projectiles flying. Several of the SoulEaters ventured too close to the fiery barrier and were roasted alive by it; and Ileana's power reeled again, as though it had been dealt a ringing slap, before she managed to regain control of it. Others of the creatures were crushed and set ablaze by the huge, flaming stones cast down by the mangonels. Hundreds more fell before Cain's sword.

He was ghastly to see, a madman, an avenging demon of the Darkness. He could feel Its power surging noxiously through his body, Its poison emanating from the very pores of his skin. He *was* the Darkness, terrible and horrifying. His black eyes shone with a vehement, unholy light; their whites were misted with a bloodred film, as though all the vessels within them had burst from some abominable force. His face was black with smoke and soot, diabolically distorted. His teeth flashed white between his lips, which were drawn and curled in a depraved grin. His baleful laughter rang out chillingly over the plains, causing all who heard to cringe in terror. Bodies lay piled in heaps about him, where he had carelessly kicked them aside to add to the mounds.

And still, the UnKind came on.

Ileana, hungry and exhausted, could feel her power starting to weaken. Now more and more of the saurians' arrows and spears began to slip through the protective barrier she had thrown up around the castle, and the cries of the soldiers struck by the missiles echoed in her ears.

Charis, seeing what was happening, ran to fetch food and drink for her mistress, while Halcyone, amazed at her own temerity, rushed to help support Ileana. Wordlessly, the girl permitted the mistress shipbuilder to reach through her aura, grateful when Halcyone's arm encircled her waist to hold her upright as she swayed on her feet.

"Hang on, Lady!" Halcyone urged, glancing at the slowly lightening sky. "Dawn will be here soon! Hang on!"

But Ileana, when she looked at the firmament, knew the day would be dull and grey, dark enough for the reptiles to continue fighting; and despair filled her heart, for she did not know how much longer she could go on.

Yet Cain was tireless, it seemed, his power magnified tenfold by the Sword of Ishtar, his strength increased by each despoiled spirit tearing itself free of a dying UnKind body.

Sensing that Ileana's power was failing, he moved swiftly to defend the northern boundary of the plains. If the wall of

warding there should fall, he would make certain none of
the SoulEaters disappeared into the forest and the Majestic
Mountains beyond to sweep across the Groaning Gorge into
Borealis.

But Woden also grasped the fact that the barriers of blue
fire were no longer invincible, and his voice grated as he
grunted orders to those who followed him. Immediately, a
wedge of creatures marched toward the fortress, punching a
hole in the aura that surrounded it. Ileana staggered wildly
from the impact. Charis and Halcyone reached out frantically to steady her, and presently, she was able to recover
her balance. But the damage had been done. Hordes of the
saurians were now gushing like black bog water through the
narrow chasm.

Vile laughter pealed forth, and Ileana saw that it was
Woden, chortling with glee. Determination swept through
her, renewing her vigor. She straightened her back, squared
her slender shoulders, and spread her palms wide, her oak
staff raised to the leaden but paling sky. Her djellaba and
violet chasuble, with its pattern of silver crescent moons
and five-pointed stars, billowed about her violently in the
winter wind; her long silver hair streamed back from her
uplifted face. Her lips moved urgently as she murmured
ancient incantations to summon every ounce of her power.
Slowly, the opening in the wall of warding closed, sealing in
those of the UnKind who had passed through it.

Now the defenders on the ramparts scrambled to drag
heavy iron cauldrons filled with hot pitch and oil over to the
embrasures. They set the liquid afire and poured it over the
walls. The dark, viscid tar and smooth golden oil cascaded
down upon the SoulEaters, burning them alive, for there
was no escape for them. They were trapped between the
keep and the aura that encompassed it. Bergren Birchbark
and Jiro Juniper sent javelins shooting down into the ranks
of the creatures; elfin crossbows rained quarrels upon them.
With his bare hands, Ulthor dropped heavy stones upon
them, pinning them to the ground, where they were devoured by the licking tongues of the blaze.

Woden's eyes were like red-hot embers of hate in his black
face as he spied the carnage done to the UnKind. At last, he

lifted one massive fist to gesture curtly at those who followed him. Slowly, the SoulEaters on the ravaged moors began to fall back, their losses overwhelming.

Noting with a peculiar, mixed relief that her husband still stood, Ileana waited until the saurians had retreated into the Hollow Hills before she collapsed, oblivious of all else. Seeing her fall, Ulthor hurried to her side and caught her up in his arms. Charis and Halcyone following hard on his heels, he carried Ileana to her chamber, where he laid her upon the bed, shaking his head with pity as he gazed down at her. She was as pale as death, he thought, and so gaunt that her skin seemed stretched like taut leather across her bones.

"Is she—is she dead?" Halcyone asked, her voice a terrified whisper.

"Nay," the giant replied. "But she is weak—very weak. Ye there!" he shouted at a petrified handmaiden hovering outside in the hallway. "Bring food and drink. Hurry, damsel! Hurry!"

Then, seeing there was nothing else he could do, Ulthor left the sleeping girl to the care of the women and returned to the ramparts of the keep. There, the defenders were busily regrouping. Under Tarragon's direction, the elves were conveying the dead and wounded below to the great hall, where those who survived would be treated by the healers. Gerard was forming the remaining warriors into new units. Those soldiers too exhausted to continue had been sent to chambers to rest; others were checking supplies, replenishing ammunition, and stacking weapons where they would be close at hand. Rosemary and Syeira were overseeing the removal of debris. The King Lord Arundel was conferring with his advisers and issuing further orders to his subordinates.

"The Lady Ileana . . . how is she?" he inquired soberly as he turned and observed Ulthor.

"Resting, Lord," the giant responded gravely. "I fear her power has been utterly drained. I hope the UnKind wait a while before their next attack." His eyes scanned the far horizon worriedly.

"Do not fret, Ulthor," said Gerard, who, along with Tarragon, had joined the two men. "Surely, we will have a little time; even the SoulEaters must eat and rest and reassemble their forces."

"Still," Tarragon said, shaking his head skeptically, "I don't believe they'll waste any time about it. They must know that every hour they delay, the Lady Ileana's power renews itself. And Woden has realized it is she who holds his army at bay. If she falls, I think not even the Lord Cain shall be able to destroy all the creatures in time to save us—and even he must tire sooner or later."

But when the four men, with some concern, looked at the solitary figure on the plains, they saw he was pacing the ground restlessly, his power barely restrained as, eagerly, he awaited the UnKind's next assault.

"He is mad," Ulthor muttered uneasily.

"He is our only hope of victory," Gerard rejoined tersely.

"Yea, but when the battle has ended, what then?" Tarragon queried, his fair brow knitted in anxious frown. "What then? Surely, he will turn on us!"

No one could deny the truth of the elfin Prince's statement, and it was with heavy hearts and a sense of foreboding that they returned to their posts, wondering what was going to become of them all.

At midday, the SoulEaters resumed their attack.

Ileana, having slept and eaten, had regained a great portion of her power, and the walls of warding she now raised held firm against the reptiles. But Woden, shrewd and cunning, had foreseen this. He motioned with one fist, and a group of creatures bearing shovels ran forward and, with difficulty, began to dig up the snow-laden ground beyond the fortress walls.

"Look!" Syeira cried, pointing at the UnKind scooping up the frozen dirt. "What are they doing? What are they doing?"

"Great God Daeggawode!" Ulthor roared. "They're sappers! *Sappers!* Gerard!" he shouted at the Finisterrean Prince. "Tell the warriors to aim their weapons at the saurians who are digging! They can't be permitted to succeed at what they're attempting."

Gerard nodded as he, too, grasped what the UnKind intended. They meant to gouge vast tunnels under the earth to the walls of the keep. Then they would set the passages on fire. The intense heat beneath the ground's surface would sap the strength of the land, drawing it downward until it caved in, taking the walls with it. It would be much as though the castle's defenses had been destroyed by an earthquake. It was a time-consuming process but one that could prove most effective. Normally, the entrances to the tunnels were dug some miles away from the actual target; but the SoulEaters—apparently counting on being able to shield themselves from their opponents' missiles—had started at a point so close to the fortress that they would burrow through its defenses in less than a week!

Hoarsely, Gerard began yelling commands, and the soldiers hastened to obey. In moments, the huge war devices were hurling their projectiles at the sappers, driving them away. But it seemed that for every reptile who ran or fell, ten more sprang up to take its place.

Realizing what was happening, Cain shifted positions again, the Sword of Ishtar thrusting, hacking, parrying, mowing down the sappers right and left until, finally, they gave up, dropping their shovels as they fled. But instead of demanding they return, Woden only smiled mockingly and folded his arms across his immense, muscular chest as, from his vantage point atop a small knoll, he watched and waited.

"What is he waiting for?" Rosemary questioned sharply, biting her lip. "What is he waiting for?"

"Ileana's power to fail," Gerard answered grimly. "Then Cain will be drawn back to the northern boundary and our warriors will be busy fighting those creatures who manage to penetrate the protective barrier around the keep. Then the sappers can get on with their work."

Simultaneously, Ileana and Cain reached this same conclusion. For a fleeting moment, their eyes met and locked, and the girl saw it was her husband—not the beast within him—who gazed at her so intently, so longingly, as though there were much he would have said had he been able.

There is yet hope, Ileana thought eagerly. *He loves me still! I know it!*

And then the beast was there, grinning at her slyly, and she turned away, feeling more helpless and alone than she had ever felt before in any LifePath.

They were lost after all, the two of them—and Tintagel as

well. There was nothing either she or Cain could do to halt the sappers. She could not call forth power she did not have; he could not be in two places at once. Soon the UnKind would overrun the castle—and then the very land itself.

Slowly, the day gave way to twilight, and then the three moons of Tintagel rose in the night sky. Ileana's power faltered. Cain swung to the north to compensate for the failing wall of warding stretched across the Strathmore Plains. The SoulEaters slithered through the cracks that appeared in the blue fire around the fortress. The sappers resumed their digging.

All through the night, the heated battle continued. But still, somehow, Ileana hung on, her face visibly drawn from the effort, her body wasted, drained, and fatigued. At dawn, moaning and hallucinating, she collapsed—and her aura vanished.

Before the UnKind could sweep forward, however, the rhythmic chanting of a thousand voices raised in song rang out in the distance, causing all eyes to turn toward the forest that edged the plains.

"*Uig-biorne, märz ana!* War-bears, march on!" the voices cried in the language of the Boreals.

The sound grew louder and louder until it rolled over the heaths like thunder, causing the earth itself to tremble; and at last, out of the thin veil of morning mist that cloaked the land, an army of giants came marching down from the north, hundreds of them, their weapons held at the ready, their boots thudding against the ground like hammers upon anvils.

The SoulEaters and the defenders alike stared with disbelief. Then, suddenly, led by Ulthor, a great cheer rose from the keep, and shouting their battle cry, the Boreals broke into a run, fearlessly closing ranks with the UnKind.

"I knew they'd come!" Ulthor yelled boastfully, his eyes shining with pride. "By the Great God Daeggawode, *I knew they'd come!*"

Steel clashed upon steel as the colossal sledgehammers and enormous battle-axes of the giants slammed against the shields of the reptiles, sending the smaller, weary creatures reeling. Even their thick, tough, scaly black hides, impervious to arrows, spears, and swords, were not proof against the gargantuan force of the Boreals' blows. With their sledgehammers, the giants staved in the heads of the saurians, causing brains, blood, and bones to fly in every direction. With their battle-axes, they decapitated and dismembered the SoulEaters. Heads and limbs tumbled crazily through the air and rolled like marbles upon the ground.

In desperation, the reptiles threw away their useless weapons and, with sharp teeth and claws, tore into their opponents like rabid animals, ripping the flesh from their bones. The deadly umbilical cords of the dying UnKind whipped forth in a frantic attempt to create others like them. With their shields, some Boreals deftly fended off the ropelike appendages. Even those who could not avoid the sting of the umbilical cords went on fighting until the saurians, in their unreasoning lunacy, dragged them down, tearing them limb from limb.

Heartened beyond measure by the giants' bravery, the defenders of the keep renewed their onslaught against the reptiles with a vigor they had not known was yet within them. The spears of Bergren Birchbark and Jiro Juniper sang as the dwarfs aimed the shafts and released them. The taut strings of elfin crossbows snapped. The catapults, ballistas, and mangonels loosed a barrage of projectiles against the creatures.

And in the midst of it all stood Cain, indefatigable, undefeated, the Sword of Ishtar seeming to burn brighter and sicklier in his hand as the hours wore on. His aura now stretched jaggedly across the wide expanse of terrain—to the heavens themselves, and to the very core of the planet, as though he were no longer Kind but a monstrous sunburst. Fire coursed wildly down his blade, flames shooting from its point, sparks flying from its metal. It was as though Cain had so much power that he could no longer contain or control it. The saurians that sought to slay his body were now no more bothersome than flies—and he swatted them just as easily. Row upon row of the reptiles fell until at last, on the night of the third day, out of all those who had ravaged the land, only Cain and Woden remainded standing on the Strathmore Plains. The Boreals had perished valiantly to the last man.

Still, the stout-hearted giants had not given their lives in vain. They had provided Ileana with a much needed respite, and now, having eaten and rested, she stood upon the ramparts, made ill unto death by the carnage that had been wrought. Tears streamed from her eyes as, by the light of the First Moon and the stars, she saw the hundreds of Boreal bodies, scarcely recognizable as such, strewn upon the moors, alongside hundreds of equally mutilated SoulEaters. When her power had failed her, the giants had prevented Ashton Wells—and the world—from falling. Until the end of time, Ileana knew, they would be remembered for the heroic deed, their tragic tale handed down from one generation to the next by the bards who would sing of them so none would forget their courageous act.

By the girl's side, Ulthor wept unashamedly, and the soldiers stood with their right hands clenched and pressed to their breasts in silent tribute to the brave Boreals.

There should be time now to mourn, Ileana thought, an overwhelming fury suddenly welling inside her, making her tremble and sob. *Hasn't there been enough killing? Hasn't there yet been enough?*

But even as her mind cried out the question, she saw Cain, grinning malevolently, beckon the leader of the Un-Kind forward, and she knew that there was still one last battle to be fought—and that afterward, alone, she must meet its victor. She could not use her strength against Woden, who had once been Kind; her power would rebel, as it had before, and she would be lost. Cain, then, must destroy him. But what of her husband? How could she defeat him, when he, too, was Kind? Somehow she must avoid fighting him; somehow she must find a way to turn him back to the Light—but . . . how?

Her heart in her throat, Ileana watched as, slowly, sensing he was about to face something even more evil than he, Woden advanced across the plains, his huge battle-ax and shield held purposefully before him.

His stride measured to match his foe's, Cain, too, moved forward until at last he came to a halt some paces away from Woden. Then, warily, Kind and UnKind began to circle each other, watching, waiting.

"Are ye ssso afraid of me, then, sssorcerer, that ye mussst

continue to ussse your magic againssst me?" the reptile taunted.

Cain shrugged, his dark eyes as red as Woden's.

"Even without it, the end result will prove the same, SoulEater," he spat in reply. "Say your prayers, Woden, for soon ye shall join your master, the Foul Enslaver. It is waiting for ye."

"And for ye alssso, sssorcerer, I think," the creature hissed, grinning.

Ileana gasped as, abruptly, the brilliant sunburst that was Cain's aura vanished and the Sword of Ishtar dimmed until the iron blade was as cold and dark as though it had never shone with that terrible chartreuse light.

What is he doing? she wondered, suddenly so smothered by fear that she thought she would suffocate. *What is he doing? Cain! Cain! Are ye mad . . .?*

He did not hear her soundless wail. His attention was riveted solely on Woden, who now towered over him menacingly since the white-hot shield of his power no longer warded him against the saurian. But still, unafraid, Cain faced his enemy unflinchingly.

"Come," he said, smiling wolfishly. "I am waiting, SoulEater."

There followed a duel the likes of which those looking on had never seen before and devoutly hoped they would never see again—a duel between the Darkness and Itself.

Slowly, relentlessly, the two opponents closed on each other to engage weapons, and the clash of steel striking steel broke the stillness of the night. As the sound echoed ominously across the plains, a black cloud began to descend inexorably from the heavens to enshroud the land, blotting out the First Moon, the rising Blue Moon, and the stars, so nothing could be seen but the red eyes of the two foes and the even more terrible, unnatural, blacker-than-black silhouettes they cast against the peculiar ebony sky. A putrid stench befouled the air, as though every grave in the universe had opened up to disgorge its awful, rancid contents and every urn had turned upside down to spill forth its cremations. An unworldly wind moaned with the cries of a legion of ghosts; and the earth moved as though it crawled with millions of rotten worms and parasitic maggots. The pools and rivulets of blood that covered the ground boiled and bubbled, like some witch's poisonous brew; and fox fire glinted on the decaying corpses.

As she watched the battle unfold, Ileana's fingers clutched the crenellated wall before her so tightly that her knuckles grew white as death. Her breath caught in her throat as Woden's battle-ax slammed brutally against Cain's shield, nearly knocking him to his knees; and it was all she could do to stifle the screams of fear that threatened to erupt from her throat. Quick as a cat, her husband recovered, and a shower of silver-gold sparks trailed away into the darkness as his sword scraped savagely down the length of Woden's hastily raised buckler, driving the reptile back.

Again and again, blade and battle-ax slashed and swung furiously at each other, the clanging and clattering of the metal ringing out over the moors portentously, sending chills down Ileana's spine. Woden was bigger, heavier, but Cain was nimble and swift, and the beast within him fueled his body with an exceptional strength. Time and again, he evaded Woden's blows and lunged forward to deliver his own. Thrusting, parrying, he stalked his prey lightly and gracefully, in sharp contrast to Woden, whose movements were slow and ponderous—but dangerous nonetheless. More than once, his battle-ax narrowly missed Cain's body, bouncing off his shield, now battered so badly that Ileana did not see how it remained in one piece. Still, Woden's own long buckler did not look much better, for the Sword of Ishtar was a weighty weapon. Beneath his kurta, Cain's biceps bulged as he wielded the blade; the tendons in his forearms strained like sinewy cords; his pectorals heaved.

Strange, Ileana thought with an odd detachment, how those muscles rippled now as they did when her husband made love with her, poised his body above her own. . . .

Deftly, Cain sidestepped a wicked onslaught, and Woden, unable to halt the plummet of his cumbrous battle-ax, drove the weapon straight into the ground. Thick globs of blood-stained snow and strips of scaly black flesh flew up at the impact, spattering him, momentarily blinding him. Rapidly, Cain pivoted, using his impetus to bring his sword around and down, so its keen edge bit deeply into the backs of Woden's knees. The titanic creature toppled, growling with pain. Cain lifted his blade high, then brought it down with all his might, intending to cleave Woden's head in two. But the saurian blocked the deadly blow with his shield, using the great buckler to shove Cain backward into the snow. For a moment, Cain lay sprawled upon the frozen earth, and Ileana's heart lurched to a breathtaking stop. Then, recovering, her husband sprang to his feet, while Woden crawled to his battle-ax, yanked it from the ground, then slowly stood.

Briefly, the two combatants were motionless, their breathing labored. Woden was limping, Ileana saw; Cain had crippled him, then. Now, making the most of his advantage, her husband began to press his attack determinedly.

Time passed—Ileana did not know how much, though it seemed like hours—and still, the battle raged. The Sword of Ishtar sang, cutting a wide swath through the air. Woden hobbled back, nearly losing his balance, and before the reptile could deflect it, his adversary's blade came down hard upon his left shoulder. For an instant, Woden felt nothing; the shock and agony of the blow were so incredible. Then, as he watched his shield go sailing through the air, he realized dimly that his arm was still attached to it. The limb had been severed from its socket. He started howling then; waves of excruciating pain stabbed like hot needles through his body, and blood began to pump in sickening spurts from his torso.

He is done for, Ileana thought, feeling as though she were going to retch as she stared at the gruesome, one-armed creature. *Now, surely, he is done for.*

But still, Woden kept on fighting, though he reeled on his feet with each mighty whack of his battle-ax, the loss of his limb having affected his sense of balance. But Cain, scenting victory, was merciless now, and as time wore on, Woden grew frantic and reckless. Hissing and slavering, caught in the throes of madness and rage, he rashly threw away his weapon and flung himself at Cain, only to discover his enemy had eluded him. He stumbled and fell facedown on the ground, and lay stunned. Then, sluggishly, he rolled over.

Cain loomed above him, and in a last, desperate attempt

to save himself, Woden lashed out with his deadly umbilical cord at his foe. The ropelike appendage impacted against Cain's buckler as he expertly maneuvered the shield to protect himself. Then, with his blade, he viciously sliced the cord off at Woden's waist. The saurian shrieked and writhed with agony. He held up his remaining hand as though, knowing it was the end, he yet sought to defend himself. Cain laughed, a devilish, mocking sound.

"*Now* it ends, SoulEater!" he snarled before he plunged his sword into Woden's heart.

The reptile's vital organ ruptured instantly; his torso burst with a horrendous explosion that rocked the very bowels of the earth. A second loud blast shook the land as Cain's aura once more fulminated into being and began to blaze brighter and brighter, as though he were draining every last ounce of evil from Woden's body, absorbing it with his. The Sword of Ishtar burned so intensely with that cankerous yellow-green light that Ileana thought she would be blinded by it. The wind rose with a roar. The Great Cerulean Sea started to churn turbulently, overflowing its banks. The heavens echoed with thunder as they were shattered into a million pieces by dazzling forks of lightning.

Then, suddenly, horribly, a jagged, sharp-toothed maw in the ghastly black sky opened up without warning, as though the Foul Enslaver Itself had unhinged Its jaw to devour all in Its path; and a monstrous, utterly deafening *whoosh*ing began. Heads without torsos, decapitated and dismembered bodies, disembodied limbs, bits of flesh, congealing blood . . . all were brutally sucked from the ground and born aloft upon the savage whirlwind that whipped them up through the forbidding, yawning aperture that had formed in the firmament.

"Heaven's Light!" Ileana cried, stricken. "Heaven's Light! Hold on!" she shouted to the others, the gale tearing her words from her throat and swallowing them. "Hold on, and don't look into the mouth of the thing! Don't look into its mouth!"

The wind flogged the defenders unmercifully as they grabbed merlons, catapults, ballistas, mangonels, iron door handles—anything that would keep them from being drawn up into the terrible orifice that greedily consumed all in its path.

Ileana had no thought or care for herself as she cast away her staff and rushed from the ramparts, down the steep, winding stairs that led to the great hall of the castle. It was Cain who filled her heart, mind, and soul. It had always been Cain.

Frantically, she tugged at the massive wooden doors of the fortress, ignoring the bewildered, terrified cries of the wounded who, not understanding what was happening, were attempting to rise from the pallets that had been strewn upon the floor. Muttering prayers and issuing remonstrations, the priests and healers moved among the warriors, pressing injured but defiant men and women back down upon their makeshift beds, comforting babbling manservants and screaming handmaidens, and shushing bawling children, who clutched piteously at their mothers' skirts.

At last, to Ileana's relief, the doors of the keep opened, and she left the great hall behind, only to encounter even more panic and pandemonium in the courtyard. Soldiers and townspeople ran this way and that as they glanced about wildly to find something firmly anchored to the ground. Beasts that had broken free of the stables galloped amok, their shrieks of fear adding to the cacophony and confusion. Ileana saw a man nearly trampled to death by a horse; still, she did not pause, but raced on, yelling at the guards to open the gates.

Whether the sentries simply didn't hear her or, in their fright, refused to obey, the girl did not know. But despite all her commands otherwise, the portals remained tightly closed; and at last, desperately, she summoned her power and, with the blue fire of the Druswids, blasted them wide apart.

As she passed through the now blackened and broken gates, a twisted iron rod caught hold of her djellaba, ripping and entangling it. Ileana tore the ties at her throat, shrugged free of the cloak, and rushed on, gasping for breath and fighting to stay upright as she struck out determinedly across the violently windswept heaths.

Cain! Cain! her mind sobbed.

Laughing wildly, like a madman, he stood there upon the

Strathmore Plains, nakedly exposed to the evil, sucking force and filled with exhilaration by it. With morbid fascination, he stared at the gaping maw in the firmament, unable to tear his eyes from it, for it seemed as though it were himself who looked back at him slyly, his every flaw, his every fear reflected upon the hazy, shadowed face that surrounded the terrible mouth.

Then, without warning, just as abruptly as it had opened, the orifice suddenly snapped its jaws shut and disappeared. The wind died instantly; and in the hush that fell upon the land, Cain turned menacingly toward the solitary girl in the distance, his eyes burning like red-hot coals, his aura blazing like wildfire, the Sword of Ishtar aflame with that venomous yellow-green light. Ileana's heart shriveled into a cold, hard knot of fear. He meant to destroy her. She was all now that stood in his way.

For every force in the universe. . . . A significant balance. . . . The symmetry of the cosmos. . . . An equal and opposite force. . . . The Power. . . . The key. . . . So was there nothing before the Immortal Guardian brought forth the Light into the Darkness. . . .

The words rang in her mind. Somewhere between them was the answer that would save both her and Cain. And then, suddenly, Ileana had it, and she knew what she must do. It was so simple, she marveled that she had never grasped it before. The beast within Cain was the Darkness; the love within her was the Light; and she must do as the Immortal Guardian had done in the Beginning, when It had given unto the Kind the freedom to choose between Itself and Its antithesis, the Foul Enslaver. She must give unto Cain the freedom to choose between her love and the beast within him.

Slowly, Ileana closed her eyes and summoned her power. Her aura began to shimmer about her, darkly at first, a swirl of purple mist that became, finally, a halo of streaming, white-hot coruscation that engulfed her with its light. Nay. She *was* the Light, pure and shining with her love as she began to walk toward her husband, her sure step never faltering, her steady eyes never leaving his face.

The First Moon shone like a silvery pearl cast against the black-velvet facade of the night sky; the Blue Moon glowed like a sapphire, and the Passion Moon, just now rising above the far horizon, glittered like an amethyst as it ascended into the firmament. The stars sparkled like diamonds; and now Cain's aura was a bloodred ruby, illuminating his visage as Ileana continued toward him, her Flame Prince, the son of the Darkness. But she, who was a child of winter and the daughter of the Light, was not afraid.

A few yards away from him, she stopped, spread her palms wide, and raised them unto the heavens; and into the darkness, the nothingness of the night, she brought forth the light, the essence of her love. Slowly, snow began to fall, and with the flakes came images from her mind, images that danced like wraiths before inexorably taking shape on the barren plains. They were pictures from Time Past, when she and Cain had been one, two halves gifted by the Light to form a perfect whole; pictures from the battle just ended, when they had stood apart, separate and alone, and the Darkness had lain between them.

Through the scarlet flames of his aura, he saw the vignettes; and some small part of his heart, mind, and soul that was still his—only his—understood them and recognized the choice that was being offered to him.

CAIN/'kān/ n[Bd Qayin, fr. Obd Qanah]: "One who is given a choice. . . ."

Oh, Ottah, this is the truth ye tried to make me see, he thought, *that there is always a choice.* Slowly, an intense, unbridled struggle started to take place inside Cain as he grappled with his chaotic thoughts and emotions. *Can it really be that simple?* he wondered. *Can it really be that the whole of a man is determined not by the sum of his parts but by the sum of his* choices? *Yea, it is so. It* is *so!*

And because it was, he chose.

The beast within him staggered at the choice, for it had received a vicious blow. Baring fangs and claws, it struck back violently, tearing at Cain so ferociously, he doubled over from the excruciating pain of its attack. Still, he fought the beast with all his might, determined to prevail. His insides felt as though they were being ripped apart as the beast slashed him with teeth and talons, gouged him with its horns, lashed him with its tail. Flames erupted from its throat, burning him. Poison dripped from its tongue to ooze through his veins. Cain writhed in agony, his body contorting grotesquely as he battled the beast, strove to overcome it. His eyes were like beams of fire; sweat streamed down his horribly twisted face. But still, his grim resolve did not falter. Torturously, he managed to wrap his ethereal essence around the beast's throat. Then, inexorably, Cain began to squeeze harder and harder, choking it. The beast rasped; the terrible noise was like the rattling of bones—a death knell. Its glowing eyes bulged from their sockets; its serpentine body thrashed sickeningly. Its angry, anguished shrieks dinned in Cain's mind until he thought he would pass out from the cruel, unKind sound. But still, he kept on contracting his ethereal essence until at last, with a low, tormented growl and a convulsive shudder, the beast lay unmoving, conquered.

The crimson aura that encompassed Cain abruptly vanished, and he seemed slowly to awaken, as though from a bad dream. His eyes momentarily filled with confusion, he glanced down at himself wonderingly, as though he could not quite believe he was real; and slightly startled, he realized he was just as he had always been, a man, just a man like any other—alone, uncertain. The sword he held in his hand was cold and dark; and now he could see clearly that it was just a sword, like any other, no more powerful than the one who wielded it. Its work was done, he thought, and slowly, he slid it into his scabbard.

For a moment, he stood silently, letting the deep sense of inner peace that gradually filled his body and mind wash over him gently while he reflected on all that had passed and watched the Passion Moon that had presaged his and Ileana's LifePaths reach its zenith in the heavens. Then, at last, he turned to his wife, who was waiting quietly for him to gather his thoughts. Her aura was gone now, and she was just a woman like any other. But for Cain, there was no other woman, would never be anyone but her. He would love her with his body's last, dying breath—and beyond. Once, there had been a time when he would not have told her that. But that time was past. He was free now to speak what was in his heart.

"Ileana," he breathed, his dark eyes alight with his love for her. "Ileana, beloved."

She came into his arms then, her love for him overflowing her heart; and what they said to each other as they stood upon the snowswept plains together was only for themselves to know.

But long afterward, those who knew the tale claimed that each year thereafter, for a single night in the dead of winter, a strange and beautiful flower, lilac as the Passion Moon, bloomed on the moors where the two lovers had embraced.

THE WANING

Passion Moon Rising

Chapter 33

The Zephyr Ocean, 7274.9.16

We are going home now to Khali Keep. Mistress Halcyone designed us a ship—not so great as the Moon Raker, but a serviceable vessel all the same. The elves of the city of Bergamot in Potpourri built it, and being highly skilled artisans, they did a beautiful job.

As I look out over the moonlit sea through the window of the cabin I share with Cain, I am glad to be returning home. But still, it is not without a deep sense of regret that I leave the far side of Tintagel.

I have made so many friends here; I shall miss them all, each and every one. Yet I know their LifePaths will be happy ones, ones lived by the Way, for they have pledged themselves to spread the Word and to honor, serve, and defend the Light that forever holds the Darkness at bay so long as even one of the Kind believes the Immortal Guardian is.

The night is still; and as I write, I can feel Cain's thoughts reach out to me, his essence touch mine. I am a woman who loves and is loved. I do not need to look into the fires and mists to know that the special moment when the Passion Moon rose high in the sky above the Strathmore Plains shall live on in our hearts and memories forever, that we shall grow old together in this LifePath, and that, as a poet of another world far away once said, the best is yet to be.

The land is at peace now; the Darkness has slunk to

Its lair in retreat, though I know It is but sleeping, only sleeping, giving the grievous wounds we dealt It time to lessen and heal.

Someday in Time Future, It will once more awaken and I will have to do battle with It again, I know.

But Cain, my beloved, is at my side, and I am not afraid.

—Thus it is Written—
in
The Private Journals
of the High Princess Lady Ileana I

Here ends
PASSION MOON RISING
Book I of the Chronicles of Tintagel